I0673083

Stolen Spirit

PSI Sentinels: Book One

Pamela Moran

PSI Sentinels: Guardians of the Psychic Realm
Extraordinary senses in a world full of danger.

Protectors and hunters, PSI agents lay their abilities,
sometimes their lives, on the line. They defend and
shield unwary victims against the twisted underside
of a psychic society bent on exploiting an
unsuspecting, mundane world.

Stolen Spirit
Copyright © 2013 Pamela Moran, LLC
Publication December 2013
Print Edition

PamelaMoran.com

Cover design by Novel Graphic Designs
Formatting services by BB eBooks

All rights reserved. No part of this work may be reproduced in any fashion without the express written consent of the copyright holder except in the case of brief quotations embodied in critical articles or reviews.

All characters in this book are fictitious and are a product of the author's imagination. Any resemblance to real persons, living or dead, is purely coincidental.

Acknowledgements

M.A. Taylor and Janelle Denison
The wild ride continues … thank goodness
you two are keeping me moving forward!

Stephanee Ryle
Thanks for being there!

Warren – Always!

Dedication

Mom, this has always been for you.

Miss you.

Chapter One

"**D**AMMIT.**" Jake Carrigan slouched at his wooden kitchen table and ran the edge of his thumb along the rim of a shot glass full of whiskey. "You should be here, Hannah. With me."

Heavy with the scent of recent rain, a stiff spring morning breeze blew in through his open kitchen door. The metal screen rattled against its frame. Lace curtains, ones Hannah had picked out a year ago, fluttered above his kitchen sink.

He twisted the shot glass between his thumb and forefinger and studied the play of amber shadows swirling though the liquid.

One drink, one quick shot.

"Jake." Soft and utterly feminine, his name breathed through the cool air to slip over his skin and down his spine.

Already tight muscles at the back of his neck clenched. He took a wary glance around the empty room.

Shit. Why the hell was he already hearing Hannah's voice?

He hadn't tasted the booze. Not yet. Not a drink in months. On the table in front of him, only a single shot low, sat the bottle of whiskey.

Jake pushed away from the table, the legs of his chair scrapping over the scarred, hard wood floor. He stood and shoved both hands through his hair. Hair desperately in need of a haircut.

Close to four months since he'd had a drink.

New Year's Day resolutions and all that crap. Promises to his worried sister, promises to himself.

A promise he was about to break.

Over six months since he'd discovered Hannah had died. Alone. Without him. He hadn't even known she was sick.

She didn't tell me, didn't let me know.

With both hands splayed at his waist, he glared at the shot glass.

She could have reached him, if she'd wanted. If she'd bothered to try.

He'd been puttering around the Caribbean, soaking up the sun, telling himself he was better off without her. Until he convinced himself all she wanted was a ring, marriage.

Commitment.

Something he wasn't too well versed in.

The blue velvet box holding the platinum diamond ring he'd bought in the islands sat square on the table next to the whiskey bottle.

Mocking him.

Commitments and promises.

He rubbed at the knot centered between his neck and shoulder blades. He'd gone on a bender after … well, after. Hearing her haunting voice, then, had come close to driving him insane.

Hannah's voice.

Deep and throaty.

Sexy as hell.

God, he missed her voice.

"Are you going to stare at that or are you going to actually drink it?"

Jake spun around.

Shit. Shit. Shit.

There was no one there.

He scrubbed a hand over his mouth, along the stubble of his jaw. Why the hell was he doing this to himself *now*? Hannah sounded as if she stood right behind him. As if she looked over his shoulder, her sarcastic words a mocking tease across his skin.

During his drunken bender days he'd sworn she'd done just that. But like today, there'd never been anyone there.

Hannah was gone.

Dead.

Over seven months ago.

Seven and three quarters, if he was counting.

God help him, he was counting.

"Jake, come on." Weariness lined that sexy voice. Lined it and slithered to coil tight in his gut. "Haven't you spent enough time drowning in pity?"

His lip curled over the growl rising in his throat. He spun back to the whiskey, downed the single shot of throat burning liquid and slammed the shot glass on the table. The sharp echo of glass on wood reverberated through the room.

"Happy birthday, Hannah." He snatched the whiskey bottle on his way to the back door. "Now leave me the hell alone."

"DAMN YOU, Jake Carrigan." Hannah Dixon, her stance wide and her chin lifted, fisted her hands on her hips. "Running out on me isn't going to solve anything."

Jake's screen door slammed hard against its frame then bounced once with a hollow metallic clang. He waved his free hand backwards, completely dismissing her along with anything she had left to say.

And she had plenty.

Jackass was at the top of her mind.

She sucked in several calming breaths, or at least they were supposed to be calming. Energy vibrated up and around her spine, left her edgy. Restless. She paced to the screen door then spun away to pace back through the kitchen.

Damn insufferable man.

She had a good mind to leave.

"Give me a reason to stay, Jake." Her whispered words echoed through the empty room. "Fight for us. I can't save *us* by myself."

Hannah stopped mid kitchen and swiped at her eyes. She damn well would *not* cry for that jackass.

She shook her head once then rubbed her fingers over her temples. She'd had enough of being closed out, of being pushed away and treated as if she didn't matter.

Yet, this whole episode felt déjà vu-ish. As if they'd already done this. Right down to the slam of the back door.

But not the whiskey.

Jake didn't drink whiskey. He never had more than a couple beers. Rarely anything harder.

And what the hell did he mean with that Happy Birthday nonsense? They had months to go until her birthday. Fall barely had a hold on the Oregon coast. The colors scattered amidst the deep green of the pines had just begun to change. The crispness of the autumn air promised colder weather.

"Damn it, Jake." Hannah paced to the back door then stood smoothing the skin at her wrist and the thin gold bracelet Jake had given her on her *last* birthday. She stared out through the screen at a landscape marked by all the signs of spring. "Oh."

Spread between the pines lining the far edge of the property, the leaves of the deciduous trees held the young, fresh green that spoke of newness. Even the tips of the pine boughs were a brighter color – lighter, newer. Along the barn, the row of pink azaleas she'd planted on her last birthday had just begun to bud.

Springtime.

Not autumn.

She'd lost … months.

How?

Tension spiked across her forehead. Bracketing her head with her hands, she rubbed at the spot between her brows with both her ring fingers and narrowed her vision to where Jake strode across the rutted dirt yard.

He moved like some big cat stalking its way across a mountain ridge with the fit of his worn jeans tight over his muscular legs. The whiskey bottle gripped in his right hand, he spun to the left, towards the big pine on the far side of the barn.

Sunlight strained through a partially cloudy sky to grab at the gold sparking through his light brown hair. If he would just look back at her she knew the dark green of the T-shirt stretched over his wide shoulders would deepen the pure green of his eyes.

But he didn't so much as glance back at the house.

Not once.

That same sunlight glinted against the whiskey bottle.

Pain pressed behind her eyes, searing tiny pinpoints of flame burst in her head and throbbed beneath her cheekbones.

This had to be one of those weird, lucid dreams. A nightmare. Brought on by her worry about Jake's downward spiral along with the knowledge she had to confront him over the way he'd been isolating himself, shutting her and everyone else out.

She bit her bottom lip.

I can get through this, go through the motions until the alarm clock goes off. Getting through each day was something she had become quite good at. Making it through those moments, one after the other.

She *would* get through this.

On a disgusted groan, she spun away from her view of Jake and paced to the center of the kitchen. The frilly curtains she loved moved with the breeze drifting in through the open window. Light danced along the wood floor.

She glanced at the empty shot glass sitting squat on the table. So why, in this dream world she'd constructed, was Jake drinking whiskey?

The sound of shattering glass echoed sharp from outside. Startled, she hurried to the back door and peered through the screen.

Jake's rigid stance mirrored the tension radiating across his broad shoulders. He stood, hands on his hips and legs braced apart, staring at the mess he'd made. The remnants of the whiskey bottle lay scattered across the ground beneath the nearest pine tree. Light sparked off the broken glass, glistened across the liquid dripping down the tree's trunk.

Dream or not, fall or spring, some things prevailed. Like Jake's temper and his deep seated anger.

Mostly at himself.

On an exasperated puff of breath, she settled on the floor and wrapped her arms around her legs. If she had to wait for the alarm clock to go off, she might as well be comfortable.

Besides, frustrated or not, watching Jake was never hard on the eyes. Her soul, maybe. But not her eyes.

THE SWEET SCENT of fresh cut grass surrounded Jake. He leaned on his heavy rake to let the cool, late afternoon air dry the sheen of light sweat covering his arms and dampening the neck line of his T-shirt.

He spared a glance behind, at the house. Why couldn't that same breeze blow all the cobwebs from his brain?

Hannah's birthday.

He'd known today would be hard, however he hadn't expected to go so far around the bend. The whiskey hadn't been the brightest of his stupid ideas, but the burn in his throat had almost erased the echo of her voice.

Almost.

He'd managed to get a number of chores done in the hours since he'd stormed out of the house. Anything to avoid the torment of his too-real memories of Hannah.

His grip on the rake handle a little tighter, he straightened. That's all this was. *Remnants of Hannah plaguing him, whispering to him. Driving him nuts.*

The sound of a vehicle rumbling through the far gate brought his chocolate lab, Sadie, running from the edge of the property. Nels, the old grey and tan goat that had come with this place when he'd bought it, trotted at a more sedate pace, bringing up the rear.

With a deep frown, Jake glared at his sister's red truck as it rounded the corner of the barn. She eased to a stop a few feet away.

What the hell was Rily doing out here at this time of day? She should be working, not checking on him. She had to have better things to do with her time.

Like fight crime in the sleepy little town down the road.

Rily had made detective when he'd resigned from the Eagle Crest police force. He'd already been on suspended leave, but then Hannah had died. Although the higher-ups had cleared him to return to work after he'd made it back from the

Caribbean, he hadn't been able to face going back to the station.

There had been a time when being a small town cop, making Chief one day – *here*, where he'd grown up – had been all he wanted to do with his life.

Now, after all this time away from the department, he still wasn't sure what he wanted.

Not anymore.

A part of him was glad, sincerely glad, for his sister. He worked hard to convince himself he didn't miss the daily grind of police work.

Some days he even believed himself.

Once Rily pushed open her truck door and hopped down, she let her own dog join the other animals. A round of frantic barking and baying carried the three critters off behind the barn.

"What are you up to, Sis?"

"Passing through. Thought I'd stop in and say hi."

"Right. I'm on your way through to where, exactly?"

"Testy, aren't you?" Rily pulled off her sunglasses. She pushed a lank of chin-length, light blonde hair behind her ear. "Chores certainly haven't improved your mood."

With her green, gold flecked cat eyes narrowed, she studied him. He stiffened, tucked his chin lower and refused to look away.

Whatever she was here for he wasn't going to like, not when she looked at him as if she only wanted to *understand*. Such a false pretense. He might be older, but his little sister, the sole girl, had ruled him and their older brother, Craig, with the ease of a deceptively genial drill sergeant.

Craig. Inside, Jake flinched.

"You look thirsty." A fake smile covered Rily's mouth but failed to lighten the censure in her eyes. "Why don't we go in the house and have some of that iced tea I know you have in the fridge."

Right.

Rily might look fragile and exotic, but he knew all about the iron rod running down her spine. She'd inherited that from their mother. Arguing was futile.

With a resigned glance at his house, he shrugged. He *was* thirsty and he did have fresh, made that morning before the whiskey event, iced tea in his fridge.

Maybe Rily would keep Hannah and her sexy, throaty voice at bay. Keep his ex-lover from tormenting him.

One could hope.

After stowing the rake, he led the way to the back porch. Once inside the house he pulled glasses from the cabinet, an ice tray from the freezer and tea from the fridge. Handing his sister a poured glass, he finally took a furtive, cautious look around.

For what he wasn't sure, it wasn't as if he actually *saw* Hannah. He only heard her. Besides, what he heard wasn't real, only a figment he'd found to torture himself with.

Guilt had a nasty way of eating at a man.

After taking a short sip of tea, Rily speared him with a dark speculative look. She indicated the empty shot glass still sitting on the kitchen table. "Where's the bottle?"

"I don't need a babysitter, Sis."

A sharp stab of pain flashed through her eyes before she lowered lashes. She pressed her lips together. Jeez. He wiped at the thin layer of condensation lining the outside of his tea glass.

Anything to avoid looking at his sister.

Her concern touched him, it really did. On another level it pissed him off. He was a grown man, not a ten year old.

Not that he'd acted much like a grown-up in the last several months. He *had* broken the promise he'd made to her. That damn knot tightened between his shoulder blades.

Ah, hell.

He gave his sister a half-hearted, lop-sided smile. "I smashed the bottle against that big pine near the barn."

"Because it was empty?"

"No. Except for one shot, it was full."

Her eyes closed for a brief second. The tightness in her jaw eased. Remorse sucker punched him square in the gut.

"So that really *is* why you're here?" He glanced out the window, not really seeing anything beyond the screen but not wanting to meet his sister's gaze. Not yet, not until he had his reactions under control. "To check on me?"

"It's Hannah's birthday."

"I've already said a toast." He wasn't going to apologize for that, ass or not. He forced his gaze back to hers, leaned a hip against the counter and crossed his arms. "I'm okay."

Rily paced in the small kitchen area. She stopped, picked up the ring box from the table and flipped it open. With her bottom lip between her teeth, she closed the box before setting it back down.

"Really, Jake? You're really okay?" She swung her gaze back to his. Her expression remained steady when he narrowed his eyes.

Direct. That was his little sister.

"As fine as I'm going to be for a while. Leave it alone, Rily."

"You need help."

"Rily —" A muscle twitched in his left cheek. He didn't need this from her. Not right now. Maybe never.

She set her glass on the table then pulled a business card from the back pocket of her jeans. After studying it for a moment she held it out to him. He ignored the card but held her gaze.

"It's a grief support group." With her lip curled in a good imitation of his, she tossed the card onto the table where it landed beside the shot glass. Her quick show of temper almost loosened the ire stuck in his throat. "They meet on Thursdays at the hospital."

"So." Belligerence had fast become his second language. He couldn't bring himself to care, much less stop.

"They helped me with Craig's death."

Jake's left shoulder jerked. He lifted his chin to cover the involuntary movement at the mention of their brother. "So you're over that, are you?"

"No. I don't think I'll ever —" Her head back, she sucked in a lungful of air then shoved both hands through her hair. "Come on. You aren't to blame, not for either of them. Not Hannah. Not Craig —"

"You weren't the one he called, Rily. You weren't the one who let him down." *Who wasn't there when the brother I idolized needed me. Who wasn't there for Hannah while she lay dying, alone.*

"Jake." She closed her eyes for a second before nailing him with her hot, green stare. "Craig's death was his own fault. Not yours. And Hannah was sick. She didn't tell you. She didn't tell me. Maybe she was sicker than she knew. Maybe. Why are you blaming yourself for either of them?"

As if she could understand. "What the hell do you want from me?"

"Go to the meetings. Talk to someone."

"No."

"Hannah's dead, Jake. So is Craig. Neither of them are coming back."

"Tell me something I don't know."

"Try this. You need to get on with your life. Craig died ten months ago. Hannah died nearly eight. You've been hiding for the last six. More than that if we count that stupid disappearing act you pulled on those damn islands. You need to get back to some kind of normal life."

"Normal?" He ran his tongue around the inside of his mouth, over his teeth then he lowered his chin. "What do you call what I've been living?"

"Jake —"

"I get up early every single damn morning. I eat. I work. I'm exhausted and ready for bed every night."

"What work?" Her eyes flashed and her face flushed a light pink. "On this place? You're avoiding life. Stuck out here by yourself. Isolated."

"I like it that way." She wouldn't understand so he didn't bother to explain. No people around asking how he was or what he was doing now. Isolation definitely had its perks.

"You like being alone? Completely cut off?"

"I do." With a studied, careless shrug, he crossed his ankles. "The Jeep is finished. Looking good, running even better. The repairs to the outside of the barn are done. Same with the house. There's only one wall left to paint on the backside of the barn. I'd say I'm doing pretty *damn* good."

Although he was going to have to come up with some new projects soon. He was just about out of the ones needing done outside.

Projects inside the house were the ones he avoided. They had all involved Hannah. In spite of himself, he hadn't been able to come up with anything for the interior that was any different from what they'd laid out together.

Before they'd broken up and she'd died.

Rily stared at him with her cat eyes narrowed and her pointy feline chin tucked against her chest. "That's faking it, Jake. Not living."

"Back off." He held one palm out and fought the need to curl his fingers into a fist. "Your concern is noted and appreciated. Back off."

They stared at each other for several long, heavy moments. His rigid jaw twitched before she sighed.

"Okay." She tapped two fingers against her lips. "Thanks for the tea."

"Sure." He forced the word out.

With a slight shrug, she eased forward and wrapped her arms around his waist then leaned her head on his shoulder. "I love you, Bro. I really do. Please, call me when you decide to talk to someone."

Something small and tight uncoiled inside him. He squeezed her back. She did love him. Worried about him. But no matter what she thought she understood, Rily had no clue about the demons haunting him.

And that was *before* Hannah had started talking to him again.

He watched as Rily slipped out the screen door and whistled for her dog. Once her truck rumbled down the road he picked up the card she'd left on his table. He fingered the sharp edge.

What did his sister know about his grief? His guilt? What did anyone else know about it? How could they possibly help?

He flipped the card back onto the table where it slid to a stop next to the ring box.

Before they'd broken up, after Craig's death and his own temporary suspension from the force, Hannah had suggested they get away from Oregon. Just go somewhere for a week or two. Regroup. Just the two of them.

He'd finally agreed, more to keep her from badgering him than for any other reason. Then, out of the blue, she'd picked a major fight. Called it quits. So he'd taken off on his own.

Damn her had been his motto at the time.

He didn't need her. Didn't need the police force. Didn't need anything or anyone.

But roaming around those Caribbean islands alone had quickly lost all appeal. To stop himself from brooding on his brother's death, and his role in that, he'd instead found himself dwelling on Hannah. On her reasons for ditching him.

Damn her. He cocked his head to the side, spared a quick glance around the kitchen. He was alone. No one was talking to him. Damn her all over again.

Leaving the business card on the table, he pocketed the ring box. Time to finish emptying the ice trays he'd left on the counter.

"So I'm dead?"

Jake's hand froze on the cold, plastic tray.

"I'm really, truly *dead*?"

Shit, he hated the way her voice trembled. "Yeah, Hannah. Late last September."

Double shit. Now he was *willingly* talking to the voices he heard in his head.

Voice.

He only heard *one* voice. Hearing just one couldn't be as bad as hearing lots of voices. Could it?

God. What if Craig wanted to talk to him, too?

He gripped the tray so tight two cubes jumped out and slid across the counter into the sink. Easing his hold on the plastic, he set it down. He braced his hands on the edge of the counter.

"September. Over seven months ago ... and today's my birthday."

She sounded so *damn* sad.

If he had to hear her in his head, why couldn't she sound cheerful, happy? Like he wanted to remember her. From before she dumped him.

"How ... how did I die?"

"Man, Hannah. Why are you doing this to me?"

Silence greeted his outburst. Shit, shit, shit. "You were there. I wasn't. They said you were sick. Some kind of blood disease, acute leukemia or something like that."

He didn't even know the official name of whatever had taken her life. Just that it had.

"But ... how is that possible? I've always been anemic, but that's not the same thing."

"I don't know, Hannah." Jake ran one hand through his hair. He was so not doing this.

Except he was.

"But, that can't be how I died."

"Hannah —"

"No, Jake. How can that be? I was healthy, hardly ever sick. How could a *disease* take me that quickly?"

Silence dragged until he couldn't stand it. He grabbed the trays, filled them with tap water and shoved them in the freezer. Back at the sink, he stared out the open window and let the breeze wash over him.

"Doesn't *acute* mean it came on suddenly?" Why the hell was he talking to her? She wasn't here, wasn't real.

"Yes. But wouldn't I have shown signs of something being off? Wouldn't I have known I was ill? I just don't believe I could have been sick enough to die like that." Her voice sounded weak, almost like she was hurting, in pain.

Weariness dropped over Jake, weighted his shoulders. He lowered his head to rest his chin on his chest. She seemed so damn reasonable.

Like when she was alive.

"How can you be so sure?" Crap, just like when she was alive, he rose to the bait she dangled in front of him.

"I ... don't know. I just am."

"Of course." Jake pushed away from the counter. He swung around. No one was there. Disappointment filled him. *What did you expect, Einstein? It's just you and your psychotic imagination.*

"Someone must have ... if I am really dead, then someone must have killed me."

What?

Jake rolled his jaw and stared at the empty space in front of him. He couldn't have heard her correctly.

What the hell was he thinking? *Hear her correctly?* Why was he hearing her at all? "You think you were *murdered?*"

"Yes. Yes, I do."

"Dammit, Hannah." Not sure whom he was most disgusted with, he mustered up as much patience as he could latch onto. "You were sick. You had some kind of rare blood disorder. You died."

Maybe if he said it out loud often enough he could do what Rily wanted. Maybe he could actually move on with his life.

Except – was that a soft sniffle he heard? Hannah didn't cry. She wasn't a crier. Why the hell was she doing that now?

This was *his* hallucination. No crying in his hallucination.

"What if the disease didn't kill me, Jake?" Tears definitely edged Hannah's voice.

He squeezed his eyes shut. He was going to do something stupid. He just knew it. "What do you want from me?"

"Look into it, Jake. Just look into it."

Like there was a *just* to any of this. "There's nothing to look into."

"There has to be. My body –"

"Was cremated, Baby." God. This was getting beyond ridiculous. He was calling the voice in his head *Baby*. Next he'd be singing lullabies to himself at bedtime.

Maybe then he'd actually get to sleep, maybe that wouldn't be another lie he'd told Rily.

"Cremated?" Desperation lined Hannah's whisper and slammed into his gut.

Dammit. Swallowing around the lump wedged tight in his throat, he rubbed at his chest.

"Yeah. The people at your doctor's office told Rily that's what you wanted." He forced the words out, even though they echoed through the aching hollowness inside him. "You didn't list any next of kin. Or anyone important to you, for that matter. So they took care of the cremation."

"I don't have a body anymore." A soft tremor definitely lined her words.

Now what was he going to do?

Her voice was only in his head, it wasn't real. This bordered on – Well, beyond weird.

So why the hell am I feeling this need to shield her? To protect her, to comfort her?

Even though he wanted to curl into a ball and shed a few tears himself. But he wasn't about to start doing that.

His hands fisted.

A grip on reality, that's what was required right now.

He strode from the room, away from the soft hiccup echoing through the kitchen, away from the pressure. In his bedroom he fished the ring box from his pocket then slammed it on the night stand next to the framed picture he still kept of Hannah.

He'd shot the photo himself, in black and white, on an outing to the old shipwreck out on the ocean shore. Buried treasure hadn't interested him that day. He'd been more interested in what lay buried in his lover's eyes.

Hannah.

His nerves raw, his hand trembling a slight bit, Jake picked up the photo.

She'd been laughing at him. Her fingers laced in her long dark hair, holding it away from her face while the wind whipped it around her head, her dark eyes sparkled at him from the depths of the photo.

"Dammit, Hannah." He traced the contours of her face. "Everyone loved you. No one would have murdered you."

"Jake."

His jaw tense, the nerve below the right side of his mouth twitched. He laid the photo on his night stand, face down. "It's time I fed the animals. I have things to finish outside."

If he was smart, he'd start with finding what was left of his sanity and bury Hannah's memory some place where it wouldn't hurt so much.

Chapter Two

CROSS-LEGGED, Hannah sat on the white, fake fur rug in front of Jake's living room fireplace. The night time fire had long since died down. Hazy, early morning light spilled into the room from the paned glass on either side of the front door to fall across Jake where he lay stretched out asleep on his couch.

She itched to trace the gold stubble marking his chin, his jaw. Certain he wouldn't appreciate her touch, and uncertain she could even touch him, she curled her fingers into her palms.

Last evening he'd avoided the house until it was too dark to see before he'd finally drug himself inside. He'd given his bedroom door a pissed-off glare on his way through the house.

Now he slept a fitful sleep with only his mother's crocheted throw keeping him warm.

Hannah pulled the corner of her lip between her teeth.

He was so angry. Spitting fire angry.

That was better than the numbness that had consumed him after his brother's death. The flat eyes that had lost all spark of life, that didn't give a damn about anything.

But why did she have to be dead to matter? To finally get any kind of response out of him?

Dead. Without a body. Cremated.

Shivers chased themselves over her skin. The red sweater she wore did nothing to ward off that chill.

Sadie, Jake's dog, lay curled on the floor next to the couch, her gold eyes watching Hannah, her tail occasionally twitching.

At least Sadie could see her.

Somehow.

Dead.

Every time she tried to fill the holes in her memory, pain spiked across her forehead. The last few hours had resulted in little more than a whopping headache. She braced her elbows on her knees and rubbed small circles at her temples.

Sadie whimpered. Hannah gave her a tight smile she tried to make reassuring.

The coolness of the wood floor permeated through the rug, through her blue jeans. But was that real? Or did it only seem real because she expected it to feel that way?

So many damn, unanswered questions.

On a disgusted sigh, she shoved to her feet then ran her palms down over her thighs.

These jeans, her sweater, the white deck shoes on her feet … were these the clothes she had worn the day she died?

Dammit. *If* she was dead.

She spun to face the fireplace then pressed the pads of her fingers over her eyes, against the underside of her brows. Pain throbbed just behind there to pulsate up and over her scalp.

If she wasn't alive, how could she *feel* the things she felt? The cold floor, the slow beat of her heart, the ache lancing her head?

Sadie whimpered again. Hannah knelt beside the dog. With her fingers gripping her knees, she swallowed. Sadie, her gold gaze intent on Hannah, thumped her tail again.

Oh, Lordy.

Hannah scrubbed a hand over both of her cheeks.

Okay. Reach out, touch Sadie. Rub her head, scratch behind her ears. How hard can that be?

Hannah pulled the inside of her bottom lip back between her teeth and sucked in a deep breath through her nose.

One way to find out.

Her fingers spread, she stretched out her hand, let it hover over Sadie's head. Their gazes locked, the dog's tail thumped again, the sound loud in the stillness of the early morning.

Okay. Now or never.

Hannah lowered her hand inch by incremental inch. Sadie pushed her nose against Hannah's palm.

Nothing.

Hannah's breath hitched. She couldn't feel a freaking thing. No more sensation than if she'd been petting air.

Her stomach muscles clenched. She couldn't swallow.

Jake was right.

In spite of what and how she felt, she was dead. Her body nothing more than dust and her essence simply a spirit without substance.

A ghost?

Sadie whined.

With a moan deep in his throat, Jake stirred then kicked off the throw. He blinked sleepy green eyes and aimed a slow, lazy half smile right at Hannah before his eyelids drifted close.

Her heart hammered in her chest.

Jake turned over and nestled against the back of the couch. His breathing evened out. Her movements slow, she spread her hands over her knees. She straightened her spine and blew out the breath trapped in her throat.

Had he actually seen her this time?

A few hours later Hannah still didn't have that answer.

Jake woke. He pushed himself up off the couch. She sat cross-legged in front of the fireplace, perfectly still, her gaze locked on his face.

Completely ignoring her, he stretched his arms over his head with his T-shirt riding halfway up his stomach. Soft, mid-morning light sparked gold off the slight sprinkling of hair circling his navel.

She reached out. No. She *couldn't* touch him. Didn't matter how much she wanted to do just that. She couldn't. Her fingers curled into her palm.

With the tip of her tongue, she wet her lips.

He couldn't see her, didn't have a clue she sat a few feet away. A vise constricted her chest.

After a twist of his torso to each side, he squeezed his eyes shut for a moment, then straightened his T-shirt and stumbled from the room. A few moments later water gurgled through the old house pipes.

He'd gotten into the shower.

She laced her hands through her hair, rested them on top of her head. This was insane. She was being punished.

For what?

What had she done to be so close to Jake yet unable to touch him?

Water continued to murmur through the pipes.

In the past, *when she was alive* and would stay over, they had always showered together. Always. Scrubbing each other's back ... that's where the scrubbing and rubbing would usually start, anyway.

Where *that* led had nothing to do with cleanliness.

Her breathing snagged at the center of her chest, caught on the grip around her heart. Unlacing her fingers, she wrapped her arms around her waist.

Jake. Naked in the shower. Alone. Waiting for her.

The way this seemed to work, her new and odd ability, all she had to do was think about being somewhere inside the house and she was suddenly there.

Yet, this time – in spite of her own wayward thoughts – she was positive Jake would prefer his privacy.

Did she give a damn about that?

With her arms wrapped tighter around her middle, she rocked herself forwards and back.

She wasn't a voyeur.

But this was Jake.

Her lover, her soul. The only one who had ever made her feel whole. Her other half.

Even if he had never really felt the same and she'd told him to go to hell.

Hannah scrunched her eyes closed. Opened them.

Oh, boy.

She now stood in the middle of the oversized bathroom. Steam from the hot water had the old beveled mirror completely fogged up, along with the bathroom window overlooking the forest.

Jake leaned in the shower, his hands braced against the tiled wall and the steamy glass shower door. With his head bowed forward, water pressed his hair against his scalp and sluiced down his muscular back.

Tension radiated through every line of his fierce, naked body, tension the water caressed but didn't ease. With his eyes closed tight and his mouth half curled in a snarl, his face held none of the relaxed poise it had earlier, when he'd woken for those few, brief unguarded moments and gazed at her with such pleasure.

Oh, God. Jake. What's happened to you? To me? To us?

His eyes snapped open then narrowed. He straightened as he cast a wary glance around the room.

Lack of clothing only enhanced the feline grace of Jake's body, his nudity added to the unconscious power he exuded. She lifted her hand, the ache strong to reach out and touch him, to run her hands down his back, to lightly caress the firm muscles of his butt.

His lip curled again. She could almost hear the rumble tightening his chest.

"*Leave me alone.*" His words, whispered in a single harsh breath, stabbed at the center of her heart.

With her hand pressed to her chest, she bowed her head and blinked back the sudden sting of tears.

He wanted her away from him.

She could give him that, at least for the moment.

HANNAH HOVERED in the far corner of the kitchen. If Jake sensed her presence this time, would he storm out of the house?

Again?

She pressed her fingers to her lips.

Misty mid-morning light filtered in through the open window behind Jake. The breeze teased the damp ends of his hair, hair he'd left longer than she'd ever seen it. He stood with his back to the kitchen counter, his coffee cup in one hand and a cold, distant look in his eyes.

What was he thinking? Feeling?

Sadie had finished the food he'd sat down for her and now lay curled on the mat by the kitchen door. Her worried gaze shifted between Hannah and Jake, something she'd always done whenever they'd fought. Back then, Hannah had usually ended up feeling guilty for upsetting the dog.

Now, here, she didn't know how to fix this situation.

Or even if there was a fix.

"Come on, Sadie-girl." His jaw tight, Jake pushed away from the counter then set his cup in the sink. "Let's go feed Nels. Then I think I'll head into town."

Sadie scrambled to her feet. With a long, last, sad look at Hannah, she followed Jake outside.

Hannah took one step forward.

Going to town sounded so much better than hanging here by herself, moping over things she didn't understand.

What if she was stuck here, at the house? Unable to ever leave?

A sudden chill dropped over her, raising goose bumps across her entire body. She bit her bottom lip, threaded her hands through her hair for a quick moment.

With silent steps she hurried to the kitchen window, caught sight of Jake just before he disappeared into the barn with Sadie and Nels right behind.

Hannah held out her left hand, stopped short of the window screen. That misty sunlight glinted soft on her bracelet and played across her skin. With the tip of her right index finger, she traced the pattern of light over the back of her hand.

She was a woman who sensed her entire world through touch, through her fingertips. Tactile only scratched the surface of what she was able to sense through her hands.

These hands. Both held in front of her, she studied her palms, rubbed them together then over the sleeves of her sweater. Soft. Supple.

Sensual.

Jake.

A sharp, piercing stab tore at the center of her head. She sucked in a razor-edged breath before she sank to the floor.

There she leaned forward to press her suddenly clammy palms against her forehead.

Dark grey edged her vision. Throbs of pure pain took her breath, left her gasping, until she couldn't focus on anything except the surrounding darkness.

CURLED IN A TIGHT BALL, Hannah fisted her hands against her temples. She squeezed her closed eyelids tight.

How much time had she lost?

She pressed her knuckles harder against her head, relieved the pain had receded to only a dull, throbbing ache.

After blinking several times, she eased her fists open and gingerly traced the tips of her fingers over her brows. Slow and awkward, she straightened her stiff legs. Sadie's distressed whines echoed from outside the kitchen door.

Hannah stood on shaky legs. She pushed her hair out of her face with trembling hands and took stock. The solid back door was shut and locked. So Jake must have been back inside at some point.

She could hear Old Nels pacing down below the back porch. He paused to bay every few moments. On a full, shuddering breath, Hannah eased forward to look out the window.

Late morning, at least according to the angle of the sun.

Okay. The animals were upset. Jake was gone.

Was it still the same day?

"Sadie." Hannah sucked in another harsh breath. Her lungs burned, but she repeated the process. "I'm okay."

Immediately the dog's whining stopped. Nels angled his head to look at the house. He let out one long bay before he moved on to tear at the young, green leaves budding on the small bush below the porch.

Nels had his own priorities. A sting of sudden tears singed Hannah's eyes. She swiped them away. At least she fit *somewhere* on Nels' list. Sadie's tail thumped against the screen before she was off chasing something small that had darted across the yard.

Hannah turned away from the window.

If this was the same day as her last memory, Jake had headed to town. Where in town?

She blinked.

Suddenly, she stood outside in a small, asphalted parking area holding only one vehicle. A deep royal blue, vintage Jeep.

Fine tremors ran down her spine.

Okay. She pressed her lips together. Looked like she *wasn't* confined to the house after all because this certainly wasn't Jake's home. Wasn't even his property.

How was she getting around like this?

A small, sharp bite of pain pricked between her eyes, across her scalp.

Did she really want to know? Especially with the pain that seemed to accompany all of her questions.

Wasn't *not knowing* worse?

She tucked a wayward strand of hair behind her ear.

"What the hell am I doing here?" Jake's voice, low and full of self-disgust, washed over her.

She spun towards him.

That same earlier self-loathing evident on his face, Jake stood with his arms locked across his chest, his chin tucked and his gaze on the renovated Victorian house sitting regally on the other side of the parking area.

Dr. Sheldon's office and home.

Hannah's doctor.

Jake had said she had a blood disorder. She vaguely remembered feeling tired, run down and making an appointment with Dr. Sheldon.

Anemia. Needing iron.

Pain pierced her temples.

Focus on something else.

Blinking several times, she glanced over her shoulder at the Jeep. Jake's Jeep? The last time she'd seen his, the vehicle sat torn apart in his barn. The plan had been to rebuild the engine, to put the twenty-something year old vehicle back in service.

How many months ago?

Why couldn't this all just be a bad dream gone wrong?

The Jeep in the parking lot sported new paint, sat shining in the light peeking through the gathering clouds.

She swallowed on the hysterical laughter clogging her throat.

Jake's Jeep. Some detective she made.

But being a detective was where Jake excelled. His father, the retired Chief of Police, had said so many times.

Had Jake made Sergeant yet?

She frowned. Another thing added to her list of unanswered questions.

"Why am I doing this?" Jake's low voice pulled her gaze back to him. "What difference is it going to make?"

I don't know. The words echoed in her head. More questions, no answers.

With her lips pressed tight together, she tilted her head towards the Victorian house that stood like a gracefully aging sentry from its hillside perch overlooking the Columbia River.

She'd always thought Dr. Sheldon matched his house, standing as a guardian against disease. Inspiring in the way he'd dedicated his life to finding a cure for the illness that had taken his wife so many years ago.

Hannah stole another glance at Jake. He now stood with his hands splayed at his hips, his legs braced apart and his hard gaze fixed on the house. A small, almost imperceptible tick twitched along his jaw.

He *was* going to find out what had happened to her.

The pain biting at her head sharpened and sliced into her forehead as neatly as a slick blade sinking through her skin and into the bone of her skull. She sucked in a caustic breath.

Dizzy, she swayed and stretched out her hand. Jake was already moving towards the steps, the ones leading to the wrap around veranda and the front door.

If she fell, he wouldn't know.

Unless she called out to him.

But without being able to see her, what help could he be?

Disgusted with herself, with her pity party, she ignored the dizziness and took an awkward step forward. She *needed* to be with him when he strode through that front door. She needed to hear the questions he asked, needed those answers.

Darkness, swift and lethal, cloaked her mind, robbed her breath and sucked all light from her world.

She pitched forward with no way to stop herself. A cry tore from her throat before she sank into an abyss of black, painful nothingness.

JAKE'S GUT TIGHT, he twisted around, away from Dr. Sheldon's front door. He was sure he'd heard Hannah's cry, desperate and scared, his name a harsh scrape through the air around him.

No one was there. Big surprise. No one was ever there.

"Hannah?" Straining to catch the slightest sound, he heard the myriad of noises from the river and the drone of traffic several blocks away. Honeysuckle, hanging thick and heavy over the fence encircling the side of the Victorian house, weighed down the late morning air. Bees buzzed.

No Hannah.

You're going nuts, old boy. He shook his head, turned back to the door. *May as well get this over with.* His shoulders squared, he pulled the heavy, ornate door open then strode inside.

"May I help you?" The young and pretty blonde smiled at him from behind a tall, hand carved, dark mahogany counter. Her name plate read Amy.

He smiled and forced the Carrigan family charm to the surface. "I sure hope so, Amy."

Dimples winked in her cheeks. A light blush tinged her skin. Ah, hell. He wasn't here to flirt. Still, he kept the smile plastered to his face.

"My name is Jake Carrigan. My girlfriend was a patient here –"

"Oh." Disappointment clouded Amy's eyes. "We can't share information unless the patient signs a form specifically allowing us to. Did your girlfriend sign the form?"

"Hannah … died." Damn, the words still stuck in his throat.

"Oh." Sudden tears welled in the girl's yes. She certainly wouldn't make any kind of decent poker player.

He nodded, glanced away from the pity she aimed like a dart at him. This was harder than he'd expected, and he hadn't thought it'd be easy.

"Listen, Amy." He sucked in a lungful of air. Maybe a different tactic was necessary. "I'm looking for her ashes. She was cremated and –"

"You don't already have her ashes?" A perfect little frown line marred her smooth skin.

"No." He forced down the irritation gnawing at him. How was he going to get through this if she kept interrupting him? "I was out of the country when she ... passed. Hannah didn't have any family, but my sister talked with someone in this office and —"

"I'm new so it couldn't have been me."

Never would have guessed. He bit back the retort, forced his mouth to smile. "I just need to know where her ashes are. For —" He swallowed past the damn knot stuck at the base of his throat. "Closure."

"Ohhh." Amy wiped at a tear that had spilled over her long lashes. "What's her name? I can't guarantee there's anything I can share with you, but I can at least look."

"Hannah Dixon. She died last September." He had to get this out fast, before Amy interrupted him again or he lost his momentum. "Whoever my sister talked to said this office had taken care of the ... cremation for Hannah."

"Oh. Jake. Let me look for you."

Conflicting emotions battled in his head as he watched Amy's cute, little and irritating rear-end sashay from the room.

Rily was right. He did need to do this. That didn't mean he wanted to do it. He didn't want to know where Hannah's ashes were, he didn't want to have to face the fact she hadn't bothered to make sure he knew where she was, afterwards. That she hadn't even considered he might want to have her ashes.

For closure.

He could still leave.

Being here didn't mean he *had* to get the information. Or that he had to stay. He could still turn and —

"That's the funniest thing, Jake." Amy stepped back into the room with a folder in one of her perfectly manicured hands. The tip of one pink nail tapped her bottom lip.

"There's no record in here of her death, much less anything about a cremation or ashes. And the last entry, dated just over eight months ago, says her anemia was improving."

"No record?" His insides clenched around the thick ball of dread solidifying in his stomach. He focused on Amy pouting over the folder. Hannah had been getting better? At least according to her medical records.

Then why the hell had she died?

He ran a hand through his hair. "There's no kind of notation?"

"No, nothing at all. Dr. Sheldon's the county medical examiner. A copy of the death certificate should be in here."

"Maybe she died in Portland."

"Oh, well, no." She closed the folder and set it on her desk. "See, Althea – she's Dr. Sheldon's daughter. She doubles as his nurse and his office manager. She's a paperwork bitch." Amy's baby-blue eyes widened. "Please don't tell her I said that."

"No problem. What about the paperwork?"

"Whew. I really have to learn to watch what I say." She frowned. "I probably shouldn't have said anything about your girlfriend's health or the death certificate either."

"Hannah died, Amy." *Keep on saying it, buddy.* "I doubt she'll complain."

"Oh." Amy aimed a bright smile at him. "Well, it really doesn't matter where your Hannah died, Althea would have obtained a copy of the certificate. Otherwise, you see, her files wouldn't be complete."

"I do see." *Liar.* None of this made sense. He smelled something dank. Maybe not a rat, but something stank and now he needed to get to the bottom of it. Dammit all to hell and back. "Is Althea here? Can I talk to her?"

Amy's eyes slid upward, but she pursed her pink lips. She shook her head.

"Amy, please."

"Today is her day off. And the doctor's. They're upstairs, in their home, but I have strict orders not to disturb them." She smiled. Remorse shone bright in her blue eyes. "Jake, you'll have to come back another time to talk to her. I am sorry about your Hannah, but you talking to Althea today isn't worth my job."

A short time later Jake raked his hands through his hair. He stepped onto the front veranda. As pliable as Amy had seemed, she had an invisible steel rod stuck down her spine when it came to Althea's rules. Women and their stiff backs.

He strode down the steps to his vehicle then took another backwards glance at the house. Amy was a cute, if a bit annoying, kid.

Although he hadn't learned much, what he'd come away with had sharpened his curiosity. Even if it hadn't touched his grief.

Closure, hell.

With his cell phone out, he climbed into his Jeep before he dialed his sister's number.

Rily answered on the first ring.

"How about meeting me at that coffee place you like so much?" He twisted the key in the ignition. "The one by the river. Got some thoughts I'd like to run by you."

"Jake."

One word. His name. All that damn emotion tied up with a pink bow the color of Amy's nails. He swore under his breath. If he had to deal with any more weepy females he was going to simply throw himself into the Columbia River and get it over and done with.

"Rily —" He'd thought better of his sister. "Dammit."

"I'm good, Jake. You just caught me by surprise. I have some things to clear up. Take me about an hour. Order me a roast-beef sandwich, too."

She hung up. Jake sat and stared at the phone in his hand. Women.

The breeze, ripe with the scent of honeysuckle, drifted up from the river. A chill scudded down his spine. He glanced at the Victorian house. On an upper story window a curtain settled, drawing his attention to that side of the house.

Who watched him?

Had cute, little Amy told Althea and the good doctor he'd been there after all?

The Sheldons. Father and daughter. Very curious. His brother had gone to school with Althea, but Jake didn't know much about her. He'd have to come back, see where his curiosity might lead.

Maybe there was nothing more sinister than missing paperwork.

Missing paperwork and missing ashes.

Hannah's.

She had no family left, no one except him to claim those ashes. So where were they?

He wanted answers.

First, he'd run things by Rily, get her perspective on everything.

Everything except the way Hannah's voice haunted him. That wasn't something he was ready to share with his sister.

Not yet. Maybe not ever.

ALTHEA SHELDON SMOOTHED the heavy green drapes back into place over the second story balcony window. She tucked a strand of her short auburn hair behind her ear.

Really, it wasn't as if that man down there in the parking lot actually cared about his *ex*-girlfriend.

Jake Carrigan.

The sound of his Jeep's engine revved then faded in the distance.

Good riddance. She shuddered once before tapping her index finger against her bottom lip. What an interesting conversation she'd overheard between Jake and silly, little Amy.

He wanted closure.

Maybe he should have thought about that before he'd abandoned Hannah to deal with her illness by herself. All alone.

If you loved someone, weren't you supposed to stay? Through thick and thin? Good times and bad?

The way her father had stayed with her mother.

Dedicated love, full of loyalty and devotion was rare.

Not that she was judge or jury, but Jake Carrigan had certainly proven himself completely unworthy of someone as remarkable as Hannah Dixon.

Althea rubbed her suddenly chilled arms. She was wasting time she didn't have, standing here mulling over someone else's relationship. Her father's notes needed transcribing and there were other patients to occupy her mind.

Even if it was her day off.

Chapter Three

"**D**AMMIT, JAKE." Gold flashed hot in Rily's green eyes as she pounded her fist once on the coffee shop's sturdy table.

Jake and his sister sat alone on the open wooden deck overlooking the river, the meager late lunch crowd opting to dine inside the rustic building. Considering how irate his sister was, that was probably good. "Rily —"

"What do you think you're doing? Setting yourself up as some kind of freaking white knight? Because you couldn't rescue her when she was alive? Hannah doesn't need to be saved, Jake. Not anymore."

"Rily —"

"Don't you dare tell me to listen, you blockheaded, arrogant ass." She leaned back and shoved her hands through her hair. "I thought — And yes, maybe I'm arrogant, too. But I thought maybe I'd finally gotten through to you. That you were actually ready to move on, to work on letting Hannah go. To move forward with your life."

"Rily."

"What?" Belligerence radiated through the glare she kept aimed at him.

"Where are Hannah's ashes?"

"I don't know."

"And her death certificate? All I'm asking is that you check on that, check on the cause of death. For me."

"Jake –"

"Please." He twisted the half empty coffee mug in front of him, stared out over the grey, weathered railing at the churning river.

Sunlight skidded across the water's surface to ride along the ripples from the strong current that splashed against the rocks below where they sat. The slight, dank smell of the river swelled upwards on the breeze.

No heavy scent of honeysuckle down here on the water.

He couldn't tell Rily why, wasn't sure of all his reasons himself. But now, at this point in time, he *needed* to see that certificate.

His brief run by the library and their slow internet terminal hadn't yielded a damn thing. Even after paying the fee for access to the Oregon state records, he hadn't found anything on Hannah.

Not a damn thing.

He wasn't next of kin. In the eyes of the law, he wasn't anything to Hannah, not entitled to the death certificate. Hell, he wasn't entitled to *anything* having to do with his ex-girlfriend. But he needed the proof she was truly gone.

And the why. Needed that for himself.

First order, though, even before the *why*, was to see that certificate – the long form – listing her cause of death. Rily, as a cop, had access to that one.

Hannah's ashes … he still wasn't sure he wanted those, no matter what Rily thought. Or what he'd told Amy.

Maybe, though, once he had them – if he was able to get them – he'd sprinkle those ashes out on the nearby ocean, out at sea. Like his parents had done for his brother. Or maybe Hannah would prefer the forest. Maybe.

"You told me to accept that she's gone." He swung his gaze back to his sister. "Yet that girl in Dr. Sheldon's office couldn't find any record of Hannah even dying."

Rily's eyes narrowed.

"For closure." God, he hated using that card on her. "I need to know where she is."

"You didn't give a damn about the location of her ashes yesterday."

A short laugh, more of a bark, escaped him. She was sharp, his baby sister. "No. I didn't."

"What changed?"

Now they were getting into dangerous waters he had no intention of treading. Not with her. "Doesn't matter. Yesterday's done. *Today* I need to know where she is."

Rily leaned back and scrubbed at her face. From between her fingers she looked across at him. She lowered her hands, shook her head. "Okay."

"Okay?" Too simple. Too easy. There had to be a catch.

"Okay. I'll check into the death certificate, into the cause of Hannah's death." She pushed aside the plate holding only remnants of her sandwich. Lifting her coffee cup, she took a small sip. "But once I find it, you have to promise you'll go to that support group. The one that meets on Thursdays at the hospital."

Why not? "Okay."

"Just like that?"

"Just like that." He'd force himself to go to the meeting. One time. He sure as hell wasn't committing to more than that.

She narrowed her eyes again. He could see the wheels working in her head. Behind his mug he hid the small, humorless smile he couldn't quite resist and took a swig of his own black coffee. He'd given in too easily and it bothered the crap out of her.

Sometimes he plain enjoyed messing with his sister's mind. These days he took the small pleasures where he could find them.

HANNAH COULDN'T MOVE.

She struggled to lift her arms, to press her hands to her head, but agony attacked her muscles. A heaviness sat on her, weighing her down. Panic clawed at her chest, tore at her insides while blackness swirled and pain exploded through every part of her body.

Where was she? Where was Jake?

She screamed, but no sound came out. None.

JAKE SAT IN HIS JEEP and stared at his home. Late afternoon sun glowed behind the house, rimming it and the looming heavy clouds in gold. The scent of the coming thunderstorm filled his nose. Trepidation welled in his gut. He had more questions than when he'd left this morning.

Along with no real answers.

His earlier belief something was off with Hannah's death had faded, replaced by the sense he was grasping at brittle straws. Just as his sister had more or less suggested.

Rather strongly.

He rotated his head, working on the kinks that had taken up residence in his neck. Hannah hadn't been murdered.

What reason would anyone have to harm her?

Not like Craig, who had gone gunning for the wrong people and paid for it with his life. Jake shook his head sharp, once, to force those memories away.

No. Hannah's illness had sucked the life out of her. In spite of what Amy said, shoddy paperwork had to be at the crux of this whole thing. Rily would find the certificate, the cause of death. That would be that.

He ignored the whole other issue of Hannah's ashes.

Shutting down the Jeep, he climbed out and pocketed his keys. Sadie came running from around the barn with Nels trotting along behind. Jake bent to rub the dog's ears then did the same for the old goat. He and the animals made their way to the kitchen door, although Nels stopped to chew on a new outcropping of grass.

Once inside the house, Jake stood still and took stock. The place *felt* empty. Like he and Sadie were the only ones there.

"Hannah?" The word snuck out of his mouth. He closed his eyes for a brief moment then lowered his chin to his chest to stare at the floor.

What the hell was he doing?

Like he *wanted* her to answer? To be in his head?

Maybe he did.

Shit. What a sick bastard.

He swallowed the bile lining his throat and grabbed a can of soda from the fridge. His movements determined, he snapped open his drink before slamming his way through the kitchen door to the safety of the outdoors.

Except for the whisper of his name this afternoon before he'd gone inside the doctor's office, he'd only ever heard her inside his house. This afternoon had to have been a fluke, brought on by his nerves, the stress of what he'd been about to do.

She hadn't spoken to him since last night, when he'd told her she'd been cremated. After, like the jerk he was, he'd cleared out of the house, leaving her to deal with the fact she had no body by herself.

You're getting damn close to certifiable.

Still, she'd been upset and he'd left her there.

Alone. Sad.

He kicked a rock and watched it tumble across the ruts of the wide, dirt path angling across his yard. He was an ass. Even if she was only a voice in his head, he'd been a true, arrogant ass.

This morning in the shower, he'd have sworn she stood there, watching him. With longing and despair hanging heavy in the air.

Stupid, stupid thinking. Those had been *his* feelings, not hers. He'd been indulging in some kind of stupid psychological projection, thinking she'd been there, wanting to join him in the shower.

Wanting him, period.

God, he missed her.

He took a long swig of his cola, finishing it before he turned his gaze towards the barn. Rily had cleared out Hannah's apartment and stuffed everything in a far corner of the building. While he'd been floating around the Caribbean. Drunk and alone.

He slung the soda can against the side of the barn.

Hannah had dumped *him*, dammit.

That was on her. Not him.

He shoved one hand in his pocket, fingered the ring box he took everywhere with him these days, like some kind of stupid talisman.

Hannah was gone, it wasn't like he would ever get the chance to ask her to marry him. Or that she would have even said yes, had he had the chance to ask.

She'd been pretty adamant about breaking up with him. To the point his ego had taken quite a hit and his pride had made it impossible for him to beg.

For the reason why, for her to take back his pathetic self. For her to just love him.

The way he loved her.

The velvety softness of the box against his fingers did nothing to soothe his inner turmoil. No matter what he'd told himself, he had loved her.

He still did.

Sharing that with her back then, the depth of his feelings, hadn't occurred to him. They'd been so comfortable with each other.

Almost from their first date.

He hadn't been the most romantic guy around and he knew he'd taken her for granted, thinking she'd always be there. Treating her like shit and closing her out after Craig had died. Expecting her to love him enough to stick around anyway.

Wasn't that what people did, people who actually loved each other? Like his parents. They stuck through the ups and the downs.

Was that why Hannah was still here?

One corner of his mouth lifted.

Man, he was getting morose.

And pathetic.

Hannah hanging around because he still loved her and wouldn't let go? God, he was arrogant.

Wasn't that a pisser? Rily was right. Again.

Shit.

With his shoulders stiff, he left the ring box in his pocket and headed back up the worn path to his home.

May as well face his own inner demons.

Just because Hannah hadn't answered earlier didn't mean she wasn't still in the house.

"HANNAH?"

Jake's voice came from a long way away. As if he stood at the far end of a tunnel, calling to her.

Blackness still spiraled. She curled her arms around her waist in increments, her muscles trembling from the effort. The deep breath she sucked in burned her throat.

"Hannah? Are you still here?"

"Jake?" Even to her own ears her voice sounded husky, as if she hadn't used it in days. Maybe she hadn't. She had no sense of time, no sense of anything.

Only blackness and Jake's voice.

"You are here." Relief tinged his words.

She sank slowly in the darkness, wrapping the essence of Jake's voice around her. She was so tired. So weak.

"Hannah? Say something."

"Something."

A soft, masculine laugh swept over her. Couldn't she just burrow into that sound, let it enfold her? Make her whole.

"Keep talking to me, Hannah."

Jake needed something.

Blackness eddied, sucked at her body, tightening its cloak and mulling her mind. What did Jake need from her?

"Please, Baby. Talk to me."

Hannah angled her head. Pinpoints of light exploded behind her eyelids. She tried to open her eyes. Her lids fluttered, wanted to close. So much simpler to lay here, not moving.

Movement brought pain.

Lord, she hurt.

"Hannah?"

Jake. She managed to open her eyes a small slit. Pain radiated everywhere. Through her body, from outside her body.

So much pain.

"Dammit. I don't know why I thought that would work." His voice echoed from somewhere above her.

"Jake?" She lifted her head, focused on a blur that might be his face. After several blinks, the haziness shifted to the edges of her vision.

The kitchen. She lay crumpled on his kitchen floor. Feeble, indirect sunlight shone through the partially open, thin curtains over the window above the sink.

Late afternoon? Early evening?

His footsteps heavy, Jake paced away from her.

"I'm here." With the tip of her tongue, she wet her lips. Her legs protested but she managed to get herself into a quasi-sitting position. With her head wobbling on her neck, she narrowed her gaze to focus on him.

He stood in the center of the room, staring in her general direction but not at her. Knots twisted knife-deep in her stomach. She lifted a shaky hand, pushed her hair back from her face.

What had she expected? This to all go away, to be that bad dream she prayed it was? For him to be able to see her sprawled on his floor?

Sounded good to her.

Too bad she couldn't make that one a reality.

"Where have you been?" Concern threaded though the timbre of his voice, leaving it huskier than normal.

"I don't really know." But she wasn't at all interested in a return trip. "What happened at Dr. Sheldon's office?"

Still disorientated, she zeroed in on the strong lines of Jake's face. How his brow arched at her question then lowered when he turned his head to stare out the kitchen window.

"How did you know I was at your doctor's office?" Suspicion laced each word.

Hannah frowned. How had she known? "Lucky guess?"

"Right. Of course, since you probably are just a figment in my head, why wouldn't you know?"

That stung. Hannah bit down on her bottom lip. Was she something he'd conjured up?

Or maybe he needed to get over himself and deal with her.

"What if I'm not just a figment in your fragmented head?" Letting her temper lead wouldn't help. Not in the long run. But, for the moment, for right now, it *felt* good. "Ever stop and think of that?"

The complete look of anguished surprise lining his face was almost worth the intensity of the ache gripping her head. She pressed both hands against her temples.

"If you're not something my mind conjured up, to help me deal with losing you, then what are you?"

She had no idea. None.

"A ghost? Is that any better?" Jake paced to the open back door, stood with his fists braced at his hips. He stared out the screen. "I loved you, Hannah."

Loved. Past tense. Pain as sharp as what pierced her head stabbed deep at her heart. Twisted. To Jake she was nothing more than a wisp of spirit hell-bent on tormenting him.

"I still love you, Jake."

"Right." With a deep, shuddering breath, he leaned his head back and closed his eyes. "How do you think I felt, coming home to find out you were *dead?* That you'd developed some kind of terminal blood disease? Something so obscure there are no real facts about it on the internet. That you hadn't even bothered to let anyone know? Not Rily, your best friend. Not –" His arms crossed over his chest, he opened his eyes and glanced back into the room. The bleakness in his gaze gave another twist to the knife at the center of her heart. "Me."

Hannah cringed at the raw pain radiating in waves from him.

"I bought you a ring."

She swallowed and focused on his face, on the tightness of his jaw. "The one in the blue velvet box?"

Jake stuck his hand in his pocket, pulled out the box. He rubbed his thumb over the top then turned and tossed it onto the table. "Yeah, that one. I came back to ask you to marry me, Hannah. You. Me. Happily ever after."

As if he'd smacked her across the cheek, she recoiled, away from him. "Was happily ever after ever possible for us, Jake? Would you have even cared that I was sick?"

Her head throbbed. Sudden, traitorous tears she couldn't control tracked down her cheeks but she didn't bother wiping her face. He couldn't see them.

"Oh, I cared, Hannah. Obviously more than you knew. If I'd known how sick you were, I would've come back. For you. You should've let me be there. You shouldn't have made that decision for me. Taken that away from me." Jake shoved the screen door open, shook his head on his way outside.

"Why can't I remember?" Her whispered words were lost in the resounding bang of the metal hitting its wooden frame.

Dammit. Once again he was walking away from her.

Tension lined his entire body as he stalked towards the barn.

She sent a quick, stiff-necked glare at his retreating back, wiped the moisture from her cheeks with the back of her hand.

Damn senseless tears.

How could she know *why* she hadn't told him about the illness when she couldn't even remember being sick?

Besides, he was the one who had checked out emotionally *before* they'd broken up. Who turned tail and ran off on to some island.

But if she had really thought he was that big of an ass, why was she so sure he'd step up for her now?

Throbbing pain pulsed across her forehead, spikes of it piercing her temples. Would he have come back from the Caribbean? Been there for her, held her hand when she took her last breath?

How could anyone love her enough to go through all of that?

Her own father had left when she was young, abandoning her and her mother. She barely remembered him, but her mother had loved him, obsessively, until the day she'd died. That love had left little room for anything else, almost nothing for a daughter who reminded her too strongly of the love she'd lost.

And that sounded too much like self-pity. Something Hannah wasn't going to make time for, not today, at least not about her parents.

She rubbed at her temples, at the pain banging through her head and took a tentative step towards the table. Towards the box holding the ring Jake had bought for her. Once she stood next to the table she reached out a hesitant hand.

He'd wanted to marry her.

To make a future with her.

Her hand hovered over the table and she wavered.

She *needed* to touch the box, to feel the soft texture of the blue velvet, the hardness of the box itself. Flip it open and see the ring.

Rily had done that, in this very kitchen, but Hannah had been too intent on what they were saying, on the implications of their words, to have thought about looking at what the box contained.

Now that box filled her mind.

Jake had wanted to marry her.

She lowered her hand, holding it just above the blue velvet. Touching Sadie hadn't worked. Would this be different?

With her breathing shallow and unstable, she stood for long minutes. *Dammit. Just do it.* Sucking in a deeper breath, she wrapped her fingers around the box.

Nothing. No crushed velvet texture, no hard box beneath. She pushed at the damn thing. No movement, not a fraction.

She pressed the heels of her palms against her eyes.

Sadie whined, the sound penetrating the fog of Hannah's thoughts and she lowered her hands from her face. Beyond the screen door Sadie's gaze caught and held hers for several moments before the dog lowered her head and ambled off the porch.

Hannah swayed slightly, her gaze locked on the dog until Sadie disappeared from sight.

The barn.

Hannah *now* stood in the center of *that* building.

Sadie whined again.

Hannah's breath barely more than a shallow rise and fall of her chest, she took a shaky step forward. Stopped. Jake sat on a short stool in front of an open storage box. Sadie curled her body to settle next to him. Her gaze on Hannah, her tail thumped the ground.

Hannah's jewelry box sat on the workbench. A few years ago Jake had carved the box from a piece of oak they'd found on a walk through the forest. The lid open, her necklaces, most made by her, glittered in the soft, diffused light filtering in from above the barn's overhead beams.

She had polished that oak box until it gleamed. The wood itself had sung to her when she'd rubbed her fingers across its surface, whispering of times past, grateful and proud to be something so beautiful now.

The thought might have been fanciful, but that was how she'd communicated with the world. Through her fingertips.

Or she had. Before.

Not any longer.

She fisted her hand to her mouth and choked back the moan trying to escape. All these damn emotions.

No pity party, dammit.

Jake had no idea she was here. Probably best to keep it that way, for now.

Wetting her lips, she eased to sit on the ground with her legs pulled to her chest and her arms wrapped around her knees. She huddled in on herself to try and savor the hazy, late in the day sunlight, even if its meager warmth wasn't real to her.

Jake frowned, lifted his head and scanned the barn. *What the hell was that?* His grip tightened on the small, flat stone in his hand, the hard texture real and reassuring.

Nothing in the barn looked out of the ordinary. On the surface, everything seemed fine.

That slight vibration in the air, that sudden low hum – there, then gone – he'd be damned if he called out to Hannah again.

No matter what his subconscious wanted or hoped.

His jaw rigid, he opened his hand, rubbed his thumb over the rippled surface of the stone. Hannah's favorite. He traced the wide vein of white the same way he'd watched her do in the past.

Hannah's stones. Collected from nearly every place they'd ever visited together. But this one had been her favorite. She'd sit on his porch, stroke the rock's surface and stare out at the trees.

With a deep sigh rumbling around his chest, the tenseness lining his jaw eased as he curled his fingers around the edges of the stone. The warmth and solidness of the rock eked through his skin.

He'd been upset when he'd come out here, but now, sitting here holding her worry stone with her things strewn around him, he wasn't nearly as edgy as he'd been when he stormed out of the house.

Hannah had to be a ghost.

He'd do some research on his computer, find what he could about *that* particular phenomena.

A humorless chuckle tickled the back of his throat. Now Hannah was a phenomena. What other ways would his mind find to rationalize this?

A ghost.

Rationalizing or not, it might be as simple as that.

He sat the rock next to the others and stood, stretching. "Come on, Sadie. Let's go to the house and boot up the computer."

Sadie looked up at him and whimpered. He bent, rubbed behind her ears then stretched once more before he turned to head for the barn door. Sadie stayed where she was, her gaze swinging from him to a spot on the other side of the barn.

He glanced where Sadie seemed to be looking, but there was nothing there except farm equipment. Equipment that had always been there. Nothing out of the ordinary. Not even that low hum or vibration.

"Come on girl. Let's go."

Sadie whimpered again.

He stood with his hands braced on his hips. "What's wrong with you, girl?"

"She doesn't want to leave me." Hannah's soft voice drifted across the barn, coming from the area where Sadie had been so intent.

"So." Maybe he should have expected this. "You really aren't stuck in the house."

"I guess not."

"Sadie seems to be able to —" He took a deep breath. "See you."

"Animals are supposed to be sensitive that way."

"Well. It seems Sadie is, doesn't it?" Right. That was a brilliant observation. "You really are a ghost."

"I don't know. I don't feel dead, but I guess I'm not alive, either. Considering."

His gut tightened in on itself at the weakness shading her voice.

"Are you okay?" He settled back on the stool. This didn't seem to be the time to leave.

"Define okay." A wobbly laugh ended on an abrupt moan.

"That was a stupid question." He reached into the box, more for something to do with his hands than because he wanted to look at anything else.

"Define stupid." This time she did laugh, soft and gentle.

He let his own smile spread a little and glanced down at the address book he'd pulled from the box.

"This is where my things ended up?"

"Yeah." He flipped through a few pages. "While I was gone your landlady asked Rily to clear out your apartment. Everything ended up here."

This wasn't so bad, sitting here in the coziness of his barn, casually chatting with Hannah. Weird, yes, but not so bad. An entry in the address book caught his attention. "I didn't realize you had an uncle."

"I don't. No aunts either."

"Isn't this your mom's address book. The handwriting isn't yours." He'd know Hannah's anywhere. He twisted the book, looked at its cover then back at the entry. "This is for a Benjamin Garrett, with Uncle scribbled in the sidebar. Your mom's uncle?"

"My parents were both only children of only children." Hannah's voice still sounded weary. Tired and worn out.

Why would a ghost get tired?

"There were never any siblings to be aunts or uncles." Hannah's sigh echoed through the confines of the barn, floated over his skin. "I'm the only one left. On either side."

He ignored the shivers chasing themselves over his arms. Instead, he glanced up from the book and arched an eyebrow in the general direction of her voice.

"*Was* the only one left." Hannah's whispered words ended on another soft sigh.

He swallowed the words stuck in his throat, focused back on the book. How did he comfort a ghost?

So much for coziness, this was almost as hard as when he believed she'd been a figment of his imagination. Maybe worse.

Then, she was just something his mind had conjured up.

A ghost, well, didn't ghosts still have some part of the essence of the person? Like this really was a part of Hannah and not his imagination working overtime.

Ghost or figment? Either way he was losing it so he might as well go with the delusion.

If that wasn't pure rationalization, he didn't know what was.

"So who do you think this supposed uncle of yours is?"

"I don't know." Weaker than earlier, Hannah's shaky voice alarmed him.

"What's wrong?"

"Every time I try and remember the slightest thing, my head feels as if it's going to explode."

"Ah, Baby. I could – No. I guess aspirin can't help you now, can it?"

"No."

He *hated* being so helpless. "Hannah –"

"I don't think even you can fix this." The softness of her voice teased his skin. "I think I just need time to –"

"What?"

"I really don't know." Her fatigued, gentle laugh washed over him.

He rubbed the edge of the address book with his index finger. He had to *do* something. Sitting here wasn't changing a damn thing. Frowning at the phone number listed under the assumed uncle's name, he pulled his cell phone from his pocket.

"Are you calling Rily?"

"No." With his jaw set, he dialed the number in the address book. "I'm calling Uncle Ben."

There was a reason Hannah's mom had scribbled Uncle in the margin. Maybe he was a family friend, someone who deserved to know Hannah had passed on. Even if she didn't know who the devil the man was or what he'd meant to her mother. Something was off about the whole uncle thing and it nagged at him.

"Oh." Quietness lined Hannah's voice.

He glanced up just as the ringing abruptly stopped. Maybe he should have asked her first.

"Who is this?" A harsh female voice grated in his ear.

"I'm looking for Benjamin Garrett."

Silence greeted him for a long, drawn out moment. "Who is this? Where did you get this number?"

"I'm a friend of his niece and –" A loud click sounded as the woman disconnected her end of the phone. "Well. So much for that."

"What did he say?"

"It was a she. A not very friendly she. I was just hung up on." He set his phone and the address book on the top of a packing box then bent to scratch Sadie's head. She still gazed at the other side of the barn so he directed his comments in that direction. "Maybe this Garrett guy changed his number. I'm sure it's been quite a while since your mom made that entry."

"You're probably right." Hannah's sigh was deeper this time.

He smiled again in spite of himself. He remembered *that* sigh.

"Besides, I doubt this pseudo uncle, long lost friend of my mother or father, has any bearing on what's going on now. Or to who killed me."

"Hannah. No one killed you." Why didn't he tell her about the missing death certificate? Really, though, what would it accomplish? "But you're probably right, it has nothing to do with the way things are now."

"Besides, you'd just have to tell him that I'm … dead."

"Maybe he'd like to know."

"I don't know him, Jake. Why would it make any difference?"

He didn't have an answer for her, not one that made any kind of rational sense. But then, he'd left rational behind yesterday when he started hearing her voice again. Added to that was the fact he sat here carrying on a two-way conversation with her. And was comforted by that fact.

His cell phone rang, the sound abrupt and shrill.

Saved by the bell.

He glanced down at Sadie and shrugged. Restricted number. Could be anyone. He pushed the answer button.

"Hello." His voice curt, he leaned over to again rub the dog's ears.

"Who is this?" The voice, male this time, was rich and deep. And just as curt as Jake's had been.

"That depends." Jake settled more comfortably on his stool. "Is this Benjamin Garret?"

Chapter Four

FOR A LONG, drawn out moment Jake wondered if the man on the other end of the phone, the man Jake believed to be Benjamin Garrett, was going to answer his question.

"Who I am depends on how you managed to get this number, Mr. Carrigan."

Jake's hand tightened on his cell.

Crap.

How had Garrett found the correlation between this restricted number and Jake's name so quickly? Since his early days as a cop, he'd had his own phone set to block his number on outgoing calls.

Was Garrett with some covert branch of the government?

Jake glanced at the corner where Hannah had been. Her uneasiness ebbed over him, mixed with his own. Surprised, he tucked that sensation away to examine later. Right now he needed to concentrate on this phone call.

"Well, since we seem to be at a standoff, Mr. Garrett, I'll tell you why I called earlier."

"If you would be so kind." Sarcasm dripped from the man's voice.

Jake smiled, and it wasn't a smile full of humor. Garrett was a wolf of some sort, even over the phone Jake could sense that fact. Good wolf or bad, he didn't know. At least not yet. "Hannah Dixon."

Silence greeted him for several heartbeats.

"How is she?"

"Dead." Jake flinched at the shock waves flowing over him from the far corner of the barn. He mouthed a silent sorry in what he thought was her general direction.

A harsh curse erupted in his ear. Dark satisfaction welled in his gut. Garrett hadn't been expecting this news. Whatever the man had been to Hannah's mom, he hadn't kept any kind of close tabs on Hannah herself.

"When?"

"Nearly eight months ago."

"And you're just now calling?"

"I just now found your number in her mother's address book. Uncle Ben."

"You know I'm not her uncle."

"Yeah, I figured that one out. What I'd like to know is just what you are to her. Or were."

"We can't have this conversation over your cell phone, Mr. Carrigan. And frankly, since Hannah's gone, it's really none of your business. Thank you for the call. Good night."

Once again the silence of a disconnected phone echoed in Jake's ear. He stared at the phone in his hand.

Curious as hell.

"Well?" Hannah's voice hovered just on the other side of the boxes. Sadie laid her head on her paws and closed her eyes.

"Nothing but questions." He repeated the short conversation. "He could be working for the government. Your mother didn't have any ties there, did she?"

"My mom ran the local library. I can't believe she was any kind of secret agent. You met her, you know that's pretty farfetched."

"Yeah. But your mother scribbled uncle on the sidebar. That means something. He said he wasn't your uncle."

"We already knew that."

"He didn't even ask how you died, Hannah. You're gone and to him that's the end of that." He twisted his head from side to side, working at the kinks still there. At her swift intake of air he regretted his words. Damn, he didn't want to hurt her, but he was saying everything wrong.

How the hell did you talk to a ghost? About her own death? About her past?

"My gut says this Benjamin Garrett *is* with some type of government agency." For now he ignored their mutual uncomfortableness and plowed ahead. "I keep coming back to *why* his number was in your mother's book. You've never said what your dad did, before he left you guys. For work."

"I don't know." Hannah's weary voice held a trace of sorrow.

Did she hurt, trying to remember?

Go ahead and kick yourself in the ass now, Carrigan, get it over with and move on. He was pushing her too hard.

"I'm not sure I ever really asked." Hannah's soft moan echoed through him, the sound full of pain, and centered in his own chest. "I can't remember Mom ever really saying."

"Where did your mother keep that old picture of him?" What he wanted it for, he couldn't say. But he had the strongest itch to find that photo.

Was there a way to find the man, himself?

"There in Mom's address book, in the back."

Jake flipped to the back of the book, pulled out the 5x7, black and white photograph. A dark haired, dark eyed man stared out of the photo. A man who looked quite a lot like Hannah.

Edward Dixon.

In the picture he wasn't much older than his daughter had been when she died. Young, full of life and promise.

Intelligence and humor shone from the depths of his dark eyes, eyes that seemed to have a certain way of looking at the world, one that invited others to share the sarcasm, the joke.

Hannah had that look, too. That funny way of viewing things, that ability to make him laugh from just a particular spark in her eyes or from some smart-ass remark meant to bring him back from whatever edge he'd been contemplating.

His moods were dark to her light. She balanced him, kept him centered.

Had. She *had* balanced him. He hadn't been centered since his brother died.

At best, Hannah was a ghost. He was having a grand old conversation with a ghost about her past. About her equally gone father.

Uneasiness skittered down his spine. He swallowed hard around the knot threatening to choke him.

Everything circled back to Hannah's death. She was dead. Yet he sat here as if she really stood on the other side of these boxes, going through her things with him.

He really was losing his mind.

Those conflicting emotions flickering across Jake's face alarmed Hannah. Others believed he had such a poker face, but they didn't know how to read him.

She did. Always had.

Right now he was up to his neck in turmoil. All of it her fault.

She eased a few steps closer to him.

If she truly was a ghost, as he seemed to now believe, would he want to do some kind of ritual, forcing her to go to the *light?*

She frowned, pursed her lips. Wherever the hell the *light* was, she didn't want to go there. She wanted to stay here, with Jake.

He stared at the address book, his thumb lightly rubbing the edge of the open page. She studied his green eyes so dark with concentration, so pensive.

"I wonder if your father and this Garrett guy worked together."

"How would that change anything?" She sank down next to the open box of her things, rubbed at the sharp ache pulsing at her temples then wrapped her arms around her knees. "My father's long gone. I hardly have any memories of him. I think he's dead, not that Mom ever said so. What difference does it make?"

"Because there are unanswered questions."

She couldn't resist rolling her eyes, for once glad he couldn't see her. This was Jake's *there are no —*

"There are no coincidences, Hannah."

Yeah. That lecture. She smiled, bittersweet, against her knees. "It was so long ago. I don't think I know Benjamin Garrett. I don't know why any of it matters."

She was dead. A shudder worked its way down her spine. Jake had told her that himself, numerous times in the last two days. What difference did it make if she was murdered or not? Whether this Garrett man knew her father or not? She'd still be just as dead. Just as gone.

Jake set the address book in the open box and leaned forward, bracing his elbows on his knees. "When I was cop —"

"What?" Frowning, she stared at him. Jake lived for the police department. Had grown up with the department. He'd taken his brother's death hard, but Jake's suspension had only been temporary. Just a matter of protocol. "What do you mean *was* a cop?"

Jake scowled, his brows drawn in a harsh line. "Let it go."

"But, you were so close to making Sergeant. I thought –"

"Let it go." The muscle at his jaw twitched and his top lip curled. His nostrils flared.

She'd pissed him off. Again. More than he'd been at any time over the last two days. "What happened, Jake?"

Sudden pain flashed through his eyes, pain so deep it sliced through to her core.

"You happened, Hannah." His breath shuddered. The bleak and cold emptiness reflected in his gaze shredded her heart, the anguish worse than the tightening grip at her temples.

"But, Jake –"

"After you – After I came home and found that you'd died, I went into a hard tailspin." His laugh no more than a harsh bark, he shook his head. "Worse than after Craig. I was completely out of control. I quit the force."

"Oh, God, Jake. That meant everything to you."

"It did. Once." He pushed himself off the stool, bent to gather the things he'd strewn across on the floor. "You meant more."

She swallowed against the bile closing her throat. "Jake –"

"I think I've had enough *sharing* for one day." He sat her things back into the box, tucked the address book under his arm. "I don't know what you do during night. If you sleep or – Well, whatever it is you do. But I'd appreciate it if you'd stay away from me for a while."

He gave a sharp whistle for Sadie. His stride long and purposeful, he walked out of the barn without a backward glance.

Sadie stood and whimpered, her head swinging between Hannah and the barn door.

"Go on, girl." Hannah's throat caught on the whispered words. "He needs you right now."

The sad-eyed dog hung her head low, turned and followed Jake.

Hannah stayed, her arms wrapped around her knees, until night fell and darkness completely surrounded her. She sat until the soft, early morning light caressed the damp ground outside. She didn't bother to wipe the self-pitying tears tracking down her cheeks.

Who would see them anyway?

JAKE YANKED HIS JEEP into the hard right that took him across the narrow bridge, along the back way into Eagle Crest.

Bright, morning sunlight spiked across the blue hood of his vehicle. Behind his sunglasses he squinted in pain at the sudden glare.

He hadn't slept much the night before, not even after he'd spent hours on the internet going through pages of information and drivel about ghosts. Stuff that led him to believe no one really knew much of anything.

He hadn't had a drop of any kind of booze. Not a single can of beer. Not a shot of whiskey.

Yet his head hurt as if he'd tied one on during the night. He was no closer to figuring out what the hell Hannah was — or wasn't.

Althea Sheldon had better be ensconced in her office this morning. He didn't think he could handle another go-round with Amy. Not in his current mood.

That same bright sunlight glinted on the water as he drove along the edge of Young's River. More placid than the Columbia, the river it dumped into a few miles up the road, this river's slow pace irritated him this morning. Usually he liked the calming presence, the easy flow. But not today.

Today he was raw. On edge. Somehow he needed to bury that before he stormed into that damn doctor's office. If he didn't, he would likely get the police called on him.

Wouldn't that be something?

Finding a way to explain himself to Rily.

Priceless. His mouth curved into a semblance of a smile.

He'd been an ass to Hannah last night.

Again.

He couldn't rationalize his behavior. Not this time. Couldn't forgive himself, either.

She hadn't answered earlier when he'd called out to let her know he was leaving. His place had *felt* empty.

Also again.

He didn't like that emptiness, that sensation. As much as her presence unnerved him, her absence haunted him.

He worried.

About what, he had no clue. After all, what did he know about what ghosts did? Or didn't do.

Dammit. She should have answered him.

He swung his Jeep along the road that wound over the steep hills and would eventually lead him to the doctor's office. The strong breeze whispered through the pines covering the hillside.

Hannah had always enjoyed this drive, had always insisted they slow to almost a crawl to listen to what the trees were murmuring in the wind. He hadn't heard the messages the way she had.

Still, he shifted into a lower gear, slowing the Jeep so he could hear the breeze rattling through the branches.

Where was Hannah now? Was she at his place or had she decided he was too surly and gone looking for a better place to park her ghostly rear end?

That was the crutch of it, wasn't it? His hand wrapped tight around the steering wheel. He was afraid she'd left him. Certainly couldn't blame her if she had. Not this time.

The wind picked up and ran its chilly fingers over his skin. Goose bumps covered his body. His thin T-shirt offered no warmth. Coming this way had been a mistake.

Why would Hannah's trees talk to him?

With his foot to the gas pedal, he gunned it. The Jeep sprang forward, over the steep hill.

He had an office manager to grill.

JAKE STOOD IN the foyer area of Dr. Sheldon's office, his legs braced apart and his hands on his hips. A tall, striking woman stood behind the counter examining a thick, open file she held in her long, slim fingers. She hadn't bothered to glance up when he'd pushed through the front door.

Her short, auburn hair curled around her long neck. The dark green, elegant suit she wore screamed success as did the expensive and exotic scent surrounding her.

There was no sign of Amy this morning.

"Althea Sheldon?"

Her pale, barely painted pink lips tightened but relaxed before she looked up. Icy blue eyes impaled him on the spot. "Yes?"

"Jake Carrigan." He didn't bother to offer his hand. Rolling one shoulder, he moved to stand in front of the counter.

"Rily Carrigan's older brother?" A small smile flitted across her lips, gone as quickly as it had appeared.

"That would be me."

"What can I do for you, Mr. Carrigan?" Althea closed the file and laid it face down on the desk, one hand on top, palm flat. Her fingernails trim and coated in a glossy clear coat of some kind, tapped once, stilled.

What did she not want him to see?

Maybe he was being paranoid. The file wasn't his and he had no business seeing whatever it was she had been examining so intently. Patient confidentiality and all that crap.

Still, her manner bothered him at some deep, gut level. One he tried to never ignore. "My girlfriend was a patient here."

"Hannah Dixon."

"Yes."

One corner of Althea's mouth lifted, a bare movement of her lips. The icy blueness of her eyes warmed a little. "Hannah was a wonderful woman, Jake. She blessed everyone who knew her."

What was he supposed to say to that? He never knew how to respond. Yes, Hannah was wonderful. Yes, he missed her. No, he wasn't doing okay.

Dammit.

He pasted a fake smile across his own mouth and nodded.

Althea raised one slim eyebrow. Both corners of her lips curled up. "What can I do for you today, Jake?"

Her soft, pseudo-sympathetic voice almost did him in. Even when the condolences were as false as Althea's, they still nailed him right in the stomach. He was supposed to be past all of this. Hell, he'd prayed he was past it. Focus, he needed to focus. "Did Amy tell you I was in yesterday?"

"Yes, she did." She laid a hand across the top of her chest, against the skin visible at the base of her neck. The tips of her fingers stroked a thin black ribbon she had looped around her neck and tucked into the vee of her jacket. "I know Amy also told you we can't release any information to you, Jake."

Damn all these woman and those damnable steel rods stuck down their damn spines.

"I realize that, Althea." He flashed a quick grin, nothing too charming. He went, instead, for sincere. The woman standing in front of him wanted to play games then he'd just have to accommodate her. "What I'm looking for are her ashes. Rily said your office took care of the cremation for Hannah."

"I'd have to check. If it were her wishes then I imagine we would have taken care of that for her."

"You imagine?"

"She died a while ago."

"Just over seven months."

"Closer to eight months. A while ago."

"You have so many patients die that you can't remember the details of Hannah's cremation?" Right. Maybe that wasn't the most tactful approach he could have taken. He glanced down, not as contrite as he tried to appear, then back up to meet Althea's probing gaze.

"Jake." Her fingers closed around the ribbon at her neck, gathering both sides into a loose fist. The end dangled but stayed tucked in her jacket. The black of the ribbon made a sharp contrast against the creaminess of her skin. She leaned slightly forward, the sympathy in her voice not quite making it to her eyes. "Aren't you a bit late in asking for those ashes?"

"I had issues, Althea." He narrowed his gaze and with a slight movement squared his shoulders. Trying to keep it a casual gesture, he splayed both hands on the counter's edge. "Surely you can understand that?"

She straightened, away from him, the ice in her eyes colder now than before. The hand she had resting flat on the closed folder curled into a fist, matching the one she held closed over the ribbon at her chest.

A small thrill of anticipation ran down his spine. What, indeed, was she hiding from him? "Where are Hannah's ashes?"

Althea blinked, glanced down at the folder and her curled fingers. A small, almost feral smile slid over her lips, vanishing as quickly as the last one. If he hadn't been watching her face so intently, he'd have missed her mouth's slight movement.

"I don't know, Jake." In a casual movement, she straightened the fingers of both hands, let go of the ribbon and tapped on the folder. "Not without checking her records."

"And?"

"Those records are in storage."

Liar. Amy had held Hannah's folder in her hands just yesterday. How could he bring that up without getting Amy in trouble?

He braced his elbows on the counter and nodded as if he understood the complexity of record storage. He glanced down at the record folder on the desk. The file, definitely a patient's, showed no name on its backside. He had no way of knowing whose records those were.

"Let me see if I have this straight." He let his irritation color his voice. "You don't remember if you took care of the cremation for Hannah and can't check because the records are in storage?"

"Precisely." Althea lifted her hand from the desk and crossed her arms over her chest. "Is there anything else I can do for you today?"

Frustration tightened into a knot at the base of his stomach. Knowing the lethal look in his eyes belied the easy lift of his mouth, he smiled. "You can tell me where Hannah is, Althea. And what it is you don't want me to know."

A flicker of unease flashed across her face, disappearing as fast as her earlier smiles. "Really, Jake. Why do you want to get into something as unpleasant as all of that?"

"What the hell are you talking about?"

"Jake." Althea aimed a cold, veiled look at him. He wondered at the level of ice in her veins, so thick heat couldn't touch the frozen depths of her eyes.

She leaned forward again. The exoticness of her perfume wafted between them and came close to gagging him. He fought to keep his mouth from turning downward.

"What?" He forced himself to lean forward, mirroring her stance.

"Hannah told me, when she first started treatment, that she had no one left. No one to care for her. No one to love her. That you had *abandoned* her, left her alone when she needed you the most." Althea's lips thinned and her brows lowered a small bit. "Yet you stand here calling her your girlfriend, professing to want her ashes. Why should I help you with that when you were nowhere around when she lay there dying?"

Her words, sharp as several spike edged, hard fists, buried themselves deep into his mid-section. He struggled against closing his eyes, struggled against the intense desire to close out the triumphant light in the iciness of hers.

"Go away, Jake." Althea lifted a hand in dismissal. "I have nothing to tell you. I wouldn't even if I did."

Chapter Five

JAKE LEANED AGAINST THE HOOD of his Jeep, waiting for the slow moving line of cars to make it by him as they angled past the doctor's office towards downtown.

Not quite noon rush hour in Eagle Crest. Clouds, heavy with moisture, left the earlier bright sunshine little more than a memory.

His conversation with Althea Sheldon had gotten him nowhere. Nowhere beyond more questions and a ton of heartache.

Why had Hannah told that woman she had no one?

If Hannah had actually said any of those things.

He hadn't understood her motivations back then, didn't understand them now. How could he have abandoned her if he hadn't known she needed him? She'd never said anything.

Not to him.

Stoic, keeping it all inside where no one saw, no one knew – that was more the way she operated.

Hannah saying those things to Althea didn't sound like anything she would say.

Unless I'm drowning so deep in denial, I can't see up from down.

Which was a possibility.

He rubbed his chest and glanced back at the Victorian. Behind the large, plate glass window overlooking the parking area Althea stood with one arm crooked at her waist, the other fingering the black ribbon at her neck. The distain on her face evident, even across the asphalt.

Althea Sheldon didn't like him, not even a little. The animosity of those last few minutes in the office had been palpable.

That was fine. He couldn't work up any liking for the woman either. Man-hater was what sprang to mind.

With him being her current target.

Sounded as if he'd been her target since Hannah had become ill and graced Althea's world. The woman hadn't even been a blip on his screen until Amy wouldn't let him talk to her.

He turned back to the steady stream of cars. One of the drivers waved. He absently nodded back. Had Hannah really believed the things Althea had told him?

Rubbing his chest again, he realized his heart ached, it seriously ached. As if the knife Althea had jabbed him with protruded from his skin. Hannah couldn't give him answers to any of his questions, not without intense pain that left her voice so weak he worried she'd fade away to nothing.

And he'd lose her all over again.

If she hadn't already left his sorry ass last night.

A screeching sound, metal on metal, brought him hard out of his thoughts. Twenty feet away, one car had rear-ended another. No one seemed hurt, but Jake pushed away from his Jeep to make his way towards the two cars.

He glanced over his shoulder as he twisted his way between the stopped traffic and caught movement on the front porch of the old Victorian. Althea Sheldon now stood outside on the veranda, arms crossed and a calculating look on her face.

A dark chill, as cold as the ice in her eyes, flashed through his veins.

He pulled his gaze away to focus on the red-faced man and gangly teenager who stood arguing between their cars, tried to shake off the vague sense of dread settling in his gut.

Althea ran her father's doctor's office. No one was hurt, it wasn't as if this little fender bender would bring them any business. Still, there could be any number of reasons for that look on her face, none of them pleasant.

OUTSIDE ALTHEA'S BEDROOM WINDOW the late afternoon sun struggled to break through the storm laden clouds. With the heavy dark green drapes pulled back, meager light filtered through the wispy sheers covering the wide panes of glass.

Not interested in the file folder laying open on her bedroom desk's polished surface, she paced the length of her room before pausing at her desk to switch on the fabric covered lamp.

Energy skidded up her spine, energy she couldn't seem to dissipate. And she'd tried. Her skin prickled and her fingertips tingled, almost as if that energy jumped from nerve ending to nerve ending.

She picked up the ornate, silver fountain pen her father had given her as a birthday gift. The cool metal gave her hands a minuscule amount of relief as she tapped the pen against her palm.

There had to be an answer. A solution. Elusive and just out of reach. But there.

She laid the pen on the open folder and picked up the gilded frame she kept on the corner of her desk. With the tip of her nail, she traced the edges of the frame then kissed the pad of her fingertip and pressed it against the face in the photo. "So close, Mama. We're so close."

WITH HER ARMS WRAPPED around her bent knees, Hannah sat on a boulder facing the pond. Water misted the air around her, water from the waterfall cascading several yards away. Water she couldn't feel or touch.

The pain in her head had subsided to a dull ache.

Coolness seeped through her jeans and sweater, but didn't make any impact on her comfort. The late afternoon sky, what she could see of it through the thickness of the overhead pines, was still a leaden grey from the spring storm that had blasted through earlier.

Nels munched on a bush near the falls and Sadie lay on the rock strewn ground beside the boulder, her head on her paws and her eyes closed. Content.

How many times in the past had the three of them made this easy hike from Jake's place? How many times had she perched on this boulder, thinking, mulling over things? And how many times had those thoughts been as dark as they were now?

She heaved a deep sigh and slid down to stand next to the boulder. Dwelling on the way things had been wasn't going to change them now. Sadie opened her golden eyes and lifted her head. Standing, the dog shook herself and gave a soft whimper.

"No, girl." Hannah raised her face to the soft breeze that had picked up yet didn't disturb even a single strand of her hair. What other proof did she need of her shifted reality? "I'm not quite ready to head back yet."

Sadie shook herself again and took off in Nels' direction. Hannah smiled when the dog tried to get the old goat to chase her.

With her touch light, Hannah traced a fingertip over the smooth surface of her bracelet, along the diamonds embedded there. At least she could touch one inanimate object, even if it was something she'd somehow brought with her, on her person.

Her mouth drawn into a slight frown, she turned to the small pond with its dark surface rippling from the breeze. The frothy white water from the falls usually eased before it reached this area. There were days the pond's surface was smooth as glass.

Today wasn't one of those days. The edgy turmoil of the water matched her thoughts.

She was a ghost ... or something just as final, just as dead. After all, how did one go back to being – What? More physical? Human again? Without a body to go back to?

Besides, Jake needed to get on with his life.

A life without her.

Dead or not, her heart ached at that thought.

Jake having a life without her meant she didn't have him, either.

Oh, Lord. A sob choked its way out of her throat, followed by more until they racked her body.

She sat hard on the ground, curled her arms around herself and rocked, back and forth, until the sobs subsided and her entire body ached as painfully as her heart.

Sadie sat a few feet away, whimpering. Hannah sniffled, glad, for this one moment, no one except the animals could see her. Fat lot of good crying had done.

Her hand in a fist, she rubbed the tip of her nose.

Right now she wanted to throw something. Anything.

A sudden small movement, on the side opposite the dog, caught her attention. A fist-sized, rounded rock tumbled to a stop a short distance away.

If she could, she'd pick *that* rock up and throw it at the water. She'd wrap her fingers around the smooth edges, *feel* the heft of the rock before she'd hurl it and all of her wound up angst along with it.

The rock slid farther across the other rocks then cast itself across the water, skipping over the surface and leaving visible ripples before sinking along the far edge of the pond.

Her hand to her mouth, she scrambled to a standing position.

What just happened?

Concentrated thick rings rippled outward from where the rock had sunk into the water.

Oh, Lord. Had she, somehow, actually thrown that rock?

Pressure rose, tightening her chest, choking her. She pressed her hand to the base of her throat. Her pulse fluttered against her fingertips.

If *she* had thrown it, could she do it again?

She licked her suddenly dry lips, glanced around, searching for a suitably sized rock. Kicking at the one she found a few feet away didn't budge the stone.

Her hands fisted and the tips of her nails bit into her palms. Quick and sharp, pain stabbed at the center of her hands. She stared at her open palms and the red, crescent shapes marking where her nails had dug into her skin. Maybe she couldn't touch other things, but she could definitely inflict pain on herself.

Focus.

Was she going about this wrong? If she couldn't physically move the stone, could she move the one she'd decided on with her mind? With only her thoughts?

She shook her hands out, stared hard at the rock. Bracing her legs, she lowered one shoulder, angled her elbow and visualized the rock cupped in her upturned palm. She mentally *felt* the texture of the stone's surface, worn smooth by the water, the weight of it.

On an outward breath, she screwed her eyes closed, rocked her wrist back and forth and flung her imagined stone across the pond.

A loud splash startled her and her eyes popped open.

Thick ripples widened from the edge at the other side of the water, the half circles quickly approaching her side of the shore.

The stone she'd mentally chosen, where was it?

She scrambled to her edge of the pond. The stone was gone.

Had she actually done it? Had she really thrown that rock with nothing more than concentration on her part?

Her hand over her mouth, she staggered back.

Could it be that simple?

Her mind frenzied, she chose another stone. Repeated the process but with her eyes open this time.

The rock lifted, as if held in an invisible hand, sailed across the water to land with a loud thunk amid the rocks on the other side.

Oh, my.

A giggle lodged itself in her throat. Sadie barked and Hannah's giggle turned into a full blown laugh. She hugged herself and turned in a full circle.

"Sadie, I did it." Her whisper caught on the breeze, echoed back to her. "I did it."

DUSK WAS FALLING when Jake eased his Jeep to a stop just short of his house. Standing water from the afternoon storm filled the ruts in his dirt drive, reflecting back a glorious red and orange sunset. A silver, nondescript and mud-splattered sedan sat in the place he usually parked his own vehicle.

A rental.

Whose rental?

The welcome mat wasn't something he put out. Most people, Rily excepted, didn't make the effort to visit him. He wasn't the sociable type, especially not in the last several months.

With the gear shifter slipped into neutral, Jake pulled on his parking brake, letting the Jeep idle as he climbed out. He left the pizza he bought for dinner sitting on the passenger seat.

Scanning the area he reached for his gun. *Dammit all to hell.* He no longer carried a gun.

Not since he'd quit the force.

Plan B. Think fast on his feet.

Rounding the front of the rented sedan, he skimmed the hood with his right hand. Cool, not warm at all. Whomever the car belonged to had been here awhile.

So where were they?

What did they want?

"About time you showed up." The dry, rich male voice carried from the darkened back porch. "I was beginning to think I was going to have to track you down."

Jake, fighting to keep his expression placid, leaned one hip against the sedan and crossed his arms over his chest. He recognized that voice. "Benjamin Garrett."

So much for this being none of Jake's business. A small sliver of anticipation wormed its way up around his spine.

"And you're Jake Carrigan."

Jake was struck by the man's imposing height and broad shoulders when Garrett stepped down from the shadows of the porch and into the dimming evening light. Another thirty minutes and it would be totally dark. "You alone?"

"Completely." In his worn jeans and denim button down shirt, Garrett moved with the grace of a man younger than the grey of his thick hair suggested. He stopped directly in front of Jake, his arms loose at his sides. Only his fingers flexing in and out of loose fists belied the ease of his posture.

Jake straightened, eyeing the older man with trepidation. He didn't want a fight, but there was no way he'd back down.

"What kind of game are you playing?" Garrett's rich voice held a wealth of restraint.

"What are you talking about?"

"You told me Hannah was dead."

"So?"

"There's no record of her death."

Jake arched an eyebrow. This was getting more interesting by the moment.

"No record." Garrett settled one long index finger a bare inch from Jake's chest. "No death certificate."

Heat emanated from the tip of Garrett's finger, heat that pricked at Jake's skin underneath his shirt. He pushed the man's hand away. A sharp, electric type shock ran through his palm and up his arm. "What the hell did you just do?"

"Static electricity." Garrett fisted his hand.

Right. On a damp day. Jake frowned and shook his hand out. "There has to be a certificate."

Although if there wasn't one, that might explain some of Althea's hostility. But if it *was* missing, even more questions were raised. For starters, was this why Rily hadn't yet gotten back to him?

"There hasn't been one filed." Holding Jake's gaze, Garrett flexed his fingers before dropping his arm to his side. "Where is Hannah?"

Now, that was the million dollar question, wasn't it? "As I told you on the phone, she died nearly eight months ago."

"Then where is the damn death certificate? How did she die? Where is she buried?"

"Cremated."

Garrett cursed. "Ashes?"

Jake stared at the big, angry man in front of him and made a snap decision, one he hoped he didn't end up regretting. "I have pizza in the Jeep. Why don't you come in the house? We can share what we know over dinner."

A SHARP WHISTLE carried across the field. Sadie barked once in reply. Hannah smiled, easy and real. This was once a common ritual. Jake would arrive home, find them gone and whistle. Sadie and Nels would high tail it back. Hannah would bring up the rear.

Never mind this was Jake's place and she had her own apartment in town. She'd been her own boss, able to set her own hours designing the stone jewelry she'd consigned at several upscale boutiques in Portland. Her work had afforded her earlier hours, so she would almost always beat him here.

Sadie looked back and Hannah waved the dog on. Nels had already paced himself when they'd started back and was halfway across the open field. Sadie barked again then took off running.

That bubble of excitement, of accomplishment, buoyed Hannah's steps. She could will herself to where Jake waited for the animals, but right now she wanted the extra few minutes to savor the sensation of what she'd been able to do.

Thirty.

She had managed to manipulate and throw thirty rocks.

That wasn't a fluke. With her mind – her thoughts – she *could* impact the world around her, could control something, even if it was only rocks across a small pond.

Who knew what that meant, if it meant anything at all?

Still, exhilaration rose in her and her steps were lighter than they had been earlier.

She wasn't sure what Jake's mood would be once she reached the house. Or how he would take her still being around. She supposed she could stay quiet, try and make him believe she wasn't there.

But how long could she keep that going?

When she reached the edge of the water-logged, rutted drive she paused as Jake, with a pizza box between his hands, headed inside the house with a big man, a stranger, following close behind. Tension radiated through every line of both men's bodies.

Sadie dashed inside before Jake closed the screen door.

Weight, as heavy as the accumulated rocks she'd thrown into the pond, settled thick in Hannah's stomach.

Who was that man? Pinpricks of unease ran up and down her arms while she stood motionless at the boundary of the darkening field.

"WATER OR ICED TEA is all I have to drink." Jake sat the pizza box on the kitchen table along with paper plates and a roll of paper towels. He left the back door open so the rain-fresh air could ventilate the stuffy room. "Or I could make a pot of coffee."

"Whatever you're having is fine." Garrett paced the width of the kitchen twice before he pushed up the sleeves of his shirt. He settled at the table with his back to the far, windowless wall.

Jake figured the other man hadn't missed much in his seemingly casual purview. He didn't mind, he'd have done the same. Garrett was law enforcement, he'd stake his dwindling life savings on that. One of the federal alphabet agencies if he had to choose.

"No booze in the place?"

Everything inside Jake went still. He turned his head to stare at Garrett and the slight smirk twisting the man's mouth.

"You want booze you'll have to get it somewhere else."

"Problems?"

Jake tightened his mouth to keep the smart-ass retort from jumping through his clenched teeth. The man was baiting him, pure and simple. The question was why and how much did he already know. "Nothing I can't handle. Nothing that's any of your business."

Garrett nodded once before he flipped open the pizza box. Jake set the two glasses of iced tea on the table with a thud.

Garrett's eyes unreadable, he bit into his pizza. "Good stuff. And warm. How'd you manage that out here, away from town?"

"There's a small place two miles up the road." Jake stamped down his ire, sat at the table. He pulled his own piece from the box and tossed it on his plate. "People come out from Eagle Crest for that pizza. Hannah loved it."

Garrett sat his slice down and took a long drink of tea. He wiped his mouth with his paper towel. "What happened to her?"

"Why do you care?"

The older man held his gaze then shoved back his chair. Garrett didn't stand but instead leaned back, lacing his fingers over the top of his head. His dark blue eyes held a sudden wealth of misery.

Whatever story that gaze hid, it was a beaut. Jake pushed his plate away, leaned back himself. And waited.

"Hannah's father was a good friend. I promised I'd look out for her and her mother." Garrett closed his regret filled eyes. When he opened them the sadness had banked itself. "I did a lousy job."

"Hannah and her mom did fine on their own."

"Except now they're both dead."

Jake shrugged. Hard to argue that fact.

"Or at least Kathy Dixon is dead."

"So is Hannah."

"So you say." Garrett leaned forward and crossed his arms in front of his plate. "We keep circling back to no death certificate. Was she in an accident? Was she on life support? Where are her damn ashes?"

"If I knew I'd tell you." Jake swallowed his own misery and met the older man's gaze. He told him about Hannah's illness, about her death. About not being there for her.

But he couldn't bring himself to tell him about the way her voice haunted him. Or his fear she was a ghost, stuck here because he couldn't let go. "How do you know there's no death certificate?"

"I have my ways." Garrett pulled another piece of pizza from the box. While Jake had been talking they'd managed to polish off two-thirds of the pie. An almost easy camaraderie had begun to establish itself between them.

"Right. Federal?"

Garrett's mouth lifted in a half smile around his slice of pizza. "None of your business, kid."

"Anything to do with Hannah is my business."

"Not according to the law."

"Screw the law."

"I gather you did just that." Garrett finished what was left of his tea and saluted Jake with the empty glass.

"What's that supposed to mean?"

"You left the force. You're living out here with no visible means of support."

"This place is paid for. By me. You've got no business digging into my personal records."

"Like you, Hannah's my business, Jake. Whether you like that or not. You're the only one to benefit from her death."

"*What?*" The fact there was no accusation in Garrett's voice was the only thing keeping Jake in his seat.

"Her money and some of yours are co-mingled in one joint account. Of which you still have access to." Garrett spread his hands. "What am I to make of that?"

"Whatever the hell you want." He tried to clamp down on his spiking temper. These were exactly the kinds of questions and inferences he'd make if he were in Garrett's position. The man had gathered quite a bit of information in less than twenty-four hours.

"Explain it to me."

"Hannah and I have always had the one joint account." He didn't have to clarify any of this for the man, but what the hell? Why not? "Nothing big, mostly for funding the different trips we took and the ones we wanted to take." Like the Caribbean. "Hannah had her own place, her own money. After I got back, found out she'd died, I also discovered she'd dumped her entire savings into that shared account. I believe it was every last dime she had."

And she'd had even more than he'd realized. He'd known she had money from her mother's life insurance and the subsequent sale of her childhood home. Money she'd stashed from her lucrative jewelry business. He just hadn't realized how much money she'd had. Hannah hadn't been poor by any stretch.

"So you quit the force to live high on the hog?"

Jake choked on the tea he'd been drinking and wiped his mouth with the back of his hand. "Looks that way, doesn't it?"

"Yeah. You, the dog and the goat."

Without humor, Jake grinned at the older man. "Guess I'll have to get a job pretty soon or the dog and goat will be going hungry."

"Can't let that happen." Garrett linked his hands on top of his head. "Why aren't you using any of that money?"

Jake pushed his plate away. Garrett had hit on one of his major sore points. Hannah's money and what to do with it. He shrugged. "I have my own."

"You cashed in your vacation pay and retirement when you left the department. There can't be much of that left."

Jake eyed the older man but couldn't bring himself to put any heat into the glare. "I don't need much."

"Obviously Hannah left the money for you, Carrigan."

"Why did she do that?" Jake threaded his fingers through his hair, squeezed and let go. He pushed up and away from the table, pacing to the counter before turning back to Garrett. "Why didn't she just find me, it wouldn't have been hard. Tell me she was sick? Instead she leaves me all this money as if—"

"As if what?"

"As if that would make up for her dying. For leaving me here alone. Without her."

Chapter Six

J AKE LEANED BACK in his kitchen chair, the front two legs off the floor. He gave the man seated across the table a genuine smile.

Not for the first time this evening, he wondered if he might have an ally in Ben Garrett. Someone else who believed the dots didn't quite connect.

Dusk had lengthened and turned into late evening during the time they had sat hashing over the facts they knew, speculating on what they didn't know and avoiding Jake's earlier outburst.

"A one-stop, all purpose, doctors office?" Ben stood and stretched. He took his empty cup over to the counter where the half full pot of coffee sat. "I've never heard of a doctor taking care of that for a patient."

"Small town, Garrett. I've heard of even stranger things happening in Eagle Crest." He held out his cup for a refill, sniffing at the still present aroma of fresh ground beans. "But I don't know if Sheldon had anything to do with this. I never got that far with Althea. This runaround she's giving me — What's she hiding?"

"Maybe she's nothing more than a bitch with a huge chip on her shoulder." Ben shrugged. "I'll pay her a visit tomorrow. Maybe as Hannah's uncle I'll get farther than you did."

"Except you're not her uncle."

"Althea won't know that." With his cup full, Ben settled into his chair, slouched back with his arms crossed loose in his lap. Steam from his coffee drifted upward. "What about your brother's death?"

Jake stiffened, let the front legs of his chair hit the wood floor. "Craig's ambush doesn't have anything to do with Hannah's death."

"Maybe not." Ben brought his cup to his mouth, his eyes watchful over the rim.

"What do you know about my brother?"

"What's in your personnel file, mostly." Ben wrapped his hands around his cup, shrugged. "Your brother's file in Portland. Ramon Ortega's, his partner."

"You're good, Garrett." With his chin lowered, he kept his gaze on the other man. "FBI? CIA? Agency without initials? One without a name?"

"Something like that." Garrett took another sip of his coffee. "His death wasn't your fault. Your brother pulled a stupid stunt. One that got him killed."

"So I've been told." He slouched in his chair. "Drop it."

Ben lifted his cup in a small salute. "For now."

Jake held the man's gaze until Ben nodded. With no delusions that meant anything, Jake still took the small victory.

A cool sensation washed over him, more than the open door warranted. Almost as if someone had run cold-tipped fingers down his face and neck. Hannah? Even knowing he wouldn't see anything, he twisted in his chair.

"What are you looking for?" Ben's gaze searched the room.

"Nothing." Jake didn't want the man thinking he was nuts. Besides, it might really be nothing more than wishful thinking. "Just a little chill in the air."

He shut the back door, closing out the breeze that had to have been responsible for the goose bumps running up and down his arms.

Ben's slow nod didn't erase the perplexed look lining his face. Did Garrett sense Hannah? Would the man be able to hear her if she started talking? So far, at least as far as Jake knew, he was the only person who could hear her.

How the hell did he ask Ben if he would be able to hear Hannah-the-ghost speak without sounding like a nut-job?

Jake already had Rily thinking he was operating without most of his pistons firing. He didn't need the only ally he might have found thinking he was crazy.

Sadie scurried in from the living room, gave a sharp bark. From outside the sound of yet another vehicle chugging its way around his barn scraped across his skin. The heavy engine idled a short time then shut off, leaving a soft metallic noise pinging in the still air.

Damn. Two visitors in one day. He was going to have to find whoever had put out the welcome mat and shoot that person.

Once he found a way to get his gun back.

A few moments later light footfalls echoed up the wooden steps. Jake opened the kitchen door, stepped out onto his porch. Think of the devil and she showed up gunning for bear. Or, in his case, brother.

"Hey, Sis."

"Jake, someone's sniffing around, asking questions about you. Said he was Hannah's uncle." Rily stopped in front of him with her legs braced and her hands on her hips. The porch light lit her face, the flash of angry worry darkening her eyes and highlighting that pointy chin of hers she had high in the air. "What have you stirred up with all these questions about Hannah? I can't find any trace of her death certificate.

None." She poked him in the chest. "What's going on? What have you gotten yourself into?"

"First of all, little sister, you're not my mother."

"Yeah? Well, you don't listen to her any better than you do to me."

"Second, it's not a problem."

"Not a problem –" Her words cut off as Garrett pushed open the screen door to let Sadie out. "Who's he? Is that his car?"

"Yes, it's his car. He's Hannah's uncle." Jake moved out of his dog's way then let himself back into the house knowing Rily would follow. She had barely wound herself up. *This might get even more interesting.*

"Hannah doesn't have an uncle." Rily shot pointed glares at both of them, caught the screen door before it slammed and followed him into the house.

Ben's eyebrows rose a slight bit. Humor lurked in the depths of his eyes. "Rily Carrigan, I take it."

"Who the hell are you?" She leaned back against the door jamb with her ankles crossed, her arms folded over her chest and her brows drawn down in a ferocious frown. "And don't give me that BS about being Hannah's uncle."

"Wouldn't dream of it." Ben settled in his chair, stretched his long legs out and crossed his own ankles. His lips twisted in a self-contained smile. The look he aimed at her radiated less than pure innocence. "Although I am her honorary uncle, of a sort."

Rily narrowed her eyes.

Jake, managing to contain his own grin, sat and leaned back in his chair, the front legs off the floor. "I think there's pizza left, Sis."

"Honorary uncles don't count for –" She swung her gaze, sharp as broken green glass, to Jake. "Pizza?"

"Maybe a slice or two."

Rily tucked her hair behind her ear and pushed herself away from the door. "Pizza first, answers second."

"Must run in the family." Garrett cradled his cup in his big hands, his mouth curled in a half-assed smirk.

"Priorities." Jake watched his sister pull the leftover pizza from the fridge. In no time she had it warming in the oven. No microwave heat up for her. Some cop she made.

"How did you find out I'd called the station?" Ben glanced at her over the rim of his coffee cup before he took a drink.

"Telephone, telegraph, tell a cop." Rily rolled her eyes. "Get real. You must've known that would be all over the station as soon as you hung up."

"Honestly? I didn't think too much about it." He shrugged his right shoulder, took another long sip of his coffee.

"What, exactly, is all over the station?" Jake lowered the legs of his chair to the floor. Leaning forward, he braced his elbows on the table and wrapped his hands around his warm cup.

Did he really want the answer?

"Some yahoo —" Rily stared pointedly at Garrett. "Supposedly from the State Police, called looking for info on Hannah's death. He said he was her mother's brother. Had just found out his niece had died." Rily pulled a cup down from the cabinet and poured herself the last of the coffee. After switching the machine off, she leaned back against the counter. "That dimwit in the front office spilled his guts, giving the yahoo the whole sob story about you and your lost love."

Crap. Jake rolled his eyes. This kept getting better and better.

"Then that same dimwit came running to find me, just to make sure I knew Hannah had an uncle who would, more than likely, be turning up at *your* door."

"What did you tell the dimwit?" He didn't want this answer, either. Not really.

"What do I look like?" Rily tapped her chest and grinned without any warmth at all. "Stupid? I told said dimwit I'd let you know to expect a visitor. Which, I'm taking a wild guess here, is you. Mr. Yahoo." She pointed her finger at Ben. "And I still want answers."

"Of course you do." Ben nodded and set his cup on the table. "Benjamin Garrett, said Yahoo in question. I knew Hannah's family when she was just a small kid. Back then she really did call me uncle. I only recently found out she had died."

"State police?" Jake raised an eyebrow.

"Whatever gets the job done."

"Something that's been bothering me —" Jake tapped his fingers against his cup and frowned. "Why would Edward Dixon want you checking on his family when he didn't care enough to stick around in the first place?"

Ben's shoulders dropped, although his gaze remained steady. "That's what Hannah believed? That her father left? Abandoned them?"

Jake nodded.

His mouth tight, Ben shook his head. "Kathy Dixon always knew what happened to Ed. I never kept her in the dark."

"Hannah's father is dead?" Rily's voice low, she ran a hand through her hair.

"Yes. No matter what Kathy told Hannah, she always knew."

"Why would she keep that from her daughter?" Rily took two steps closer. "Why would she let Hannah believe the worst about her dad?"

Ben rubbed a hand over his face. "I imagine it was easier than answering the hard questions about *why* he died."

More secrets. Jake narrowed his gaze. "And those answers are?"

"Nothing that pertains to Hannah's death." Ben sniffed the air. "Your pizza's burning."

Rily spun around, yanked open the oven door and rescued her dinner.

An almost chilly pressure seeped over Jake, as if someone stood right next to him, disturbing his personal space with all the coldness of an open freezer door.

Hannah.

Closed tight, the heavy kitchen door blocked any chill from outside. Although Rily had turned the oven off, she had the oven door propped open to let the heat out into the room. The kitchen itself was warm. There was no reason to be chilled.

None at all.

Relief settled deep in his gut. He ignored the implications of what that relief meant. Hannah was home and listening.

Had she heard what Garrett had said about her parents?

Was she upset? How could she not be?

Impatient, Jake glanced around the room. He was going to have to wait until later to talk to Hannah. Later, when they could be alone with no eavesdroppers on what would surely sound like a one-sided, nut-job crazy conversation.

HANNAH LEFT JAKE'S SIDE. With her hands pressed to the ache pounding at her temples, she paced across the kitchen. Bright overhead light kept the dark night contained behind the flimsy curtains but didn't stop the darkness swirling at the edges of her vision or the shadows clutching at her chest.

This man, Garrett, knew her parents. She'd once called him uncle.

Her father was dead, had been dead all along.

Her mother had lied to her.

If Garrett was telling the truth.

But why would he lie? Why had her mother?

Her head throbbed with a memory just out of reach. She laced her fingers through her hair, pressed harder against the sides of her head. The edge of her vision dimmed and blurred. She had to hang on, couldn't let herself be sucked back into that black void.

Not now.

Please not now.

She disregarded the frown marring Jake's forehead when he glanced in her general direction. Maybe he sensed her, maybe she only wanted to believe he did. She rubbed her fingertips tighter against her temples and backed away from the group.

Out in the living room she took several deep breaths. The blurring began receding. Her next breath shuddered through her.

Somehow she'd managed to fight the blackness back.

For now.

In front of the fireplace she sank to the floor. With her arms wrapped tight around her bent legs, Hannah took several deep breaths and mulled over the things she'd heard in the other room.

Those things Benjamin Garrett had told Jake.

The things Jake had said.

About her money. About his anguish over her not seeking him out, not letting him know she had been that ill.

They'd broken up, dammit. He'd run.

She hadn't owed him anything. *Not a damn thing.* He hadn't been entitled to the knowledge of her illness.

Why didn't she remember being sick?

She had to have known she was dying. Why else would she have dumped all her money into that joint account? Why hadn't one of them closed it?

Broken those ties?

God, she still loved him.

Her head throbbed with each unanswered question.

Instead of reaching out back then, she'd set herself up to die alone.

Served her right, didn't it?

Push everyone away and handle things herself, that was the way she did things.

Standard Operating Procedure.

Self-contained.

In control.

Alone.

Could that be why she was in this position now? Here but not truly able to interact on this plane except by throwing rocks with her mind.

Because she hadn't let anyone stay close to her?

Her elbows on her knees, she pressed the pads of her fingertips to her forehead.

Earlier, she hadn't been able to smell the pizza, not when the two men ate theirs nor when Rily had almost burned hers. The fresh ground coffee may as well been in a vacuum.

She couldn't smell anything. Didn't that make her the one in the vacuum?

Food held no appeal. Ghosts must not need to eat.

Yet she swore she *still* breathed, that air moved in and out of her lungs. Her emotions *still* got the best of her and her mind *still* seemed to function. Even if she was light in the memory department.

This ghost business didn't make any sense at all.

The voices from the kitchen had faded to an indistinct murmur. She let the sounds wash over her until the back door opened and Sadie wandered into the living room. Hannah rested her chin on her knees and wrapped her arms tight around her legs. She gave the dog a half smile.

Sadie settled herself on the floor and pushed at Hannah with her nose.

Nothing. Hannah choked on a soft sigh. No sensation at all. She may as well be made of nothing more than air for all the sensation that wasn't there. Sadie whimpered.

In Hannah's mind the image of her fingers running over Sadie's head bloomed. Hannah mentally scratched at just the right spot behind the dog's ears. Sadie heaved a huge dog sigh and laid her head on her front paws.

Hannah's breathing hitched. The image dissipated.

Oh my goodness. Had she really just scratched the dog's head with nothing more than a picture in her mind?

Sadie opened one reproachful eye before heaving an indignant snort and rolling onto her side. Some of Hannah's earlier elation over throwing stones across the pond ebbed back. She tightened her grip on her legs.

Earlier she'd imagined running her fingers over Jake's cheek. He'd closed the back door almost immediately afterwards.

Had she actually touched him?

Had he *felt* her fingers on his face?

Oh, man.

She threw an impatient glance towards the entryway leading to the kitchen. Rily and Garrett needed to leave. Hannah had so much to share with Jake.

All these newfound abilities.

And, heaven help her, she wanted to touch him again. Even if it was only with her mind.

HANNAH BACKED AWAY from Jake's couch. Her gaze swung from him to Benjamin Garrett then back to Jake.

They had to be kidding.

Jake was letting the man spend the night.

Here?

Jake had even raided the hall closet for sheets and a pillow.

"Thanks for loaning me your sofa tonight." Benjamin Garrett took the sheets and with his hand over his mouth, stifled a yawn.

Hannah set her hands on her hips. They didn't know anything about this Garrett dude. Nothing beyond what he'd told them. He'd lied to that officer at the station about being with the state police, about being her mother's brother.

Was he lying about anything else?

About everything else?

Why did Jake trust the man?

She opened her mouth in protest, closed it.

Would Garrett be able to hear her if she gave Jake a piece of her mind? Could anyone, beyond Jake and the animals, hear her? Should she even try?

Dammit. She spun away from the two men only to spin back and glare at Garrett.

Tonight she wanted Jake to herself, wanted to share her new ability with him. Wanted to find out exactly what he thought about this man who claimed to have known her father.

She ignored the dull ache again blossoming at her temples.

"The afghan is pretty warm. Let me know if you need anything else." Jake glanced around the room as if looking for something, then nodded at the older man and turned on his heel. "Night."

Hannah stared at the spot where Jake had been standing.

Didn't he realize she'd been waiting all evening to talk with him?

Of course he didn't.

Her own fault, really. What did she expect?

She blew out her breath, turned to gauge the older man. Benjamin Garrett was tall, as tall as the vague memory she had of her father. And broad shouldered. Handsome, in an older man sort of way. Deep crinkles around his dark blue eyes spoke of years that matched the grey of his hair and the craggy lines around his mouth. But he moved as if he were much younger.

Had he really been as close to her family as he'd said?

Garrett spread the sheets across the couch, then the afghan and tossed the pillow on one end.

"Uncle Ben." Hannah whispered the words, testing them.

With a tuneless whistle, Garrett undid his watch and set it on the end table along with his wallet and keys.

"Uncle Ben." Her voice stronger, Hannah deliberately stepped into his space a mere few inches from him.

He shuddered once and glanced around the room before he shrugged and smoothed out the covers on the couch.

Disappointment settled heavy, pressed on her chest. He might sense her on some level, but he couldn't hear her.

Not that she really wanted to have any deep, philosophical discussions with him. Ones like, *why was my dad's death such a secret? What didn't my mother want me to know?*

Like she really wanted *that* conversation.

She pressed her lips tight. A step back was what she needed, a step back and away from Benjamin Garrett.

The man rubbed his hand over his chin, the blue of his eyes dark as he glanced around the room. With a sense of irritation, knowing it wasn't rational, Hannah focused her internal gaze as she'd done earlier with the dog. She breathed deep and roughed up the afghan, managing to push it several inches down the sheet.

Garrett frowned and straightened the cover.

She knocked his watch to the floor.

"Weird place." He bent, retrieved his watch and set it carefully on the end table, away from the edge.

Her hands balled into fists at her side, with her nails digging into her palms, she took a few steps back and aimed a dark look at Garrett. Frustration welled inside her, frustration that fought with her common sense.

What she wanted was to stomp her feet, throw a fit. But what good would that do?

I'd feel good for a few moments.

She bit the inside of her lip then reached out with a simple, single thought and flicked at the grey hair touching the top of his left ear.

"All right." Garrett straightened. With his mouth turned downward, he faced her general direction. "I'm getting ready for bed now. Unless you really just want to see me naked, I suggest you go somewhere else."

Hannah blinked in stunned silence. That wasn't quite the response she'd been after.

Then again, what, exactly, had she been after? Recognition of some kind?

She'd gotten *that*, hadn't she?

An inane giggle lodged itself in her throat. As fine as Benjamin Garrett seemed to keep his physique, seeing him naked wasn't on her agenda.

Before the giggle could erupt, she grasped at the thought of Jake and focused on being with him … seeing him naked again, that was all together a different story.

IN GREY SWEAT PANTS and a black T-shirt, Jake settled on his bed. The soft light from his side table lamp illuminated the rustic room, pushing the blackness emanating from the curtainless windows to the fringes of the room. With his back against the headboard, his legs stretched out and crossed at his ankles, he studied his bare feet.

Where the hell was Hannah?

He seemed to be asking that a lot these last couple of days.

She'd ignored his calls, although he knew she was in the house. How he knew, he'd be hell pressed to explain. Something in the air, the pressure itself … maybe.

More of a knowing, a sense she was around.

If he wasn't careful he'd be neck deep believing in that woo-woo shit. Something else to give Rily a laugh.

At his expense.

"Jake?" Hannah's voice whispered over him, through him.

Tension seeped from his shoulders. He closed his eyes for a brief second. Relief expanded, swelling in his chest. God, she was back. "I was wondering if you were avoiding me."

"You've had lots of company today."

"Too much." He rubbed the stubble lining his chin. Now that she was here, he wasn't sure where to start, what he should say. *Apologize for being such an ass or jump into the stuff she must have heard?* "What did you think of Uncle Ben?"

Silence lengthened and then her soft sigh caressed the air. "I don't really know what to think. You?"

"He's here."

"And that means what?"

"You meant enough to him to ask questions. To come all the way out here when he couldn't find the answers."

"That's something to think about, I guess." She was quiet, her hesitancy seeming to taint the very air. "Does that mean you aren't happy with the answers, either?"

Now that was the crux, wasn't it? "No, I'm not real happy with what I've found. I'm getting the runaround in an area I shouldn't be."

"Althea Sheldon?"

"Yeah."

"And my ... ashes?"

He nodded.

"She was always so nice to me."

"You heard what I told Garrett about her. Did you say those things to Althea, Hannah?" Crap. He sure as hell hadn't meant to go there.

"Those hateful things she said, why would I have said them to her?" Her voice weakened and pain seeped through her words. "I don't understand why she told you I did."

"It's okay, Baby."

"No, it's not."

"Hannah —" Inadequacy flooded him, leaving him unsure of what to say, what to even feel. "Why didn't you give me the chance to be there for you? Why didn't you ask me to be?"

"I can't remember." Her words, laced so deep with hurt, pierced his heart.

"Okay." His own pain, sudden and sharp, lanced through his chest in a twin wound. He looked away from the direction of her voice. "So. How much did you hear tonight?"

"A lot. Most of it, I think." A soft sigh fluttered through the air. "You left the back door open. I sat out there until just before Rily showed up."

"That *was* you." Adrenaline trickled through his veins and he sat forward, away from the headboard. "You touched me. I *felt* you touch me."

The sound of her sudden intake of breath raised bumps along his arms. Anticipation built inside him. Along with something closely resembling fear.

What if he was wrong?

"You *did* touch me. Didn't you, Hannah?"

"Yes." Hesitant and soft, her voice edged closer. The one word caressed his skin.

His eyes drifted close. A groan snuck out of his throat. "Touch me again, Baby." *Please.* "Touch me now."

Feather light and cool, an unseen finger trailed over his stubble roughened cheek, leaving the softest awareness in its wake. His breath hitched, caught in his throat. Afraid to move, afraid she would stop.

God, Hannah.

Hands cupped his face. Touched his mouth.

His insides twisted into a tight ball of want, of need. He leaned into her touch. Fingertips traced light over his lips, he pressed a light kiss to the cool air.

"No. Please, no, not now." Edgy, laced thick with pain, Hannah's husky voice wavered just above him. "Noooo."

Jake's eyes snapped open. He sat absolutely still, testing the surrounding area with his senses. "Baby? Hannah?"

Nothing one was there. She had disappeared.

Chapter Seven

J AKE LEANED BACK against his kitchen counter, a mug of steaming coffee in his right hand. Hazy morning sunlight along with cool, damp air filtered through the open window behind him. Goose bumps raised along his exposed arms.

He probably should've dressed in something warmer than the T-shirt he'd grabbed and yanked over his head before heading into the kitchen. Not that he cared much about the temperature.

Hannah had touched him last night.

He hadn't imagined the feel of her soft fingertips on his face. The tracings of her icy caress down his cheek, over his skin.

Hannah had touched him.

Only now there wasn't a hint of her in his house. Or outside, either. He'd stood like some psychic moron testing the air for vibes. There hadn't been any.

Hannah was still gone this morning.

Wherever she was, he hoped like hell she wasn't hurting. And that she came back.

Here. To him.

Sick bastard that he was.

He raised his mug to his mouth, blew across the coffee's scalding surface before taking a tentative, slow sip. Strong and black, the fresh brewed aroma filled his nose. The near bitter taste matched his mood.

"How long has she been haunting you?" Ben stood in the open archway for a moment before he braced his shoulder against the wall's edge. He crossed his arms loose over his wide chest.

The muscles in Jake's neck and shoulders bunched. How the hell did Ben know about Hannah's ghost?

Jake took two deep breaths, willed his muscles to relax. Along with the twitch at his jaw. After a short moment, he again blew across his hot coffee. Had Hannah managed to talk to Ben last night? Why hadn't she told him?

The pain and resentment souring his stomach roiled up a notch. He wasn't Hannah's keeper. For the sake of his own sanity he should probably remember that. Otherwise, he might begin to believe all of this mattered.

Might begin to believe this was more than just an aberration, more than what it appeared to be on the surface. He might begin to believe that Hannah might stick around.

Heartache, buddy. Heartache.

He needed to remember that.

Taking another stalling sip of coffee, he glanced at the older man, taking in the still damp hair, casual jeans and long-sleeved Henley T-shirt. Not exactly Fed wear.

The man might fit in over in Eagle Crest. Maybe even manage to get a few answers.

Or maybe not.

Benjamin Garrett was a stranger. Although the town thrived on tourism, being so close to the coast, friendliness only went so far. Might be interesting to see how far. The other man was resourceful.

Right now that man watched Jake too closely, with one brow lifted, a look of total patience plastered all over his face.

Crap.

"Define haunting." Jake gave a mental shrug. Although the last thing he wanted was to discuss the latest turn in his relationship with his ghostly ex-girlfriend, he needed Ben's input. Possibly even his advice.

Maybe.

Ben shook his head and pushed away from the door. He poured coffee into the mug Jake had set out for him earlier. Inhaling the vapors without drinking, Ben leaned his hip against the counter a few feet away. "How long has she been here?"

"Since her birthday." Jake angled his head and gave Ben a sideways look.

"Only a couple of days?" A frown pulled on the rugged lines of Ben's face, furrowed his brow.

"As far as I can tell." Without drinking, Jake lifted his mug. "Why? Does it matter?"

"I'm not sure." Ben took a short sip of his own steaming coffee. "When were you going to tell me she was here?"

"I wasn't."

"You didn't think the fact her spirit is around, here – at this time, at this point – was important?"

Jake set his mug on the counter. He turned to face the open window. Keeping his gaze focused on the fluttering curtains, he let the damp air cool his suddenly heated skin. He tried to ignore the embers sparking hot in the pit of his stomach, the way the acid licked at his throat. "Why would it be important? How, exactly, should I have told you?"

The edge of the counter dug into his palms. On an out-breath of air he eased his grip. This was harder than he'd expected.

"Hey Garrett. Your best friend's daughter is dead." His throat tightened but he pushed the words out, angled his head to glare at the other man. "But, hey, her spirit decided to hang around, so no worries."

Ben smacked the counter with the flat of his palm, the sound reverberating through the kitchen. "Cut the self-pity crap, Carrigan."

"Funny. That's damn close to what Hannah said when she decided to make her birthday entrance."

Ben went still. "She talks to you?"

"Yeah." Belligerence warred with common sense. Jake sucked in what he prayed was an anger-dampening lungful of cool air. "That's not normal? For ghosts"

"No. Not really." Ben's face drawn deep in a frown, he drummed his fingers around his mug. "She's been dead over seven months, nearly eight, and is just now letting you know she's here?"

"Pretty much. If that's not normal, what is?"

"With ghosts?" Ben gave a short, terse laugh. "Who can really say? The fact she hasn't been around before, is here now *and* able to talk strikes me as unusual."

"Hannah's always been unusual."

"Maybe so, but –" Ben set his mug on the counter. His eyes intense, he faced Jake. "When she talks to you, do you hear her in your head or is it like this, a regular conversation?"

"A regular conversation. Except I can't see her." Grabbing his own mug, he stepped wide around Ben, topped off his coffee then retreated to his spot with his back to the counter. "The animals can hear her. Especially Sadie. They may even be able to see her. Sadie seems to know where she is in the room."

"Animals are sensitive that way."

"You don't think I've lost my mind?"

"No." Again, Ben gave that terse, short laugh. "If you have, then so have I."

"She talked to you?" Jake's chest tightened. Part of him wanted to be the only one she could talk to, wanted that link between them to be unique, special.

How stupid could he get?

"No." Ben shook his head.

For a quick moment Jake closed his eyes against the elation, the spark of *yes* swelling through him. Not only stupid, but pathetic. He forced himself to meet Garrett's gaze. "Then how did you know she was here?"

"I believe she was trying to get my attention last night after you left the living room. When I didn't respond she had a bit of a fit. Knocked my watch off the table." Ben rubbed his hand over his forehead then down his cheek and over his jaw. "I didn't sense anything. Or at least not much. But what else except a ghost could do those things?"

"When you say sense, what do you mean?"

"There are several different ways. The air pressure can change, the temperature drop. All the standard methods of detection."

Jake choked on the coffee he'd been sipping. "Standard?"

"Sure."

"Sometimes the temperature does drop when she's around. But not always. It's not consistent."

"That might explain why I didn't get much of a sense of her last night. Is she here now?"

"No."

"You're sure?"

Jake nodded.

"How can you be sur —" Lines around Ben's eyes deepened. He shrugged. "I don't feel her, either. There was one moment last night that might have been her, but for the most part I didn't feel her. Yet, I was positive it was her."

A small amount of the tension twisting the knots in Jake's shoulder blades eased. He still didn't know where Hannah was, but someone else believed she was around.

Of course, maybe they were both nuts.

At least he wasn't alone.

"Where is she now?" Ben swallowed the last of the coffee in his mug. "Where does she go?"

"I don't know. She's just – Gone."

Ben stared off, his gaze unfocused. "Yet you know when she's around? Does she let you know? Does she tell you?"

"That's how it started. Now I just seem to know."

"Odd." With his gaze locked on Jake's, Ben set his mug on the counter. "You don't have any idea why Hannah's ghost is here? Now, at this point in time?"

"Until yesterday I thought she was just a product of me going over the edge."

"Why would you be doing that?"

Jake crossed his arms tight over his chest, stared at the bland expression Garrett had pasted on his face. Another person trying to psycho-analyze him wasn't what he needed right now.

"Seriously, Jake. What is it you want? For yourself."

Hannah back. Safe, in my arms. Alive. "To figure out what's going on over at Sheldon's office. Why the runaround? What they're hiding."

"Yeah. I want those things too." Ben half-filled his mug and leaned back against the counter. He cupped his mug, mirroring Jake. "But what do you want for yourself?"

Jake thinned his lips and shifted his stance. He stared at the older man.

"You quit your job. Abandoned your goals." Ben shrugged, his face now blank. "Limbo doesn't really suit you."

"My brother was murdered. Hannah died." The hard, tight knot back between his shoulder blades, he set his mug down and shoved it aside. He swung away from the counter. "Nothing else mattered."

"And now? What matters to you *now*?" The words, spoken in a soft hush, still held a trace of censure.

At least that's how they sounded to Jake. Maybe he wasn't being fair, but dammit — He didn't need Garrett mimicking Rily and jamming good intentions down his throat. "What makes you such an expert on what should matter to me *now*?"

"You have no idea."

"So enlighten me." Tired of being on the defensive, Jake stuffed his hands into his front jean pockets and rocked back on his heels. "Give me an idea. What else are you?"

"What do you mean?"

"Law enforcement of some kind is a given. Probably a Fed. This psycho-analyzing, this sensing ghosts — Where do those skills fit in? It's more than just humoring me."

Garrett's eyes went flat. "Suffice it to say I know something about what you're going through. And ghosts, I know a bit about those, too. From what I do know, there's something off with Hannah's spirit."

This entire conversation was off. "How?"

"I can't quite figure it out. Not yet. Let me put some thought into the matter. We can discuss more on this ghost issue this afternoon." The lines around Ben's eyes again deepened. Light seeped back into his gaze. "After I drop into Dr. Sheldon's office and see what else I can ferret out of Althea. Maybe even the good doctor himself."

"In other words, back off and maybe we'll talk about it later."

"I truly enjoy working with a man so fast on the uptake." Ben rinsed his cup, set it in the sink. "If you don't mind company for one more night, I'll even spring for a couple of steaks to go on that barbeque I spotted on the porch yesterday."

Jake arrowed a sharp scowl at him but Ben smiled.

"Think about the questions I asked. Limbo isn't doing you or Hannah any good." With an off-key whistle he made his way outside. The screen door slammed behind him.

With a disgusted grunt, Jake pushed the curtains further aside and again let the damp cool air wash over him while he watched Ben, still whistling, pat Sadie's head. The man stepped around a puddle of rainwater then climbed into his silver rent-a-car.

Jake let the curtains fall back into place. Things were spinning faster and faster away from him, out of his control and completely away from any comfort zone he'd ever remotely enjoyed.

His dead ex-girlfriend was a ghost. Now he had a self-proclaimed expert in semi-residence. He couldn't get any damn answers from either one of them.

Some detective he made.

Lame was the word that came to mind.

He fingered the velvet box he'd shoved in his pocket earlier, after pulling on his jeans, more out of reflex than anything else.

At least that's what he told himself.

Lame was right.

Pathetically lame.

FUZZY, BLACK DOTS mixed with the dark grey clouding Hannah's vision. She struggled to keep her eyes open, to focus. On something. Anything.

She tried to lift her arms, to wipe the clouds away. Her limbs refused to move. A heaviness pressed on her, sucked at her body. Even the sob buried deep in her chest wouldn't budge.

Where was she? Blind and paralyzed?

Still a ghost?

Or had she somehow gone past that? Gone past to a place where there was nothing but pain.

Tears leaked from her eyes, their heat scalding her skin as they traced down her temples to puddle in her hair. Panic, thick and heavy as the weight pressing on her, churned hard and insidious in her stomach.

Jake? Where are you?

Her sob forced its way past the hard lump obstructing her throat. Her lips, dry and cracked, parted to let the scream tear through. No sound escaped.

HUDDLED ON JAKE'S BED, Hannah unfolded her legs, inch by painful inch. Sudden movement sent the room spinning and made her stomach heave. Each motion ratcheted the tension tighter in her body.

Outside the bare window, clouds drifted and sunlight spilled into the room. Daytime. Late morning, judging by the angle of light through the glass pane.

With her arms supporting her, she pushed herself upright. Her wrists trembled from the soreness banding deep inside her joints.

Even her fingertips ached.

Afraid of making the pain worse, she inched her fingers apart and splayed them over the surface of the bedspread. The material may as well been made of air. She couldn't feel the cloth.

Why would that change?

She ran her tongue over her bottom lip, then her top one. The dryness had disappeared. Had they really been cracked or was she the one cracked?

Where had she gone? If she'd actually gone anywhere.

Did ghosts have hallucinations? Or was this all one big hallucination?

She turned her face towards the window, towards the radiating warmth of the sun shining through the glass.

The last thing she remembered, before being sucked into the darkness, was touching Jake with her mind. *The way his head fell back, a low moan from his throat.* At that time, outside this same window, night had covered it all, as black as the world she'd been yanked into so quickly.

Where was Jake now? Was she here alone?

Still moving slowly, she eased her legs under her so she crouched in a half sitting position on the bed. Her head pounded, the beat hard with an uneven rhythm on the inside of her skull. But the grey spots and the blackness weren't dimming her vision.

At least not right now.

That was something.

Her breath thready and uneven, she wove her fingers through her hair and rested her hands at the back of her neck.

The house was so quiet.

Empty.

She swung her legs over the side of the bed and stood. Her legs wobbled and her knees almost buckled before she caught herself. With a hand to her chest, she took a few slow and shaky steps to the window.

Jake's Jeep was gone. So was Benjamin Garrett's silver sedan.

Sadie must have run off somewhere with Old Nels.

Hannah wet her lips again.

Jake, what are you doing? Where are you?

Grey dots swam through her vision. Dizziness sucked at her.

"What the hell?" Jake's voice, low and deep with an under-layer of pure panic yanked her disoriented gaze to him.

She now sat in the front passenger seat of his Jeep. He cursed and pumped the brakes. His eyes in narrow slits and his jaw tight, he downshifted, wrenched the steering wheel to the left. They careened around a sharp, downhill curve.

Oh, Lord.

She twisted in her seat, reached to brace herself. Nearly fell out.

Oh Lord, oh Lord.

What was happening?

If he didn't slow down – This was suicide.

"Jake!" Her scream filled the air.

He jerked his head in her direction.

"Hannah?" He whipped his gaze back to the switch-backed road. "Now's not a good time."

He made the curve but his speed increased with each spin of the tires. The opposite curve came too fast.

Hannah's breathing raced, matched her heartbeat. She risked a quick glance at the side. The road's edge fell away in a sharp, deep plunge. Straight down to the churning river.

"No!" She flung out her hands. A white-hot flash enveloped her.

In less than a single heart stopping beat, she stood in front of the careening vehicle as it barreled towards her.

"No!" She screamed again. That eerily bright white light surrounded her hands.

The front of the Jeep buckled, the sound a sickening metal-crunching echo that scraped the air. Jake jerked forward, snapped back by his seat belt.

The engine sputtered. Died.

The Jeep sat, utterly still. Motionless and quiet except for the hiss of white steam rising from under the mangled hood.

In front of the vehicle she stood with her arms stretched out before her. Sparks of white, little arcs of heat, pricked along her skin, abrading all of her nerve endings. Jake's harsh breathing punctuated the staccato beat of her heart.

Below them the river rushed on, as if nothing had happened.

"What the –" His eyes wide and a bit wild, he unsnapped his seatbelt, rubbed at his chest. "Hannah?"

"I'm … right here."

"What did you do?"

"I'm not sure."

"Got to get the Jeep out of the road." Jake sucked in a harsh sounding breath then twisted the ignition. A short, sick bark of laughter tore from him when the engine caught. Slamming the gear-shifter into reverse, he backed the vehicle uphill a short distance and tucked it into a narrow turnout behind them.

Once there, he left the Jeep in reverse gear and shut off the vehicle.

"Hell, Hannah." He ran his hand through his hair then gripped the steering wheel. "What just happened?"

Chapter Eight

A FEW HOURS LATER, Jake stood in his barn with his thumbs hooked into his front jeans pockets, fingers splayed at his hips. He stared at his Jeep.

Beat up and much worse for wear.

The vehicle had been old when he'd bought it years ago. Over the last year he'd restored it, taken good care of it, did all the maintenance and upkeep. How the hell was he going to get it back in drive-able shape again?

He rolled his shoulders. The tension and knots in his shoulder blades bunched in response. One big ache tomorrow, that's what he was going to be. Would probably have a hell of a dark bruise across his chest, right along the area his seatbelt usually rode. He widened his stance.

A faint odor, similar to burnt carpet, clung to the vehicle, reinforcing the idea his brakes had overheated.

Why? He'd changed them out himself. Three weeks ago.

Brand new brakes, pads, the whole thing.

The Jeep had been fine.

Yet when he'd headed straight for that cliff earlier, his emergency brake hadn't worked either. If someone had tampered with the brake line, the same had been done to the emergency brake cable.

He didn't want to think about Hannah and the way she'd stopped him, about the damage to the front of his Jeep.

About his busted radiator. Right now all he wanted was get to the bottom of the brake problem.

He'd deal with the impossible stuff later.

Hannah had disappeared again. Maybe she needed time to assimilate what she'd been able to do, how she'd saved his life.

He wasn't going to think about that, either.

Or the way Hank, the tow truck driver, had stared at his miserable Jeep. The way Hank glanced around, scratched his head but hadn't said a word. They'd known each other since grade school. Jake had kept more than a few of the man's secrets over the years.

Hopefully that meant something.

Jake hadn't offered an explanation. Hank hadn't asked.

Not going to think about those things.

Grabbing his flat dolly, Jake stretched out and rolled himself under his jacked-up, banged-up vehicle.

JAKE WIPED HIS HANDS on a rough, blue terry shop towel. Late afternoon sun slanted through the open barn doors and the barn's high beams.

"So what's the verdict?" Ben, with his hands in his pockets, strolled into the building. Sadie and Nels followed in tandem.

Jake shook his head and continued wiping his hands. "How'd you know anything had happened?"

"Your tow truck driver told Rily. She called me when she couldn't reach you."

So much for Hank keeping confidences. "Which means she'll be showing up here soon."

Ben shrugged. Patience lined his features.

"Looks like three of my brakes were loosened." Jake wadded the towel and threw it hard across the barn. "It was just a matter of time before that last brake, the right rear, heated up and went out on me."

"You're sure they were loosened?"

Jake toed the dolly, kicked it toward Ben. "Check for yourself."

His gaze unreadable, Ben stopped the dolly with his foot. He lowered and scooted himself underneath the Jeep. After several minutes, he pushed himself out. With the seamless agility of a much younger man, he levered himself into a standing position. "When was the last time they were worked on?"

"Three weeks ago. I changed them out myself." Jake had to work at keeping his jaw from tightening into a fist-sized knot. Whoever had done this knew what they were doing.

"The vehicle is too old to have disc brakes. So –" Ben ran his long-fingered hand over the back fender of the Jeep. "You're sure?"

"Hell, Ben. Of course I'm sure they were fine." He twisted away from the Jeep, pulled himself up to sit on top of his work bench. With his legs dangling, he braced his hands on the counter. "So is my emergency brake. There's nothing wrong with the cable. The connection is fine. But with the brakes themselves loose, it didn't do me a damn bit of good."

"You're saying someone tampered with your brakes?"

"What the hell do you think I've been getting at?"

"Don't jump down my throat. I wanted to make sure I understood where you were coming from."

"What's that supposed to mean?"

The lines around Ben's mouth deepened. He walked completely around the Jeep. Recognizing the ignoring tactic for what it was, Jake stayed where he was and kept his mouth shut. Ben was not going to bait him into any kind of argument.

Not yet anyway.

At the front of the vehicle, Ben paused and ran his hand across the bent frame. Soft light arced between his fingertips and the metal. "What stopped you?"

Jake stared at the hood and Ben's fingers. The weird light faded. Static electricity? Jake shook his head. Too much weirdness for one day. "You mean what did I run into?"

"No. I mean what stopped you."

This was getting too close to those things he didn't want to think about. He let his legs swing a little. "Doesn't matter."

"The tow truck driver told Rily there wasn't any damage to anything in the area. Not to any trees, any rocks. Nothing damaged. Except your vehicle." Ben stroked the hood where it met the bent and mangled front-end. "He went back and checked."

Son of a bitch. Hank really needed a lesson in keeping his mouth shut. And staying out of other people's business.

Jake managed a shrug. He kept the muscles in his face still and expressionless. The edge of the bench dug into his palms.

"He was worried." Ben rubbed the tips of his fingers together. "About you. That's why he called your sister."

"Obviously I'm fine."

"Yeah. Real obvious." Ben's fingers curled then he shook them out. His voice, though, was low and dripping with patience, as if he talked with a small child or an imbecile of an adult. "With your radiator busted you couldn't have moved the vehicle very far."

With belligerence choking him, Jake pulled off another shrug.

"I drove that section of road, Carrigan, before I came back here." Ben placed both palms flat on the hood. His fingers twitched then stilled. "Steep downgrade with a rock face on one side. The drop on the other is straight down to the river. Hell of a drop."

"Are you forgetting I was there?"

"No. I'm not." Ben leaned over the Jeep, his arms straight and bearing his forward weight. "There's no sign of impact on the road. No sign you hit another vehicle. Although there is a fresh stain just down from where the tow truck picked you up. Antifreeze. Water. Had to have been you. Hank wondered if you were trying to commit suicide."

"What?" Jake's head snapped up. He met Ben's impassive gaze.

"Were you?"

"Was I what?"

"Contemplating suicide? Joining Hannah?"

"That is the biggest pile of bullshit I have ever heard."

"Really? I thought it might have some merit."

Jake's jaw tight and his mouth twisted in a sneer, he screwed his eyes closed. Son of a freaking bitch. This was not happening.

Forcing his eyes open, his gaze narrowed, he aimed his hot stare at the older man. "Why would I do that? Why would I call Hank to tow my Jeep back if I'd intended to kill myself?"

"Cold feet?" Ben pushed away from the vehicle and pinched a bit of sawdust off the top of the bench a few feet from Jake. He rubbed it with his thumb and forefinger, watching as it drifted in the dappled sunlight on its way to the ground.

Jake's face muscles stiff from restrained effort, he fought his instinctive need to let go of the edge of the bench, to curl his hands into fists. To pound the other man into the ground right there with the damn sawdust.

Ben wiped his palms together then leaned against the bench where he stood, his elbow propped on the top for support. He met Jake's glare. "How did your vehicle wind up in that shape? What stopped you from going over that cliff?"

Jake released his stranglehold on the bench's edge, flexed his fingers. He wiped his palms over his knees. Without answers and being pissed at being asked, this was a conversation he didn't want to have.

Dammit, he hadn't figured out the answers yet himself.

He met Garrett's shuttered gaze square on.

"Hannah?" Ben's gaze didn't waver. "Did she have anything to do with it?"

"With what part?"

"Any of it, Jake." Ben's breath went out in a hiss. "What did she have to do with this *accident?*"

"She saved my life." With his grip tightening on his knees, Jake forced himself to loosen his fingers. He rolled his jaw and glared at the ceiling then back at Ben. "One minute I was losing control of the Jeep. The next I was stopped. It was like I'd hit something."

"Hannah?"

"Yeah. Maybe." He shrugged, his mind shying away from what he'd seen out there on that road. "She was in the Jeep, beside me, for a brief second. She screamed my name. Then the next time she said anything she was in front of the Jeep. Out there on the road."

"How did she do it? How did she stop you?"

"I don't know, Ben. Neither does she."

"You've talked with her about it?"

"Only then. Right after."

"Is she here now?"

"No. She's —" Jake sucked in a deep, scalding lungful of air. "I think she needed time. To figure all of this out. Assimilate it."

Hell, *he* needed the time. He couldn't even imagine this from her position.

"She hasn't been around since Hank picked me up out on the road."

"Do you want to be with her? To join her?"

"What?"

"You heard me. Do you want to be with her? Wherever it is that she is?"

"What the hell are you suggesting?" Dammit, yes, he wanted to be with Hannah. But alive, not dead. *Both* of them alive.

"Jake, even if you managed to kill yourself or let her kill you —"

"Stop right there." He held up a hand, palm out. What was wrong with this guy? "Are you actually suggesting *Hannah* tried to kill me?"

Ben's gaze lowered. He worked his jaw again before meeting Jake's eyes, the look hot and intense. "Look. Hannah's signature is all over that damn Jeep."

"Hannah's signature?" Now he was a damn mimic. What the hell was Ben getting at? The static electricity? "More woo-woo shit?"

"You can call it that, if you want. Hannah is dead. You've said so yourself."

Inside, Jake flinched and hated that he did.

"*If* this is her ghost *and* she managed to stop your vehicle from careening down that cliff face, then she's got a hell of a power supply."

"Not if."

"You need to understand something." Ben stared at the two animals lying in the hay across the barn. A shaft of sunlight played across the area. "Even if you managed to get yourself killed or you let Hannah kill you, there's no guarantee you'll end up with her. Here. Or anywhere else."

"Why would she try —" His face heated, Jake pushed off the bench. From where Sadie rested she lifted her head, her posture tense and alert. He shook his head. She settled, her gaze intent on them. He turned back to the older man.

Ben hadn't moved.

"Jake, we don't know *why* Hannah's essence is still here. Just because hers is doesn't mean yours would be also."

"This whole discussion is ridiculous. How do you even know these things?" He paced the length of the Jeep before turning and facing Ben. "I didn't try to kill myself. What reason would Hannah have to kill me?"

"Vengeance, retribution, love. Why do people who are alive kill anyone else? Any number of reasons."

"Hannah did not try to kill me." Broken record, that's what he was. He rubbed his sore chest. First he'd had to keep saying Hannah was dead, over and over. Now he had to keep repeating she hadn't tried to kill him. And she *hadn't*. "She saved my life."

"Maybe she got cold feet, too. For all I know, the two of you made a pact. Then you both chickened out."

"Dammit, Garrett. Are you trying to make me take a swing at you?"

"You won't get far if you do." Ben rubbed his chin. "Hannah's energy is all over those brakes. The same signature that's on the front of the Jeep, which by your admission has to be hers. Muddled on the brakes, but it's the same base line signature."

"Hannah didn't tamper with my brakes."

"You keep believing that."

Jake twisted his head at an angle, rubbed at the side of his neck. The knot lodged there refused to budge. Hannah had saved his life. He didn't care what some self-professed expert had to say on the matter.

How the hell did you read an energy signature, anyway?

And how could you trust the info even if you could read it? Facts were what he needed, not more mojo, woo-woo or any of that other psychic crap.

"Did you want to talk about anything else?" His hands loose on his hips, his feet flat and shoulder-length apart, Jake faced Ben. "Or are you done here?"

The man smiled, warmth seeping past the coolness in his eyes. "Denial's a hell of a place to be, kid. Been there. Done that."

Jake lifted his chin.

With a dry laugh, Ben straightened. "Yeah. Okay. I do have more to discuss on this, but I'll leave it for another time."

Load of bullshit and Ben had to be full of it. Tension ebbed out of Jake's muscles in a trickle, too slow to do him much good.

"I spoke with your cute little Amy this morning." Ben wiped his hands together.

"Did she let you get a word in?" Jake let part of his breath out, settled back against the Jeep. He crossed his arms loose over his sore chest.

"A few. Turns out Dr. Sheldon's on his way to Boston. Some medical seminar. He's pinch-hitting for a buddy of his who is supposed to be teaching but came down with some kind of mysterious illness."

"Sick, like with the flu?"

"If it was the flu it wouldn't be mysterious, now would it?" The lines around Ben's mouth creased but there wasn't any humor in his grin.

"Sounds hinky."

"Convenient is the word I was looking for. Speaking of convenient, Althea was also out of the office today. Delightful little Amy had no clue where she went or when she'd be back."

"Maybe Althea took her father to the airport in Portland."

"Nope. Amy said he took his own car."

"She's just a fount of information."

"That she is. She suggested, rather strongly, that I come out here and talk with you."

"Why?"

"She's worried about you." Ben covered half the grin spread across his mouth. "This has been so hard on you and it might help if you could talk with someone in Hannah's family."

"Oh geez, Uncle Ben. Help me get through the pain."

"Thought you'd appreciate that."

"So you're – What?" Jake shoved his fingers through his hair. "Looking at some kind of conspiracy theory here?"

"Aren't we?"

"Yeah, maybe. It would be nice to get some simple answers to a few simple questions." Be nice to have answers for the hard ones, too. But he wasn't holding his breath on that, either. He rubbed his chin, his thoughts lingering on the Jeep behind him. "Speaking of answers, how did you –"

"What?"

"That energy signature thing." He couldn't believe he was going there. He ran his hand over his face. What happened to ignoring things? "Why are you so sure you're right?"

Ben's gaze shuttered.

"*What* are you, Garrett?"

"Late." The craggy lines of his face set, Ben pulled his cell phone from his front pants pocket. After checking the face, he stuffed it back into his pocket. "I have a few things to handle. I'm going to owe you a rain-check on those steaks. Do me a favor."

"What?"

"Stay alive while I'm gone." His eyes still hooded, Ben gave him a small salute. He turned and strolled out of the barn, whistling that same hapless tune from earlier in the day.

Well. Jake puffed out a breath, stood where he was and listened to Ben's car start, then the sound of the car's engine fading as it went along its way down the dirt road.

What kind of secrets was Ben keeping? And why?

And why, in spite of those obvious secrets, did Jake trust the man? Hoping it was good people instincts and not simple relief at having someone believe him, he shook his head.

Sadie ambled over, nosed Jake's leg. Uncrossing his arms, he scratched behind her ear. She leaned against him. Such a small thing, but he found immense comfort in the dog's touch.

Maybe Amy wasn't so far off after all.

Uncle Ben. Shit. The internet search he'd done earlier during the morning had turned up nothing on the man. Nada. Zilch.

His hand motionless on the dog's head, Jake stared at his Jeep. What the hell kind of business did Garrett have to handle? And what did it have to do with Hannah?

HANNAH HESITATED AT THE BARN DOOR. The warm reddish glow of the setting sun coated the pasture and the buildings behind her, but she found no joy in the beauty.

She'd abandoned Jake with Hank. She was such a coward. Even now a fine tremor ran through her body. All she wanted was to run and hide. Curl up in a corner somewhere and pretend nothing had happened.

Disregard all the implications about things she couldn't answer. She hadn't wanted to hear how Jake explained what had happened. What she'd been able to do.

Or *how* she'd been able to do what she'd done.

Her skin cool to her own touch, she pressed the back of her hand against her forehead. At least the mind-numbing pain hadn't returned. When Hank had shown up, she'd fixed the image of the waterfall in her mind, found herself there in a blink. She'd stayed for hours.

Thinking.

Trying to come up with some kind of answer. Something, anything that made sense.

"Hello, Hannah." From inside the dark recesses of the barn Jake's soft, deep voice jolted over her nerve endings.

He knew she was out here.

How?

"Are you hurting?" Concern laced his words.

"Not too much." Her chin down, she stepped into the building. She wanted to vomit, but since she didn't have any food in her system, how was that an option? Dry heaves maybe? "How did you know I was here?"

"That's a good question." He stood, facing the open barn doors, and wiped his hands on a tattered blue rag. "I don't have the answer. I just know."

His eyes, such a deep green in the shadowy light, pierced through her and nicked her heart. He might not be able to actually see her, but she still looked away from the pain in his gaze.

Around him lay pieces of his vehicle. The damaged radiator sat propped against the bench. Brake parts scattered the floor.

"What are you doing to the Jeep?"

"Trying to figure out what happened."

"Oh." She eased a few steps closer. "Any ideas?"

The corners of his mouth tensed. His eyelids fell to half mast, shuttering his eyes. "No. Not really."

Had he just lied to her?

Why?

"Jake —"

"I saw you, Hannah." His words, soft and silky, slid over her. "Standing in front of the Jeep."

"You …?"

"For just a brief second. I've been over it again and again in my head. I didn't imagine it. White light surrounded you, so bright it hurt my eyes. I *saw* you." He sat the rag aside and lowered himself to sit on the floor. His arms dangled over his drawn up knees and he leaned his head back against the Jeep.

Stress lined his face, pulled at the corners of his eyes and his mouth. Her fingers curled into a small fist, she covered her heart. *What am I doing to you, Jake?*

No longer looking in her direction, he closed his eyes. "It was so quick, I had wondered if I'd imagined it. If I just *wanted* to see you so badly my mind made you up."

"But you hadn't?" In spite of the vise around her heart, a small thrill scudded though her veins. She stamped it down. Hard. She had no business being excited.

He was haggard, worn out. And she'd bailed on him.

Her movements stiff, she sat cross-legged on the floor near where he sat. With her arms tucked close to her side, she leaned forward. Right now, the only thing she wanted was to touch him, to wipe the frown lines from his forehead, from between his brows.

To gently rub the stress from his temples.

In her lap, she laced her fingers together tight.

"No. I didn't make you up." A sigh rumbled in his chest. "You screamed. Then I saw you standing in the middle of the road. You had your arms straight out. Panic all over your face. I was headed right for you. I couldn't turn the wheel fast enough. Then I jerked forward. Stopped. And you were gone. But still there."

"You didn't hit me, Jake."

"No, I don't think I did." He took a quiet, deep breath. "But I saw you. God, Hannah. You're still so damn beautiful."

Behind her, Sadie gave a small whine and padded through the barn. Without opening his eyes, Jake lifted his arm. The dog settled against him, resting her head on her paws, her big golden eyes fixed on Hannah.

"Jake –"

"Tell me what happened. From your perspective."

"Okay." She could do this, although inside she screamed, demanding to know why he didn't ask her where she went. Why she'd left him to deal with it all by himself. Why she'd abandoned him *this time*. She focused on the lines between his brows and took a deep and not-so-steadying breath. "I was in the Jeep, with you, for just a few seconds. You'd made it around the one curve but the other one was coming so fast."

She sucked in another breath, this one shakier than the last. The image of the edge of the road looming so close filled her mind, and the Jeep heading directly for the cliff.

Through blurred, moisture-ridden vision she stared at Jake. His eyes still closed, he continued to rub Sadie behind her ears.

How close had she come to losing Jake? "I didn't even think —"

"I've been meaning to talk with you about that." Jake's voice purred from low in his chest, sending a warm trail of sensation over her skin, down her belly. "Don't stop."

Stop?

He stretched his neck, tipped his head back. A sense of shock sparked at the nerve-endings in her fingertips.

She'd been mentally stroking Jake's forehead, rubbing the tension away at his temples. Touching him without a conscious thought.

The same way he rubbed Sadie's ears.

Oh, Lord. Jake.

She reached out, deliberate this time, and tentatively touched his cheek. A slow smile curved his lips upward. He leaned into the touch, pressed a slight kiss onto her invisible fingers.

Her hand lifted, stretched out. She wanted him to kiss *her*, to brush his lips over *her* skin. But he couldn't. He could feel her fingers caressing his skin, tracing the lines of his cheek, the hard edge of his jaw. She couldn't feel him.

Not physically.

Mentally, though, she stroked his neck with a light, soft caress. A small thrill whipped through her entire body when his head tipped farther back.

"This is all that matters, Baby. Right now. This moment." A rough moan escaped him. "Touch me."

Chapter Nine

NIGHT FELL FAST, pulling the last of the dim light from the sky outside the wide barn doors. Hannah held her breath as she watched Jake where he sat with his back against his Jeep. The shadows cast by the lamp over the workbench played across his body.

"Hannah. Don't stop, Baby. Touch me."

Hesitant, half afraid she'd be sucked back into that black void, she stretched her thoughts and touched the hem of his T-shirt. Inching it up, small amount by small amount, she scrunched the fabric in a fist-sized ball.

In her mind she ran the image of her own fingers, warm and soft, skimming over his skin. Just the barest of touches.

His stomach muscles contracted. He moaned and little tremors skittered across her already heightened nerves.

She'd missed this. Missed touching Jake, missed hearing those groans growl deep in his chest.

"Hannah."

His gruff voice stole over her, through her and centered in the warm, fluttering liquid core between her legs. With her head tipped back and her eyes half closed, she pressed a hand to the base of her throat to keep her own moan from escaping.

Jake.

The rumble of a heavy vehicle making its way up the fur-rowed drive yanked Hannah forcibly back from the edge she'd been hanging over.

Nooo.

Her breathing ragged, she stilled the images in her mind and barely contained the harsh cry cramming her tight chest.

"Dammit." Jake's voice husky and his eyes still closed, he lowered his chin to his chest. "It's Rily."

"What —" Hannah drew in a lungful of cool air and ran trembling hands through her hair, threading her fingers along its length. "What do you think she wants?"

"Hank called her, so I imagine she wants to give me a piece of her mind."

"And make sure you're okay." She pulled her knees to her chest, wrapped her arms tight around her legs. She barely stopped herself from rocking back and forth.

"More than likely." His shoulders sagged, his eyes opened and a glint of light reflected across them, the color undetecta-ble in the shadows. "If I just sit here really quiet and don't move, maybe she'll go away. I've had enough company to last the rest of the year."

The slam of the truck's heavy door echoed across the yard.

"Jake?" Rily's call followed the echo.

"I don't think that's going to work." Hannah tightened her grip on her legs.

"No." He straightened his T-shirt. "Please don't leave again, Hannah. Stay, okay?"

Her throat tight, she nodded then choked out a laugh. "Okay."

"Jake?" Rily strode into the barn, her hands tucked into the front pockets of her red pullover sweatshirt. "There you are."

"Here I am." His words slow and sardonic, a humorless smile crossed Jake's mouth. "Wondered when you were going to show up."

"Funny." With her gaze downcast, she scuffed the toe of her boot across the sawdust coating the cement floor where she stood.

Rily must have truly been worried. Hannah had rarely seen her friend without a torrid of words, always willing to speak her mind.

"Where's Garrett?" Rily glanced around the barn.

"Gone. For the moment anyway." Jake pushed himself to his feet before he twisted a side switch on the workbench. Bright light flooded the area. He blinked several times before turning to focus on his sister. "Says he'll be back but I'm not sure when."

"Oh."

"Didn't he call you?" He picked up the rag he'd discarded earlier, wadded it into his fist. "After all, you sent him out here to check on me."

"I got a text message that said your sorry ass was fine." Hands on her hips, Rily lifted her chin and aimed her hot gaze at her brother.

Hannah lips curled. *Give him hell, girl.*

"Yet you came out here anyway?" Jake's eyes shuttered to narrow slits. A twitch pulsed along his jaw.

"I won't apologize for worrying about you."

"We've been over this before, Rily. I don't need a babysitter."

"Then quit acting like a baby and answer your damn phone so I'll know you're okay." A light sheen of tears filmed her eyes. She blinked furiously.

"Ah, dammit, Rily." Jake slammed the rag back onto the bench. "Come here."

Her stiff posture wilting, Rily shuffled forward into her brother's begrudging embrace. His arms wrapped around her.

A sudden binding in Hannah's chest tightened the lump low in her throat. She couldn't swallow past the damn thing.

Rily's sniffles filled the quiet in the barn.

"I'm sorry for worrying you, Sis."

Rily hiccupped. Looking away from the two of them, Hannah squeezed her own eyes closed for a moment.

Damn these tears. Damn her promise not to leave this time. To stay.

Jake leaned away from his sister and wiped the moisture from her cheeks. "I really am okay."

"I can see that." Rily scrunched her face into a frown and took two steps back. "At least physically you are."

"Ah, hell. Not you too."

"I drove that section —"

"Shit." Jake raised his hands into the air then shoved his fingers through his hair. "Does *everyone* have to go check it out?"

"Just be glad we actually care about you, especially since you're such a jerk."

"Do Mom and Dad know yet?"

Hannah started. Jake's parents. She hadn't thought about them since she'd been ... well, back.

"That you're a jerk? I've told them often enough. About what happened earlier? No." Her face set, Rily spun around and stalked over to the stack of boxes containing Hannah's possessions. She stared at them for a long moment then swung around to face her brother, her hands slammed onto her hips. "They're still on that rail portion of their tour. Out of phone or even email range. But it's only a matter of time before they check in with me. I'm not going to lie to them."

"You're also not going to ruin their time in Europe." Jake leaned against the bench, his jaw tight and his mouth set in a firm line. "I had an accident, Rily. I'm fine."

They stared at each other. Hannah paced between them and Jake's gaze flicked towards her. Rily frowned and rubbed her arms.

"Cold?" Jake again sent a quick glance in Hannah's direction, a question marking his face.

Rily shrugged and moved forward, almost into Hannah's personal space. Hannah held her ground. What difference did it make anyway? Rily couldn't see her, didn't sense her, didn't know she was even around.

"Not really cold." Rily shuddered then side-stepped to stand a few feet away. "More like a sudden chill. There, then gone. Not sure where it came from."

"Hannah."

"*What?*"

"What?" Rily's voice echoed Hannah's and they both stood with their hands splayed on their hips.

Sparing a quick glance at Rily, Hannah crossed her arms over her chest instead. What the devil was Jake up to?

"According to Ben, an unexplained chill could indicate you felt Hannah's ghost."

"Excuse me?" Rily pulled back as if she'd been hit.

Hannah balled her hands into fists. "What are you doing, Jake?"

He glanced in her direction then back at his sister. "Hannah's ghost. Her essence still here, on this plane. That's what you felt."

"I know what a ghost is." Rily paced away then whirled around to face her brother. "What I want to know is what the hell you're talking about."

"Hannah's ghost —"

135

"Jake, are you nuts?" Hannah moved to stand right in front of him, in his space, her arms wrapped around her waist.

"Maybe." His eyes crinkled at the corners, the look tender and then calculating when he shifted his gaze back to his sister.

"Maybe Hannah's a ghost?" Rily's hands fisted and she planted them on her hips, her feet spread and solid on the floor. "Jake, make up your mind or I really am going to believe you've gone over that edge."

"Are you sure you want to do this?" Hannah turned back towards Rily.

"Yes, I want to do this and yes, Hannah's a ghost." Jake crossed his legs at the ankle and his lips twisted into a semblance of a smile.

"I know Hannah's birthday threw you a wild curve-ball, Bro, and I know you miss her terribly —"

"Cut the crappy talk-to-him-like-he's-a-moron-because-he's-nuts voice, Sis."

"Jake —"

"She is a ghost. She is here."

"Really? How are you going to prove that?"

"I'd like an answer to that one myself." Hannah laced her words with syrup, thick and gooey. His sister was right, he really had slipped over that edge. Rily couldn't even hear her. Jake himself hardly accepted her presence. How was he going to convince his sister she actually existed?

"Hannah, why don't you step up to Rily? Let her know you're here?"

Jeez. She set her shoulders. This was dumb. So dumb she couldn't believe she was going to actually do it.

She took the couple of steps, leaned into Rily's personal space. She imagined a kiss from her own lips grazing across the other woman's cheek. Rily shivered, raised a hand to her face before she stumbled back.

"How the hell did you do that?" Rily caught her footing and whirled around in a tight circle, her gaze darting around the barn.

Hannah blinked. A small thrill twisted around her spine. Her focus was getting tighter. The results seemed to be faster, more immediate.

And, so far this evening, no mind-numbing headache.

"I didn't do anything. Hannah did." Jake frowned and pushed away from his workbench. "Whatever it was she did."

"You know what she did." Rily's brows drew together. "I mean you know what you did."

"Ask Rily if she's wearing the red lace, satin bra and panties."

"What?" Jake spun around, his face a mask of comic disbelief.

Hannah bit back a sudden bark of laughter. He wanted to prove her presence to Rily, fine. Why should she make it easy or comfortable for him?

"You heard me." Rily, her mouth set in a thin line, glared daggers at her brother.

"Go on. Ask her." A small smile played across Hannah's lips. This might be fun, after all.

Jake shifted away from her general direction. He swallowed once, his Adam's apple working around whatever he'd found stuck there. "Um, Sis. Hannah says you're wearing red lace and satin panties. And bra."

"That's not what I said."

"*What?*" Rily's face lost color. Her eyes wide, she pressed her palm against her chest. "How do you know that?"

"You mean you *are* wearing red lace and satin? Rily?"

Hannah couldn't stop the snicker bubbling in her chest.

"She can tell what I'm wearing under my clothes?" Pink tinged Rily's cheeks.

"No." Hannah shook her hair back, let out an exasperated puff of air. "I was with her when she bought them and since her sweatshirt is red, I guessed."

"I *guess* she can." With a pained look settling on his face, Jake turned away from Rily. "My little sister wears red satin lace?"

"Too much info, big brother?" Hannah grinned. Looked like she was the only one who thought this was funny. Too bad. "The black ones are pretty sexy, too. And the baby blue ones –"

Jake shot a dark look in her direction. She shrugged one shoulder, glad he couldn't see the glee she knew shone in her eyes.

"It's really none of your business." Rily lifted her chin and crossed her arms at her waist. "At all. I can't believe Hannah would tell you about … my undies."

His eyes still troubled, Jake shrugged and spread his hands. "Me, either."

"She told you before … before she died. This was just a lucky guess on your part."

"No she didn't, Sis. She kept your little secret." He shot a glare in Hannah's general direction. "I've only *just now* found out you don't wear standard issue, white cotton granny underwear."

"Standard issue?" The pink in Rily's cheeks darkened. "Grow up, Bro."

"I'm not the one blushing, Sis. I'm just the one in shock and denial. My little sister's not supposed to wear stuff like that."

"Really? That was the same shopping trip Hannah bought that little, dark blue –"

"Enough already." Jake pressed his hands to his ears. "I really don't want this conversation with you."

"You started it. Not me."

"No. Hannah started this." He aimed another deadly glare in Hannah's general direction.

"She's really here? Now?" Rily's voice soft, she rubbed her arms and glanced around the barn.

"Yeah." Jake's gaze followed his sister's. "Somewhere."

Hannah kept her mouth closed.

"Jake?" Rily worked her bottom lip between her teeth. Hannah couldn't remember ever seeing Rily this hesitant before. "*If* Hannah is really here –"

"Not if, Sis. *Is*. Hannah really is here."

Rily ran the fingers of her right hand over her face. "Okay. Why?"

"Why?"

"Why is she still here, Jake? What does she want from you?"

Jake was silent for a drawn-out moment, his gaze locked with his sister's. The pit at the center of Hannah's stomach churned, twisting in on itself. Tremors quaked along every inch of her skin.

This was important but she didn't know the answers.

How could Jake?

"I don't have to know why." One corner of his lip curled, only a slight movement. His nostrils flared. "It's enough that she's here."

"Listen to yourself." Rily stepped forward and reached out, her fingers light on Jake's arm. "Really listen. She's dead –"

Hannah flinched, backed further away from them.

"We've been over this ground before." Jake cupped Rily's hand and removed it from his arm. "You need to stop."

"I can't." She pulled her hand free from his, balled her fist. "Not when you're doing this to yourself."

"What, exactly, am I doing to myself that's so terrible?"

"Staying here, locked in the past. Not moving forward. Killing yourself slowly —"

"Killing —" His jaw tight, Jake closed his eyes for a brief second. "You too?"

Hannah pressed her hand to her face, her palm covering her mouth. Jake was alive, too much *here* for Rily to be saying these kind of things. He would *never* kill himself.

Never.

"You have to look at this from my perspective." Rily reached out, her hand again grazing her brother's arm.

"No." He took one step back, away from his sister. "Actually, I don't."

"So this is how you want to live out your life?" A muscle twitched along Rily's jaw. With her palms up, she swept her arms in a wide arc. "Alone out here with your ghost girlfriend?"

"Harsh, Rily. Really harsh."

"What about Hannah?"

"*What* about her?" Eyes narrowed, Jake pinned his sister with a darkened glare.

"Is this what she wants?" Rily spun in a slow circle, her right arm outstretched, fingers spread. "Does she even have a choice? Are you keeping her soul, her spirit, here? Or is *she* keeping *you* from moving on?"

"What difference does it make?" His voice low and dangerously deep, Jake crossed his arms over his wide chest. With his gaze locked on his sister, he raised one eyebrow.

"A hell of a lot, I'm thinking." Rily again glanced around, her eyes troubled and her brows drawn together. "How are either of you supposed to move forward if her spirit is keeping you both locked here, stuck in place?"

Oh, no. Hannah pressed her palm tight over her mouth. Rily was right. How could Jake move forward when all she did was tie him to the past?

Their past.

A past without any kind of possible future.

A gasp, small and involuntary snuck out of her suddenly dry throat. She cringed.

"Hannah?" Jake spun around, his dark green eyes flashing with panic. "Don't leave. You promised you'd stay this time."

"No." The whisper, torn from her, echoed across the small space separating them. Her steps tiny and unsure, with her hand still pressed tight over her mouth, she backed away. "I can't."

"Dammit, Hannah." Jake stood facing her direction, his legs braced, his arms rigid and his hands fisted in front of him. "Stop running away. Stop pushing me aside."

HANNAH STARED AT THE CHURNING WATER.

Moonlight ripped across the black surface of the pond. A strong wind rented through the pine branches above her, surging with furious screams, almost managing to cover the angry calls from the open field to the north.

"Hannah!"

The wind shifted, grabbed and threw Jake's cries at her, along with Rily's curses. She ignored them.

She wished she could ignore her friend's words.

But Rily was right.

She usually was, although it was rare for anyone to admit that to her. But Rily *was* right.

About Hannah. About Jake. About them being locked in this place. Locked in this time. Neither of them moving forward. Only looking back.

Tears leaked over the rim of Hannah's lashes. She ignored them, too.

Pain pierced her temples, lancing through her with its suddenness. Her hands trembling, she pressed her fingertips at the pressure building under her skin.

Grey dots mingled with the blackness of the night. She squeezed her eyes shut tight. The pressure intensified. Stumbling, she fell onto the rocks, curled in on herself at the edge of the pond's shore. Her breath came in harsh gasps.

No. Please not now.

But then, why not just give in?

Hannah? A voice, not Jake's and not Rily's, whispered through the pine branches, barely audible above the howl of the wind. *Stop fighting, Hannah.*

"What's happening to me?" Her own voice, thin and barely clear even to herself, carried no force, no will. She was a coward.

Always running.

Never stopping to face whatever it was that needed facing.

A touch, soft and soothing, floated over her, caressing her hair, her cheeks, kneading at the tension tightening her shoulders.

Relax. The gender-less voice echoed in her head, the order soft with a solid firmness braiding the words. *Accept.*

Relax and accept what?

Death?

Maybe she should.

Simply close her eyes, allow herself to drift into the greying darkness.

That's it. Smugness laced the words. The voice sharpened. *Good.*

No. Hannah, her head heavy and bowed forward, pushed herself up on her arms. Focus. She had to focus on the voice.

Male? Female? She couldn't get a fix, couldn't tell. Where was it coming from? Inside herself, bouncing around inside her head?

The light, lingering touch along her arm tightened into a pinch, digging deep into her skin. She gasped and rolled away from the sudden pain. Away from the water.

The wind swept down. Dry, brittle leaves left from autumn swirled in a crackling circle around her, skimming over the surface of the pond on one side and completely surrounding her.

Her hair blew hard across her face, slapping and stinging her skin. What was happening?

For the last few days, she'd been able to feel the warmness of the sun, the coolness of the breeze, but nothing beyond those sensations.

How was the wind whipping her hair around now?

What was different?

What had changed?

Stop fighting, Hannah. The voice whispered across her skin, through her mind. Cajoling and sickeningly sweet.

"No." Hannah's jaw clenched. She pushed herself to a standing position. None of this was right.

Her legs trembling, the leaves still swirling around her, she turned in a slow circle. A slight pinching sensation pricked the backside of her right hand. Startled, she covered it with her left.

Soft light flittered in and out of the darkness surrounding the area. In the flickering light, something deep and dark red oozed down what appeared to be white walls.

Blackness dimmed the edges of her vision, overcoming the white, red and grey before sucking her into the edges of the black void.

A wild scream echoed across the pond and through the overhead trees, drowning out Hannah's own cries.

Chapter Ten

J AKE PACED ACROSS HIS BEDROOM. He barely resisted the urge to pound his fist straight into the wall.

The only light in the room, his small bedside lamp, glowed in the corner. Night blackened the sky outside his bare windows. He paused to brace his hands on the window sill. To stare at his own bleak reflection. Behind him, Sadie whined.

Where the hell was Hannah?

He'd been out for hours looking for her, most of that spent with Rily following behind yammering about him being a fool. He didn't need his little sister telling him what he already knew.

When Hannah's scream had ripped across the field, he thought he may as well have died with her. Even now his gut twisted in anguish about what had made her scream.

With his fist, he pounded once on the sill before he turned to face the bed. Doubting he'd sleep, he stretched out on top of the comforter, crossing his ankles and cupping the backside of his head with his intertwined fingers. Sadie sighed and settled on the floor beside the bed.

Why was Hannah always running away from him? With his eyes closed, he frowned at the thoughts and images bombarding his mind.

Hannah, her face a mask of nothingness with no expression at all, uttering those lifeless words that changed the direction of his entire life. Pain flickering through her eyes when he told her he was going to the Caribbean anyway. Without her.

That small sense of satisfaction welling inside that at least something he did, something he said, still meant something to her.

Even if all it did was upset her.

But that wasn't right. Hannah had been angry, had told him to go to hell. Her face had never been expressionless. Almost chilly maybe, but never without expression.

Jake shook his head. Frowned deeper. But the images kept whirling through his mind.

Hannah, standing in front of his Jeep, hand outstretched, trembling. A bright, white light surrounding her. Agony lining her face.

Gone. No one there.

Hannah, laying in a hospital bed. Her dark hair spread out around her, framing the whiteness of her face. Her chest barely moving. The sheet covering her body slowly turning red as blood seeped from her chest and stained the white cotton.

No.

Jake twisted his head to the side, trying to dislodge that image. A moan caught in his throat, choked him. Blood flowed down the walls of Hannah's hospital room.

A large pane of flat, black glass. Sudden, sharp impact, shattered lines spider-webbing across the entire surface.

No.

He cried out, his throat raw.

Wetness coated his cheek. He brushed at it with the back of his hand.

Sadie whimpered. The sound pierced Jake's consciousness and he came to, sitting up, his arms full of trembling, anxious dog.

"God, Sadie." His hands shaky, eyes sticky with sleep-dust and dried tears, he rubbed the dog's ears then rested his forehead against hers.

Where the hell had that nightmare come from?

LOW, EARLY MORNING GOLDEN LIGHT filtered across the open field stretching out past the barn. Jake sat on the steps of his back porch, bundled in an old, worn and greyed sweatshirt underneath his brown leather jacket with a scarf Hannah had once bought him wrapped around his neck. Steam, along with the aroma of fresh coffee from the full mug he held, drifted upwards in the chilled air.

Damp pine scented the air, the faint sound of the water-fall reached across the distance. Sadie stretched out next to him while Nels chomped on grass a few feet away.

The three of them were alone. Hannah hadn't returned. There wasn't any sense, any *feel*, of her in the house, the barn or anywhere else on the property.

She had died from her illness. Not from any form of vio-lence. She hadn't hit a windshield, hadn't shattered a plate of glass. And she certainly hadn't bled to death. Not the way his brother had. The images he'd seen last night hadn't happened. They weren't real.

No matter what the dream implied.

In his grief, he was mixing both deaths together.

He wasn't psychic. He wasn't anything except frustrated.

The nasty dream was simply a remnant brought on by yesterday's accident, his worry about Hannah. Add in his brother's death and it was no wonder he'd had a nightmare.

End of story.

But still, beyond the understandable uneasiness the nightmarish images had left him with, a darker, more insidious worry gnawed at his insides. On edge, he lifted the mug and blew across the coffee's surface.

He'd go back into town, once the sun came up fully and people began stirring. Once Dr. Sheldon's office opened he'd have another chat with Amy, maybe grill Althea again.

After he checked out the waterfall area in daylight.

Hannah's scream had seemed to come from that direction, but his meager little flashlight hadn't been able to penetrate the darkness last night. With Rily insisting on following him, they'd made it down to the waterfall, but any trace of Hannah had been gone.

He hadn't known where else to look.

Taking a sip of hot coffee, he stood and motioned to the animals. "Come on you two. Let's go for a walk."

"GOOD MORNING, AMY." Jake eased Dr. Sheldon's front door closed behind him. Technically, though, it was closer to noon.

"Jake." Amy's smile lit her face and her blue eyes crinkled in the corners. She leaned forward, her elbows on her desk with the heels of her hands cradling her chin. "Did Hannah's uncle get hold of you?"

In a manner of speaking. "That's actually part of why I'm here. He wasn't able to speak with Althea."

"No, I was the only one here that day." With the edge of her bright pink bottom lip between her teeth, she shrugged. "I thought he was going to come back, though."

"He was called away. Business."

Movement behind Amy caught Jake's eye.

Althea Sheldon stood there, her head tilted slightly to the side.

"Hello, Mr. Carrigan." Althea's lips, a deep and dark red today, twitched when Amy jumped.

His gaze narrowed.

From the carpeted hallway Althea moved into the room. Her high heels clicked on the wooden floor of the front office. Smoothing a hand down her dark green skirt, she then fingered the green satin ribbon that disappeared down the neckline of her pale green blouse. After a moment, she tucked a strand of her short auburn hair behind her ear.

One cold, calculating, well put together woman.

"Althea." Jake glanced behind her. How long had she'd been standing out of sight before she let herself be seen?

"How are you?" False concern seeped from her voice. Then she laughed, a low and sultry sound that skimmed across his nerves.

Jake frowned at the bumps raised on his arms.

"I heard about your Jeep. Hank's mother is our neighbor." She waved a manicured hand to the right. "Hank told her and she told me about your *accident.*"

Really? Paranoid City, his new hometown.

The Jeep might look worse for wear, but it was running again. And stopping like it was supposed to when he braked.

"A few issues with my brakes, but they're all fixed now." That had taken him all morning, after his walk and thorough – probe – of the waterfall area. Where he'd come up with zilch. Hannah was still gone.

"Accident?" Amy squeaked, her hand in front of her mouth. "Brakes? Jake, were you hurt?"

"Amy." Althea raised her eyebrows and disdain eked from her voice. "He's standing right here, in one piece and no obviously broken bones. He must be okay."

"Oh. Right." A small, self-conscious half-smile touched Amy's lips and she shrugged. Her eyes shimmered with moisture. "Well, I'm glad you're all right, Jake."

"Me, too." He aimed a real smile at Amy, one he actually meant, before turning back to Althea. He let his mouth form a stiff, straight line. Not quite a frown, but close. "I'd actually hoped to speak with you. If you're not too busy."

Be nice. Be polite. Don't let your real thoughts show. Those certainly wouldn't get him anywhere. Not with I-can't-stand-your-guts Althea Sheldon.

"Of course." Althea gave him a half nod and turned away but he caught the sudden jerk of Amy's shoulders and the small frown lining her forehead. "Why don't you come into my office, Jake?"

With a wink for Amy, he followed the other woman down the short hallway. At her office door Althea waved him into the room.

A heavy, dark cherry wood desk dominated the center of the room. The desk sat squat on top of a thick, green tapestry type rug covering a portion of the polished wooden floor. File cabinets of that same cherry wood lined one wall. Healthy and lush green plants sat on top of the cabinets, under the tall window and in the far corner of the room.

Floor to ceiling curtains, matching the green of the rug, framed the beveled, sparkling panels of the window and were tied back with what looked to him like burnished, gold braided rope.

Fancy.

With all the wood and greenery, Jake had visions of being in the middle of a freaking forest. Of course, maybe that was the look she was going for. Under other circumstances he might have even enjoyed the room. Found peace there.

Today it made him claustrophobic.

"Jake, why don't you sit down?" She indicated one of the two overstuffed, *green*, wing-backed chairs in front of the desk. "Hot tea? Something cold to drink?"

"No, nothing for me." He eased his long frame down onto the chair, its comfort surprising him.

Althea gave him another of those smiles that didn't quite reach her eyes before she settled behind her big desk. She ran the tip of her fingernail, blunt and coated with clear polish, along the ornate, silver framed photo of an older man that sat on the far edge.

Her father? Dr. Sheldon?

A similarly framed photo of a young woman sat next to the man's photo. Not Althea, but close enough to be a relation.

Her mother? He remembered something about her dying when Althea was young. Sketchy on the details, he was going to have to check with Rily on that little fact.

Althea drummed the nails of her other hand on top of the only file folder on the desk. Closed and upside down.

Deciding she could start this, he let her fidget while he continued to study the room. And her.

Her red lips pursed and the edges of her eyes crinkled, not in pleasure. Good. He wasn't too happy to be here, himself. Even though he had been the one to initiate this visit.

Fingering the satin ribbon at her neck, Althea eased the file-folder to one side. She leaned her elbows on the desk's polished surface and stared at him over her steepled fingers. Filtered light from the window shone across her eyes, giving them an unnatural, pale glow. "What can I do for you today?"

The temptation to tell her what he wanted from her, *the truth would be a good place to start*, had his jaw tightening. "I understand Hannah's uncle was in to see you."

"Yes. Amy said he stopped in." She straightened a little and pulled the file closer. "Unfortunately, I wasn't here at the time."

"So you weren't able to release Hannah's ashes to him."

"You know we didn't, Jake."

"Althea." He worked to unclench his jaw "All I want is closure." *Liar.*

"I can understand that. And if her uncle had shown up sooner, we would have been able to arrange the release of those ashes to him." She picked up the lone pen on the desk, tapped the end on the file folder. "However, because they went unclaimed for over a hundred and twenty days, which is all the time required of any funeral home, those ashes would have been ... disposed of before now. They are no longer available for him to claim."

Tension knotted the space between Jake's shoulder blades, radiating upwards, ending in a hard twitch in his cheek. *Hold it together, Carrigan. Blasting her won't get you anywhere.*

"There's nothing left of Hannah, Jake. Nothing at all." The icy blueness of Althea's eyes speared him right in the center of his chest. "I am sorry, Jake. If her uncle had come by sooner...."

"Which funeral home did you use?"

Her mouth tightened a fraction but she held his gaze. "Jake –"

"Which funeral home, Althea?"

Her eyes even icier, she glanced away. On a sigh, she opened the folder, flipped through several pages.

Jake crossed one leg over the other, his ankle resting on his knee and his hands loose on his crossed leg. Patience. He could wait a bit longer to see where she was taking this damn game she played.

He had no doubts she was stringing something together.

Him, most likely. At least in her mind.

He focused on the papers she riffled through. Several seemed to be a series of medical records. The one on top looked to be some kind of official form filled in with a long, scratchy script. A flourished signature scrawled across the bottom.

The missing death certificate?

Jake sat a little straighter in his chair. His fingers gripped his ankle. Althea frowned then tapped the papers together before she settled them back in the folder. She closed it and pushed it away before she met Jake's deliberately noncommittal look.

"That information isn't in the file. I'm not sure who was used." She stood, her chin raised, her palms flat on her desk. "Are you sure you wouldn't like a cup of tea?"

"Sure." Jake nodded, careful to *not* glance at the folder. What was she up to? This was too easy and she wasn't that stupid. What did she want him to see? The certificate? "Plain would be fine."

"All right. I'll see if I can find out which company we used while I get that tea."

At the soft click of the door behind her, he straightened, leaned forward to stare at the file sitting square on the desk. He rubbed a hand across the back of his neck, turned the folder over.

The words *Hannah Dixon*, in bold black type, sat on a white tab in the upper right corner of the manila folder. He glanced at the closed door. Definite set up. Still, he might as well see what it was the woman wanted him to see so badly.

He flipped open the file, did a quick scan of the top document. The missing death certificate or at least a copy of what the doctor submitted to the county? *Dr. James Sheldon* scrawled across the bottom in a forward slanted signature. The date matched what Jake knew of the facts.

Cause of death Acute Leukemia.

That wasn't exactly what Rily had been told. A similar disease, one without a cure, was what the receptionist had told his sister.

He twisted his head to the side. His nostrils flared. Ignoring the slight trembling of his hands, he flipped past the first page. Lots of senseless medical jargon filled most of the pages, along with information on Hannah's stats for each visit.

A long, hand written paragraph on one of the last pages caught his attention. The writing seemed to match that on the first page.

Dr. Sheldon's notes?

A fist sized knot clenched Jake's stomach. According to what he read, Hannah had been responding well to the treatments. The date of the notation was a mere week before she'd died.

Had she really taken such a drastic u-turn? In such a short period of time?

He worked at the kink in his neck, squeezing at the tension just below his skin. Of course she had taken that turn. She was dead. Hard to be more definitive than that.

If this entire file wasn't a complete crock of shit.

Jake scrubbed his hand over his mouth, along his jaw.

Pushing the papers back into messy disorder, he tossed the folder on Althea's desk. She'd wanted him to read the file, he certainly didn't want her to have to guess if he'd taken the bait. Why disappoint her?

He leaned back in his chair with his hands behind his head, his fingers linked. A few moments later the door pushed open. Althea came in with a tray loaded with two dainty cups and an elegant tea pot.

She sat the tray on the table, glanced at the folder. For a quick, barely noticeable moment, a sharp and predatory glint shone in her icy blue eyes. She lowered her lashes and bent to pour hot tea into the fragile cups. Satisfaction oozed from her when she sat his cup in front of him then settled into her own chair on the other side of the desk.

"Thank you." Without sipping, he lifted the cup to his mouth. The warming aroma of orange, spiced tea filled his nose. "Nice."

She leaned back, cradled her own cup in two hands and stared at him over the rim.

"So which funeral home did you use?"

"I couldn't find that information." Althea lowered her chin. "Good help and all that."

"Amy seems competent enough."

"She wasn't working for us then. The woman that was, is now gone."

"Good riddance?"

"In a manner of speaking." Setting her cup on the desk, Althea straightened, pulled the folder closer. Tapping the edges, she ran her fingers along the sides, righting the pages and smoothing the file. "Did you enjoy your extracurricular reading?"

"Matter of fact." He nodded towards the file. "Why?"

"I was … cruel to you the other day, when you were in here." She kept her eyes lowered. Her fingers smoothed the green satin ribbon where it touched her blouse. "I didn't think about the fact you were hurting. I didn't think about any of this from your perspective. Not until you'd already left."

"I appreciate that, Althea." He sat his untouched tea on the desk in front of him. "But you were pretty definitive about me not being family and not deserving this information."

"You will have to forgive me, Jake." Her eyes met his and her fingers twisted the thin ribbon. A slight tremor echoed along her hand. "I had become very fond of Hannah, had felt you'd abandoned her when she needed you. Seeing you standing there, wanting her ashes ... hit me as wrong. I'm afraid I took it out on you."

Jake kept his gaze locked on hers.

She was saying the right things, pushing the right buttons, but the whole exchange seemed off.

Wrong.

"I didn't take into account the fact you'd had two great losses so close together." She tilted her head to the side, stroked the ribbon. "With the loss of Hannah following so closely on the heels of your brother's death ...."

Craig.

Sorrow sucker punched him, tightened the muscles in his stomach, constricted in a thick band around his chest.

God, he had to get out here. Away from the confining claustrophobia of her office, the cloying scent of her exotic perfume, the spicy tea.

"Thank you for your time, Althea." His legs a little wobbly, he pushed himself to a standing position. Not bothering to offer his hand he nodded at her. "Let me know if you figure out which funeral home you used."

Her mouth lifted in a semblance of a smile, still not quite reaching her eyes. "I will do that."

He inclined his head again then made his way out of her office, closing the door behind him with a soft click. His legs shaky, he made it past Amy's empty desk and out onto the front veranda then down to his Jeep.

Honeysuckle scented the air he sucked in, cloying and sweet, thick in his throat. Hard to swallow.

Where the hell had all of *that* come from? That unexpected up-swelling of grief over his brother?

A by-product of almost dying himself?

Probably. But he didn't like it.

He raked a hand through his hair and glanced towards the neighboring house. Sure enough, Hank's truck sat square under the carport.

Jake's breathing somewhat steadier, he glanced at his watch. Lunchtime. Hank was checking in on his mother.

Like a good son.

Could Althea knowing about his accident be as simple and innocent as it seemed on the surface?

Should he run next door, check on Hank himself? Have a little chat about minding one's own business.

Man, he was getting paranoid. But almost ending up as part of the scenery out on River Road, and not the pretty part, could do that to a person.

Jake wiped a hand over his mouth then swung his gaze back to the doctor's house.

Had Althea stayed in her office, at the back of the old house? Amy was out, probably also at lunch. No one stood on the porch or behind the big picture window to watch him this time.

So why did the area between his shoulders twitch?

ALTHEA LEANED BACK in her chair, her tea cup cradled in her hands. She pulled her gaze from her closed office door.

That had been … difficult.

Warmth from the cup seeped into her hands but didn't spread past her fingers. She was cold.

And out of sorts.

Her hands still curled around her cup, she leaned her head back against the support of her chair and stared at the pair of framed photos on her desk.

Jake Carrigan was hurting. From loss. Grief.

She knew how that felt. All consuming, until it colored and controlled every aspect of a person's life.

Which was worse, though? Watching someone you loved waste away from the disease or having that person taken so quickly you hadn't even realized she was sick?

Her movements sharp and sudden, Althea sat forward and shoved her fragile tea cup to the side of her desk.

Jake Carrigan didn't know how lucky he was.

A clean break. There and then gone.

First his brother, then Hannah.

With her elbows braced on the desk top, she fingered the satin ribbon at her neck.

Jake Carrigan wanted answers. Closure.

Didn't he realize that wasn't really ever possible?

Chapter Eleven

L OW ON THE WESTERN HORIZON, early evening sunlight skipped across the crests of the river, sparking gold and red over the wind driven surface.

Those waves slapped against the underside of the rotting wooden pier. They wobbled the planks where Jake stood. Behind him a long abandoned warehouse loomed. He didn't have to look to know the glow from the setting sun would be swallowed by the burned exterior, the blackened surface sucking at every small bit of light.

The fire had been extinguished nearly ten months ago. How much of the strong phantom odor of charred wood was based in the reality of now, and how much was in his mind?

Mixed with the freshness of the river breeze, the scent of the surrounding pines seemed wrong.

Too pure. Too clean.

With one hand in his pocket, his fingers gripped the velvet ring box. He shoved his free hand through his hair.

Man, he really needed a haircut.

Narrowing his eyes, he looked down river, towards Eagle Crest. Evening lights flickered in the distance, miles away, and added to his sense of isolation.

What the hell was he doing here?

Craig was long gone. Dead.

Just because Hannah was a ghost didn't mean his brother had met that same fate. Jake was alone out here. No ghosts except the ones in his head.

Like he was some kind of expert.

His eyes burned from the residual smokiness. He had to blink several times just to clear his vision. Or maybe they burned from memories. He wasn't sure any more.

With his lips in a tight, straight line, he turned to confront the shell of the building where his brother had been shot and left to bleed out. Or burn to death. The bastards hadn't cared, as long as Craig died.

He hadn't been able to stop that from happening.

"Jake."

He started at Hannah's voice. Where had she come from? He angled his head, stretching his senses out, the way he'd been doing at home whenever he looked for her.

There, just at the edge of the pier, a few feet away, her presence strong now that he looked for it. Strong and somehow comforting.

How sick was that? Comfort from his dead, ghostly girl-friend.

"Hannah." He pulled his attention back to the warehouse. "What are you doing here?"

"I seem to be able to center on you. I think of you and then wherever you are, that's where I am."

He snorted, the sound loud in the quietness of dusk. "Re-ally? Didn't notice."

"Stop being such an ass."

Her words, spoken in a calm and direct manner, eased a small bit of the tension at the back of his neck. "Okay."

"Where were you? Just now? You're here physically, but you were gone."

"I was thinking."

"About your brother?"

His chest suddenly tight, he ignored her question and fisted both hands in his jeans pockets before lifting his face to the bitter breeze.

"This is where he was ambushed?"

"Yeah." The word stuck on the damn knot tied at the center of his throat. He pulled his fists from his pockets and spread his hands to take in the warehouse, the pier. "Here."

A hard swell hit the pilings and shook the planks.

Pain radiated from Jake in waves and swept over Hannah. She lifted her hand. In her mind, she ran her fingertips over his cheek.

He flinched.

She sucked in a breath then crossed her arms over her stomach. So futile. He was hurting and what kind of comfort could she offer him?

Instead, she ran her hands up and down the sleeves of her sweater, not really cold but not warm, either.

"I let him down, Hannah. He needed me and I let him down."

"Jake —"

"No." He closed his eyes for a short moment. When he opened them a shimmer of tears coated their surface. Working his jaw, he stared at the warehouse with his gaze unfocused. "I thought —" He shrugged. "I really thought I had talked him out of going through with it."

"It?" Her voice low, she moved a few steps closer. The ache at her center clenched in on itself. *Oh, Jake.*

"Going after the bastards who put Ortega in the hospital."

"Ramon Ortega? Your brother's partner."

"Yeah. After they ambushed Ortega, Craig set the bastards up. Big drug buy, here at this place. Abandoned warehouse. Hours away from Portland. Middle of the night. Perfect." His nostrils flared and the edges of his lips curled downward.

With her gaze locked on him she wet her bottom lip. He'd never talked to her about any of this before. He would always change the subject or simply walk away. Now, his suffering was palpable.

A living, breathing torment eating him alive.

"Pieces of shit. Asshole drug dealers, both of them. But Craig *needed* to follow protocol. That's what I told him. Follow protocol, Bro. Do this one right." Jake shoved his hands back into his pockets and rocked slightly backwards. "He agreed. Said I was right. Then that night all hell broke loose."

"You didn't know, Jake. You didn't know he was going to go through with the setup."

"No. But I should have known."

"Jake —"

"It's what I would have done if it had been my partner. It's what I should have done for my brother."

"But you weren't Craig's partner. You —"

"Bottom line. He asked *me* for backup. I let him down."

"You believed you'd convinced him to wait and do it right."

"I was a damn fifteen minutes away when he called. While he lay shot and bleeding out in that shithole warehouse." The heat in the glare he sent the building should have boiled the water slapping hard against the pilings.

Watching Jake, Hannah bit back the words clogging her throat. Anguish lined the planes of his face, long shadowy crevices stark against his skin.

"He sat there in the corner. His back against the wall. His own blood a black shadow surrounding him. God, I didn't know what to do for him. I had an ambulance coming. But I didn't know if those bastards who'd shot him were still on the premises.

"If I waited on backup, on the emergency crew – He wasn't going to make it. I had to meet the ambulance. Cut the time in half."

With her hands clasped in front of her she waited. Lost in the hell of that night, Jake barely seemed aware of her. She sniffed back the choking sob wanting to escape.

"I wrapped him in that blanket I kept behind the seat of my old truck. Everything seemed slow motion. I hurried. As much as I could. Then I smelled the smoke.

"Those bastards had set the place on fire. I shoved Craig in the truck and the bullets started flying." He frowned. "Shattered the windshield."

"Rily said you got them, those men."

"Yeah. Nailed them both. Craig still died."

"Jake –"

"No. I should've been there. I should have backed him from the start."

"Then you both would have been dead."

He angled his head in her direction. "That would have been so bad?"

"Jake –"

"You left. You died. Craig's dead. I may as well be."

"Damn you, Jake Carrigan."

"No more than I deserve." With his hands still shoved in his pockets he shrugged. "Go back to the house, Hannah."

"What?"

"Please go on back to the house. I'll be there later."

She pursed her lips, blinked against the watery veil of sudden tears. Dismissed, just like that. Stupid, dumb tears. She stared out over the river, the setting sun nothing more than a slight dark gold glimmer across the deepening blue of the water.

An unexpectedly hard wave hit the pilings and the pier shook, rocking Jake back a few steps. His hands out of his pockets, he turned towards Eagle Crest.

"Jake." She had to try to reach him again.

"I'll be okay, Hannah." With his face turned to the western sky, the lowering light expanded the harsh shadows lining his face. His sharp laugh startled her. "It's not like I'm going to jump into the river."

She bit the edge of her bottom lip.

"God, Hannah. Don't you think if I was going to kill myself, I would have done it already?"

WITH HER ARMS WRAPPED TIGHT around her legs, Hannah sat on the floor in the far corner of Jake's bedroom. She watched moonlight play across his face. The white sheet, tangled around his bare legs, glowed in the pale light.

Vestiges of his grief at the pier still echoed in his restless sleep. He had never willingly talked about the night Craig had died. Not to her, not to anyone as far as she knew. He'd gone stone-faced, filed his report, answered the investigators questions and completely closed himself in.

Even the temporary suspension hadn't seemed to touch him. In such a short amount of time, that stone-face he showed the world became the only one he ever wore.

Getting through the days back then had seemed to be his only goal. With as little emotional contact as possible.

Dammit Jake.

With a huff, she angled her head to rest her cheek on her knees and watched moonlight stream into the room.

Maybe she should have been more understanding, more patient. Waited him out of the funk.

But every time he'd turned those stony green eyes towards her, eyes without a single shred of compassion or concern, she'd died a bit inside.

She'd left him before he could leave her.

Had it only been two days ago that he'd said he'd loved her?

With a sniff, she wiped at the moisture tickling her cheek. For a woman who hardly ever cried, she sure as hell was doing a lot of it lately.

Jake moaned and the lines around his mouth deepened. She'd take away his pain if she could. Take away the suffering, take away the hurtful memories.

She caught her lower lip between her teeth. Maybe she *could* ease his sleep, even if she couldn't erase the rest of it.

Why not try? What did she actually have to lose at this point?

She pushed herself upright, wiped her hands down her jeans. At the foot of his bed she tipped her head slightly to the side. On an inward breath she focused her thoughts, imagining her fingers brushing back the lock of hair that had fallen forward from his forehead. Her phantom fingers traced the contour of his cheeks.

Jake moaned again. He turned his face into her illusionary touch.

She pressed her own fingers across her mouth. She wanted so badly to *feel* Jake's skin. The rough texture of the stubble on his chin, the light caress of his lips on the tips of her fingers.

A shudder ran down her spine.

Okay, focus.

This wasn't about her. She wiped at her nose, sniffed once, squared her shoulders and sucked in a deep breath. Reaching out mentally, she again brushed at that stubborn lank of hair drooping over his forehead. She threaded it back where it stayed.

This was going to work.

A small thrill of triumph washed over her skin and dried her sniffles.

Okay. She licked her bottom lip and focused again.

With the image of her fingertips firmly in her head, she massaged small circles at his temples, gradually adding a bit more pressure until he sighed and his body finally let go of the tension.

Once his breathing steadied out and stayed even, Hannah backed away from the bed.

Oh, Jake.

STEAM ROSE FROM JAKE'S MUG, white in the early morning chilled air. He tipped back the porch chair he sat on, brought the cup to his mouth.

Warmth caressed his cheeks and the freshness of coffee brewed from fresh ground beans filled his nose. Still too hot to drink, he lowered the mug to rest on his knee, the heat radiating through the material of his jeans. From where she lay sprawled against his chair, Sadie snorted in her sleep and thumped her tail before settling again.

Clouds hung low over the pine trees bordering the meadow to the east. The sun struggled to lighten the morning dawn. A major storm was coming, the scent of it heavy in the air.

He really should check the generator before the rain arrived, something he hadn't done in a while. There were a lot of things he hadn't done in a while.

Last night's restlessness had smoothed out sometime during the long hours. He actually felt rested this morning.

Taking a cautious sip of coffee, he couldn't remember the last time he'd greeted the dawn with any semblance of enjoyment.

There had been a time when sunrise had been his favorite part of day. The peacefulness of it, the quietness before the world woke and the day really began.

But that was before Craig had been killed.

He shook his head and tipped it back to stare at the overhead beam of his porch. Yesterday evening, out at the pier, he'd really dumped on Hannah. Now, he couldn't work up any regret.

Not sure if that made him an ass or just selfish, or maybe a selfish ass – that was more his speed lately – he puffed out his cheeks then let go of the breath. Sadie lifted her head and he dropped a hand to rub behind her ears.

Talking about what happened to his brother, with Hannah, maybe that was something he'd needed to do, after all.

Maybe.

Hannah hadn't yet made herself known this morning and he hadn't checked. He wasn't going to dwell on her or his brother.

Not this morning.

Time to check that generator.

MORNING DEW COVERED the green metal of the generator. The cool air was still. Calm. The sky right above Jake was clear of the surrounding clouds and had just begun to seep with blue in the earliness of the day.

He hunched his shoulders under the leather jacket he'd shrugged on before trudging out here. Even the scarf around his neck wasn't warding off the sudden chill. With a spare glance for the clouds hovering behind the pines he shot another glance towards the lightning rod that stood halfway between him and the trees.

The back of his neck prickled but everything appeared as it should. Nothing out of sorts. No one hovered along the line of trees. He turned in a full circle, taking in the entire area and letting his senses broaden and span his surroundings.

Like when he looked for Hannah.

Woo-woo man.

He snorted at the thought, but that didn't stop him from his scan.

There wasn't any sign of Hannah or anyone else. No predator on the horizon, none hiding in any unseen crevice. At least nothing he could pinpoint.

However, something was off. He let the prickle settle between his shoulder blades, let one part of his mind keep track of his surroundings, and squatted next to the generator.

Only a few seconds passed but the prickle intensified, biting into his flesh. He stood. Again, he scanned the area with his senses.

Nothing tangible.

Dammit.

Sharp and electric, sudden pain speared through his body, arcing around him and slamming him to the ground.

What the hell?

JAKE OPENED HIS EYES. The motion sent sharp shards of pain tearing through his body.

He lay flat on his back, prone, with his arms by his side. His motions slow, he lifted a finger a fraction of an inch, wincing at the shock of tremors clenching every muscle in his body.

That hadn't been such a great idea.

He blinked. Taking stock of his surroundings, as well as he could without moving, he tried to blink the dark haziness from his eyes.

Dusk?

There were no discernable shapes, nothing except him and this blue darkness surrounding him. What he lay on, he had no idea. The surface wasn't hard or soft, it just was.

Made no sense.

The ground, a bed, the floor? He couldn't tell.

The last he remembered, he'd been outside checking the generator because of an upcoming storm. And he'd been hit by ... something.

What?

Granted, he wasn't going to move too fast right now, not with the way the pain shot through his body every time he did. Still, he needed to figure this out.

Gritting his teeth, he lifted his head. His neck muscles tightened in protest. Clever little pricks of sharp electric current swept down his spine. His breath in short gasps and his eyes screwed close, he lowered his head.

Now what?

"You're awake?" Hannah's low, throaty voice eased and flowed over his skin.

Strange, he hadn't started when she spoke to him. He tucked that away to examine later. He ignored the venomous bite of pain and angled his head a slight amount to the right in the direction of her voice.

She sat a short distance away, her legs drawn close to her chest with her arms wrapped around her knees. The dark blueness shadowed her but he saw her face in sharp detail.

How many times had he seen her sit just that way? Especially in winter, in front of the fire, staring into the flames. Thinking.

But this wasn't winter, nor were they in his house.

At least he didn't think so.

Oh, shit. Jake blinked again.

"Hannah?" His voice was harsh, sounding rusty and full of pain. Like he hadn't used it in a long time. "I can see you."

Did that mean *he* was dead, too?

Or had he taken hallucinating to a new and different level?

Hannah blinked several times in quick succession. She sat straighter. Her arms tightened more around her legs.

"I can see you, Baby." The words croaked past the lump sitting square center in his throat. "I can —"

She dropped her grip on her legs and scrambled to him. Unshed tears made her eyes shimmer in the weird, dusky light. With her legs tucked under her, she leaned over him. Her hand hovered just above his cheek. With her bottom lip caught between her teeth, her fear lurked in the darkness of her eyes.

"Touch me, Hannah." He had to know, had to feel her fingers on his skin.

Maybe he really had died, too. He didn't care. Right now, there was only her and him.

Here. Now. Together.

He *had* to feel her touch.

She nodded, swallowed once and gave him a tight half smile.

FINGERTIPS, COOL AND WARM at the same time, lightly scrapped over the stubble on his cheeks, down his jaw-line. His eyes closed. A small groan worked its way up his throat.

God, Hannah.

She traced his mouth, her fingers light and sending electric tremors straight to his groin. Tremors he welcomed.

HE LIFTED HIS HAND, but the sharp protest from his arm muscles contracting had him gasping.

"Jake?" Her hand moved away from his face while her eyes glistened with concern.

"Don't stop, Baby." To hell with the pain.

She leaned closer. The curtain of her long, dark hair isolated them, cocooned them. With their gazes locked, she traced her fingertips over his eyebrows and down his cheek. In a slow, graceful motion, she lowered her head. Her gaze still locked on his, she brushed her lips over his mouth.

He angled his head, groaning with her touch and grimacing in pain at the same time. "Hannah."

"Shush." She spread her fingers, ran her hand over his chest, along the ends of the scarf and underneath his leather jacket.

He sucked in a deep breath at the contact, warm through the material of his T-shirt. Running her hand down his arm, she lifted his hand, pressed her lips to his palm.

No pain. A small part of his mind registered that fact. Hannah touched him, she moved his arm and it didn't hurt.

He cupped her cheek and ran his thumb over her lips. So warm. So soft. He was *touching* her.

"Jake." With her eyes closed, she tipped her head back.

He let his hand slip down her arm. Even through the soft material of her red sweater, he felt her tremble.

Like a sinuous cat, she stretched her body out beside him. He wrapped his arm around her, pressed her against him. Tangled his hand in her hair.

"Hannah."

The sweet wildflower scent of her hair filled him. She rubbed her cheek on his chest. A shot of pure desire ran like molten wildfire through his body.

With his pain-free arm wrapped tight around her, he pulled her on top of him. Warmth spread from every point their bodies made contact. Even through their clothes.

"Baby, this is going to sound weird, but I think your touch takes away the pain."

"You're hurting?" Hannah lifted her head and met his gaze with her troubled one. "Why didn't you tell me?"

"Why would I?" He let his fingers trace her spine, settle at the small of her back.

"Jake."

She twisted. He clenched his teeth and bit back a groan. Not from his muscles hurting, but from his body's response to her touch.

"Lay still for a couple of minutes." *Please.* "You've got to stop squirming."

"What?" Even in the dusky blue shadows, the pink staining her cheeks was visible. "Oh."

"Yeah. Oh. Looks like that part of my body works just fine."

"Does it now?" Her throaty voice lowered.

Those tremors again shot through his body, again arrowed straight to his groin.

Her hand brushed over his T-shirt, pausing over his stomach. "Where do you hurt?"

"Everywhere."

A low, soft and feminine chuckle fanned over his cheek.

"Then I'd better take care of that, hadn't I?"

He *had* died. This place must be heaven. Although it hurt and might be hell controlling his body. "I don't know if I can handle that."

"Let's find out."

Chapter Twelve

HANNAH HESITATED, her hand poised between her and Jake's bodies. Butterflies bumped into each other in her stomach.

She didn't know where they were or how they'd ended up here.

Or why.

Jake didn't seem to care. He was completely focused on her. The way he once had been.

Before.

Right now, she could *feel* Jake. His touch. His skin beneath hers.

Light, afraid this would be taken from her, would disappear in an instant, she untied the scarf at his neck and pushed it aside before she smoothed her fingers over the edge of his shirt hem. She pushed the fabric up to expose his stomach. The taut skin, firm muscles.

Jake.

Those stomach muscles of his tightened and he groaned. She didn't bother to stop the small, pleased smile crossing her lips.

He'd said he hurt all over, that her touch stopped the pain. She'd just have to touch him.

Everywhere.

She slid to his side and gave the laugh bubbling in her throat free rein. His fingers curled around her wrist but she pushed his arm away. "Come on now. I'm just trying to make you feel better."

"Baby, if I *felt* any better, we'd both be naked."

Her breath caught and she pressed her lips together to keep her moan from escaping.

Naked. Both of them.

Blinking the sudden image away, she pushed Jake's T-shirt up to his chest. Her thumbs caressed a trail on the trip upwards.

"You trying to kill me, sweetheart?"

"Only trying to ease the pain, my darling."

"Right." He tipped his head back and the cords in his neck tightened. With his brows suddenly drawn together, his mouth tightened into a thin, straight line.

Pain, a thick and taut string, stretched between them. She *felt* the way his body hurt inside her own muscles. The center of her chest constricted, as if her heart was being squeezed by a fist.

Abandoning his T-shirt, she scurried into a sitting position. Jake hurt and she had the power to alleviate that pain. She leaned over him and eased her hands under his neck. With her fingertips she massaged the knot she found there.

He tensed, a sharp gasp stiffened his jaw. Then his neck muscles relaxed and he let out the breath he'd held. The tangle of knots wadded up inside her loosened when his mouth curved into a rueful smile.

"You've always had the touch, Baby."

Afraid that other reality would come swooping down at any moment, she smiled but spared a quick glance around. Nothing had changed since she found herself here. Time and reality didn't seem to have a presence. Blue darkness stretched out in all directions. No borders, no real shadows, no light source. Just her and Jake, almost suspended in space.

Wherever this was, he was with her and she was grateful for that. Grateful she *did* have the touch.

Here. Now.

Eased back on her heels, she let her gaze run over Jake's prone body, caught herself lost in his hot, green gaze. On a hard breath, she leaned forward to run her palms over his shoulders, over the supple leather of his jacket and down his other arm. She caressed the top of his hand. Warmth from his bare skin seeped into hers.

To be touching him, when she'd thought she never again would be able to was more than she could handle in that moment. Sudden tears coated her eyes, her vision swam for a few seconds.

He twisted his hand and captured hers. His thumb rubbed the back of her hand. Though the film of moisture, she stared at their linked fingers, watched the small circles he traced on her skin. Skin warmed by the heat of his touch.

Jake.

She lifted her gaze and met the intensity of his.

"Baby." He squeezed her hand. His eyelids drifted down for a short moment. "Don't stop. Keep touching me."

With a low and throaty laugh, she untangled their fingers and ran her hands over his jacket. She spread her fingers underneath the leather at his shoulders and pushed the jacket back. The material slipped over her skin, soft and worn. "Take this off."

With a grunt, his gaze holding hers, he lifted his head. She cupped his shoulders, pulled him into a sitting position.

"God." His breath came in sharp pants. He shook his head. "I feel like an invalid here."

"Then let me play nurse."

"Please." His deepened voice scrapped over her nerves, the pulsing currents heading straight to her core. Her insides throbbed, erratic and uncontrolled.

Raw and jagged, her breathing matched her pulse, beat by wild beat. Slow. She needed to slow down. Savor this for however long it lasted.

With her hands still under his jacket, she pushed it down his arms. She let her fingers linger over the way his muscles twitched and then firmed under her hands.

The jacket bunched behind him. Not on the ground, not on the floor. This place had no discernable dimension, no boundaries, nothing to mark reality. After the hell of the last few days, this had to be paradise.

At least for now.

His arms finally free, Jake wrapped them around her and pulled her, sideways, onto his lap. He rocked his hips against her bottom.

Lordy, but he was right. *Some parts of his anatomy didn't seem to be suffering.* Her heart thumping madly in her chest, she squirmed a little before settling herself more solidly on his lap.

He groaned. With his eyes locked on hers, he cupped her face. His calloused thumbs caressed her jaw-line, her cheeks, ran over her lips. The light touch from the rough skin of his thumbs sent spirals of heat spreading outward from each sweet sweep of his touch.

Jake.

Low, aching tremors from deep in her belly vibrated throughout her body. Her head tipped back, her neck supported by his warm hands. Eyes half closed, she flicked the tip of her tongue across the pad of his thumb.

His sharp intake of breath echoed along every one of her nerve endings. She clenched her knees tight together against the heat scorching her insides. Heat that threatened to consume her.

Jake.

A guttural groan, from a long way down inside his chest, erupted and with his hands still holding her face, he crushed his mouth against hers. Parting her lips, welcoming his thrusting tongue, she twisted her upper body to press against his chest.

They had too many clothes between them.

"Jake." His name came out in a short, breathy gasp against his mouth. She didn't care.

"Baby. Don't stop." He angled his head, threaded his fingers through her hair and kept his mouth hard against her lips.

Fumbling between them, her hands grasped at the hem of his T-shirt. She shoved the fabric upwards. "Take it off."

With a short, sharp nod, he pulled away and yanked his shirt over his head. Tossing it behind him, he reached for the bottom of her sweater. "This too."

His hands trembling, he slipped his fingers under the material and she sucked in a breath. A tensing heat spread from his fingers across her skin as he pushed the sweater up her stomach and over her breasts.

Her gaze on his, she lifted her arms. In one smooth movement, he had her sweater off and thrown behind her. He broke their gaze and teased his thumbs over the thin, black lace of her bra.

Her nipples tightened into hard buds. Her stomach clenched. She couldn't stop her breath from gushing out.

"Oh, God. Jake."

Her back arched and he leaned forward. With his hands covering the dark material of her bra, his tongue followed the same path his thumbs had across the top edge of lace.

Hot and prickly sensations swirled inside her chest, spiraling downward, fueling the fire in her belly. She braced her hands on his shoulders and pushed her upper body against him.

Closer. She had to get closer.

His touch barely there, he squeezed her breasts and through the lace he skimmed her nipple with his teeth.

A soft moan escaped, but she didn't care. All that mattered was *this*.

She twisted to straddle him, to get as close as she could while still wearing her pants.

"My legs." For a quick moment his grip on her tightened and he hissed, the sound harsh in the stillness. He leaned his forehead against hers while his breath came in short puffs.

Her own breath not too steady, she rubbed the tip of her nose against his then spread her fingers over his cheeks and his jaw. The roughness of his beard stubble sent piercing little pinpricks throughout her body. "Let me help."

His throat worked, but he didn't say anything. Instead he gave a short nod then pressed his mouth to hers in a hard, quick kiss.

Still straddling him, she eased backwards and let her hands caress the top of each of his legs. *Oh, Lord.* She could *feel* the rough texture of his jeans beneath her palms, the firmness of his muscles beneath.

Her breath hitched.

She really could feel.

She threw a quick glance at Jake. He caught her with the intensity in his shadowed eyes and the taunt lines of his face.

Okay, he needed her to do this. She was going to do this.

For him.

In tight, small circles, she massaged his legs through the jeans.

He groaned, deep in his throat. His eyes closed and his head fell back. Looking away from his face, she bit her bottom lip and concentrated on his thighs. Scooting back, she ran her hands under and over his legs.

At his feet, she pulled off his tennis shoes, hesitated, then pulled off his socks. She glanced up to find Jake watching her.

"Has that helped?"

"Some."

"The pain's still there?"

He bent his right knee. A spasm tightened his body. "Yeah."

She rubbed the sole of the foot she still held in her hand. The movement tentative, he flexed his toes.

"That doesn't hurt." He pushed his foot against her hand. "My leg, that's another story."

With her thumb, she continued to rub his ankle, her fingers massaging the top of his foot. "Maybe the material's too thick for this to work through your jeans."

"Yeah. They're going to have to come off so you can actually touch me." He tipped his head back, his eyes half-shuttered. "Touch my skin."

Take his pants off?

Her brain latched onto that one thought. Strip him and run her hands over his completely naked body?

Her breath hitched in her throat again.

That was where this was headed, where she wanted it to go, so why did the thought make her so giddy?

"Hannah?"

She let a slow and wicked smile ease its way across her lips then she licked them.

"For the pain." His voice deepened and his half-closed eyes went even darker.

"Right." On her hands and knees, her gaze on his, she inched her way up Jake's body. "To ease your pain."

Without moving, he watched her. The muscle in his jaw twitched. A spike of pure adrenaline scored her veins.

He was hers. At least for now.

She'd ease his pain, then have him inside her. And they'd both ease each other. Reaching his chest, she pressed her lips to his then pushed at his shoulders.

"Hannah." The sound choked, he laid back, his body prone with her astride him.

Lifting her own hips, she reached between their bodies and slipped her fingers into his waistband. The stubborn fastening refused to budge and the bulge underneath her swelled more. Jake rocked his hips upwards, pressing into her bottom. Her fingers slid off the metal button.

"Dammit." So much for sexy seductress. She rocked backwards. Damn button jeans.

"You're going to kill me, sweetheart." He stilled her hands.

At his touch, a flare of heat scalded through her body.

"Let me." With several, quick movements he had the buttons undone, but his chest heaved and his breathing raced.

Barely resisting the urge to run her fingers along the swollen ridge pressing against his jeans, she spread his pants open and slipped her hands inside, under his hips. She squeezed his bottom through the material of his underwear.

"Oh. God." Jake swallowed once and arched his neck.

"Does that hurt, darling?" She squirmed back, giving herself more access to his mid-section and trapping his legs.

"Different kind of pain."

Oh. Well, she'd work on that in just a bit. "Lift up."

When he followed her order, she pulled at his jeans to slide them down his hips. The white of his underwear, and the bulge they contained, drew her focus.

"Baby, please."

"Right. Focus." She pulled at the denim, tugging it down his legs. Once she had the jeans off, she tossed them aside.

Starting at his feet and moving upward, her touch hardly there, she caressed his skin. At his knees, she leaned forward to press her mouth to the right side dimple. His body jerked and then he moaned.

After a cautious glance at his face, she scooted up his body then spread her hands over his thighs to deepen the massage. At the top of his legs, she slipped her fingers underneath the edge of his underwear.

Jake lifted his head, his shoulders, before he threaded his fingers through her hair. "You are killing me, Baby."

"No pain, Jake. I can't leave an inch of your body untouched."

"Like I said, different kind of pain all together."

He cupped the back of her head, pulled her to lie on top of him. His arms like bands around her and his mouth hungry, he latched onto her lips and shoved his tongue deep inside.

Centered at his mouth, the warmth of him wrapped completely around her. Rolling them onto their sides, he ensnared her with one leg over hers, the weight heavy and welcomed.

And still he attacked her mouth.

Her elbows trapped between them, her own starving needs sprang loose. She managed to shove her fingers through his hair and crushed her mouth back against his.

Jake ran his hands over her bottom and pressed her tighter to him. He rubbed his naked chest over the thin lace of her bra. Unable to move, she groaned at the coiled heat between her legs.

"Too many clothes, woman." His growl against her cheek sent more heat spiraling through her mid-section and straight to her hardened nipples.

Oh, Jake.

With one arm wrapped tight around her, he undid the hooks at the back of her bra and leaned away enough to pull it down her arms and toss it aside. Then he pulled her back against him, naked skin to naked skin.

"Your jeans have to go, Baby." His words skimmed across her cheek. "They're in the way."

She brushed her lips over his. Arched her neck, her back. His low groan, deep in his chest, tightened the thick strands of heat writhing low in her belly.

He reached between their bodies and undid her jeans with a quick flick of his fingers. Rubbing his bare foot over her calf, he eased back to push her pants over her hips and down her legs. He tossed them behind him along with her panties and his underwear.

Her skin suddenly chilled and hot at the same time, she pressed her body against his. He wrapped both his arms around her. His hands warm, he trailed his fingers down her spine, over her bottom and then back to her shoulders.

She rocked her hips tight against his, closing her eyes briefly at the naked hardness of him pressing against her.

"Hannah." One word, her name, soft and pleading. His breath whispered over her cheek while his mouth touched hers, brief, before he nuzzled her neck. Sharp pinpoints of electric heat sparked at each place his tongue touched and his lips caressed.

She spread her hands over his chest, her fingertips kneading his skin. *She was touching him.* With her back arched, she pressed the lower part of their bodies tighter. He groaned before pushing her onto her back, his weight heavy and welcomed.

With his elbows braced on either side of her head, he tangled his fingers in her hair, his thumbs a light pressure at her temples. Lost in the darkness of his gaze she splayed her own hands across his chest.

The fast thump of his heart against her palms pounded through her. He bumped his knee against hers and she wrapped her legs around him. Her breath caught. Tears spiked her eyes when he settled there, cradled against her.

Jake.

Wet and beyond ready for him, she pressed her heels tight against his rear. She lifted to meet him.

This is real, it has to be. And if it wasn't, she didn't care. Right now, this was all that mattered.

Just this.

Jake paused, his breath labored, the green of his eyes even darker. "Hannah?"

"Now, Jake." She gripped his shoulders. When his hips rocked to meet hers, she pressed her mouth to his. "Now."

"SO YOU'RE AWAKE." The censure in Benjamin Garrett's voice penetrated the cloud hazing Jake's mind.

Barely.

"Hannah?" He screwed his eyes shut tight.

This wasn't where he wanted to be. He wanted to be back with Hannah.

Just the two of them. Nothing, no one, except him and Hannah in that endless, border-less piece of time.

Space.

Wherever the hell they'd been.

Except he must have found the border because that sure wasn't Hannah's hand gripping his shoulder so tight. Through his T-shirt and leather jacket he wore.

He tried to pull away, but thick, piercing needles of pure pain shot through his arm. All the way to his fingertips.

Crap that hurt. His entire body hurt. Ben needed to leave him alone, let him go –

If Ben was here, where was Hannah?

"I'd like the answer to that one myself."

The grip on Jake's shoulder tightened a fraction then dropped away. Shit. The man was a mind reader now?

God, he hoped not.

"What?" Jake's own voice sounded muffled, full of cotton and from a long distance away. But he was pretty sure the word had come from his mouth.

"You asked where Hannah was." The implied patience of Garrett's deep voice underscored the censure.

And disappointment.

That Jake heard loud and clear.

What the hell did Ben have to be disappointed about? He wasn't the one who'd been torn away from Hannah. At least Jake thought he'd been torn away.

Otherwise he'd still be there.

There was no way he'd have left her voluntarily.

On his own.

She had lain next to him, his leg draped over hers, their naked bodies pressed closed. He'd been playing with her bracelet, the only thing she wore. With her other hand between them, she'd been rubbing small circles on his skin, right under his navel. The thought of pulling her on top of him, of sliding his hand down her spine, over her rear had just crossed his mind.

Then he was here.

Just that fast. Just that abrupt.

He swallowed, tried to work moisture around that wad of pure cotton stuck at the base of his throat. But the damn thing wouldn't budge.

Where the hell was Hannah?

He tried to extend his senses, but he couldn't arrow in on anything. Not even himself. Nothing beyond the pain racking his entire body. Certainly not even the man sitting right next to him.

At least he thought Garrett was right next to him.

At this point, he wasn't trusting *any* of his perceptions.

"And –" Garrett paused for an extra long moment.

Or he had slipped away, Jake wasn't sure which.

"I said I would like an answer to that myself."

Jake, with his eyes still shut, lifted his hand to brush the man's words aside. Pain shot straight through to his chest. The groan tearing through his body ripped a wide hole in its wake.

"Easy, Jake."

"Whe –" He tried to angle his head to the side, but the scream of his muscles stopped him. "Hannah?"

"Jake." Ben gripped his shoulder, spread the fingers of his other hand over his temple and forehead. "Rest."

"Han …." Darkness swirled through his mind and bit at his thoughts, sucking him into a black and blue, Hannah-less void.

Chapter Thirteen

HANNAH SAT NEAR THE FIREPLACE in the corner of Jake's living room with her knees pulled to her chest and her arms wrapped around her legs.

Back to being invisible.

Jake lay on his couch, stretched out and unconscious, his chest hardly moved and his face oddly still.

Too still.

She tightened her grip on her legs. When had she ever felt so damn helpless?

Why didn't Ben do something? Anything beyond sitting there, stretched out in the recliner a few feet from the couch?

Rily had shown up several minutes ago, checked Jake's pulse and brushed his hair back from his forehead. Both Rily and Ben knew as well as Hannah that Jake wasn't simply asleep.

She bit her bottom lip as the wind outside rattled through the trees, battering rain against the bare panes of glass on either side of the front door. The storm had finally arrived and although it was barely dusk, the heavy greyness of the day had given way to black, sucking any remaining color from the sky.

"Why the hell didn't you call an ambulance?" Rily pushed away from the couch and paced from one end of the room to the other. The glow from the fire played across Rily's face when she swung around to glare at Ben.

Exactly. Hannah curled forward over her knees to keep herself from rocking. Worry thickened in her stomach, twisted in on itself and tightened in ever increasing slow increments like one of those vise grips on Jake's workbench.

"Well?" Rily stopped directly in front of Garrett.

With his fingers laced and behind his head, Ben shrugged.

"Take him to the hospital?" Rily, her face set in a murderous scowl, stood with her legs spread and her hands splayed on her hips. "*Something* beyond hauling his ass inside and dumping him on the couch."

Hannah wet her bottom lip, pulled it between her teeth. Her body still hummed from her time with Jake, from their lovemaking, whether that had been real or she'd just been indulging in some kind of fantasy, it had *felt* real.

But had her indulgence, *their* indulgence, done this to him?

How did she fix it? How did she make him better?

"There wasn't any need." Ben's voice pulled her startled gaze to him.

"No need?" Rily exploded from her stationary position, whirled away from the man, then spun back to tower over him. She jabbed her finger at his chest. "*My brother* is lying there, unconscious. You don't know why. Yet you say there's *no need?*"

A muscle twitched along the right side of Ben's jaw. His movements slow, almost casual, he wrapped his hand around Rily's finger. She jerked back, but Ben didn't let go.

"I didn't say I don't know *why.*" His dark blue eyes flat, he pushed her hand away.

Rily stared at him a moment longer before shoving her hands through her short hair, leaving it mussed when she spun away.

The fear, the panic, in Rily's voice twined around Hannah's own fear, aimed straight from the pit of her stomach to lodge in her throat.

Rily stopped to stand in front of the fireplace, the glow from the flames flickering along her jeans and green sweater. She had her hands braced on the mantle, her head angled towards Ben. From where Hannah sat, she had an up-close view of Rily's anguish torn face. Of the distress shimmering there, darkening the golden tones of her green eyes.

Staring up at her friend, Hannah reached out with her mind to soothe the worry lines marring Rily's forehead, to stroke a light touch over her cheek.

Rily's eyes widened. She jerked back from the mantle as if the fire had reached out and licked her skin. Spinning around to face Ben, she planted both hands square on her hips. "What the hell did you just do?"

"Absolutely nothing." His expression impassive, he quirked an eyebrow. "What do you think I did?"

"Cut the crap, Garrett."

"No crap here."

Rily stared at him, the muscle in her right cheek twitching. Hannah squeezed her fingers into tight fists. *Don't touch.*

Rily wasn't Jake or Sadie.

After several long moments, Rily swung away from Ben to face the fireplace. Her eyes still more gold than green, tears glistened on her lashes. She pushed away from the mantle, moved to stand over her brother, facing Ben. With one hand threaded through her hair, she wrapped her other arm around her middle and hunched her shoulders forward. "Then why? Why is he here instead of already in a hospital?"

Ben held Rily's gaze. "Jake was struck by lightning –"

"What?" Hannah's voice mixed with Rily's and echoed across the room.

Ben's brow lowered in a frown, he rubbed his right ear and cast a suspicious look around. Then, with his lips in a thin line, he focused on Rily.

Hannah pressed her fingertips to her mouth.

When had Jake been hit? Had that lightning strike sent him into that borderless blue space or had it taken him away from it? Away from her?

She hadn't known where to find him, and just like the other times the thought to be with him had taken her to him.

Only in that space he'd been stretched and unconscious. Much like now. She hadn't known what or why they were both there, so she'd settled down to watch over him. To wait.

Now he lay on his couch, prone and unconscious.

And the only thing she could do now was again wait.

She rested her chin on her knees. Without wiping them away, she let her tears leak down her cheeks.

"You're saying Jake was struck by lightning?" Rily faced Ben.

He rubbed a big hand over his eyes. "Yes."

Rily visibly flinched, turned away from Garrett. Hannah's chest constricted.

"It wasn't ordinary lightning, Rily." Ben's voice softened and he grimaced.

"What do you mean?" Rily stared at the ceiling, her eyes glistening with unshed tears. "How many types of lightning are there?"

"This was psychically induced."

"Psych —" Rily's arms at her sides, hands clenched in tight fists and her narrowed eyes damp with moisture, she swung to face the man still stretched out in Jake's recliner. "Bullshit, Garrett. Are you where Jake is getting all this crap? First Hannah's ghost, then —"

"It was a psychic booby trap. Waiting on the last ingredient. Jake."

"But —"

"No buts, Rily." Ben forced the footrest down, leaned forward with his wrists braced on his knees, his fingers loosely entwined. "After I brought Jake in here, after he came to and said —"

What? Frowning, Hannah lifted her chin.

"He came to?" Rily set her fists on her hips. "You didn't tell me that."

"You didn't exactly give me an opportunity to tell you much."

"You weren't exactly forthcoming, were you?"

Still leaning forward, Ben propped his elbows on his knees and rubbed a hand across his eyes. "I went back outside to check the area. To try and find out what had happened."

Rily wrapped her arms around her middle and rocked ever so slightly. "And?"

Hannah slouched forward, sniffling and blinking at the moisture clouding her vision.

Damn tears.

"The lightning rod lay on the ground." Ben's dark blue eyes stayed locked on Rily. "Bent in half."

"It was fine yesterday. I saw it."

"As I did the day before."

"So?"

"It was set, for lack of a better word, to trigger when Jake came within a certain range."

"Set?"

"Grab the lightning and redirect it."

"Towards Jake?"

"Yes."

"That's ridiculous. How can you tell that? How could someone know *when* there would be lightning? How would they know when Jake would be around? And how can you be so sure Jake was a target and that this wasn't just ...?"

"Random? Do you really believe that, Rily?"

"Sounds a hell of a lot better than someone out to get my brother with all this woo-woo bullshit."

"Rily. You're a cop. A damn good one according to Jake."

"So?"

"So. Use your head. Think."

"I am. And this is just so much crap."

"Jake's brakes."

"What about them?"

"You are as stubborn as that brother of yours." Ben raked his fingers through his thick, grey hair then smoothed his palm over the surface. "Do you really think your brother could make such a drastic *mistake* with his brakes?"

There was no way. Hannah shook her head.

Rily's nose flared. She heaved a disgusted sigh. "No."

"Then what happened?"

"He never really gave me an answer." Rily lifted her chin, rotating both shoulders before casting a sideways glance around the room. "I was worried about – He fed me all that crap about Hannah's ghost."

Hannah flinched. *Ouch.*

"You mentioned something about that. I'm surprised he told you about Hannah."

"So, you know about the ghost thing, too?"

Ghost thing? Hannah rubbed both hands over her damp cheeks. She wasn't a *thing*. A ghost, maybe, but not a thing.

Ben nodded.

"You buy it?"

Again Ben nodded.

"Why? Who are you? What are you? How do you know all of this? Why the hell should I believe you?"

"You sound like your brother."

"You didn't answer my questions."

"I'm not going to."

Rily scrubbed at her face. "You want me to be a good cop, but you won't give me anything real to work with." Her voice held no real heat. "How about I haul your ass down to the station?"

The enigmatic look Ben aimed at Rily set the hairs on Hannah's arms to attention. She glanced back at Jake. He lay as still and unmoving as before.

Dammit.

Those two should be doing something more than arguing. Calling an ambulance, the paramedics. A doctor. Someone.

Ben wouldn't let Jake die, would he?

Rily wouldn't. Hannah let go of the breath she'd been holding.

"Because he came to —" Rily rubbed her hands over the sleeves of her sweater. "That's why you didn't call for aid? He's going to be okay?"

Ben arched his neck, closed his eyes for a brief moment then aimed his intense gaze directly at Rily. "Jake has to make that decision. Live or die."

"What the hell do you mean?"

Hannah swallowed hard.

"I'm not sure this isn't something Jake has done himself. Something he and Hannah cooked up between them —"

Hannah erupted upward, her legs shaky and her arms trembling.

Ben frowned, turned his head towards her position. "Rily. Did you feel that?"

"Feel what?" Rily yanked her cell phone from her front jeans pocket. "You're wrong, Ben. And even if you're not, Jake doesn't get to make that decision. Not as long as I'm able to stop him. Not as long as I'm able to save his sorry ass."

"No, Rily." Ben pushed himself out of the chair. In two steps he stood beside her, his hand covering the phone. "They can't do anything for him."

"But —"

He took the cell from her, tucked it back into her pocket. "He has a *psychic* wound. Not a physical one. He has to decide to come back."

No. Hannah held up both hands. This was wrong. All wrong.

"You said he came to." Rily shook her head. "That means he's already made that decision."

"No, it doesn't." Ben cupped his big hands over Rily's shoulders. "He was here, with me, only briefly. Then he slipped back. I can't tell if he's simply recuperating, if he's hiding in subconsciousness. Or if he's traveling to places we can't get him back from."

"Nooo." Rily's eyes locked on Ben's, her cry slammed into Hannah, leaving her shaking.

Ben was wrong. Jake was in shock. He needed medical care.

Rily covered her eyes, but Hannah could only stare at Ben.

He pulled Rily to him and wrapped his arms around her, resting his chin on her head.

No, dammit. Hannah stamped her foot. *Why* was Rily listening to him? Jake needed a doctor.

Lightning strike.

Psychic lightning strike.

Someone targeting him? Specifically targeting him.

No. Ben had to be wrong.

He shouldn't be standing there, comforting her friend. Jake's sister. Not when he was going to just let Jake die.

No. This was completely wrong.

In her head Hannah shoved herself between Rily and Ben. She pressed a palm flat against each of their chests. Shoved.

Rily stumbled back. Ben didn't budge.

"Get the dog." His face set, he turned in a full circle. "Sadie can see her. Get Sadie so we can tell where Hannah is."

Rily eased backwards towards the kitchen.

No.

In the archway between the two rooms Hannah set a door in her mind. Slammed it shut.

Rily backed into the invisible door, swung around and hit it full force. Knocked on her rear, she scrambled up, her eyes wide and mouth half open. "What the hell?"

"Hannah." Ben stood with his arms stretched over Jake's prone body, his fingers spread. "Rily, give me a moment and then try again. We need Sadie."

"Hannah wouldn't hurt —"

"Now's not the time to argue, Rily. You need to get the dog."

Hannah cast her gaze back and forth between the two of them. Rily had her arms behind her, her hands flat on the invisible door, her eyes still wide. In shock or disbelief, Hannah wasn't sure.

Didn't care. Not right now.

She shifted her gaze to Ben. This bastard wasn't going to get away with letting Jake die.

Her mouth flat and nostrils wide, Hannah gathered her thoughts around her, focused on Ben.

"Now." His deep voice calm, he moved his hands over Jake in a smooth, slow wave.

Nooo.

Hannah threw all the energy she'd gathered inside her at the man standing over her lover, aiming right for the middle of Ben's back.

"Oomph." He arched his body, but held firm.

A wave of pure energy rebounded, knocking Hannah to the ground. Sprawled on the floor, she shook her head, but the ringing in her ears didn't stop.

"You're not going to hurt him anymore." Ben turned to face her general direction. "Not today."

Hurt him?

She loved Jake. Why would she hurt him?

Damn Garrett.

Hannah scrambled to her feet.

"Get away from him!" The scream burned her lungs. Mentally, she grabbed the empty coffee mug off the end table and hurled it at Ben.

The mug bounced off a few inches from his chest and hit the hard-wood floor, breaking into several large pieces.

"I sure hope that wasn't one of Jake's favorites." Ben stood facing her, his legs spread. His arms, bent at the elbow, stiffened. He spread his fingers and a pressure built against Hannah's skin.

Sadie barked, bounding into the room with Rily hurrying behind. The push on Hannah eased a fraction, although Ben's face still held an intense stillness. Except for the slight, almost imperceptible, twitch of his upper lip.

But that was okay. Hannah's own breath came in short, deep gasps. She was pissed, too.

"What happened?" Rily stood staring at the broken shards of the white mug. She bent to gather them. Sadie barked once then whined. The dog squirmed her way between Ben and the couch to rest her head on the cushion next to Jake.

"That's it, Sadie." Ben, his arms still stiff and his fingers still spread, turned in a semi-circle. He kept Jake behind him.

"Garrett?" Rily crouched low with the ceramic shards cupped in her hands.

"I do believe we've managed to tick Hannah off."

Not we, asshole. You.

Hannah threw a stack of magazines at him, the pages riffling in mid-air, hitting the spot just inches from his face and then scattering across the floor.

"Whoa." Rily eased to her feet and backed away. "What just happened? Why didn't —"

"Sadie?" Ben kept his voice low.

Hannah narrowed her eyes. Sadie whimpered.

"Rily, get Sadie out in front of us."

"Ben?" Rily dumped the ceramic shards on the table at the end of the couch. She wiped her hands down the side of her jeans. Her gaze in constant motion, she eased in behind Ben and slipped her fingers under the dog's collar.

Hannah spared a quick glance for the dog. Sadie whimpered again before sneaking her tongue out and running it over Jake's cheek.

He didn't so much as flinch, he just lay there with his chest barely moving.

Jake, please. Wake up.

Hannah scrubbed her hands over her eyes.

"I don't believe Hannah will hurt Sadie." Ben shifted his stance, bent his knees. "But the dog can show us where she's at."

With a single thought she lifted several of the magazines scattered around Ben's feet and held them there, suspended in air.

"Garrett." With Rily's gaze locked on the magazines, the muscles in her throat worked. She still held Sadie's collar, but now she wrapped her other arm around the dog and hugged her close. Sadie nuzzled Rily's cheek. "You might want to make up your mind. Whatever Hannah is right now, either she's an attempted murderer or she's not."

"Attempting murder and loving dogs isn't exclusive from one to the other." Ben flicked a finger at one of the magazines and it fluttered to the floor. "You know that, Rily."

Hannah wrapped her arms around her stomach and rocked. The magazines thudded on the floor. *I wouldn't hurt, Jake. Why don't they understand that?*

From the end table behind Rily, a book lifted and flew to smack Ben on the back of his head. Hannah, with her arms still wrapped around her stomach, fisted her hands and stood shaking with her breath coming in short gasps.

She hadn't meant to hit Ben with the book.

"Dammit, Hannah." Ben spun to scan the entire room.

A choked bark of laughter had him facing Rily.

"Hey, Garrett." Her arm still around the dog, Rily shrugged. Humor lurked in her wide eyes, but the light smattering of freckles across her cheeks stood out against the paleness of her face. "I guess you forgot to protect your backside with whatever hocus-pocus you're pulling."

"Looks that way." Ben's eyes narrowed. Rubbing his scalp, he went back to scanning the room.

That same book hovered a foot above the floor. He crouched down and wrapped his fingers around it before glancing up at the fireplace.

Hannah set her mouth in a flat line but let go of her mental hold on the book. Ben's eyes widened a slight fraction.

"*What* are you, Hannah?" With his gaze still on the area in front of the fireplace he set the book on the floor behind him. "Hannah?"

He couldn't see her, couldn't feel her, couldn't hear her.

Damn him for acting as if he knew where she stood.

Energy coiled tight inside her belly. Lordy, she had to move, had to get away from the man's intense stare. She swung away and shoved the fireplace equipment aside with a simple flick of her mind.

The clank of metal crashing against stone loud in the room, Hannah spun around and stared. She hadn't meant to push quite that hard. Her fingertips tingled and she rubbed them together. Small sparks arched between them.

What's happening to me?

Lifting her hand, she spread her fingers and faced her palm towards Ben. Still crouched, he jerked backwards, bumping into Rily and the dog.

Sadie yelped.

"Hey." Rily pushed at him. In a squat with her back to Jake and her gaze moving across the room, she had her right arm behind her back. "What the hell is going on here?"

"Hannah's having a temper tantrum." Ben settled on the floor with his back against the couch and his legs crossed. "This could get interesting. But your gun isn't going to do any good."

"It might if I decide to shoot your ass."

"There is that."

Hannah advanced two steps with her palm still out-stretched. The air in the room swirled, ruffling the pages of the magazines littered across the floor.

Oh, Lord. How am I doing this?

"What the hell?" Rily pulled her gun from the small of her back.

"That's not —"

"It's my security blanket."

Moving faster, the air tangled Rily's hair. She shoved it out of her face. Ben's eyebrow arched.

Damn him.

Hannah, lifting her head, raised her other hand. Wind gushed through the room, pushed against the man, lifted magazines and rattled the windows from the inside. Sadie cowered, curling her body tight between Rily and Ben.

"Hannah." Jake's voice, sharp and insistent, cut through the noise pressing against her ears. "Stop."

Chapter Fourteen

SLOUCHED ON HIS COUCH, Jake spread his fingers across his forehead. He rubbed his temples with his thumbs. The extra-strength aspirins Rily had given him a short time earlier hadn't touched the pain in his head, but at least now he could actually make small movements on his own. His body protested, but not enough for him to care.

The bare side windows flanking his front door showed nothing more than a black reflection of the room. Night had fallen sometime while he'd been unconscious.

Unless he'd been out for more than this one day.

He didn't think so, otherwise his sister would have had him in the hospital no matter what Garrett thought or tried to convince her was the best option.

Rily paced the room. Every once in a while she stopped to stare at him, but all that contained energy didn't allow her to be still for long.

She was definitely upset. Probably at him. He couldn't work up any real concern.

Garrett sat on the recliner with his elbows propped on the chair arms and his fingers laced, all the while tapping a small beat on his mouth with his index fingers.

The man wanted to say something. Jake figured it would come out sooner or later. He was opting for later, if he had a choice.

Hannah....

Moving his own fingers, slowly, to rub at the ache centered at the base of his head, he scanned the room one more time.

Just to be sure.

Hannah sat on the floor, just off to the right of the fireplace. Probably with her legs drawn up and her chin on her knees.

How he knew she sat on the floor instead of standing or pacing the room, he had no clue. But he knew, absolutely, she sat there. Her tantrum finished.

And it had been a hell of a tantrum.

Alive, she'd rarely lost her temper. But it had always been quite a show when she had. He wondered, briefly, just what had set her off this time. He'd bet Garrett had something to do with it, yet he couldn't bring himself to focus on that, either.

Now, she sat where she could see everyone, taking it all in. Observing. The stunt with the wind behind her, for now.

Maybe, somehow, his time in that other region – wherever the hell that had been – had heightened his tracking ability as far as Hannah was concerned. He still couldn't see her, not here in his living room, but his awareness seemed *more*, somehow.

His body throbbed, thinking about that other place. About Hannah. The pain didn't matter. He wanted her again.

Never mind that last time had been a gift he had never expected. He *wanted* with everything he had in him. Wanted her beneath him, wanted inside her.

Just the two of them.

Forever.

"Jake." Ben continued to tap his fingers against his mouth.

Here we go.

From the kitchen archway Rily whirled around and nailed Garrett with a glare. "He should go to the hospital. Get checked out. Make sure there's not something really wrong with him."

A small spark of energy washed over him.

Hannah. Agreeing with Rily?

Stupid question. She *always* sided with his sister.

The knot between his shoulder blades tightened. He wasn't going to the damn hospital. He was staying right here on this damn couch. Even if he could *feel* whatever message Hannah had for him, he was going to ignore the *damn* thing.

His arms too heavy to hold up behind his head, he lowered them to rest his hands in his lap. Sparing a sideways glance at Ben, he closed his eyes against all of them.

"Jake." Ben's voice, deep, patient and insistent, pressed at him from where the man sat.

Dammit all.

Jake frowned when Rily moved, like a lithe cat on the hunt. He'd kept his eyes closed, hadn't heard her steps. But he knew she now stood in front of him, ready to pounce.

He sniffed, but the perfume she splashed on in the mornings was now little more than a distant whiff of musk. Not enough to have alerted him to her movements.

As a cop, he'd taken his instincts for granted, always aware of what was happening around him. But that hadn't been anything like this *awareness* that sprang into his head, full blown, along with the knowledge, the absolute certainty, he was right.

"Jake, you need to go to the hospital." Rily's barely restrained frustration washed over him.

That again.

"Sis." His voice sounded rusty, unused. Not strong, as it had been when he'd told Hannah to stop. How long ago was that?

He was losing track of time.

"No hospital." Opening his eyes a small slit, he stared at his sister.

Pain flashed through her green eyes for a brief second then flared into burning temper. "Damn you, Jake."

"Damn me all you want."

Ben leaned forward in his chair. He braced his hands on his knees. "Do you remember what happened to you?"

Which part?

Like he was going to share what went on between Hannah and him. He shrugged then grit his teeth at the pain radiating down his shoulders to center as a throbbing ache in his wrists and at the small of his back.

"Jake?" Her eyes wide, Rily sank down on the couch to sit next to him. Her touch whisper-light, she laid the tips of her fingers on his arm. "Ben says you were struck by lightning."

"*Lightning?*" That might explain the black-out. The headache. The way every muscle in his body ached. "Shouldn't I be dead?"

"Probably." Ben pushed out of his chair. He stood with his fingers splayed at his hips. "If it had been normal lightning. Rily, where'd Sadie get off to?"

Normal lightning? Sadie? Lifting an eyebrow – *damn even that hurt* – Jake gave his sister a sideways look. Her touch light and warm, she tapped his arm.

Ouch. He managed to keep the grimace small and tight.

"Garrett wants Sadie to function as a pointer." Rily sent the other man a veiled look. "To point out Hannah's location."

"Why do you need to know where Hannah is?"

"He doesn't trust her."

"I trust her with my life."

"Obviously you are." Garrett cocked his head to one side.

"What is that supposed to mean?"

"You said yourself, you should be dead. But you're not."

Belligerence, Jake's old companion, reared its head. "And that has *what* to do with Hannah?"

"You were the target, again –" Garrett settled back into the recliner. "Of a psychic booby trap."

Jake rubbed the shell of his ear, wincing at the pain radiating down his arm. "What the hell?"

"Did that bolt scramble your brains, Carrigan? You're not usually this slow."

"Neither am I. And I'm still not sure I'm buying this bullshit." Rily slammed her back against the couch, bouncing once on the cushions while she crossed her arms in front of her.

Jake flinched at the sudden shift of the couch cushions behind him, but his sister settled and that extra jab of pain subsided.

Beside him, Rily scalded Garrett with a glare. The man seemed oblivious. *Must be made of Teflon.*

But then, Rily wasn't Garrett's little sister.

"Psychic booby traps." Ben let his hands dangle between his knees. He pinned Jake and Rily with a teacher's look straight out of high school math class.

Rily straightened and squared her shoulders. Irritation flashed hot through Jake. Garrett wasn't their teacher and they were all a long way out of school.

Jake lifted his lip in a snarl.

Laughter winked in and out of Ben's cool blue eyes.

Maybe they *were* back in high school math class.

Or science. Lack thereof….

"As I was saying." Ben, with his hands still dangling between his knees, entwined his fingers loosely together.

Jake yanked his stray thoughts back.

"These psychic booby traps, laid out specifically for you, Jake, are some particularly nasty ones. Made to look like accidents, intended to take your life."

Someone wanted him dead?

Icy cold blood coursed through Jake's body, leaving sharp, frozen pinpricks in its wake. "The Jeep brakes —"

"Sabotaged."

Rily leaned forward, laced her fingers between her knees in a mirror of Garrett's. "There wasn't any way Jake *forgot* to tighten his lug-nuts. That just isn't going to happen. But this psychic stuff? Come on, Garrett."

Ben raised that damn eyebrow again, this time with a slight lift of one side of his mouth. "Are you forgetting the last few hours?"

Rily frowned. She leaned back against the couch with her fingers still twisted together and pressed to her stomach. "There is all of that."

Jake kneaded his forehead and his temples again. He didn't have the energy, wasn't in any shape to argue with Ben about the man's belief Hannah was behind the brake tampering. Or the lightning.

Especially after the windy fit she threw.

But it was crap, all of it.

A touch, not much heavier than air, feathered across his forehead. Invisible fingertips, light and barely there, massaged his temples. His eyelids fluttered shut.

"Jake?" Alarm threaded through Rily's voice.

He patted at the air in her direction, wincing at the sudden jab of pain. An unseen palm stroked down his arm, kneading through the material of his shirt. *God, Hannah.*

"Did you give him any pain-killers?" Ben's voice came from a distance away.

Jake ignored the man's question. He was talking to Rily, anyway. Whatever Hannah was doing with that mind of hers, it was taking away the hurt and leaving a trail of pleasant sensation in its wake.

Not like in that other place, but then they had an audience now. Besides, he couldn't see her or touch her, not here.

Sadness washed over him.

Why had he come back? He would have been quite happy to have stayed there. With Hannah in his arms.

"Nothing except those aspirins earlier." Rily's voice echoed over him. "He hates taking medicine and not knowing what, exactly, was wrong, I didn't think I should give him anything stronger. Why?"

"Look at him. It's like he's on something and it just kicked in."

"I'm still with you guys." *Unfortunately.* Jake forced one eye open. He motioned with the hand that no longer hurt. "Keep going. Psychic booby traps on my brakes or … something or another."

"Okay then." Ben's voice held something, annoyance maybe.

Inside, Jake shrugged.

"The lightning was also a trap."

"Okay."

"One Hannah set."

Jake's eyes snapped open. "Bullshit."

"Thought that might bring you around." Garrett's mouth moved a fraction, but his eyes were still that dark, cold blue. "The rod was set to trigger when the two ingredients it needed were present. Unstable air and you within a certain distance."

"Set?" Jake rubbed a hand over his face. "Its purpose is to *deflect* lightning. Not redirect it."

"True." Ben tapped his fingers together. "But add in psychic intent and you have a hell of a trap. One that was supposed to leave you dead."

"Why didn't it?"

His mouth set in a grim line, Ben shrugged. "I was hoping you could give us an explanation for that."

Not bloody likely. The touch on his shoulders squeezed and patted in a comforting motion. Tamping down the urge to reach and rub a hand not really there, he instead smoothed his fingers across his mouth.

"Garrett believes Hannah set the rod, Jake." Rily swiped her hands across her eyes, made a face. "That she wants you to join her in ghost-hood or whatever you call it."

"No." Quiet and firm, Hannah's voice came from above and to the side of Jake. He glanced in that direction. As if he would be able to see her there.

"Well, then." Ben stood and scratched his index finger over his ear. "We don't need Sadie after all, do we, Rily?"

Jake swung his head to stare at the tall, towering man. *What the hell?*

"Sweetheart." Ben ignored him and spoke to the spot just over Jake's head. "What is it you want?"

"You to go to *hell.*" Hannah's voice, low and husky, shook.

"She's not too happy with you, Garrett. Is this how you got her upset earlier?" The ache in his body now manageable, Jake pushed himself upright, away from the soft comfort of the back cushions. "Goaded her into that fit?"

"Priceless, Carrigan. She throws a temper tantrum and I'm to blame?"

"Aren't you?" Rily stood and faced Ben with her weight on one foot, hands on her hips and an eyebrow raised. "I can't believe I'm standing here talking about ghosts and psychic booby traps. We're all out of our minds."

"Maybe." Jake forced himself off the couch. He swayed. His sister rushed forward. She wrapped her arm under his and around his back.

"What do you think you're doing?" Rily's words hissed over him.

"Standing. I told you I was fine."

"Yeah. You look fine." She glanced at Ben and cocked her head at Jake.

"Actually, he looks a lot better than he did." Ben, his brows lowered, scanned the area behind Jake. "What did Hannah do? Just now? She took your pain, at least part of it, away. How did she accomplish that?"

Jake steadied himself then eased from his sister's grip. The pain *had* receded. Not gone, but not nearly as agonizing or mind robbing. He stared at Garrett.

"You know –" Ben, his gaze thoughtful, scanned the entire room once more before focusing on Jake. "We won't figure out what's going on here if you insist on fighting me every step of the way."

"Hannah didn't –"

"Sit back down, Jake." His lips drawn downward, Ben waved a hand at him. "Before you fall."

Jake opened his mouth to argue, but Rily raised her own brow and gripped his elbow.

Shit.

"Why the hell not?" He lifted the corner of his top lip and shoved Rily's restraining hand away.

Her eyes darkened, the gold more prominent. He didn't care. He wasn't an invalid. Unsteady, he lowered himself to the edge of the couch.

"Jake, I found you prone on your back, on the ground. Next to your generator. So far gone I wasn't sure you weren't already dead." Ben settled onto the recliner, kicked the foot rest up then crossed his ankles.

"So you hauled my sorry ass in and dumped me on the couch."

The corner of Ben's mouth quirked. "True enough. You had no pulse. At all."

"What?" Rily spun around and faced Garrett. "Then why didn't you –"

He lifted a hand, palm toward her, for a brief moment before he laced his fingers together over his stomach. "You still breathed, Jake. Barely. But had no heartbeat."

"That's not possible." Rily, with her hands splayed on her hips and her chin in the air, swung her head between the two men.

"You'd be surprised at what's possible." Garrett tapped his index fingers together.

Jake ignored the desperate laughter Hannah choked back.

"All right, Garrett." He leaned back to let the couch cushions support him. "Inform us. What is possible? What the hell are you involved in and why is it impacting us?"

Ben's lips curved, that icy smile that never quite reached his eyes. He rubbed his hand over his mouth before again lacing his fingers across his stomach. Rily's eyes narrowed.

Yeah, little sister. Right with you on this one. Whatever they were about to hear certainly wouldn't be everything. Could be interesting, though. Jake folded his hands over his lap in a deliberate mirroring of the other man's body language.

The corner of Ben's eyes crinkled, but the flash of humor was gone quickly. "You don't need –"

"More *need to know* bullshit?" Rily crossed her arms over her chest.

"Pretty much." Ben aimed a dark, humorous look her way. "As I was saying, my work has no immediate impact on either of you. However, because of what I do, my knowledge should be of some help in figuring out all of this crap."

"Meaning this psychic, mumbo-jumbo ghost crap?" Rily's eyebrow lifted.

"Yeah." His eyes flat, Ben nodded. "That crap."

"So?" Jake shrugged. "You feel ghosts and energy signatures. Somehow that's going to lead to the break in the case of who's trying to kill me? Enlighten us. Who are you?"

Ben's dry chuckle underscored the way Hannah's restless energy washed over his skin, seeped into his veins and settled in his chest. He resisted the urge to talk to her. To comfort her.

He had to focus on here. On now.

Focusing on her would only distract him. The mush in his brain was doing a bang-up job of that.

"Hannah's still in the room?" Garrett cocked his head slightly to one side. "She hasn't left?"

Maybe the man really was a mind reader. "Why? You *read* ghosts. You sense their presence. Can't you tell?"

"Belligerence isn't going to get us anywhere. And, just for the record –" Ben untwined his fingers and picked at a piece of nonexistent lint on his jeans then nailed Jake with a blank look. "I'm here for my goddaughter, not for either of your two sorry asses."

Hannah wished, desperately, she could believe that. But she didn't.

With her arms wrapped tight around her waist, she spared them all a quick glance. Jake and Rily exchanged an unreadable look. Ben's gaze moved between them both.

Ben Garrett. Her father's friend.

Every once in a while she actually *felt* some kind of energy from him. A searching, probing type of energy. Nothing she'd ever sensed before, nothing she let touch her. How she stopped the probe, she had no idea. But, as if it were a tangible thing, she had managed to stop it a few bare inches from her skin.

By her will alone.

Weird. But on a one to ten weirdness scale, that hardly registered these days so she filed it away to think about later.

"I repeat. Who are you?" Jake angled his head to look at Ben. "Who do you work for?"

Ben, his mouth a thin line, scanned the room with narrowed eyes. He pulled a small, slim sliver case from his front pocket and slipped out a white business card. Rily, her own mouth tight, took the card and gave it a quick glance over before handing it to Jake.

"What the hell is IPS?" Rily turned back towards Ben. With her hands again at her hips, a frown drew down her brow.

"Institute for Psychic Studies." Jake read from the card, flipped it over once and then back to the front. He ran his thumb over the raised print. "In Minnesota. You're the man in charge of this place?"

Ben, now settled back in the recliner, nodded.

"Psychic Studies?" Rily swung her gaze between Jake and Ben. "How does that give you any leeway to impersonate an Oregon State Police officer, *Uncle Ben*?"

Hannah wrapped her arms tight around her middle. Institute for Psychic Studies. He'd said he worked with her father.

Had her father been part of this Institute?

"There's more to this, Rily." Jake's voice a little more weary, he set the card on his thigh.

His sister rounded on him. "I can't believe you're listening to *this*. Much less buying into it. It's all bullshit."

Was it? Hannah ran the tip of her tongue over her lips. Queasiness, like soft waves along the pond's shore, lapped at her stomach. Ebbed and flowed. Maybe Ben really did know what he was talking about.

"Jake's right." Ben made a face, the grimace deepening the grooves at the side of his mouth. "We also do quite a bit of what you might call side work for the U.S. Government. Consulting you might say."

Rily spun to face him. "What does any of that have to do with us? With Hannah?"

"Nothing at all. But I do have considerable resources at my disposal. I told you, I'm here for my goddaughter. I will find out what happened to her. And if we're able to, we'll keep Jake from actually getting killed."

"Gee, thanks." Dryness lined Jake's voice. "You know we'll both be checking into this."

"No problem." Ben lifted one shoulder in a loose shrug. "Just don't expect to find much."

Rily scowled.

"Tell him I'm here." Hannah moved to stand behind Jake. If he was willing to listen to Ben, maybe she should, too. "He already knows, anyway."

Hoping she wasn't making a mistake, she bit the edge of her bottom lip.

His chin low, Jake sighed. Tiredness seemed to be overtaking him again, leaving his skin pale and his eyes dull. He glanced in her direction, then back at the man reclining in the leather chair. "Hannah wants you to know she's in the room."

"Good." Ben nodded, a pleased light sparking his eyes. "She should be part of all of this."

Big of him. Like she was going anywhere now.

"So back to business. The facts first." Ben stared at the ceiling, then met Jake and Rily's gaze in turn. "Hannah's dead and her ghost talks to you."

"You call that a fact?" Rily paced to the fireplace, turned to face Ben. "Hannah's a ghost and haunting my brother? And you may or may not be who you profess to be."

"I am who I say I am. And yes, I do call those facts. We've been over this, Rily. Catch up."

Rily's mouth tight, eyebrows drawn into a frown, she stalked back to the couch and flopped down on the far end. "Excuse me if I attempt to be the voice of reason in this ever-expanding loony bin."

Ben shook his head. He spared a glance in Hannah's general direction before focusing on Jake. "If Hannah isn't behind the two attacks on you, then obviously we need to figure out who is responsible."

"Obviously." Jake leaned his head on the back cushion. Exhaustion lined his face, his eyes were open no more than a slit. "It's not Hannah. If someone wanted to kill me, why not just use a gun? Much more effective."

"And just think of all that lovely evidence we could gather off your dead body, brother dearest."

"Exactly." Ben directed a beam at Rily, conspicuously ignoring her deepening scowl. "Killing with psychic intent is so much cleaner, evidence-wise."

"Ohhh-kay." Rily rolled her eyes. With her legs crossed, she settled deeper into the corner of the couch. "This should be good."

Ben flicked a disgusted look at her. Hannah understood her sarcasm. That was the place her friend retreated to whenever things got to be too much. Right now, Hannah wanted to retreat, too. She pressed her hand to her stomach, but the queasiness still roiled.

If Ben was right, someone actually wanted Jake dead.

Could ghosts vomit? That was another question she didn't have the answer to, either.

"While I was away I checked into that gang involved with your brother's death." Ben stroked his chin.

Jake flinched. His small, sharp movement sent slivers of pain slicing through her shoulder.

"And?" A hesitant, almost panicked look replaced the frown on Rily's face. She pulled her legs up, looked at Ben over her knees. "What were you looking for?"

"Any kind of affiliation with the supernatural world, a psychic on the payroll."

"Okay." Rily puffed out a breath. "I'll bite. How do you figure that out?"

One corner of Ben's mouth lifted. "I have my ways. But there's not much there. At least not on the surface. I have people checking deeper."

"Of course you do."

"We may have to head to Portland. Check into that gang ourselves."

"Right." Rily lifted both hands for a brief moment before shoving them through her hair. "And we would be so much better equipped to discover psychic motivations than the *people* you have looking into all of this."

Jake, his eyes closed, chuckled. "Give it up, Rily."

"Sure. Why not? So if it's not revenge motivated, at least not from that angle, what else is there?"

"Hannah —"

"It's not Hannah." His jaw tight and his lips drawn together, Jake opened his eyes. His heated gaze focused on Ben.

The man met Jake's glare. Hannah tore her own gaze away, rolled her head against the tension in her neck before pacing to the end of the couch.

Jake believed in her, in her innocence.

She wasn't sure if she did.

She'd blacked out both times, just before Jake had been in danger. Yes, she'd stopped the Jeep, but *where* had she been in the moments before?

And the lightning strike?

She'd found Jake in that void, laid out, his body prone. Where had she been, before, when he'd been struck?

What if she was responsible? For these psychic accidents? These attacks against Jake, against his life?

Was all of this her fault?

Chapter Fifteen

WITH FRUSTRATION BINDING HIS CHEST, Jake leaned his head against the back cushions of his couch. While the actual pain lancing his body was now manageable, stress knotted every one of his muscles.

Outside, the night wind howled and slammed rain against the panes of glass on either side of his front door. Nature was as pissed as he was, although probably not for the same reasons.

"Whether you accept it or not, Hannah is at the center of all of this." Ben, his fingers linked with his hands resting on his stomach, stared at Jake with hooded eyes.

Although a muscle twitched along his jaw, Jake simply stared back. Hannah wouldn't hurt him. He was damn tired of going over that again and again.

A soft, lingering chill traced across his cheek, along his tight jaw.

Hannah.

Rily pushed up from the couch. She paced to the fireplace and back. Twice. "Maybe —"

"No." With his voice low, Jake put in as much force as he could muster.

"We're back to this." Garrett forced the footrest of his recliner down into the locked position. He leaned forward to rest his elbows on his knees and held his hand up, palm forward. "Let me finish. Then you can play the injured boyfriend defending his girl. Or whatever role you're into playing these days."

Rily snickered. Jake scowled at her. Her grin bright and false, she wiggled her fingers back. At lease someone was getting something out of all of this. At his expense.

"Dammit, Carrigan." Gruffness coated Ben's voice. "That lightning rod, just like with your Jeep, holds Hannah's energy signature. Not light, not lingering and left over from some past encounter. It's strong. It's recent. And it's all over that damn area out there."

Jake swung his gaze from his sister to stare at Garrett. This was the most emotion he'd seen on the man since they'd met.

But it was still all so much bullshit.

"So if Hannah's not the one doing the dirty work, then how did any of this happen?" Rily spared a quick glance at Jake, her eyes dark and unreadable. "This psychic intent? Is it enough to just want him harmed or is there more to it?"

"Harmed isn't what this person wants."

"*Person?*" With his gaze locked on Garrett and conscious of the razor-sharp pain scrapping along the entire length of his spine, Jake eased away from the cushions. "Not ghost."

"Right." His mouth in a thin line, Ben glanced between them. "I've been giving this a lot of thought. Although playing devil's advocate has been quite entertaining, I believe someone has actually hijacked Hannah's energy."

"*What?*" At Hannah's quick intake of breath Jake threw a hasty look in the direction of her voice.

"*I believe.*" Ben lowered his head and raised his clasped hands. He rubbed his temples with his thumbs then shoved both hands through his hair. "I can't prove it. Can't get a read past Hannah."

Rily shook her head. "We keep coming back to who would want to hurt Jake."

"Not hurt." Ben looked directly at him. "Kill."

Wonderful. The twitch in Jake's cheek matched the one along his jaw. "So looking at the bastards responsible for Craig was smart. Except why use Hannah? Why not Craig?"

"Is he also talking to you?" Both of Ben's brows raised.

In front of the fireplace Rily swung around, her eyes wide and dark, her fingers cupped over her mouth and chin. In that instant, with her other arm wrapped around her middle, she looked ready to bolt.

The vise around his chest clamped hard. Shit. He couldn't help his sister any more than he could help himself.

"No. He hasn't." Although Jake almost wished Craig would. So he could tell him – What? He was sorry he hadn't gotten there in time? Sorry he hadn't saved him?

Sorry didn't begin to touch his regrets.

"Has Hannah seen Craig?" Ben's narrowed gaze zeroed in on him.

"I don't –" That hadn't occurred to him.

"No." Hannah's voice whispered over him and he let his eyelids drift close. "I haven't. And I ... looked while we were at the pier."

"She says no." Opening his eyes, Jake caught Ben's startled glance towards Hannah's position.

"Right." Frown lines pulled Garrett's brows downward. "So, as we thought, this is someone connected to Hannah and not your brother Craig."

"Everyone loved Hannah." Rily ran her hands over her cheeks and neck, threaded her fingers into her hair at the base of her skull.

"I'm fairly sure not everyone loves Jake."

"You got that did you?" The corners of Rily's eyes crinkled.

"Loud and clear." Ben aimed a gentle smile at her.

Humor. Ha-ha. Great. Jake shook his head. Again, at his expense.

"Who has he pissed off, say, in regards to Hannah?"

"Althea Sheldon."

Jake frowned at the quickness of his sister's answer. "That's recent. Only in the last couple of days."

Her arms spread, Rily spun around to face him. "That you know of. You said she jumped your ass about not being there for Hannah at the end."

"That's interesting, that she still has that much emotion tied to Hannah dying after all these months." Ben swung his gaze between them.

"Interesting, yes." Jake had to reel these two in before they jumped off that slippery river bank. "The woman's a bitch and I don't trust her. She's hiding something. Using that as a reason to want me dead? I don't think so."

"Still." Rily stood a few feet away from him, her hands still open. "These ... attacks on you started *after* you paid a visit to her office."

"That's reaching." Jake shook his head at the determination settling over her face. Turning toward Ben, he frowned at the alertness lining the other man's face. "You, too?"

Jake let his body slump. He leaned his head back on the cushion.

"Has Althea always been her father's office manager?" Ben's voice was thoughtful.

"Far as I know. Amy said Althea's also a Registered Nurse, but I think she's worked for her father her entire career." This was stupid. "How could she possibly pull off what you're talking about?"

How could anyone?

"Was she close to Hannah?"

"Not that I'm aware of." But then, obviously there was a lot he hadn't known. "Hannah?"

His senses wide open to her, he knew she was still in the room. She hadn't *touched* him in the last few minutes, but she was here. Listening.

"Not real close." Pain radiated from her voice.

"Dammit. Baby, I didn't mean to make you hurt."

Ben raised a brow but Jake brushed him off.

"Whatever it takes to figure this out." Hannah's deep sigh cut across his skin, sliced at his heart. "She's always been good to me, concerned. Other than that, no. We weren't close."

He repeated Hannah's words for the others.

This wasn't much different from being an interpreter. That he was a go-between for a ghost, he ignored.

"So what's Althea's motivation?" Rily settled further into her corner of the couch. "Why put so much effort into killing Jake?"

"Again, if she hates me to that degree, why not just shoot me?"

His gaze unfocused for a moment, Ben stared into space. "What would she, or anyone else, stand to gain?"

Jake shared a quick glance with Rily, jerked his head in her direction. "Little sister there is now my beneficiary. The only one who would actually gain anything, money-wise, if I were to drop dead."

"Thanks, Bro." Rily's sarcasm practically dripped and he let go of a dry chuckle.

"Financial gain is one of the chief motivators for murder."

"Excuse me." Rily's chin jutted upward.

The corner of Ben's mouth lifted. "Revenge and getting someone out of the way are two other strong motivators."

"Revenge, that one's wide open." Jake rolled his head from side to side, let his upper lip curl. "But, in spite of the tourist population passing through on their way to the shore, this is a small town. Speeding and parking tickets aren't enough reason to kill someone."

"That's when you were a beat cop, Carrigan. What about after you made Detective?"

He shrugged. "There have been a few dead bodies here and there. Again, people passing through, thinking they could use this area as a dumping ground."

"Solved? The killers behind bars?"

"Pretty much. There are a couple bodies who are still John Does, plus two locals who dropped dead for no reason we could discern. When I left the department, those four were the only open cases. Nothing to warrant wanting me dead."

"Rily should probably look into those. See if there's any personal angle you didn't catch at the time."

"Already on that." She met Jake's gaze direct. "Doing my job, brother dear."

"Which one? Satisfying your curiosity or poking your nose in my business?"

The smile she gave him serene, she blinked twice. "I love when my actual job dovetails with irritating you."

"I bet you do."

"Children."

Jake rubbed his hand over his face. "*Acquaintances* of the bastards who killed Craig are the only ones who would want me dead. You've ruled them out."

"Only on a cursory look. As I said before, that's being looked into at a deeper level." Ben held up a hand, heaved a deep, put upon sigh. "All right. I do run the Institute. On the

Agency side, the side that consults for the government, we employ psychics and others with some interesting talents."

"Psychics? Working with our government?"

"Yes." Ben's eyes turned chilly. "I have access to quite a few resources. Official and otherwise. That's as much as you're going to get."

"For right now." The smile Rily aimed in his direction held no humor. "So you really do have a lot of experience with this weird shit?"

Ben turned that deep blue, cold gaze on her. "You're a good cop. Back off."

She shrugged one shoulder. With a slight twist to her lips, she settled against the couch.

"Going beyond revenge and financial gain –" Ben turned his head and directed his gaze at Jake. "Whose way are you in?"

"Althea Sheldon's." Rily tugged on the afghan and balled it onto her lap. "Possibly her father. Dr. James Sheldon."

Jake scrubbed both hands over his face. "Why?"

"Personally, I'm thinking they might be good for it, Carrigan."

"Yeah. Earlier you were thinking Hannah. I'm still having trouble with the idea anyone would want me dead. Again, why?"

"You know how this works. If we had the *why*, we'd have the *who* tied up in a nice bright bow." Ben tugged at his earlobe. "As for Hannah, I'm not ruling her out. She may just be the vehicle. Possibly an unknowing vehicle."

"So, in this scenario you're building, Althea wants me dead. She's using Hannah's energy *signature* to do it? Trying to frame a ghost for murder?"

"Something like that. Except she's setting it up to look like an accident."

Shit. Jake let his head rest on the back of the couch's cushion and blew out a breath. "How is she doing this?"

"No clue."

"Figures." He crossed his hands over his belly, his gaze on Garrett. "I saw Althea yesterday."

The startled jerk of Ben's body satisfied some small quirk in Jake's psyche. Petty, maybe. He didn't care.

"And?"

"Miraculously, the good doctor's copy of the death certificate was in Hannah's folder."

A soft moan whispered over his skin. *Sorry, Baby.*

"What?" Hands tangled in the afghan, Rily leaned forward. "How did you get to see it? There's no way she would have —" Rily leaned back. "She did, didn't she? What game is she playing?"

"Good question." Ben shook his head. His gaze narrowed and his mouth tightened. "Doctor's copy or not, it still hasn't been filed."

Jake straightened and filled them in on his visit with Althea.

"You need to actually meet her, Garrett. Do your woo-woo magic on her." Rily tossed the afghan onto the back of the couch.

"I thought you didn't believe the woo-woo stuff." Ben pushed to his feet and paced to stand in front of the fireplace.

"Whatever means available." She hunched then rolled her shoulders.

"I was thinking the same thing." Ben checked his watch. "Don't you have the early shift in the morning?"

"Yeah." She stood, stretched and glanced at Jake. "I could sure use a decent night's sleep."

"You worry too much, Sis." With his arms limp and his hands loose in his lap, Jake again leaned his head back against the couch. Any energy he'd mustered had petered out. "Go home. Sleep. Maybe this whole mess will make more sense in the morning."

"Do you really believe that?" Rily stood and faced him with her hands balled into fists on her hips.

He didn't even have enough energy left to shrug so he simply stared at her.

She arched a brow then turned to Garrett. "Are you staying here tonight? Or do I need to bring in my overnight case?"

"I'll stay."

Jake glanced from one to the other one. "I don't have any kind of choice here?"

Ben swung his gaze to Jake. "You want your sister hovering?"

"Hey. I don't hover." Rily shrugged. "Much."

"No." Jake closed his eyes. "I don't want anyone hovering. Go home, Rily. Get some sleep."

"After I check out that lightning rod."

"In the dark?" Ben turned in Rily's direction.

Jake still hadn't figured out how he could tell, beyond the direction of their voices, where the two of them were with his eyes closed. But that puzzle was going to have to wait until tomorrow. He was wiped. "Let her show you her uber flashlight, Garrett. Should impress even you."

"I would like another look at that rod, myself." Concern coated Ben's voice. "You —"

"I'll just stay right here." Without bothering to open his eyes, Jake held up a hand. "Both of you need to stop. No hovering. Go check the damn lightning rod."

"Twice in three days, Jake." Ben's words drifted as he moved towards the kitchen. "The next time you might not be so lucky. Especially not knowing what to watch for, or where the next strike will come from."

"Yeah, yeah. I know. Attempted psychic murder." His eyes still closed, Jake gave them a small wave. "Now we've heard everything."

IN THE CORNER near the fireplace, Hannah huddled in on herself. Rily and Ben fussed between themselves on their way through the kitchen to go recheck the lightning rod. The back door slammed behind them.

Her blackouts worried her. She was responsible for the attacks on Jake. Somehow or another, this was on her.

Where had she gone? What had she done while she was there? Wherever *there* happened to be. The energy signatures, *her energy signature*, all over the Jeep, the brakes, the lightning rod.

She had to get away from Jake. Leave before she managed to get him killed.

"Hannah?" Jake's voice yanked her thoughts back to the room, back to the present.

"Hey." Her voice sounded small, even to herself.

"Missing you."

"Jake –"

"Hannah." Jake still sat on the couch. His head rested on the back cushion. He had his hands folded in his lap and his eyes open a bare slit. "Tell me our time in that blue void actually happened. That I didn't dream it. That we touched."

She drew in a deep breath. "Okay."

"Just okay?"

"No, not just." Her chuckle, lacking any trace of humor, still managed to be low and throaty at the same time. "Touched might be a rather tame word."

A small, sad smile flitted across his mouth. "What we did, wherever it was we were, doesn't even come close to everything I want to do to you. With you. Together."

She swallowed around the tightness clogging her throat.

Oh, Lordy, this was so hard. "Jake, however we managed that, I don't think it's going to happen again. We're both right back here. The same place we were yesterday."

"I'm not anywhere near where I was yesterday. Neither are you."

"You *have* to stay alive. Don't —"

He held up a hand. "I'm here, aren't I?"

"That lightning, the psychic angle Ben was talking about, that had to be what sent you into that space. That void. That's why you're leaning back on that couch as if you'll never move again. If —"

His face hard and the spot in his right cheek twitching, he pressed both palms onto the couch and pushed himself up straight.

"Jake —"

"No. None of this is your fault. You had nothing to do with this."

"Yes, I did. Somehow, I did." Her insides twisted in knots, but she had to make him understand. She had to make this right.

Without him ending up dead.

"I'm a bit hazy on how this psychic shit works, but I do know you wouldn't do anything to physically hurt me, Hannah."

"Not on purpose. What if Ben is right, though, and someone is using me? Using me against you?"

"Back to what I told Ben." With a slight tremor in his locked arms, Jake used his hands to scoot to the edge of the couch. "There isn't anyone who wants me gone that badly."

"Someone has to be using me –"

"Maybe. But answer a question. How the hell would this person know about you?" He took a deep breath, the harshness echoing through her own chest. "Ben and Rily are the only ones who even know you still exist."

"But –"

"As pissed as you might get at Ben Garrett, he's not behind this."

"I know." Sometime in the last few hours she'd accepted him. More or less. "That doesn't mean I have to like him."

"No, you don't. I do, though. He wants to find out what happened to you almost as badly as I do. He's going to help me with that." Jake stood on wobbly legs.

"What are you doing, Jake? Where do you think you're going?" She jumped up and stood next to him. *Hovering.* If he fell there wasn't a damn thing she could do to help.

"Going to the bathroom." He lifted one corner of his mouth, the look grim, and took a shuffling step forward. "And then my own bed. I've had enough of that couch."

She gripped her hands tight and watched him make his unsteady way across the room. His words hadn't been lost on her. He was going to find out how she'd died.

Why she'd died.

Right now, though, she was more worried about what might happen to him than what had happened to her.

No matter what Ben might think, she didn't want Jake dead.

JAKE LEANED ON THE THICK BRANCH he'd grabbed from his stack of uncut wood. Not the best cane, but under the circumstances it worked.

He stood over the prone lightning rod and took another quick scan of the surrounding meadow. Unlike the last time he'd been out here, today the late afternoon sky was blue and completely clear.

No threatening clouds. The storm had moved off.

Ben had left early that morning, leaving a note on the kitchen table. He'd be back later. Jake had slept several more hours.

Now, out here in the meadow, the bright sun shone across the forest's edge and had chased away any lingering shadows. Everything appeared peaceful and relatively quiet.

But the hair on the back of his neck stood at attention. Pinpricks of awareness that had nothing to do with the strong breeze slapping at his still too-long hair, raised bumps all along his arms.

The heavy tang of burnt grass hung in the air.

He wasn't sure if those pricks or that smell were real or simple residue from his earlier experience. Like the phantom scents that plagued him out on the pier where his brother had been shot.

Here, the grass in the meadow was as green as it had been yesterday, the shadows from the tall pine trees along the meadow's western edge nonexistent. His legs weren't quite as unsteady as they'd been just an hour ago, but they weren't a hundred percent either.

Everything appeared normal. Still, something was off.

Something more than the rod on the ground, something more than his injuries. Such as they were.

Not because Ben had planted that thought in his head.

No. The very air around him seemed off.

Wrong.

He turned in a full circle. No birds. No sound beyond the wind through the pines.

Even that sound seemed wrong.

Off key.

Sadie sat silent next to the fence bordering the field, her gold eyes alert, watchful.

Not sure he wasn't making himself a target for whatever lurked, Jake crouched beside the rod. Glad to be lower to the ground and not sure it would make any difference, he poked at the metal with his stick.

Nothing. The rod lay on the ground, bent in half, but he didn't *feel* anything off the metal. Nothing at all.

No *sense* of Hannah. Although she was back at the house, he'd wondered what he'd find out here. If he would be able to feel this signature Garrett talked about. He didn't. The relief swelling through his gut surprised him.

He hadn't wanted to admit he'd been worried, not out loud. That would have given power to the thought.

Ben had harped on that particular one enough for everyone.

There was nothing out here to suggest she had anything to do with the lightning strike. He wiped his hand over his face. After a quick glance towards his house, he used his stick to push himself into a standing position.

Sadie whined.

His dog was right. He scanned the area one more time. He needed to get back to the house. Back to Hannah. Being out in the open wasn't doing anything constructive to his sense of self preservation.

HANNAH STOOD ON THE PORCH, her gaze locked on Jake as he made his way towards her from across the meadow. Not really cold, she crossed her arms over her chest and rubbed her upper arms.

The material of her red sweater soft under her fingers, the memory of the two of them alone in that blue void slammed full force into her head. Jake's hands running over her bare skin, cupping her breasts....

Her nipples tightened.

The two of them. Naked. Jake inside her, their bodies moving together.

Had that only been yesterday?

They shared the memory, but was it real?

Sadie bounded up onto the porch, barked once, the sound sharp in the quietness of the late afternoon. Old Nels looked up from his sampling of fresh grass in front of the barn.

How many times in the past had Jake stood right here on this porch, waiting for her and the animals to finally make their way back from the waterfall?

The grill going, a bottle of wine chilling in a bucket of ice.

Normal life.

But that had stopped after Craig had been killed.

Pain arched across her head, centered at her temples.

The dog whined.

Needles pricked at her skin. Other memories fought through the murky depths, hovering there just under the surface, swamping her as pain spiked through her head.

Right there. Memories of....

If she could just touch them, reach them.

Her fingers curled into her palms.

Everyone leaves. Her mother's words whispered across the breeze.

No. She shook her head.

Ben had said her father had been sick, had died.

Everyone leaves. She left Jake before he could leave her.

But he already had left. Maybe not physically, but emotionally she'd been completely alone.

She cringed at the stab of pain across her scalp. Maybe she had been alone, but he'd been hurting. Even then, she'd known *why* he'd pulled away, but she hadn't stayed the course, waited him out.

Then she'd been sick.

Oh, Lord.

That memory crashed into her leaving her breath shallow and rapid, her heartbeat erratic.

She *had* been ill.

Anemic. Exhausted, lethargic.

Dr. Sheldon had recognized the symptoms, the same ones that had taken his wife so many years before. His kind, watery blue eyes swam through her mind. The excitement lining his face.

He'd found a cure, was positive he could save her life.

Her knees buckled. She crumpled on the porch. Dark grey spots pulsed at the edge of her vision.

No.

With trembling arms, she pushed herself up on her hands, let her head hang low with her chin tucked against her heaving chest. The spots darkened, swarmed into a tight spiral. She focused on the narrow grey board beneath her hands. On slowing her breathing.

In. Out. One breath at a time.

Stop fighting, Hannah.

The words, spoken in a harsh whisper down a long tunnel, seeped over her skin. A chill scudded down her spine.

I can't stop. Her throat closed in on itself. *If I do, I'm really dead.*

Sadie whined again. Hannah lifted her head. She tried to center on the dog. The dark greyness solidified from the edges inward, reducing her vision to a dim pinhole of hazy light. The middle continued to pulse. Dizziness enveloped her.

No.

Fingers, barely there, swept down her cheek, leaving a cold trail in its wake. Oh, God. Someone touched her. Not Jake, but someone else. The pit in the center of her stomach seized tight. She jerked her head away from the prickly sensation of that illusive touch.

A hand clamped around her chin. Fingers dug into her skin. *Stop.*

Black closed in to block all light. Shrapnel exploded through her head.

"No." Her moan echoed, hurt.

"Hannah?" Jake's voice, alarmed and so far away, tangled with Sadie's whine.

Oh, Lord. No.

Chapter Sixteen

WITH TWO FLICKS OF HER RING FINGER, Althea tapped the syringe twice. Holding the plastic tube to the light she nodded and slipped the tip of the needle into the IV.

"Shush." Althea patted her restless patient's shoulder. "You're going to be fine."

A few more minutes before the upped dosage of medication would take hold then the patient would once again be calm. Her last chore for the evening before she had her own peace, her own calm.

Thank goodness. The last few days had been less than pleasant. But now, everything was back on track. Or as close as it could be, all things considered.

Her father had finally landed safely in Boston, was even now settled in his hotel with the room service she'd ordered for him on its way to his suite. The red wine should leave him mellow, help him sleep after such an arduous journey. Although she wished the unscheduled overnight layover in Denver could have been avoided, he was where he needed to be, now.

He fretted and she worried. About him, about the toll of his research. His once square shoulders seemed more hunched these days, more worn down.

Rotating her own shoulders, Althea allowed a sigh to break loose. She wasn't sure how to fix that, how to bring her father back from the edge of depression he closed in on, inch by inch. Day by day.

Although not angry at Hannah Dixon, she understood their work with the woman had done this to him. Althea and her father had both had such hopes with Hannah's response to the treatment he'd devised. That last ditch scramble, all his research culminating down to one point in time.

Hard to walk away from that, to admit defeat.

With a last look at her patient, Althea tilted her head to each side before disposing of the syringe and lowering the lights. Maybe she would actually get some of her father's research transcription done this evening.

JAKE WIPED A HAND over his blurry eyes and across the stubble marking his jaw line. How the hell had Garrett gotten him out of town and into the outskirts of Portland so friggin' early?

Sunrise was little more than a glimmer on the eastern horizon. Even the thermos of coffee, which was now close to empty, hadn't made his mind any less fuzzy.

Lack of sleep was fast catching up with him.

There was a pattern here he wasn't too pleased with.

Hannah disappeared. He didn't sleep.

She would be back, though. He had to believe that.

Otherwise –

"How far out of Portland is this place?" From the driver's seat Ben's voice cut across his thoughts.

Jake shrugged. Dwelling on Hannah and where she went wasn't helping his muddled mind. He took a fortifying gulp of lukewarm coffee. "Only been there once. A long time ago."

"Are we headed in the right direction?"

"This all looks familiar." Well, as familiar as it could in the near darkness. He nodded toward the windshield. "Should be the next left then maybe twenty more miles out."

As if Ramon Ortega, his brother's old partner, would be happy to see them so damn early. Without advance notice.

Yeah. Like this was going to be fun.

Ortega protected his privacy – more successfully than Jake had been able to, given the last few days. In spite of what Rily said, being a hermit suited Jake.

Was that how Ortega felt? The man had been in the hospital, in a coma, when Craig had died. The doctors had believed Ortega himself would die without ever waking up.

He hadn't. Ortega had eventually made a decent recovery. While not yet cleared for active police duty, the man put a few hours a day in at his office, chained to a desk and biding his time.

Jake wasn't sure he would have been able to handle that.

GARRETT'S PEOPLE hadn't been able to find all the answers he wanted about the gang responsible for Craig's death.

So a visit to Craig's old partner had been in order.

This morning Garret and Jake had both been awake, up and pacing hours before sunrise. Ben had suggested they take off and Jake had shrugged. Beat the hell out of the two of them staring at each other on each pass across his small kitchen.

Or worrying about Hannah.

But showing up here at Ortega's, why had he gone along with that insanity? He took another drink of his tepid coffee. Lack of sleep was getting blamed for a lot of things this morning.

That and lack of better judgment.

Ben turned onto the narrow road. Tall pines lined both sides, blocking any remnants of the burgeoning dawn.

How the hell did they ask the questions they needed to ask without sounding like complete nut jobs? Showing up at Ortega's door unannounced. And say what?

Hey, by the way, someone is trying to kill me using psychic powers. Happen to know anyone with that ability?

Shit.

Maybe that was the whole answer to the trepidation gnawing at his gut. He hadn't seen Ortega since the man had been released from the hospital. Rily had. She kept Jake up to date on Ortega's progress.

Whether he wanted the info or not.

Yet here he was, in the early predawn hour, heading to Ortega's house to ask him about the people responsible for Craig's murder.

If that wasn't a pisser, Jake didn't know what was.

Right now, at this moment, there was only one thing clear in his mind.

To face Ramon Ortega was to face his own internal demons.

PINE TREES AND EVERGREEN SCRUB OAK shrubs lined the compacted dirt path leading to Ortega's front door. Not visible from the road, even in the grey early morning light, the house sat camouflaged by its own mini forest.

With his leather jacket doing nothing to block the chilled wind, Jake stood at an angle to the large wooden door. Ben rapped on it for the third time. Obviously Ortega didn't want to be bothered.

Or he was still asleep.

Maybe Jake would get lucky. Maybe the man was out of town.

"Are you two lost?" Ortega's voice gruff and full of warning, he stood a few feet behind them. "If not, what the hell are you doing here? This time of morning?"

Jake hadn't seen him approach. Hadn't heard him.

A frown marked Ben's forehead as he turned and slid a single glance at Jake before focusing on Ramon Ortega.

Ramon stood, feet braced shoulder width apart, fists on his hips. Black sweats covered his lean body and matched the black hair and eyes. Lethal. Predatory. One eyebrow raised, he nodded at Jake without taking his gaze off Garrett.

Ben bristled and lifted his chin. His top lip pulled away from his teeth. Tension crackled the air between Garrett and Ortega. They eyed each other for several long moments.

Two wild animals standing their ground.

Shit. This was not a good idea. At all.

Not that Jake feared for their actual *physical* safety. It wasn't as if Ortega was the person wanting him dead. Still, the man wasn't someone you wanted for an enemy.

Why the hell had he let Garrett talk him into this visit? Oh yeah. Lack of sleep and better judgment.

Shit.

"Ramon." Jake's voice firm, although his legs were still shaky from the generator incident – he didn't know what the hell else to call it – he took a wobbly step forward. "This is Ben Garrett. Hannah's Godfather."

Both men swung their gazes to Jake before they again focused on each other. Neither extended a hand. After another tense moment passed before Ben nodded and lowered his chin. His dark blue eyes glittered in the low morning light. Not defeat by any means.

Glad he wasn't one of the testosterone charged males involved *this time*, Jake let his chin drop to his chest. Exhaustion lapped around the edges of his mind. Maybe he should just let them duke it out and pick up whatever pieces they left behind.

Challenge still strong in Ramon's nearly black eyes, he moved between them with a slight limp on his right side. How had he snuck up on them with a bum leg?

Ramon unlocked his front door. He turned to face them both. "Why are you here, Jake?"

"Someone may be trying to kill me." So much for the sidelines.

"Really?" Ramon's gaze impassive, he looked between Garrett and Jake. "This involves me how?"

"Cold, Ortega." Jake chuckled, the sound dry in the quietness of the morning. Even the wind had stopped. "Real cold."

Ramon shrugged his left shoulder. He glanced again between the two of them. "Let's take this inside. I have coffee made. That should warm us all."

When Ramon turned to push open his door, Ben gave Jake a wary look and motioned for him to go ahead.

Great, throw me into the den.

Once inside, Ramon waved them into the wide kitchen before he excused himself. The room, in colors and a style more reminiscent of the country of Ramon's heritage, was certainly warmer and more welcoming than Ortega himself. Jake would bet Ramon's grandmother, the woman who had raised him, had more to do with the decor than he did.

The only other time Jake had been here he'd come with Craig. They'd dropped by to retrieve some paperwork. Along with freshly made tamales and salsa. Which had been more to the point, if he remembered correctly. A dedicated city-dweller, Craig had still seemed at home out here.

Comfortable and at peace.

He'd said it was different from his apartment in Portland. An oasis of calm. He'd also bitched about how far out of town it was, that Ortega was a damn recluse who lived alone and liked it that way.

Craig had been the social one in that partnership.

Jake's chest tightened, constricted in on itself. He rubbed a hand over his mouth. Damn this was hard.

Coffee scented the air along with a hint of cinnamon and another spice he couldn't pinpoint. Brooding on the past wasn't going to get him through this. Neither was coffee, but at least that gave him something to do. He pulled three mugs from a cabinet over the granite counter and poured coffee into each.

Ben stood in the center of the room with his eyes narrowed and intent. The constriction across Jake's chest cinched another inch tighter. If this kept up, he wasn't going to be able to breathe at all.

What the hell was Garrett looking for with that woo-woo shit. Getting a read on the house? The way he, himself, did when he looked for Hannah?

Jake glanced around the room. *He* didn't feel or sense anything out of the ordinary.

Not yet, anyway.

Of course, Ramon might throw them off his property once they explained what they were after. But then, Jake really didn't fully understand what that really was, what Ben hoped to accomplish with this visit.

Jake turned to lean against the counter, brought his mug to his lips. At least Ramon made good coffee.

Not looking forward to the upcoming conversation – at all – he crossed his ankles and settled more solidly against the counter. Ben took another visual scan of the room, his blue eyes seeming to take in all the details. He nodded once before his shoulders lost a measure of tension.

About damn time.

Jake handed him a mug of coffee. He wasn't going to ask what Ben had sensed. Not now. Not here. Garrett had relaxed, that was enough. To a degree anyway.

"What is this all about?" Ramon reentered the room, his black sweats changed for black jeans and a dark blue shirt. With his black hair slicked back from his face, the dark stubble along his jaw heightened the paleness of his skin.

The man was hurting. Physically. Maybe mentally, emotionally. Jake wasn't going there if he could help it.

Ben, his gaze sharp, bought his mug to his mouth. He blew across the surface of his coffee. Steam swirled from the cup.

"Why would someone try to kill you?" Ramon glanced at Ben but focused on Jake. With his hands loose at his hips, Ramon's stance slightly favored his bum leg.

"*May* be trying to kill me." Shit. Let's just jump right to it. Whatever happened to small talk and leading up to a subject? Jake shoved his free hand through his hair. "We don't know for sure."

Ramon pinched the bridge of his nose before picking up his full mug from the counter. "Not that I wish you harm, I still don't understand why this has anything to do with me?"

"It might not." Ben shrugged and rubbed the lobe of his right ear.

"But it might." His dark eyes solemn, the corner of Ramon's mouth lifted. "You two can stand there all day if you would like, but my earlier run has done my leg in for the time being."

Pulling out a chair from the table tucked in the near alcove, Ramon settled himself with his back against the wall.

Ben followed suit, angling his chair so his own back was against the adjacent wall. Jake stayed leaning against the counter, legs crossed at the ankle, his mug in hand. Able to watch both men from a safe distance.

Silence prevailed, stretching for a few moments.

"*Mi hermano.*" Ramon's voice held a trace of affection. He glanced at Jake before extending his bad leg. "You look worse than I feel."

Brother? Jake tore his gaze away from Ramon to stare at the top of his mug. A slight fluttering in his chest, the tightness returning there, constricted his throat.

How could Ramon sit there and call him brother when Jake had all but abandoned him after he'd gotten out of the hospital? Him and everyone else who'd meant anything before his brother had died.

"Who wants you dead, *mi hermano?*" Ramon's voice, quiet yet firm, cut across Jake's thoughts.

He slanted his gaze towards the table. Ramon kneaded his bad thigh. A grimace lined his face, but his black eyes stayed focused on Jake. Ben had leaned back in his chair, his cup on the table, and now sat with his hands folded on his stomach.

Watching. Waiting.

"*May* want me dead." Jake gave him a half smile, shrugged his shoulders. "The jury's still out on that."

"I admit you have me intrigued." Ramon took a sip from his mug before cradling it between his hands. "Who is it that *may* want you dead? And what does that have to do with me?"

"The men that killed —" Shit. This was difficult.

"No." The one word, hard and final, filled the quietness of the kitchen. Ramon's eyes were lethal shards of flint.

Jake exchanged a quick, sharp look with Ben. "I killed two of their men." That was undisputable. The two men responsible for Craig's death were dead themselves.

"Rogue members." Ramon's nostrils flared. "Striking out on their own. If you hadn't killed them, their own people would have done the job."

"Those were the men who put you in the hospital?" Ben, his fingers still linked, lifted his hands and rubbed his thumbs over his mouth.

"I believe so." Ramon shrugged one shoulder. "However, on that issue they were following orders."

"To kill you?" Jake frowned.

Ramon nodded once. "Which had nothing to do with you. Or your brother."

"Bullshit." Jake's voice shook. Dammit. He pulled in a scalding breath, pushed away from the counter. "Craig is gone. How can you sit there and say it had nothing to do with him?"

"This is part of a vendetta against my family. One that started before I was born. Craig ended up collateral damage."

"Collateral —" Jake slammed his cup on the counter. Liquid sloshed over the brim. "That's *my* brother you're talking about. My *dead* brother. He was more than just collateral damage."

Ramon lifted his chin. "He got in the way."

"He was more than someone who died by mistake." Jake's nostrils widened. His fingers tightened into fists. "My brother's life counted for something. He shouldn't be dead. Not Craig."

"But he is." Ramon's flat gaze didn't waver.

"Because his own brother didn't back him. Not because he was simply in someone's way." Jake worked his jaw, willed his fingers to uncurl. "Shit."

With his gaze straight ahead, he wiped his hand down his face.

"What do you want me to say?" Stone-edged, Ramon's voice remained even. "I know about the guilt eating at your soul. Devouring you from the inside. A hidden, festering wound others can't see. Questioning and re-questioning. Going over every single moment. Every single decision. Knowing *you're* the reason Craig is dead. I know all about that, *mi hermano.*"

His breathing uneven, Jake angled his head, caught and held Ramon's gaze. The man's eyes glinted with the razor sharp edges of obsidian. Just as cold.

He'd wondered if Craig's death haunted Ortega.

He had his answer. "Craig is not collateral damage."

"Not to us." Ramon lowered his gaze, his chin. He wet his bottom lip. "But he was to the people who did this. Just as the two you killed are. My *family* is the reason behind this. The cause."

"Why?" Ben's voice, quiet and steady, swept over Jake's skin.

Startled, he glanced at the man. He'd forgotten, for a brief moment, Ben was even in the room.

Garrett's eyes narrowed, he sat forward in his chair with his elbows braced on the table. His chin rested on his linked fingers, his gaze on Ortega. "The official record is that you were caught in the middle of a drug deal gone wrong."

Jake's pulse pounded in his ears. He rubbed his forehead. "Craig had said it was a drug deal."

"That's what he thought it was." Ramon slouched in his chair. He leaned his head back, his eyes focused on the ceiling. "What I thought it was."

"What changed your perspective?" Ben picked up his mug and sipped his coffee.

Ramon lowered his gaze and met Ben's oblique stare. "Events. Realizations."

"What Craig set up outside of Eagle Crest *was* an undercover drug deal. How does that have anything to do with your family?" Jake slouched back against the counter, letting it support his weight. Otherwise he was going to fall down where he stood. "Unless your family is into dealing drugs."

One side of Ramon's mouth lifted. "Hardly."

"Why are you so sure I'm not on their target list?"

"You're wondering if they have a hit out on you."

"Something like that."

"Let me ask you, why now?" Ramon lifted his mug to his mouth, his gaze on Jake over the rim. "It's been over ten months. Why would they come after you now?"

"Events. Realizations."

One corner of his mouth lifted in a half smile, Ramon rubbed the bridge of his nose. "In our community, *mi abuelita* – my grandmother – is considered powerful. With many enemies. More than I knew."

Jake frowned. Maybe he should have sat down.

This *was* something new. Different. Weird.

Ramon's grandmother?

Powerful? That could mean so many different things. None of which were reassuring.

Ben ran the back of his fingers along his jaw. "What kind of power?"

Yeah. Cut straight to the chase. More woo-woo shit.

Beat the emotional crap, though. Any day of the week.

Jake rubbed at his chest and spared a glance for the ceiling. The knots in his neck matched the ones between his shoulder blades.

He hadn't wanted to come here. Next time he needed to listen to himself.

Ramon shrugged one shoulder. "She is who she is. Many do fear her. Just as many come to her for –" He pinched the top of his nose then shook his head. "Help. Advice."

"As in a local wise woman?" Ben arched one eyebrow.

"In a manner of speaking."

"These people – this gang – put you in the hospital because of your family." Jake rolled his head, rubbed the back of his neck. "By family, you mean your grandmother?"

"Yes." All light drained from Ramon's eyes, again leaving them flat opaque discs. His mouth tightened. "*Mi abuelita* is my family. She and I are all we have left."

"This gang is after your grandmother, but they targeted you." Ben cast a narrowed sidelong look at Jake. "Why?"

"They attacked me to strike out at *mi abuelita*. The fact they killed my partner, that is *my feud*. The ones responsible will pay."

"Ramon –" Jake caught and held the man's emotionless gaze. He dropped his hand from the back of his neck and straightened. "They're dead."

"Those two. Yes. Wild cards. Acting alone. Had it not been for the vendetta of their elders, Craig would never have been on their radar. He would still be here."

"Vendetta is the operative word, Ortega." Ben picked up his mug. "And why we're here asking about that gang."

"As I told you, there is no interest in Jake from that direction. Besides, for you, they are no longer important." Ramon brought his own mug to his mouth. His lips curved, but his eyes remained flat. "There aren't many members left of that particular family. The ones remaining have more important matters to worry about. More important than putting a hit out on you. Important things like seeing to their own survival."

"Ramon –"

"Look at me, *mi hermano*." Ramon held his cup over his bum leg. "I am not even allowed active duty."

Jake held Ramon's cool gaze for a long moment. Looking for what, he wasn't sure. Reassurance? That Ramon was right, no one from Portland wanted him dead? Or that Ramon wasn't playing rogue himself? "And when you are?"

"I will cross that when it happens."

The front door opened then closed with a whisper that managed to echo through the house and into the kitchen. Ben's head came up. His brows drew downward in a frown.

Something invisible yet completely tangible skimmed Jake's skin. The hairs on his arm stood at attention. He wiped his hand down his arm then spared a glance for Ramon. The man's face was still and his eyes appeared as if a shutter had dropped over his face.

"Ramon." A deep and sultry feminine voice called from down the open hallway. "Are you in the kitchen, *mi nieto*?"

"My family, gentlemen." Ramon raised his mug in a mock salute. "*Mi abuelita.*"

Chapter Seventeen

J AKE SQUINTED AT THE SMALL DYNAMO of a woman who breezed into Ortega's kitchen, her arms laden with canvas tote bags she dumped on the counter a few feet from where Jake stood. He straightened. The woman's presence seemed almost tangible. That somehow he could reach out and *touch* the heat burning around her.

Odd, considering how cold the morning was and the fact she'd just come from outside.

Jake sent a wary glance towards the other two men. Ramon's expression held the complete blankness that had dropped over his face the moment the front door had opened. Ben's face was also blank, the careful kind of non-expression he used to cover whatever the hell he was thinking.

Her own expression enigmatic, the woman's dark eyes scanned the room. Not missing much of anything, Jake was sure. The touch of her gaze over his body sent sparks skittering across his skin. He resisted the urge to rub his arms.

"Abuelita." His gaze on his grandmother, Ramon's voice held a small level of censure.

Humor shining from her dark eyes, she lifted her left eyebrow. The pressure rasping along Jake's skin eased, became almost cool. Like the ebb of water lapping along the shoreline, teasing his skin. There and then gone.

What the hell?

Jake glanced at Ben, but the man sat immobile, his face a careful mask of neutrality. Except for the small twitch in his right cheek.

So he had also felt — whatever the hell it was — from Ramon's grandmother. Jake wasn't completely alone in this.

She slipped away from the counter. Her flowing red skirt swayed around her slim form, her soft soled boots almost silent on the tile as she moved towards her grandson. The bangles at her wrists clicked out their own metallic melody.

Her grandson might be in his early thirties, but the smooth skin of her face belied the woman's age. Even her black hair, with its narrow streaks of white framing her face, made her seem younger than she could possibly be with a grandson Ramon's age.

With her hand on Ramon's shoulder, she turned towards Ben and Jake. Ramon lowered his chin and drummed his own silent beat against the mug cradled in his hands.

"Abuelita, this is Jake Carrigan. Craig's brother. And Jake's friend, Ben Garrett." He angled his head. "Gentlemen, my grandmother, Elena Ortega."

Ben stood and bowed from the waist. Jake nodded also. Elena stayed where she was, her hand on Ramon's shoulder. But she inclined her head at them each in turn.

His posture alert and on guard, Ben regained his seat. He braced his elbows on the table, bracketed his cup with his hands. Watched Elena.

"Your brother, he was a good man. A good friend to *mi nieto*. A true grandson to me." Elena's gaze, filled with sadness, rested on Jake. "You miss him very much."

True empathy, so different from what Althea dished out, emanated from the woman. Jake's chest squeezed tighter. "I do."

"Ma'am." Ben cleared his throat, the sound barely discernable. "Mrs. —"

Her lips curved a fraction, she slid a sly sideways glance at Ben. "Elena, please."

Ben's eyebrows went up before he nodded once. "Elena."

Her smile widened but the slyness remained. Like a self-satisfied, dark eyed cat. One with a twitching tail.

With the tips of her fingers, Elena kneaded Ramon's shoulders. She continued to stare at Ben.

"Abuelita, someone —" Ramon frowned at Jake. "Although they've not shared the details, it seems as if someone *may* be trying to harm Jake. They worry it might have something to do with Craig's death."

"Why?" She pulled her gaze from Ben to stare at Jake. "A vendetta against the Carrigans? For what purpose?"

Ramon reached up and stilled his grandmother's hand. He covered hers with his own and kept his gaze on her. "Jake killed the men who killed Craig."

Her eyes widened. "I had forgotten that."

"Have you heard anything?" Ramon patted her hand. "Is Jake on their target list?"

"No." Her mouth curved down in distaste. In turn, she speared each of the men with her dark stare. "They have only one name on their list. Mine."

Silence carried for several heart beats.

"What about your grandson?" Ben broke the reigning quiet.

"No. He is no longer their target. They now know I will do worse than kill anyone who harms my family."

"Abuelita."

She pulled her hand from her grandson's. "I speak the truth. Even if you choose to ignore what is in front of your face."

"What truth is that?" Ben leaned back in his chair.

Her skirt flowing around her legs, she moved away from Ramon. She shook her finger at Ben in passing. "None of your concern, Mr. Nosey."

Ben's eyebrows shot up. Jake's jaw clenched, not sure if he should laugh or be shocked. Even Ramon's eyes held a small measure of mirth.

Her movements graceful and seemingly unselfconscious, she set about rinsing and sorting the vegetables she'd brought in her canvas tote bags. Jake shared a glance with the two men. He thought about moving to the table. Away from Elena Ortega.

"Jake." She dried her hands on a dish towel then laid her hand on his arm. Warmth spread across his skin, heat mixing with a calm type of comfort.

From just her touch? That couldn't be normal.

But in a world turned on its head with not-normal-shit, this wasn't bad. At least it didn't *feel* bad.

She tilted her head. Her near black eyes softened and seemed to go out of focus. Okay, maybe that wasn't so good. Prickly cold followed the warmth, pinching at his skin, leaving him with the sensation of a cold burn spiraling out from Elena's touch.

He moved a step to the side and pulled his arm across his stomach, away from her touch. She blinked before patting his shoulder. Warmth again traced the pathways she'd burned with the biting chill.

Shivers chased down his spine. He cast a quick look at the other two men. Ramon's brows were deep in a censuring frown. Ben's mouth tightened, the blue of his eyes intense in the well lit room. Catching Jake's glance, one of Ben's eyebrows shot up in question.

Jake shrugged. He had less than no idea what had just happened.

He didn't want a repeat performance, though.

Getting a cup from the cabinet, Elena poured herself coffee and topped off Jake's mug. He nodded his thanks but kept his distance.

That cat smile across her lips, she moved away. Her skirt swaying, she settled against the opposite counter.

"Abuelita –"

She spared a quick, sideways glance at her grandson before focusing on Jake. "Someone wants you to go away. Although your death may not be the ultimate goal. You are a nuisance to that someone."

Jake licked his suddenly dry lips.

She sipped her coffee and glanced at Ben. That sly smile again touched her lips. "You know I'm right."

Ben inclined his head. He matched her smile.

Ramon blew out an exasperated breath. "Abuelita."

"What *mi nieto*?"

"You take this too far."

"Do I now?"

"Yes."

"Maybe you don't take it far enough, *mi hijo*." She stared at Ramon, her eyes dark and her sharp chin tilted upwards.

If the world Jake had inhabited with Hannah held remnants of the Twilight Zone, they'd just fell through the rabbit hole in Wonderland. *Alice should be showing her face at any moment.* He shook his head and glanced between the other three people.

Ortega was supposed to be the sane one. But then, why the hell did he think that? Jake rubbed the still chilled spot on his arm.

Ramon's mouth tight, he worked his jaw. "These men are here about a hit on Jake. Not to get in the middle of our disagreement."

Elena shrugged. "Maybe one has to do with the other."

"Grandmother."

Her eyes shone bright, as if glitter had been tossed into their dark realms. "Whoever is after you, Jake Carrigan, that person is not from Portland. Nor does this person have anything to do with your brother's death. Of that I am sure."

"You won't mind if we check that out through other channels?" Ben gave her a sardonic smile.

A dimple winked in and out of her left cheek. "By all means."

"My lieutenant should be able to answer any questions you have." Ramon stood. Although he addressed them, he watched his grandmother. Anger, banked deep, emanated from Ramon in thin, barely visible red-coated sheets.

What the hell? Jake straightened, set his mug on the counter behind him. He blinked, squinted. The image around Ramon stayed for several more seconds before it seemed to fold in on itself. Disappearing. Into Ramon's body.

Shit.

With his forefinger and thumb he wiped at his eyes before running a hand through his hair. One more weird thing in a string of weirdness. This was all too much too early in the morning.

Ben angled a narrowed look at Jake before he stood. He nodded at Ramon. "Thank you. For the time and the coffee."

Yeah, time. Jake gave Elena a weak smile. *Past time to go.*

Ramon took Jake's hand and met his gaze. Shadows ebbed in the dark recesses of the other man's eyes. Shadows and demons. One and the same.

"I don't know what help I can be." His voice gruff, Ramon waved a dismissive hand over his leg. "But call me when you can. Fill me in on what the hell this is really about. Keep me informed."

His chest tight, Jake nodded.

"I don't want to lose another Carrigan." Ramon pulled Jake into a one-armed hug, lightly slapped his back. He turned to Ben. One corner of his mouth curled into a half snarl. "Stay away from my grandmother."

Elena's laughter followed them down the hallway and out the front door.

"A *WITCH*?" In the front passenger seat of the rented car, Jake twisted to face Ben. "What the hell are you talking about now?"

Ben, his gaze on the road in front of him, slowed the car around a banked curve. "Bruja, the Mexican version."

"Right. Different varieties." Jake scrubbed at his eyes, leaned back in his seat. "So you are calling Elena Ortega a witch"

"Yes I am."

"Why?"

"Come on Jake. You felt, when she walked into the house, all that power."

"That's what that was, power?"

"What else would you call it?"

"Presence. Strong personality."

"She does have that."

"And Ramon told you to stay away." Jake kept his eyes shut. Garrett had the directions to Ramon's station. Traffic was light this early in the morning. He didn't need to navigate.

Ben chuckled. "We'll see."

"You might be good, Garrett, but my money's on Ortega."

Ben's smile widened.

"Back to the witch part." Not that he wanted to go there. These days it seemed he couldn't let anything go. Even with most of the answers eluding him, he still pushed. "Why is that important? Her being a witch? And why are you sure she's right? That what happened to my brother has nothing to do with what's going on now?"

"When did I say I thought she was right?"

"You didn't. But it was obvious."

"If Elena Ortega is a bruja and this group of people are after her, then maybe – possibly – they have their own bruja. If so, that could explain the psychic angle of the attacks on you."

"So you're saying Elena is wrong?"

"No. I'm thinking it's an angle that needs to be looked at." Ben shrugged, slowed around another curve. "I believe she *read* you when she touched you. That Ortega doesn't necessarily agree with his grandmother invading people's auras to do that. I also believe she's right, that whoever is after you has nothing to do with what happened to your brother. Althea Sheldon is our best bet for this."

"But we need to rule out the other possibilities." Even if they involved a feud between warring witches. How much weirder was all of this going to get? He wasn't going to touch what Garrett called being *read*. "If someone is actually trying to harm me."

"That lightning strike should have killed you. Yet here you are, worse for wear but not as bad off as you should have been. Considering."

"Considering what?" Jake threw him a sidelong look. "First it was Hannah, then Althea wanting me dead. Then there's the possibility of being, somehow, caught in the middle of a bruja war. Which, I might add, one of the concerned parties dismisses. Now we're back to Althea."

"Yes, we are."

A wide yawn took Jake by surprise. He wiped his forearm over his brow.

"Get some rest, Jake. I'll wake you when we get there."

HANNAH FLOATED IN A PEACEFUL COCOON. Calm, free from pain. A deep sigh, from the bottom of her lungs, overtook her.

Her eyes closed, she was content to simply exist in this moment. To just drift, no worries. No concerns.

No Jake.

She turned her head to the side and moaned.

Jake.

ON THE WAY ACROSS THE PARK between the river and the Portland police station, Jake worked the kinks from his neck. He'd actually slept on the drive from Ramon's place. Too bad he didn't feel refreshed.

Restless. Edgy. But not rested.

Months had passed since he'd been to his brother's station. There had been a time, after Craig died, when Jake had haunted this place. Making the drive from Eagle Crest every few days. Phone calls hadn't been enough. Hadn't gotten him the answers he wanted.

Needed.

Now he was back. Still looking for answers to impossible questions.

Ben swung the heavy door open and waited for him to pass through. Jake led the way through the maze of corridors.

"Carrigan." The lieutenant met them at his office door. He clasped Jake's shoulder. Shook his hand. "Ortega said you'd be stopping by."

"Lieutenant Dodds –" Jake focused on the big man in front of him. The easy comradery eased the words past the lump stuck square in his throat. "This is Ben Garrett."

Dodds eyed Ben then nodded. "My captain called. Said to give you what you needed."

Captain? How much pull did Garrett have?

"I appreciate that." Ben inclined his head.

"Makes it easier on me." Dodds shrugged. "On his head, not mine."

He waved them into his office, to two chairs with non-existent padding situated in front of a dominating, old and scarred desk. File folders and case files sat stacked to one side next to an overflowing ivy plant with thick vines trailing off the desk and onto the floor.

From his wife, if Jake remembered right. Dodds kept it alive because he feared her wrath if he killed the damn thing.

In the center of the wide surface a file with Craig's name typed across a white tab lay open. Jake's breath hitched in his throat. He swallowed once then stretched his legs out in front of him, glad the slight tremble of his muscles wasn't evident.

Dodds sat on the edge of that monster of a desk, one foot flat on the floor, his hands clasped and resting on his other thigh. He focused on Jake. "Ortega indicated you were interested in any additional info we have on the gang that killed Craig. Why? I thought you'd worked yourself past that."

"Their recent activity may have bearing on what we're investigating." Ben leaned back in his chair with his hand on the ankle of his crossed leg.

"Not sure how that's possible." Dodds glanced between them. Shrugged. "They've had some kind of war going on.

Internal or otherwise, their numbers have dropped considerably. Not sure they have enough members left to have *any* kind of activity going on. But then, I guess anything is possible."

You'd be surprised at what's possible. Jake kept his expression bland.

"Glad to see you're back to work." Dodds gave him a nod.

"I'm not." Jake caught the side look from Ben. "At least not with the PD. I'm working with Garrett. For now."

"As long as you're working."

Jake nodded. He eased his mouth into a semblance of a smile. Not going there, not with his brother's LT.

"Keep us informed." Dodds ran a hand over the back of his neck before he gave Ben a pointed look. "With what that gang did to Craig and Ortega, we have a vested interest in that slime."

"Understood."

"Carrigans are good cops." Dodds smiled, the look grim. He leaned over, closed the folder before tapping it against his hand. He stared at Jake. "Each and every one of them."

Jake kept his gaze locked on Dodds.

"You could do a helluva lot worse than having one on your team." Dodds spared another quick glance at Ben before he handed Jake the folder. "With regards to your brother, in spite of what went down, he was an excellent cop. A good man. I hope whatever it is you're looking for is here. I had summaries on the gang investigations added for the five years prior to losing Craig in addition to the time since."

Jake found his voice, cleared his throat. "Thanks, LT."

"Glad to be able to do it."

JAKE HELD THE CASE FILE loose on his lap, unsure if he wanted to dig right in or just hold it, afraid to look. Information he'd managed to glean on the investigation into Ortega's shooting and his own brother's subsequent death had never been official. In any way.

His grip tight on the folder, he slid a sideways look at Garrett. He owed him one. For this. However it turned out, he owed the man.

Glimpses of late morning sunlight flashed across the windshield of Ben's rental car, danced in and out of the trees lining the road as they flew past. The clean scent of pine filtered in from the open vents. Maybe there wouldn't be anything of any importance in the file, nothing to help. But maybe there would.

Jake opened the folder. Ben sent him a side long look then returned his attention to the road. The first few pages held the summaries the lieutenant had mentioned. Escalating violence followed by quiet periods.

Then Ortega's ambush and Craig's death.

Jake stared out at the passing trees for a brief moment before he squeezed his eyes shut.

Damn.

He blinked to clear his vision then glanced back at the page he held in his hand. "Cut and dry. Nothing to indicate Ortega had been hit for anything more than a drug deal gone wrong."

"They made him as a cop?"

"No indication of that."

"Simple drug deal gone wrong. Ortega in the hospital and your brother on their case?"

"That's the way it reads."

"And your brother?"

Jake shuffled the pages, found the one with his brother's name and case number. He scanned the pages. "Nothing new here either."

He shifted the pages and found another report. This one from the department shrink. Jake's breath caught on the sudden knot centered in his throat.

Why had the lieutenant included this?

He scanned the one page, went back and read it at a slower pace. Then he read the lieutenant's response.

Shit.

"What did you find?" Ben slowed to take a sharp curve.

"After Ortega was attacked, the department shrink wanted Craig pulled off duty."

"Because?"

"He threatened to kill the rat bastards."

"And?"

"Dodds went to bat for him, according to this response." Jake wet his lips. "Craig convinced him his threats were simply in reaction to the extent of Ortega's injuries. That Craig was ordered, and agreed, to stay away from the case."

"That's it?" Ben threw him a quick sideways look.

"No." Jake rubbed one hand over his forehead then shoved his fingers through his hair. Both of his legs ached, the pain pulsing in time to the rotating of the car's tires, but he'd be damned before he let that show. "There's an addendum from the Chief. Says he agreed with Dodds, but that Craig was to be put on administrative leave if he was found anywhere near the case."

"Explains why he didn't ask his own guys for help."

"Yeah." Jake let the pages settle on the folder on his lap. He stared out the window, not really seeing the passing scenery.

"Jake —" Ben blew out a breath heavy with agitation.

"I know." Jake, his fingers drumming on the side of his throbbing leg, continued to stare out the passenger window. "Not my fault."

Chapter Eighteen

J AKE, SITTING ON THE TOP STEP of his porch, eyed Althea as she moved around the front of her sleek sedan. Early evening light skimmed across the hood's dark blue surface, sparked off the front emblem. The car, like its owner, was understated elegance.

Beautiful, exotic and cold all wrapped in one tight package.

Now he was getting poetic.

He needed to stop. Both with the poetry and all these damn people dropping in on him.

"Hello, Jake." Althea's black, spiked heels dug into the soft dirt of his rutted yard.

Ben and Rily's suspicions lurked in the back of his mind. Along with the fact they'd found nothing in the file to indicate any concerns from the Portland direction.

"Evening." He stood, shoved his hands in his pockets. His fingers brushed over the ring box before he leaned against the porch post. "Nice time of day for a drive."

"Yes it is." Althea faltered over the uneven ground. Stopping, she looked up at him before she tucked a loose strand of hair behind her ear. Her smile slight, she ran her palm down the length of pale green satin hanging around her neck. Her fingers curved over the edge and she patted the spot where the ribbon disappeared under her fancy white blouse. Sunlight glinted off the deep red of her blunt nails. "I hope I'm not bothering you."

He shrugged one shoulder and didn't move.

She flicked the tip of her tongue over her lips. "I found something I thought you might like to have."

He cocked an eyebrow. No sense making this easy for her. Regardless of his own curiosity.

"Our old receptionist, the one before Amy, must have tucked this away in the file cabinet." Althea glanced behind him, towards the screen door.

Whatever she held, whatever it was she wanted, he didn't want her inside his house. Might be for stupid reasons, but his stomach clenched at the thought of her inside his home.

Her lips tightened a fraction, but instead of saying anything else she held out a hand. Gold flashed in her palm.

His movements slow and deliberate, he pushed away from the post, took the two steps down without too much protest from his aching body. "What is it?"

"Hannah's bracelet."

Vicious, a fist-sized knot twisted his gut, the sudden pain sucker-punching him. He struggled to keep his reaction from showing.

Hannah's bracelet. Molded gold with small diamonds scattered along the thin surface. The bracelet he'd bought her for her birthday a year ago. The only thing she'd worn when they'd made love in that endless blue void.

Why was Althea bringing this to him now?

Ignoring the way his legs objected, he took the extra steps to stand in front of her. Without taking a breath and careful to avoid touching her, he lifted the jewelry from her outstretched hand.

The gold was warm. His throat worked to get past the golf-ball sized knot lodged there. He closed his fingers into a fist over the bracelet.

"I thought you'd like to have it." Althea laced her fingers, loose, in front of her. She shrugged her shoulders. Once.

The effect should have been uncomfortable nonchalance. The slight gleam in her eyes ruined the effect.

Think, man. Stop reacting.

Hannah's bracelet. The one he'd played with when she'd lain next to him, her arm stretched over his chest and her breath caressing his skin.

God.

"Thank you." He could be polite. He wanted Althea the hell away from him. Now. But he could be polite.

"Are you all right?"

Maybe polite only went so far. "Why?"

"Excuse me?"

"Why are you asking that?"

Althea blinked twice, but that fake smile never faltered. "You looked a little peaked, that's all."

Jake shrugged his left shoulder, tried to keep from swaying. His legs threatened to buckle. He couldn't allow that to happen. "Hard day."

"Well." She angled her head to the side and flicked a glance to the house behind him. "Anything I can do to help?"

Oh, you've helped enough. The bracelet bit into his palm.

The silver car pulling around his barn saved him from answering. Saved him from telling her there was no way she was getting inside his home.

He spared a quick glance for the newest arrival. This place was fast becoming Grand Central. Right now, though, he was okay with having one more person here.

Her perfect brows drawn together, Althea turned her head towards the vehicle. While her attention was elsewhere, he eased back to sit on the top step of his porch and cradled Hannah's bracelet between his hands.

The silver car's engine came to an abrupt stop. Silence stretched until Ben Garrett levered his tall frame out of his car. He slammed the door.

"Jake." Ben nodded once in his direction then turned towards the woman standing between them. "Althea Sheldon? You're a hard woman to track down."

"And you are?"

His hands tucked in his pockets, Ben jerked his chin in a short nod. "Benjamin Garrett."

"Hannah's supposed uncle."

"No supposed about it."

"She never mentioned you. Not once."

"The two of you were close?"

"Extremely. Especially towards the end."

"How nice. Her mother and I didn't exactly get along."

Althea's chin lowered. She crossed her arms over her chest. "Amy told me you'd been in a couple of days ago."

"And yesterday." Ben moved to stand a few feet away from her. He mirrored her stance. "And an hour ago."

"Really?" One brow arched, she threw a quick glance in Jake's direction.

He leaned his shoulder against the porch post for additional support but kept a benign look plastered on his face.

Ben smiled, the look predatory. He moved a step closer. "Why are you avoiding me, Althea?"

A flash of impatience, so quick Jake would have missed it if he'd blinked, darkened her eyes for a brief moment.

"How ridiculous." She held her ground. The smile on her mouth didn't touch her eyes. "I'm a busy woman, Mr. Garrett."

"Too busy to give me a call?" Ben lifted his own brow. "I know Amy gave you my number."

"We have nothing to talk about, so why bother?"

Now the dance was getting interesting. Jake shifted his position on the step to ease the ache running down his right leg. The bracelet in his hand warmed.

He opened his fist. Waning sunlight glinted off the diamonds. Ben's frown deep, he shot a quick look in Jake's direction.

Althea moved back. Her stance reminded Jake of an alley cat hunching her muscles, gathering her energy and readying herself to strike at her prey. He closed his fist tight over the bracelet.

The woman blinked and lowered her chin. "I need to get back to town." Without taking her gaze from Ben, she nodded in Jake's direction. "Let me know if you need anything else."

"Right."

That raptorial smile still in place, Ben held out his hand. "Call me, Althea."

She glanced at his outstretched hand then back at his face. "We'll see."

With her posture stiff she took a step backwards, turned and made her way to her car. Once in the vehicle, without a glance in their direction, she backed out and pulled her vehicle around Garrett's.

Ben raised his proffered hand and flicked a wave at the back end of the car. Brake lights glinted just before the car rounded the barn.

"She didn't want you touching her." Jake's movements slow, he stretched his leg to rest his heel on a lower step.

"Rather astute of you."

"You wanted to touch her."

"Again, rather astute. She holds herself in tight, not much of her essence gets out of her personal sphere. I'd have liked to have had at least a taste of her."

"A taste?"

"Psychic jargon. Means I wanted to sample her energy signature. If I can tell the difference between the two signatures, I should be able to tell if Althea is laying Hannah's over her own."

"Wait a minute." Jake rubbed his knee. "The hijacking you were talking about yesterday? I still don't understand how that is even possible?"

"I admit that with Hannah not having a body, it would seem to be somewhat trickier."

"Somewhat?" Now he was a damn mimic.

"Usually blood is used. No body. No blood."

Jake stared at Ben. "You're shitting me."

"No, I'm not. It was Hannah's signature I felt. She's either doing all of this on her own or someone is using her."

"Someone like Althea?" The bloodied walls from his nightmare filled his mind.

"Yes."

Jake blinked the images away. He stared across his yard. "Althea maintained a pretty sedate front for how pissed you made her."

"She's a piece of work. I want her for this just on that alone." Ben strode over to the porch. He pointed at the bracelet. "What is that?"

"A piece of jewelry."

Ben lifted a brow.

"Hannah's. Althea said her last receptionist must have filed it away." Jake rubbed his thumb over the edge. The gold was warm to his touch. "It's definitely Hannah's. I gave it to her for her birthday last year."

"Can I see it?" Palm up, Ben held out his hand.

Without meeting Ben's gaze, Jake closed his fingers over the bracelet. "She was wearing this the last time –"

He didn't want to go there. The whole idea of explaining the void and what he and Hannah had shared in that place seemed wrong. Sacrilege.

"The last time?"

"That I saw her." The truth, such as it was. "She had this on." Jake dropped the bracelet in Ben's hand and leaned back against the post.

Ben examined the jewelry. His fingers hovered over the edges. "This doesn't feel right."

"Like it feels like Hannah, but not quite?"

Ben cocked his brow and the corner of his mouth lifted. "Right. Her energy signature is quite strong on this. It underlies everything else. Maybe too strong. Curious how Althea just happened to find it. Now. At this time."

Jake wanted to kick himself. If he hadn't let the bracelet sucker punch him, if he hadn't been so hell-bent on keeping the woman out of his home, maybe he would have been thinking straighter and gotten a few more answers.

"Is it booby trapped? Like the lightning rod?" Jake shook his head. "I don't believe I just asked that question."

"We all have issues, son. I can't tell if there's a trap attached. Not for sure." Ben turned the bracelet over, ran his fingers over the inside surface. He frowned and ran the bracelet between his thumb and forefinger. "Her signature shouldn't be this strong. Not after so many months."

"What you're doing is something like psychometry?"

Ben sent a quick glance his way, then returned his attention to the bracelet. "Been researching on the internet?"

"Yeah." No sense denying that. "I had some free time this afternoon."

"Yes. It's a bit like psychometry,"

"Her essence could last several lifetimes. What's a few months in comparison?"

Ben turned his head and leveled his gaze on Jake.

"According to what I've read." Out of his depth, Jake plowed forward anyway. "Isn't her signature the same thing as her essence?"

"Yes and no."

"Real definitive there, Garrett."

"The reality of it is just about that solid." Ben shrugged, his fingers still rubbing the jewelry. "The essence you've read about, what hangs on, is somewhat like a memory the object retains. Like a quick snapshot of that point in time mixed with what the person was feeling."

"A part of that memory is the essence of the person holding the object?"

Ben nodded with his eyebrows drawn downward. "Like an imprint. Especially if the emotion is strong."

"A signature is different how?"

"There's the crux of the matter. A signature is part of the person. Like a psychic fingerprint, it's unique to each individual. Objects, like this bracelet, can retain a sense of the owner's signature. Especially things important to the person.

"Without continual contact, the signature fades over time. Hannah's been gone too long for hers to be this strong. Especially if this has been sitting in a file somewhere."

"Wait a minute. You said the Jeep and the lightning rod had her signature. She's dead, so if it fades, how is that possible?"

"That's part of what's been bothering me. I had wondered if was possible for her ghost to have that much power.

Enough to retain that strong a signature. But Hannah hadn't really manifested much in the way of talent before she died. At least according to what I'd picked up from you and Rily."

"Her ghost?"

Ben nodded. He held the bracelet up between them. "See, this has a touch of your signature, your energy. Not because you gave it to her, but because you sat here holding it with such strong emotion. Shock. Longing. Passion and anguish. Pain. In short time, all of that will fade. At least on the bracelet."

Jake pressed his back against the porch post. What the hell? The man read what he'd felt? From Hannah's bracelet? His feelings had really attached themselves? He stopped himself from sticking his hand in his pocket, from touching the ring box. "Back to the ghost thing."

"Hannah's doesn't feel right."

"You've said that before."

Ben nodded. "She's not like any other ghost I've come across. It's like she's not really there. But she is. It's the same with the signature left on your Jeep and that lightning rod. It's definitely her. But it shouldn't be."

"Ghosts don't have signatures to leave behind? Because I know it was Hannah who stopped the Jeep."

"Yes, ghosts can have a signature. In those cases I can usually feel them. I get nothing from Hannah's. Nothing at all."

"It's not just a case of you being off your game?"

Ben aimed a narrowed glance at him. "No."

Jake shrugged. "Had to ask."

"Umm." Ben held the bracelet up to the fading evening light. "This hasn't been tucked away in a file. A flesh and blood, live person has been wearing it."

"What?" Jake blinked twice. "Hannah —"

"I'm not saying it's been on Hannah." Ben lifted his other hand, palm outward. "But it's been on someone's wrist. And there isn't another signature. Nothing on here from Althea. There are so many variables, so many ways to hijack Hannah's energy. That might be why I'm having trouble sensing her ghost."

"She was wearing the bracelet yesterday morning."

"What?"

"Yesterday. Hannah wore her bracelet yesterday morning."

With deep lines between his brows, Ben's mouth opened then closed. His gaze locked on Jake, he lowered his chin. "What are you talking about?"

"I saw her. After that lightning hit me." His hands dangling between his knees, Jake shrugged. In too deep to back out now, he wet his lips and plowed ahead. "Before you hauled me inside, I was someplace else. Everything was dark with a weird blue light. No shape to anything. Nothing distinctive. But Hannah was there."

"God, Jake." Ben rubbed his hand over his face then stared at him, the blue of his eyes dark and intense in the dusk. "You did die."

He shrugged one shoulder. "I wondered."

"And? Any particular reason you didn't share any of this earlier?"

Jake wet his lips again. *Because it's none of your damn business.* He sucked in a deep breath. "It felt private."

Ben's gaze still locked on him, he nodded. "I'm sure it did. However, this is obviously important. You're sure Hannah wore this bracelet?"

"Yes, I am." Jake had been the one playing with it. It was all she'd worn. He was sure.

"You actually saw her? Talked with her?"

"Yeah."

"Were you able to touch her?"

The knots in his neck tightened. "Yeah."

"That changes everything." Ben sat on the top step of the porch, next to Jake. He sat the bracelet on the board between them. With his elbows on his knees, he linked his fingers and tapped the pads of his thumbs together. "Is Hannah here now?"

"No. I haven't sensed her for a while."

"But she was here earlier today? Inside the house?"

Jake shook his head. "Not today. Yesterday. You and Rily pretty much freaked her out."

"She's an adult."

"She's a ghost."

"I wonder."

"Now what the hell are you wondering?"

"Jake, none of this is normal. It's almost as if Hannah isn't really dead."

"Ben –" The muscle in Jake's cheek twitched. This wasn't happening, no matter how much he wanted the words to be accurate. "Don't go there. Don't play me with that."

"I'm not playing you. But, I don't have anything except a gut reaction. This whole thing has been off from the beginning."

"That doesn't mean Hannah's not dead." *What if Garrett was right?* His throat too tight to swallow, he angled his head to stare at the other man.

"No it doesn't." Ben leaned forward. With his elbows still on his knees, he rested his chin on his clasped hands and stared out across the darkening fields. "But you died or at least passed into another dimension of some sort. And Hannah was there."

"Pretty much what I already said."

"Thinking out loud here, son." Ben chuckled, the sound low. "And now you're here."

"She saved my life again."

With a slight cant to his head, Ben threw Jake a sideways look. "Because you *were* dead?"

"In that other realm —" Geez, with every breath he seemed to be getting further and further into that strange land Garrett lived in. "I couldn't move."

"Similar to the way you were on the couch yesterday?"

"Worse." Jake picked up the bracelet, ran his thumb around the inside. "I couldn't move at all. I lay flat on my back and my entire body hurt. I don't think I've ever hurt that bad. Hannah touched me. Every place she touched the pain disappeared."

"She healed you."

"Saved my life. I believe I was, if not already dead, then dying." He met Ben's gaze. "And you're right. That makes twice in a short number of days."

"Let's hope you're as lucky with attempt number three." Ben nodded at the bracelet. "I'm curious. Is Hannah still wearing that, now that it's here. Essentially in this world and not hers."

"I don't know." Jake cradled the jewelry between his hands. "You really think Althea is behind all of this?"

"I do. And that bracelet is, somehow, part of the next attempt on your life."

Chapter Nineteen

BLACKNESS EDDIED AROUND HANNAH. Swirled and mixed with the deepening blue, surrounded her and pressed heavy on her chest. Dark grey pulsated at the edges of her vision.

The lure of rest, of just giving in, pulled at her, merged with the overwhelming desire to close her eyes. To let the heaviness take her under. To just drift.

But she couldn't. Not yet.

Not until Jake was out of danger.

Her chest heaving with exertion, she sucked in short, blistering pants of air and forced her eyes to stay open.

Stop fighting, Hannah. The voice came from far above.

Above and to the right? Male or female?

Why couldn't she tell?

Gritting her teeth, she strained to turn her head.

Hannah. Stop. This isn't getting either of us anywhere.

Cool fingertips ran down both sides of her face. The backside of those fingers caressed upward, over her cheeks, sending cold shivers in their wake.

Shush, sweet Hannah. Just relax. Our little problem will soon be taken care of and won't cause you or me any more grief.

A soft chuckle settled in the air and pulsed with the dark grey.

"Nooo." The sound guttural, even to her own ears, Hannah thrashed her head away from the icy touch's stain. Hard, cold fingers gripped her chin and held her head in place.

Stop.

"No." She had to get away. Find Jake. Her fingers curled into a loose fist, she swung her arm upward. Made contact. The jolt vibrated downward to convulse through her weakened muscles.

That's enough. The words, low and harsh, breathed across her ear. A hand grabbed her wrist and twisted it, sending spasms through her body. *Hannah, this is for the best. We need to work together. That's the only way this will work.*

Using the pain to fuel her refusal, Hannah focused on the grip on her arm. Like the idea of her flinging rocks across the pond, she pushed outward a vision of nails raking the person's skin.

The grip loosened. *Bitch. How did you do that?*

An image of Jake hovered at the front of Hannah's mind. She grabbed at the picture. The air pulsed around her.

Sprawled in a heap on a hardwood floor, her entire body trembled.

Away from that voice, away from the darkness.

Big, quake like tremors shook her from the inside out, leaving her lungs screaming for air, her harsh gasps of breath sounding as if she'd just run a major marathon at a high altitude without being prepared.

Breathe. She focused on each breath. In, then out. Several moments passed.

Still shaking, although not as hard, she pushed up on her hands. Through the curtain of her hair she slid a glance around.

Light from a small lamp cast a soft glow through the room.

Jake's bedroom.

With his back against the headboard, he sat with his legs stretched in front of him and crossed at the ankles. Her breath quickened again, in relief this time.

Here was safe, at least for this moment.

"Hannah?" His voice, deep and concerned, matched his frown. Wearing jeans, with his chest and feet bare, he had never looked so good.

"Here." Hating the way her voice shook, she gathered herself. Although her legs were wobbly, she stood and rubbed her hands up and down her arms. The friction helped a little. She wasn't cold, not on the outside.

Inside was a different matter.

This was the second time, third if she counted Jake, someone had touched her since she'd regained her senses. Or whatever the hell it was that had happened on her birthday.

"Are you all right?"

"Define that, would you?"

"That good?"

"Yeah." She stared out the bare window. The thin, grey line of dawn glimmered over the pines in the distance. Rain splattered hard against the pane, sliding down the glass in long, jagged rivets of water. "How long have I been gone this time?"

"A day and a half."

She shivered.

"You disappeared when I came back from checking on what's left of the lightning rod. You were there and then you weren't."

"I should probably stop doing that."

"Yeah." His lips twitched. "I'd appreciate it if you would. My heart stops every single time you *vanish*."

"Please." A ripple of hysteria bubbled low in her throat. "*You* need to stop doing *that* heart stopping stuff."

"Doing –" A grimace pulsed along his jaw, tightening his mouth. "My best."

The ache of his pain echoed through her body, settled at her nerve endings, spread through her muscles.

"You're still hurting." She eased onto the edge of his bed. Her legs protested, but she sat cross-legged anyway and rubbed her knees.

"Yeah, well." He shrugged, the movement slow and cautious.

Unwilling to stop herself, she stretched her senses out, wrapped them around him. The sharp, piercing pain radiating through his body throbbed even more fully in hers.

With that pain in the forefront of her mind, she focused on it, on the shape and denseness of the throbbing red color, on the *feel* of it vibrating between her body and his.

After several long seconds, his pain receded to a point low in her gut, to a small swirl of dull residual ache that tightened in on itself.

"Wow." Jake blinked several times before he shoved his fingers through his hair. "Everything still hurts, but it's manageable. Thank you for doing whatever it was you did."

She let out the breath she'd held and rubbed at her knees again.

"Are you still wearing your bracelet?"

In reflex she covered her bare wrist with her other hand. "It's gone."

"When did you lose it?"

"I don't know." Her stomach sank in on itself. How could she have lost her bracelet? She pressed her lips together to keep them from trembling.

One more thing taken from her by this strange existence.

In and of itself, the jewelry didn't matter. But Jake had given it to her. The last tangible piece she had of him.

Now she'd lost that, too.

Pain spiked across her scalp, stealing the air from her lungs. Jake grimaced, drawing in his own sharp breath.

"Baby —"

"No." She held up her hand, her fingers spread wide then curling. *He felt her pain.* The link wasn't one way. That couldn't be good. She closed her eyes and concentrated on evening out her breathing. Counted to ten. Opened her eyes.

"I don't know what you're doing, but whatever it is, we should bottle it and make a fortune." Jake uncrossed his ankles. His movements slow, he brought his legs up to plant his feet on the bed. He draped his arms over his knees, letting his hands hang lose. "I couldn't have done that even ten minutes ago. Thank you, Baby."

With her bottom lip between her teeth, she searched his face for any lingering signs of tormenting pain. *I'm so sorry, Jake.* Easing his hurt was one thing, him feeling hers was another.

The lines marking his face eased. His breathing settled to a more peaceful rhythm. The rise and fall of his bare chest evened out.

"How did you know my bracelet was gone?" She pushed herself off the bed. Jake was too damn close. Instead of watching him, she paced to the window. "Do you know where it is?"

"In the barn."

She swung around to face him. "Why is it there?"

"Because Ben thought it was safer if it wasn't here in the house."

With one hand still rubbing her wrist, Hannah stared at him. "You're not making any sense."

"I know I'm not. None of this makes any sense."

Drawing in a deep breath, she massaged her temples, hoping Jake couldn't feel this new spike of pain. She gave up staying away from him and perched back on the edge of his bed.

"There you are." He sighed and rolled his head. The knots in his neck made a soft pop in the quietness of the room.

The way he sensed her presence eased a small portion of the ache inside her.

"Althea brought the bracelet over yesterday evening."

"But I had it on when we –" Her cheeks heated. "When you –"

"Yeah. You did." Jake exhaled a deep breath and closed his eyes. He leaned his head back, the exposed lines of his throat taunt. "Maybe the bracelet wasn't real in that void."

"Any more than I am."

"I didn't mean –"

"Yes you did." Her words, simple and without inflection, hung between them.

He swore soft under his breath.

"Maybe you're right. Maybe I'm not real, either." No matter how she felt. Now or before, in his arms. In that void.

"What difference does it make? Whether you're real or not? Or whether the bracelet was actually in your world or here in mine?" With his head angled down and his eyes open a small slit, Jake stared in her direction. "At this point?"

She shrugged. The corners of his eyes crinkled.

"Why are you smiling?" She frowned at him.

"You shrugged. The way you always do when I'm being dismissed."

"Dismissed? I don't –" She swallowed around the bubble stuck in her throat. "You can see me?"

"No. But I'm able to sense you." Self-satisfaction laced his words. "More than I could before. Where you're at, your movements. Your pain."

"You *do* feel me?"

"Probably something to do with the way you blew my mind in that void." A purely masculine chuckle settled over the edges of her nerves. "I feel you, Baby."

A spiral of heat caught and swirled in her belly. She couldn't stop the moan gathering in her throat.

Jake.

Just like that, she wanted him again.

With her hand pressed to her chest and her head back, she swore his fingers traced down her neck, over the back of her hand. The touch soft and slow.

But that couldn't be real, either.

She leveled a glance at him. He still sat forward, his chin tucked against his chest, a small smile on his mouth. She lifted her hand from her chest. In her mind she touched that mouth, lingered over his bottom lip.

His lips parted. Mentally she slipped her finger inside his mouth, stroked the tip of his tongue once.

"God, Hannah." The groan tore from him and vibrated through her body. "I need you in my arms."

Her thoughts snapped back. She couldn't be in his arms.

"Hannah?" Jake lifted his head, his eyes narrowed and staring in her direction. "What's wrong? Why did you pull away?"

"We can't do this, Jake."

"Hannah —"

"I'm not real. You said so yourself. More than once."

"But —"

"Rily's right."

"Don't go there."

"She is. All I'm doing is holding you here. In place. In time."

"I have a choice in this." Jake pushed off the bed. He stood with his naked chest heaving, his jaw tight. "It's not all on you."

"This isn't healthy."

"Let me worry about that."

"I can't." She lifted her hand, the urge to smooth that spot on his jaw, to touch him and sooth away the panic darkening the green of his eyes, welled inside.

She fought to resist, when it would be so easy to give in, to reach out. But she couldn't, no matter what she wanted. No matter what he wanted.

To protect her own heart, she'd left him once. Now, she needed to find the strength to leave him again. To protect his life.

Jake, panic blossoming full blown in his chest, turned in a circle with his hands in fists at his side. *Hannah. No.*

"Don't leave me. Not again. Not now." He choked the words out of his tightening throat. "Please don't."

Silence swelled over him, mixed with the emptiness of the room. He spun around, his fist ready to swing at something.

Anything.

Dammit all to hell.

His breathing jagged, he shoved his fingers through his hair, gripped the back of his neck. Shit. He glanced at his bed. At the glowing clock on the night-stand. At the rain drenched, bare window.

Dawn had crept over the tops of the trees. A wet, grey dismal dawn. Promising a wet, grey, dismal day.

She was gone.

He rubbed his chest, his skin cool in the cold morning air. Ignoring the ache centered at his core, he grabbed a T-shirt from his drawer and jerked it over his head. His muscles protested, but he ignored that ache, too, and shoved his feet into his running shoes.

He left the stick he'd used as a walking aid on the floor beside his bed. Right now he didn't want any help, not even from a damn piece of wood.

Sprawled out on the couch, Ben still slept. Good. The last thing Jake wanted right now was that man awake. With his hooded eyes looking right through him. No, Ben Garrett could stay asleep and leave him the hell alone.

His movements stealthy, Jake shushed Sadie when she joined him. The two of them made their way outside. She yawned wide and settled in the corner of the porch, her head on her paws, her gold eyes watching him. He stood on the top step with his legs braced apart. His hands on his hips, he drew in a deep breath.

The rain had finally settled into a light mist, it tangled the air, mixed with the heavy scent of pine. Water covered the ground in the barely dawn greyness, leaving everything soaking wet. A damp, cool breeze ruffled his hair.

His gaze swept the field. Nothing out of place. Nothing menacing. No Hannah.

He pushed his senses outward, searching the tree line, the path beyond leading to the waterfall. A few short days ago he would have laughed at the thought of what he now did so effortlessly.

Woo-woo, his ass.

There, along the trail, his senses found Hannah. On her way to the waterfall? Maybe.

He took the steps two at a time, limped halfway across the rutted yard before he stopped. The tremble in his weakened knees hardly registered.

What was he doing? In the past, forcing the issue had never worked with Hannah. Why did he think it would now?

His fingers spread, he rubbed his chest again. He knew where she was, where she was headed.

She might not be speaking to him, but she hadn't left. Not for good. Not yet. He would let things lie for a short time. Give her space. Figure out what to say to her, how to convince her to stay. This time.

Blowing out a puff of breath, he arched his neck and stared at the heavy grey sky.

Now what?

He angled his head to glance at his house. His empty bedroom held no appeal. He wasn't in the mood to answer any more of Ben's pointed questions. Besides, he didn't have the energy it would take to evade those same questions. Added to that, the man needed his sleep.

Right. Like he cared if Garrett got his eight hours. His mouth lifted in a humorless smile. With a last look at the tree line hiding the start of the waterfall trail, he swung his gaze to the barn.

He had chores to do. Chores had always been good for what ailed him. Good thing he had a lot of them backed up because what ailed him right now wasn't going away any time soon.

Three steps closer to the barn Jake stopped again.

That damn bracelet was in there. Somewhere. Last night Ben had done something to it, something that had dampened Hannah's signature. Hell, whatever he'd done had left the thing feeling as if it didn't even really exist. Then Ben had stashed it somewhere in the barn.

Jake stole another glance at his house before he swung his gaze back to the barn. Did he really want to go in there?

Not that he seriously believed a bracelet could hurt him.

But then a few days ago he hadn't believed a lightning rod would knock him out, either.

Maybe he'd concentrate on chopping wood.

Outside. Should be safe.

He glanced at the field and the downed rod still lying on the ground. An eagle flew overhead, its lonely screech echoing inside his head. He followed the bird's path across the gloomy sky.

He wasn't a fool. At least not most days. He wasn't a coward, either. But all this stuff about booby traps and someone wanting him dead made the hair on his arms stand to attention. And it was more than the cold morning air giving him goose bumps.

Paranoid or not, being out in wide open didn't seem to be the best course of action. His knees protesting, he made his way to the side of the barn, skirting the woodpile. He snatched his axe from where he'd left it against the stack of wood.

The weight of the handle in his hands, the solidness of his grip, began to settle his thoughts. He readied a log on the post for splitting.

"Jake!" Ben's yell rent the air, punctuated by Sadie's frantic barking. "Where the hell are you?"

The axe clutched in both hands, poised over his shoulder, Jake swung to face the direction of Ben's panicked approaching voice.

"Get away from the barn!"

Twisting away from the woodpile, the axe still in his hands, Jake spun. His left knee buckled.

Crap.

He staggered, struck the top edge of the axe into the ground to catch himself, to push away from the barn.

Heat and exploding wood strafed him, knocking him off his feet. He lost his grip on the axe handle. Reddish, yellow light burned into his eyes, filled his vision.

"Jake?" Ben's voice came from a long distance. Rough hands clasped his chin. "Boy, don't you leave now. Stay with me."

He tried to listen to Ben, to focus on the man's voice, but everything darkened. The weird reddish light began seeping away. Blackness edged his vision.

"Hannah? Oh, God. If you're here, Hannah, anchor Jake. Don't let him go."

HER ARMS WRAPPED TIGHT around Jake's limp body, Hannah struggled to lower him to what passed for the ground in the swirling blueness of the void area. Frantic, she kept a hand flat on his chest and tapped his cheek with her other one.

"Jake?"

His chest didn't move. He didn't breath.

She tapped his cheek harder.

He couldn't be dead. She spread both hands over his chest and stomach. *Please don't be dead.*

Her own breath hitching, she scanned the area around them. But everything was dark. The blue glow illuminated nothing.

She swung her gaze back to Jake. Her fingers scrunched the material of his T-shirt. "Sweetheart? Please answer me."

Smoothing his shirt in quick, sharp movements, she searched her mind for the distant memory of CPR. Her breath in short, panicked puffs, she angled his head back, pinched his nose closed and laid her mouth over his.

Laughter, dark and vile, filled the air.

Hannah's shoulders tightened. Her entire body tensed. But she continued the CPR.

"Like that's really going to work." The feminine voice, full of vicious satisfaction, scrapped along her spine. "He's dead. Finally."

"No." Hannah sucked in another breath and with her hands one on top of the other on Jake's chest, pumped.

"That's quite enough, Hannah. I know how it feels, to lose someone." The voice lowered, softened. "I am sorry this had to happen to you. But there is a time when you have to accept. To let it go."

"No." She couldn't give up. Jake couldn't be dead. She wouldn't let him be dead.

"Hannah." The voice hardened, surrounded her, pressed at her with an invisible weight. "Now."

Prickles bit at her spine, banded to become more solid, to scrape down her back with an ominous stroke. She threw a desperate glance over her shoulder.

What felt like fingers still touched her, but there was nothing there.

She choked past a bubble of hysterical laughter, spread her arms over Jake's prone body. Whatever the hell that was, she wasn't going to let it touch him.

That invisible hand clutched her sweater, yanked.

"No." She hunched forward to brace herself against the pull.

Air thickened as invisible arms snaked around her waist, tightened, wrenched her away from Jake.

"Noooo." She grabbed at him. Her fingers brushed his T-shirt.

The arms around her squeezed and the invisible fingers dug into her stomach. She struggled, twisted and pushed at the unseen arms.

Like passing through over-thickened sugar water, Hannah couldn't manage a solid connection with whatever held her.

She shoved her hands through the syrupy air, reaching for the other side of the arms.

Her struggles made no impact on what held her tight in its grasp.

Frantic, she swung her gaze back to Jake. He still lay where she'd left him. Absolutely still. Not even his chest moved.

If he was dead, why did he just lay there like that? Here in this blasted void he should at least be awake.

Like her.

Shouldn't he?

"Let me go." She flung her body, hard, to the left. One of the arms loosened. The other locked tighter around her waist.

This wasn't working.

She let her body drop, becoming dead weight. Both unseen arms lost their grip. Scrambling to her right, away from the fingertips she could feel reaching for her, she crouched and kept her body compressed. Made herself a smaller target.

Her breathing ragged, she flung her hands in front of her. The mental picture of a solid wall sprang into her head.

Why the hell not? That had worked once, when she'd wanted to stop Rily from leaving Jake's living room.

Fixing that image firmer in her mind, she solidified it and imagined it several inches thick.

A loud thump sounded. The air in front of her vibrated hard against her hands. Her body wobbled with the second thump.

But the invisible fingers didn't grab her again. Not yet, anyway. For right now, whatever the hell she was doing was working. Her mouth set in a thin line, she mentally added another couple of inches to the picture in her mind, thickening her invisible wall.

Against an invisible enemy.

That gurgle of rising hysteria threatened to drown her. She swallowed past it and stole a quick glance at Jake's prone body.

He hadn't moved.

She needed to check his pulse, needed to lay her hand flat over his chest, continue the CPR, but she didn't dare.

Not with whatever was out there stalking her.

How was she going to protect them both? When she had no idea what direction the threat would come from next.

Easing in front of Jake, she sculpted the mental image of her wall into a thick bubble encapsulating them both.

With her lip between her teeth, she did a quick visual scan of the surrounding area. Nothing had changed. Black darkness mingled with that dark blueness, almost pulsing with its own dim eerie light. The edges indistinguishable. Indistinct.

"Hannah." The voice, definitely female, oozed from the dark air. "Enough of this. You can't save him. Leave him there so we can move forward."

Ben and Rily's suspicions loomed in her mind. "Althea?"

"Yes." Pride, like a teacher's for a prized student, welled in her voice. "Right first guess. I'm impressed."

A small, subtle tingle along the edge of Hannah's shielding bubble sent quivers through her body. With a quick reinforcing thought and a flick of her fingers the sensation disappeared.

She drew in a shaky breath.

"Hannah, please. This is getting old."

Try it from this side of the equation. Hannah scooted back the last few inches until her heel touched Jake's arm. Once there, she focused, sending more fortifying thoughts into her invisible bubble.

How long the shield would hold, she had no idea. She wasn't even sure how she'd managed to construct the thing in the first place. Figuring that out had to wait until later.

There had better be a later.

Right now, she needed another option, before she ran out of alternatives.

"Why are you doing this, Althea?"

Like fingers across a chalkboard, a long, low sigh scrapped across the surface of the bubble. "Do we really need to go there?"

"I don't see why not." Was this how Jake had felt, talking to what amounted to thin air? And being answered. "We're not going anywhere just yet."

"You really should come back to your body."

"What? My bod –" Small spasms convulsed along Hannah's spine, radiating sparks of pure pain to each nerve ending.

"Hannah." Impatience hung heavy in the air, clinging to the outside of the bubble with an almost tangible existence. "We have important work to finish. Today. I can't do that work if you're floating around out there."

"What are you talking about?" The words choked her, leaving her sounding hoarse and unsteady.

I have a body?

"You're an important part of my mother's legacy." Althea's disembodied voice, edged with anger, sharpened. "Without you, our research can't continue."

A chill scudded over Hannah's skin, giving an icy mix to the small electric convulsions piercing her spine. She swallowed. "What are you talking about?"

"Our research into your illness. Jake Carrigan was threatening everything. Snooping around. Asking questions. As if he really ever cared about what happened to you."

"Maybe he does."

"God, Hannah." A soft, feminine and almost delicate snort filled the air. "So pathetic. If he *cared*, then where was he when you were sick? Hmmm? Where has he been all these past months since you *died*?"

Jake's arm brushed the back of Hannah's heel. A jolt of pure energy sizzled up her leg, coiled at the pit of her stomach.

He wasn't dead.

At least not here, in this place, at this time.

She couldn't let the other woman know.

"None of that is any of your business, Althea." She pressed her palm to her stomach. Energy pulsed there, throbbed in time to her heartbeat.

From Jake's touch?

Could she use it? Redirect it?

How?

"Avoiding the subject isn't going to change things." Understanding coated Althea's voice.

In the past, why had she allowed herself to believe in the woman's sympathy? To accept the compassion without question?

"No, it doesn't change anything, does it?" Hannah wet her lips. She had to alter something soon. This standoff couldn't last forever.

Her hands cupped together, she mentally gathered the energy at her core, the jumbled mix of what coiled in her stomach from Jake's touch and what she dredged from inside herself. The image of that energy balled between her palms and pulsed with its own silver tinged eerie glow.

In these circumstances, it was quite beautiful, would be even more so if it helped protect them.

On an out breath, she tossed that throbbing light up and into her bubbled shield. Golden glitter scattered across the pseudo surface then dissipated.

Had it done a damn thing?

A sharp crack sounded in the air, like a palm smacking a hollow surface. The bubble of her shield shuddered but held firm.

"Give it up, Hannah." Irritation raked Althea's voice. "Whatever you're doing isn't going to work. Not for long."

Another crack whipped across the shield's surface, followed close by a delicate, muted curse.

Jake's fingers wrapped loose around Hannah's foot. His thumb rubbed a circle over her ankle. A bolt of pure power coursed through her body, whirled over her skin, pulsed at her fingertips.

"Do you feel that, Hannah?" Jake's gruff voice rasped from behind her. "That flow of energy between us? Can you use it? Direct it?"

"How is it going to make any difference?" Her voice low, she scanned the area again. With each stroke of Jake's thumb, power again coiled tight in the pit of her stomach.

"Can you tap into me? Mix our energies like you just did. Blast her."

"She's not here. Not physically." Hannah's entire body hummed, thrumming with their combined power. "There's no one to blast."

"Who are you talking to?" Althea's words, sharp and vicious, hovered over the shield.

"Myself, you bitch."

Chapter Twenty

"**D**O IT, HANNAH." Jake's momentary spurt of strength gone, he slipped his hand off her foot, loosely wrapped his fingers around her ankle. Somehow, in this blue void, he knew they were stronger if they stayed in physical contact. "Use me. Use my energy. Blast that bitch."

If he had any energy left to share.

Dammit Ben. You'd better be right about all of this shit.

Beyond his arm and hand, which Hannah had touched when she eased backwards earlier, he couldn't move. Mind searing pain radiated through every other part of his body. His jaw clenched, he breathed as deep as he was able through his nose.

"How?" Hannah's voice, low and barely audible, shook. "I can't control this energy sharing we're doing."

That was the million dollar question.

What the hell was the answer? Where was Ben when he needed the man's know-how?

Jake swallowed the curse biting at his throat, flexed his fingers over her skin. This had better work. "You're good with the mental thing, Baby. Imagine pulling *my* energy into you. Fix an image of Althea in your head. Attack that with everything *we've* got."

A low vibration stirred inside him, deep in his gut, then eddied and expanded to throb just under his skin. The air around his fingers and Hannah's ankle glittered gold in the darkness.

Hot and stinging, tiny pinpricks of awareness skittered over the entire surface of his body. The glitter spread out, growing to completely encompass them before settling in around their bodies.

Without moving his head, he eyed the sparkling structure. He tried to find the edges but the glitter simply faded into the bluish darkness without any kind of real border marking the fringe.

"Jake, I think I'm going to have to drop the bubble to do this."

Bubble? He twisted his head towards her while his leg muscles tensed and bunched. Pain stabbed sharp throughout his body. His legs still wouldn't move. How the hell was he supposed to protect her when he couldn't even stand? "Do it."

The dark glitter coating the air above them expanded, scattered and then contracted. Sudden, sparkling light spilled into the shadows to illuminate the blue span of space.

He screwed his eyes closed against the brightness. Tried to slow his breathing.

With her heels in contact with him, Hannah pushed herself upwards and stood. Now that her feet touched him, he let go of her ankle to cover his scalded eyes with his arm. Still, the only thing he could see was that brilliant light.

Illuminating everything and nothing.

He eased his arm away from his face. The air surrounding them pulsed. He could feel the energy gathered in and around Hannah. The light compressed to a tiny point.

And then exploded.

JAKE OPENED HIS EYES.

Dark grey clouds pressed down. Heavy with moisture and threatening to let loose, they hovered just there. Overhead.

He blinked. The image stayed the same.

A shallow breath rattled his lungs. His chest protested the movement. The acrid smell of wet, burned wood lined his throat.

Like when Craig had died.

"We got him." A male, soot covered face with his head covered in some kind of yellow helmet loomed in to block his view of the clouds. "He's breathing."

Sounds filtered in, getting louder and more irritating. Jake tried to turn his head, but the overwhelming need to just close his eyes again was too much to resist.

"Jake Carrigan." Ben's deep, worried voice hovered a few inches from his ear. "Come on, son. Open your eyes."

Fingers smacked his cheek, lifted his right eyelid.

He brushed away the offending hand. "Leave me alone."

A sigh, full of relief, sounded above him. "Can't."

"Sir, you need to back away and let us work." The commanding voice replaced Ben's.

Jake slit his eyes.

Ben frowned. His sooty face disappeared. A clean male face with dark, shuttered eyes came into view.

"Mr. Carrigan?"

They all needed to go away. Leave him alone.

He had to – What? What was it he had to do?

"Hannah?" His fingers slipped on the man's jacket, but he managed to grip the material. "Where's Hannah?"

The man swung his gaze behind him. "There's someone else in there?"

"No." Ben's voice echoed from somewhere to the side. "There's no one else in the barn. Hannah died months ago. From an illness."

"You're positive no one else is in there?"

"Yes."

"No." Jake's fingers clenched over the man's wrist. "She's not dead."

"Jake." Ben came into view over the other man's head. "Don't send these men back into that burning barn on a goose chase."

But, Hannah – Right. The ghost thing.

He nodded and forced the words past the taste of smoke clogging his throat. "Hannah's a spirit that talks to me."

The man, probably a paramedic, threw Ben a quick glance.

Ben shrugged. "He still misses her."

"My barn's burning?" Jake forced his attention to Ben. Must be why the air held so much heat. So much light. In spite of the heavy clouds. "All of Hannah's things are inside there."

Ben gripped Jake's shoulder. "I know, son. And I'm sorry we couldn't save any of it."

The paramedic stared at Jake then nodded. "Okay. Let me check you out."

What the hell happened? Weary, Jake closed his eyes again. Where was Hannah? Was she all right?

ALTHEA SAT ON HER ROLLING STOOL and braced her elbows on the bed's thin mattress. She scanned the equipment recording Hannah's vitals and brushed an errant lock of dark hair away from her patient's face. If there was more she could safely do to ease the restlessness of Hannah's sleep, she would.

But no more meds, not right now. Even though it wasn't yet noon, she'd already had to medicate Hannah twice. The woman seemed to be building a resistance to the sedative.

Something Althea tried to take into account. She had to be careful she didn't over medicate her.

As it was, she was going to have to wait until some of what she'd injected Hannah with wore off before she could continue with the testing.

Blood heavy with sedatives didn't do her a damn bit of good, that only forced her to take things at a slower pace than she wanted.

However, patience was a skill she'd acquired a long time ago.

Years' worth of patience.

Ever since the marker had first made its presence known in Hannah's annual physical. The marker she and her father had looked for once they'd realized *just* who Hannah's father had been.

Such a slip and Hannah had had no clue what she'd so innocently divulged.

So many years ago.

Althea adjusted the leather straps. A shame, really, having to use them. Hannah had more strength than she'd expected.

Outside, the wind shook the tops of the pines, loud whispers echoing across her roof, swirling around the house. Heavy rain beat on the window panes. Funny how the weather matched her mood, matched Hannah's restlessness.

Althea sighed, ran a hand over Hannah's forehead. "Shush. You'll feel better once you sleep this off. You won't even remember Jake is gone. I promise."

WITH A PARAMEDIC'S BLANKET wrapped secure around Jake's shoulders, he sat on the top step of his porch. Firemen wandered between the two fire engines, the paramedic truck still on the property and the blackened shell of his burnt-out barn. The smell of sopping wet, charred wood permeated the air.

So similar to that lingering smell of death out at the pier where Craig had died.

Craig, who had been a loose cannon – out for revenge.

Regardless of the consequences.

Jake lifted his face to the light early afternoon breeze blowing across his property. The clouds had finally let loose earlier. The heavy downpour had helped put out this fire.

Not much was left of his barn.

But the rain had kept the fire from spreading. That was something, at least.

He couldn't bring himself to care one way or another.

A few feet away, Ben stood talking to the Fire Chief, but Jake couldn't muster any real curiosity about that either. The entire morning was one hazy, incoherent fog.

He didn't remember going outside, much less the explosion that had rocked his barn or the fire. Now, instead of listening to Ben and the Chief, he scanned the area, expanding his senses outward.

Where was Hannah? Why did he have this overwhelming, urgent *need* to find her?

Besides the obvious ones.

The barn, the fire. The fact she seemed to be missing.

He'd told the paramedic she wasn't dead.

What had he meant by that? Was it only speculation, what he and Ben had talked about last evening? Or something more?

His body stiff and uncomfortable, he shifted his weight. A spasm of pure pain rocketed through his hips and down both legs.

His low, uncontrolled groan snapped Ben's attention his way.

"Excuse me." Ben shook the Chief's hand before making a direct line towards Jake.

Not what he wanted right now. The man had been mother-henning him since he'd – what? Woke up? Came to?

Where the hell was Hannah?

That desperation gnawed at him. Something important skittered around the fringes of his mind.

Ben clasped his shoulder and Jake cringed from the shock of fresh pain. Tingles cascaded down to his fingertips, taking some of the ache away with them.

"How did you do that?"

"Take the hurt away?"

"Yeah. Like Hannah."

His brows drawn together, Ben studied him for several moments and then nodded. "The pain you're feeling now is a type of psychic overload. Like the lightning rod."

"If you say so."

With exaggerated patience marking his face, Ben shook his head once. "Because it is rooted in the psychic realm, I'm able to take a small bit of it away. I'm not a healer, per se. Hannah may be. I'm not. What I took just now is as much as I can help you with." He sat on the step next to him, dangled his clasped hands between his knees. "You were dead, Jake. This time you were truly dead. There wasn't a damn thing I could do to bring you back."

He swallowed, shrugged. "Then why am I here? Now?"

"Hannah? Did she save you again?"

Jake angled his head towards the other man, ignoring the shot of pain twisting his neck muscles.

"I'm thinking she somehow anchored you to this dimension." Ben lowered his chin to his chest. "I was hoping you could tell me how she did that."

"No clue." He hunched his shoulders, shrugged again, the hurt a little less than before. "I don't remember any of it."

"Is she around?"

"No." His stomach churned and clenched in on itself. Her absence this time scared him more than any time before. "I can't find any trace of her. Do you think –?"

God, he didn't even want to think the thoughts pressing in on him, constricting his chest. But he had to ask. "Do you think this hurt her?"

"This?" Ben, his eyes dark and intense, frowned.

"Saving me like she did." The breeze kicked up, stronger now, increasing the heavy burnt odor. The damp chill penetrated through the blanket's layers. "This time."

In his lightweight wind breaker, Ben hunched his shoulders. He turned his head to stare at the activity in the yard. "I don't know."

"I feel like I'm missing something. Something really important. It's right there, but I can't grab it."

Ben angled his head towards him. "To do with the fire?"

"With Hannah." He ran his tongue over his upper teeth, grimaced. "Something … right there."

"Go back over what you do remember."

"That's just it. All I remember is talking with her in the bedroom. I told her –"

"What?"

"About the bracelet."

"And?"

"It wasn't on her wrist." Jake wet his bottom lip. "She didn't have it. Not anymore. And we had – Words. About the bracelet being real, about whether she was any more real than the bracelet."

"It was real. We both held it."

"Yeah, we did. What does that make Hannah?"

"I never said she wasn't real, Jake."

"I have this urgency building up inside." He spread his hand over his chest and leaned his head back to fill his lungs with the damp, charred air. "That we need to find her. Before it's too late."

"Too late for what? Her to die again? You told the paramedic she was alive."

His movements slow, Jake turned his body to lean against the porch post. He cushioned his shoulder with the blanket and gripped it tighter around his body. His thoughts ran in circles and came back on themselves. "I know. But I can't remember."

"Then let's step away from actual memories for now. Focus on what you're feeling. What you're sensing."

"That *need* to find her." Jake scanned the immediate area without actually seeing what was around him. "Ghost or alive. It keeps pushing on me."

"Then we need to find her."

He swung his gaze back to Ben. "Just like that? Let's find her?"

"Yeah. Just like that."

"How?"

"Any kind of impressions? Anything lurking with that need?"

"No." Jake rolled his head from side to side. "Wait. Althea. Right? We think she's behind this, so –"

"Last time we talked about that woman, you scoffed at the idea of her wanting you dead."

"I know I did, but –" What? He was positive she was involved. "Now I don't find it so unlikely."

"Good enough for me." Ben pulled out his phone, punched in a number.

"Who are you calling?"

Ben held up a hand and spoke into his phone. He nodded before he disconnected the call. "Althea's not at the office. Hasn't been since before she showed up here yesterday."

"You have someone watching her place?"

"Seemed like a necessary precaution."

"Well." Jake blinked. "Thank you."

"Don't thank me yet. Obviously that didn't help." Ben made another call. He frowned and stared towards the sky in the distance. Nodded and disconnected again. "She slipped by the team I had following her. They're not sure how. She was there then she wasn't."

"How far away did she get before they lost her?"

"Turns out, not too far from here. Not far at all." Ben tapped on his phone then studied the screen. "I had some files sent over last night. That Victorian house of theirs is the only property listed in either of the Sheldons' names. In this county. Or this state."

"So you're thinking she's gone to ground somewhere?"

"Maybe. Maybe not. It depends on how threatened she's feeling. How smug she is to have slipped by my crew." Ben nailed him with a dark look. "And how fast she finds out you're not dead."

Well.

There *was* that.

Jake scanned the immediate area again.

"Her father is still in Boston." Ben continued to tap on the phone screen.

"You have people on him, too?"

Ben nodded.

"All because of Hannah?"

Over his phone, Ben leveled another look at him. "For her. Yes. For her mother. Her father."

Jake nodded. He understood regrets. Letting someone down.

Right now he could use all the help Ben could muster. For whatever reasons Ben had. "So where else could Althea be?"

"You're still not remembering anything?"

"Nothing beyond that sense of pressing time."

"And that Hannah's alive."

"Yeah." The muscle in his left cheek twitched. Why the hell did he think she wasn't dead? He was more positive on that score than any speculation they'd done before.

She was alive.

"Then we need to find Althea. She may very well be the key."

"Again, how?" That urge to just do something, anything, bit at his nerves. "If she has Hannah —"

"I know." Ben stood. He bent to clamp a hand on Jake's shoulder. "My team is less than ten miles south of here."

"South? That would be near the old trail."

"Narrow dirt road? Not much else out there except trees?"

"Yeah. There are a few small vacation cabins scattered off that road. And some abandoned buildings the forest is reclaiming."

"Tell me more about the area."

"That dirt road ends several miles in, right at a cliff overlooking the ocean. It's the fastest way in or out of that immediate area. Unless you hike. The terrain can get demanding out there. Especially along those cliffs. Everything is overgrown and treacherous."

"Well, let's head out there and see if you pick up anything from Hannah."

"So now I'm a blood-hound?"

"We use what we have at hand, son."

"Her mother." Jake shook his head. The memory of something important hovered just out of reach. "Althea's mother."

"What?"

"Research. And a legacy." He grimaced. "I don't – Shit, Ben. I can't remember. There's something there, that stuff I can't quite grab, about research. Hannah's important to it."

"Crap." Ben shoved his phone into his pocket. He gripped Jake's hand, pulled him to a standing position. "That doesn't sound good, any way you look at it." Ben wrapped his arm around Jake's shoulders. "Bring the blanket. Let's get moving."

"I'm moving." He tightened his hold on the blanket's edges.

Ben urged him down the wooden steps and over to the silver rented car. They both glanced at the tight grouping of firemen a short distance away.

"Go along with me here." Ben opened the passenger door.

Jake barely managed a nod before the Fire Chief broke away from the two other firemen he had been talking with. A frown lined the man's sooty face.

"I've managed to convince him to at least see his own doctor." His movements on the cautious side, Ben helped Jake into the passenger seat. He then stepped forward to offer his hand to the other man.

"Good job, Mr. Garrett." The Chief shook Ben's hand then leaned on the open car door. "Jake, you're not invincible and this was quite a shock your body took."

"Yes, sir."

The Chief nodded. "I'll talk with you about all of this later." The man studied Jake's face for a few more long seconds. "Tell your parents hello when you call them."

"I will, sir."

The Chief nodded again before he headed back to his men.

Ben settled into his seat and pulled the car door shut before starting the car. "Guess it pays, living in a small town."

"As long as you're not getting into trouble. I was just put on notice." With his head back against the headrest, Jake wiped a hand over his mouth. "The Chief and my father will be having an extended chat about all of this once Dad is home. Either over breakfast at the diner or a beer at the pub."

Ben snorted, slipped the vehicle into gear. He eased around the equipment and engines. "Small town dynamics."

"Yeah." Which had been one of the reasons his brother had escaped to Portland. "Are your men backing us up?"

"I originally called them in strictly as surveillance, but they're available if we need them."

"Can I use your phone?"

Ben fished it out of his pocket and handed it over. "Calling Rily?"

"Yeah."

Craig hadn't called for backup, had done the lone wolf thing. Jake wasn't looking for revenge, but he wasn't going to make that same mistake.

He punched his sister's number into the cell. "Why isn't she already out here?"

Never taking his gaze from the muddy, grooved dirt road, Ben shrugged and ran his tongue over his bottom lip. "Because she was out on a call. I told her you were alive, to hang on where she was. That we might need her."

"Bet she liked that."

"Bastard was a word she used several times. But she's hanging tight."

Rily answered. Jake had to hold the phone away from his ear for a couple of loud moments.

"Are you done?"

"Bastard." Rily's voice roughened over the word.

"Yeah." He spared a glance at Ben then returned his attention to the phone and his sister. "Can you break away? Meet us out near the main highway, down at the turn off for the old trail to the ocean?"

He glanced at Ben, who nodded and pulled the car onto the paved road. Jake told Rily about Ben's men holding their position in the vicinity.

"And Sis? Wait for us. Don't –" Thoughts of his brother's last hours slammed into his head. He stared out the passenger window at the thick stand of trees whizzing past. "Just don't."

"You either." Rily's voice thickened.

"Yeah, well, I have Ben."

"And if anything happens to you, I'll have his balls served up on a skewer for lunch."

A bark of laughter choked him. "I'll be sure and tell him."

He disconnected and handed the phone back.

"What did she threaten me with?"

His smile grim, Jake shared his sister's threat.

"She probably would, too." Ben eased the car to a crawl and turned down a narrow dirt road. Mud sucked at their tires.

To the left a small, nondescript grey sedan sat pulled over to the far edge of the road. Mud splatter, thick and still wet, covered the bottom half of the vehicle.

Ben pulled to a stop in the middle of the furrowed lane. He glanced at his rear view mirror. "Speaking of, there's Rily."

Jake spared a glance at the side mirror. She must have already been close by, probably headed to his place regardless of what Ben had said to her. Rily eased her truck in behind the grey sedan.

"If we end up moving too far out from here my guys will keep this perimeter secure." Ben slid a gun across the seat. He met Jake's gaze. "We don't know what we're up against. Or what we'll find."

Damn if that wasn't the truth.

With a nod, Ben pushed out of the car, navigated his way in the mud to the edge of the road. Jake watched in the side view mirror as Ben headed back to talk with his men.

Jake's gaze snapped back to the Glock.

Damn.

He wrapped his fingers around the gun's grip. The heaviness felt right in his hand. A missing part of him.

Like Hannah.

With his door shoved open and the paramedic blanket left on the seat, he eased his aching body out of the car. His feet sunk a few inches into the mud.

This wasn't going to be easy.

He checked the Glock before he slipped it in at the back of his waistband. With a soft click, he shut the car door.

A turn-off for what was once a local small produce farm was only a hundred feet up the muddy trail. He'd been out here quite a few times as a kid. With his brother. He shoved the thought of Craig into a far shadowy corner of his mind.

He couldn't afford to be distracted now. This weakness in his limbs was enough of a hindrance. No one needed his guilt getting in the way.

Not now.

Away from the low voices behind him, he glanced up the muddied pathway. If what he remembered was correct, the dilapidated farm house itself was at least a half mile further away down an even more rutted road.

Instead of the odor of wet, scorched wood, the light breeze carried the briny scent of the nearby ocean mixed with the pine of the surrounding trees. Along with the promise of more rain.

He spared a glance at the sky, at the heavy cloud cover, dark behind the line of pines towering over the road. A trio of small birds clattered overhead, probably ticked-off at the intrusion. He glanced at them, but with a last squawk the birds settled on a top pine branch to observe the intruders.

In his peripheral vision he caught movement. Rily nodded at the men in the grey sedan as she came around the side of Ben's car, her own gun out and at her side. Her mud boots already caked, she eyed Jake's feet.

His running shoes would have to do, considering his own boots had been in the barn. He doubted they'd survived. Ben's tennis shoes weren't going to fare any better.

He didn't think the man cared any more than he did.

"Game plan?" Ben stepped in, quiet, behind Rily. He pulled his weapon, checked it before glancing between the two of them.

"Barreling in there, guns drawn. Isn't that what you two cowboys have in mind?" She cocked her head to the side and batted her eyelashes several times.

"That's not really a viable option." Jake scanned the area. "We don't know if Hannah's out there or not."

"What —" Rily spun to face him. Disgust lined her face and she threw Ben a veiled look. "The hell?"

"Right now it's a theory in progress." The corner of Ben's mouth twitched.

"I thought the *theory* was nab Althea Sheldon for attempted murder. Jake's." Rily's frown deepened.

"Yes, but without putting Hannah in harm's way." Jake took two painful steps to stand in the middle of the muddy road. "She will not be *collateral damage.*"

He ignored his sister's scowl. Right now he had a more urgent need.

Hannah.

With a deep breath, he closed his eyes and opened his mind, widening the range of his senses in an attempt to detect the slightest trace of the woman who was more a part of him than he'd ever allowed himself to realize.

"Are you picking up anything?" Ben stood two feet away. His gaze narrow and sharp, he zeroed in on Jake's face.

"Not really sure. I can almost feel her."

"Almost?"

"Yeah." Jake kept his head angled for another moment. He grimaced then expelled the frustrated breath he'd held. "Almost. Like she's there, but it's more of a resonance. Like a drum beat being bounced back at me. Like an echo."

"We'll convert you yet, son."

He threw Ben a sharp look before he shook his head.

Ben stared out at the forest. "Narrow in on that echo."

Jake exchanged a glance with his sister but ignored the skepticism marking her face. Who was he to tell her any different?

He also ignored the trace of worry buried deep in her gaze, along with the quick once over she gave him. No, he wasn't up to par. Yes, he prayed his weakness wouldn't hinder them. But he also had something neither of them did.

A direct link to Hannah.

He lowered his chin, narrowed his eyes and focused on the faint thread holding what he sensed of the woman he loved.

This was like following her muted perfume trail. He jerked his head sideways. "That way then."

Ben, his eyes hooded, nodded once.

Jake pulled his borrowed weapon from his waistband. The grip fit snug in his palm.

"So again –" Rily eyed his gun then raised an eyebrow. One side of her mouth pulled down in a half frown. "Do we actually have a plan?"

"Follow his connection." Ben jerked his chin in Jake's direction. "If she's actually out there somewhere –"

"She, meaning Hannah? Based on *my brother* feeling this echo? From a ghost?"

"Yes." Ben aimed a hard look in her direction. "Or a live, breathing person. One of the two."

"Right. Just looking for clarification, is all." Her own eyes shuttered, she shrugged. "If Althea is out there? Waiting to ambush this posse of ours?"

"We take her down."

"Okay." Rily pressed her lips together. "Sounds simple enough."

Not.

Jake heard the unspoken word in the look she threw his way. He lifted his eyebrows and shrugged.

Hannah *was* out there somewhere. Possibly weak, but alive.

Maybe.

He swallowed once, nodded at Ben. "Let's go."

With Jake leading, they moved south, between the trees, keeping close to the edge of the side road. The muscles along his jaws clenched tight with pain, but he ignored the way his knees wanted to buckle with each deliberate step.

We're coming Hannah.

Chapter Twenty-One

HER ARMS HEAVY, Hannah stopped struggling to lift them. Exhaustion pooled in every pore of her body. She had tried to open her eyes, but beyond a slight flutter, they refused to respond. Almost as if a pound of sleep dust glued her lashes together.

Added to that, a thick weightiness pressed against her, held her down. She managed to turn her head a slight bit to the right. Something soft brushed her cheek. Or her cheek brushed something soft. Not sure which, she frowned.

She was on her back. Lying flat with her body prone.

Did she lie on a bed? Was she *alive*?

Althea had said something about getting back into her body. Was that were she was now? Back in her physical body?

Not cremated?

She wet the inside edge of her lips with the tip of her tongue. Even that small movement left her lungs aching and her breathing nothing more than painful gasps for air.

"Oh, Hannah." Althea's voice came from somewhere to the right. "What have you done to yourself?"

Hannah tensed. Her muscles protested. She renewed her struggle to open her eyes, but they refused to budge.

Go away. She tried to part her lips, to force the words out, but her throat wouldn't work. *Leave me alone.*

Something hovered, the weightiness of the displaced air pressing down on her and constricting her chest.

Althea?

Hannah struggled to fix an image of the woman in her head. The way she'd done earlier, in that void with Jake.

"Oh, no, my sweet Hannah." A hand, the fingertips cool against her forehead, brushed her hair away from her face. "Whatever it was you managed to do earlier, we don't want a repeat of that. We really don't."

The hand lifted from her face, then gripped her arm. Something sharp struck her skin just above her wrist. The sudden prick of pain radiated outward, like thousands of tiny red ants biting their way across the surface of her body.

No.

Hannah fought to hold the image she conjured of Althea in her mind. Inside that image she reached up and smacked her. Hard.

The hand gripping her jerked. The fingers loosened then dropped her arm. "You bitch."

A slap landed on Hannah's cheek. Her head snapped to the left. The march of red ants intensified across her skin, the pricks of pain closer together. Her breathing shallow and fast, she fought to keep from hyperventilating.

She had to stay in control of at least that much.

Oh, Lord, she hurt.

Hannah again tried to pry her eyes open, to focus on Althea's image. On anything beyond this pain.

Jake.

THERE.

Jake turned in a slow circle. Swollen muscles gripped his knees, protested the slippery mud. He held the arm Ben stuck out to steady him.

They had passed an abandoned home a while back, one with no sign of occupancy for at least the past several years.

There had been no sign of anyone passing through by car or foot, either. While there were other ways in, without knowing the end destination, they had nothing but Jake's link to guide them.

And this was the direction of Hannah's echo.

The boughs of the overhead pine trees darkened an afternoon already dreary with heavy clouds, although a patch of pale sunlight streamed through the open area to their right. The breeze had stilled and the birds were quiet.

"Hannah?" No one answered. Not Hannah. Not Ben nor Rily. Jake glanced at the two of them. "I *felt* her."

"And?" Rily whispered, the sound sharp in the hushed quietness.

"No response. But we're heading in the right direction."

Ben nodded then sent a pointed look at Jake's leg.

Jake shrugged. What could he say? His weakness didn't matter as long as they found Hannah. He'd try to stay out of the way once they did, once they breached whatever structure they discovered. Once they found where Althea actually held Hannah.

Because Hannah was still alive.

Bottom line.

He wasn't going to let her down. Not this time.

Not the way he had before. Not the way he had Craig.

"This way." He ignored the look Ben and Rily exchanged. With a shove, he pushed Ben's arm aside, limped off in the direction he'd sensed Hannah's cry.

A short time later, deep in the woods and far away from the rutted, muddy road, Jake stopped. With one hand held up in a fist, he signaled the other two.

He braced his other palm on the trunk of a huge, towering pine. Both his knees burned as if on fire. His lungs tightened with each harsh breath. But he'd made it this far. He wasn't quitting now. With his chin, he motioned towards the glimpse he'd caught of a rundown farm house between the trees.

Ben nodded before he broke out a small canteen filled with water. After taking a swig and passing it on to Rily, Ben turned back towards the farm house.

"She's in there?" Rily pointed with the canteen. "Althea? Hannah?"

"I don't know." Jake fisted both hands then spread his fingers. "I don't —"

Ben cupped his shoulder. "This is where her echo leads?"

"It feels … stronger here. At least more so than anywhere else today." He turned in a full circle, but the direction of this house held the strongest pull. With a grunt, he pushed away from the pine.

"Not meaning to sound like a broken record here, but what the hell is our plan of attack?" Rily slapped the canteen into Jake's hand. "Drink."

With the canteen to his mouth, he met Ben's gaze and raised an eyebrow.

"Tell me we're not just going to push our way in there." Rily moved a few steps away to check their back trail.

"No. We're not." Ben took the canteen from Jake. He swallowed another swig of water. "For starters, we have no idea what's in there."

"No shit." Rily spun around to stand with one hand on her hip, the gun in her other hand down at her side. She swung her gaze between them and the surrounding area.

"Something's off there." Ben stared at the house.

"Again." Rily speared him with a sharp glance. "No shit."

Jake stretched his senses further than the farm house. The pull centered there. But Ben was right.

This was off, somehow.

"Echo is the right word." Jake lowered his chin, not quite touching his chest. "It's just a really strong echo."

As compared to what, though? He sucked in a breath. He couldn't deny what he felt, what he sensed.

Ben, his eyes hooded in the dim light, nodded. "I'll check the perimeter, see what I can see. Feel. Then signal the two of you if there's any reason to breach the building."

"Not sure that's much of a plan." Rily rolled her shoulders. "But it'll have to work."

The corner of Ben's mouth lifted a fraction. He handed the canteen to her before he pushed his way through the thick undergrowth. Jake followed. Rily fell in behind him.

Once at the edge of the clearing Jake and his sister crouched low under the trees. They traced Ben's movements to the outer boundary of the half cleared property around the dilapidated farm house.

Over the years nature had started the reclamation process. The old, wood-shingled roof had caved in along with the west facing wall. Wild vines, their red flowers muted in the gloomy light, covered that side of the structure.

The echo bothered him. Hannah, but not Hannah. Then there was the fact this building was unusable in this condition. Single story without any sign of a basement. Hannah wasn't in there, at least not physically.

And the echo still didn't feel quite right. Not wrong either.

Dammit. He was too new to this woo-woo stuff to understand the damn nuances.

In the meantime Hannah was out there.

Somewhere.

Ben reached the left side of the structure. He squatted with his back straight and rigid. With his right hand extended he remained unmoving for several long moments.

Waves of low level energy swept over Jake then dissipated in soft rolls over his body.

"What the hell?" Her eyes narrowed, Rily angled her head towards him.

Jake shrugged one shoulder. He locked his gaze on Ben. The man eased backwards, crouching low, away from the structure but staring forward. Once he reached the edge of the trees, he straightened. At a quick clip he made his way back to them.

"Booby trap." Ben crouched down beside them. He rolled his head back and side to side. "Of a sort."

"Is that what we felt?" Jake scanned the area behind Ben with his gaze and his senses.

"You guys got that, did you?"

Rily nodded. "We got something."

Ben spared a glance for Jake. "Like a wave of some sort?"

"Yeah."

"Early warning system. Good news is that we're on the right track." Ben indicated the farm house with a curt jerk of his head. "Bad news, Althea knows we're coming."

"So it is Althea?" Rily rocked back on her heels. "You're sure?"

"As sure as I can be." Ben wiped the back of his hand across his mouth. "The signature is definitely Hannah's. But Jake is right. Here, it's more an echo than anything else. Like it's being redirected to this point. To this place."

"And Althea's signature?" Jake glanced back at the farm house. "How can you be sure it's her?"

"Technically, I can't." Ben's jaw tightened to the point a muscle in his cheek twitched. "But it feels like Althea. The entire area feels like her. As if she stood there, cloaked in Hannah's essence, in front of the building, and —"

"Sucked the life out the area?" Her brows drawn down, Rily scanned the region around them.

"Yes."

"The birds stopped what little chattering they were doing when he set off whatever it was waiting there." Her mouth tight, Rily met Jake's gaze. "And the breeze. It's completely stopped, too. Even the air feels weird."

He held his sister's gaze for several seconds. She was right. The emptiness of the area vibrated tight inside him. Almost as if the oxygen had leached out of the air, along with everything else. All Althea left behind was a weird vibration, like too much ozone in the air.

"Will it come back?" Rily held his gaze, but directed her question to Ben. "Or will it stay like this?"

"It should come back. Although I'm not sure how long it will take. Hopefully in just a few hours or a day or two." Ben eased forward on his knees. He tucked his gun in his waist band. "What she did, I believe, was anchor her alarm to the natural resources around here."

"Using nature as a battery?" Jake broke his gaze away from his sister's and the worry simmering there.

"Exactly." Ben pulled several pairs of thin, black gloves from his back jeans pocket. He handed a pair to each of them. "Put these on."

"Why?" Jake took the gloves, fingered the material. Weird. Not latex, although that's what they looked to be.

"If she's powerful enough to harness nature this way, and to redirect Hannah's energy the way we're suspecting she's done, then we really don't want to be touching her skin with our bare hands."

"Once we apprehend her." Rily's upper lip curled. She jerked the gloves on then speared Jake with a pointed glare.

"Whether Hannah is alive or not, we have to take Althea down. We have to stop whatever it is she's doing."

Jake shoved his hands into the gloves and held her gaze. He didn't give a rat's ass about apprehending Althea. She could rot in hell. While he was tempted to make sure she did, finding Hannah was his priority.

Anything else was gravy.

"Which way?" His gun back in his gloved hand, Ben stood.

Jake spared a glance in his direction then pushed himself upright. He drew his borrowed Glock out from his waistband, checked it then closed his eyes. With his attention turned inward, he scanned the area with his heightened senses.

A small, almost undistinguishable, invisible thread tugged at the center of his chest. One he hadn't felt before Ben tripped the alarm.

Hannah. Real this time. More substantial. Not an echo.

Jake focused on the silky feel of the thread. In his mind he rubbed it between his thumb and forefinger. Energy arched and his nerve endings tingled. His eyes snapped open. "That way."

JAKE.

Awareness seeped into Hannah's mind. A thin, taunt line that stretched beyond the darkness encasing her.

She still lay prone on her back, her arms too heavy to lift. Her eyelashes still seemed glued together, but the pinpricks of red hot pain had faded.

She strained to hear anything beyond the quietness surrounding her.

Althea? The word stuck in her throat. Her lips wouldn't move. This was getting old. Like she had a choice in the matter. A sob clogged her throat.

Dead.

Jake was dead.

Althea had said ... hadn't she? Jake was dead. Gone.

A touch, feather light, whispered over her forehead. She tensed. Her nerve endings flared.

Again the touch, hesitant and barely there, traced across her skin. Almost as if nothing had touched her at all. Almost as if....

Jake?

The touch traced her lips. Her breath stuttered. She could almost hear a shush rustle across her ear to tangle in her hair and caress her cheek.

Jake.

He was here, with her. Somehow.

Not dead. He couldn't be dead.

She stretched her senses out, fanning the area around her.

There, hovering just above her, she found a thin thread. There, but not there.

She tried to focus, to actually see the image in her mind, but the thread shimmered in and out of view like glitter on a dark, moonless night. A bitter laugh gagged her, as stuck in her throat as the words she couldn't speak.

See. View. She couldn't even force her eyes open a small slit, yet she lay here thinking in terms of vision.

The thread snapped the air above her. In her mind, energy, so much like that illusive glitter that had covered her bubble shield in the void, misted down and coated her skin. Sparks of that electric energy nipped at her, settled along her nerve-endings.

Soothed the tenseness straining her muscles.

What had just happened?

Her heart fluttering in her chest, she yanked her focus back to the thread. With her thoughts she reached out to run the fingers of her left hand along the edge of a short length of that thread.

A low level prickle quivered at the tips of her fingers then radiated down to swirl in her palm. Mentally she let go of the thread and curled her fingers over the sensation in her hand. The power remained, centered there.

A door slammed somewhere to her right. With the sensation still whirling in her palm, she tried to turn her head.

To open her eyes.

She still couldn't move.

"All right. Show time." Althea's voice, edgy with suppressed excitement, scrapped over her. "Your little group of would-be rescuers is on their way."

JAKE SPARED A GLANCE at the trees towering over them. The heavy scent of pine mingled with the saltiness of the nearby ocean. Afternoon clouds pressed down, their weight keeping the air chilled and thick with humidity. Moisture dripped from the overhead branches.

A heavy downpour was coming.

Soon.

His knees ached. Hell, his entire body ached. He kneaded the base of his neck and forced his attention back to the nonexistent trail and the wet, slippery vegetation covering the muddy ground.

Hannah was nearby. The thread coiled tight in the middle of his chest. He spread his palm over his T-shirt, rubbing the material at the center. In his mind he could almost see a shimmery thin light stretching outward from him, out through the trees. He tugged, his mental touch light.

And Hannah responded. A soft, there and then gone, moan flashing down his spine.

"That way." He jerked his head to the right. "We're close. A few hundred yards at the most."

Ben nodded. He moved off a few feet in the direction indicated then knelt down on one knee next to the wide trunk of a tall pine tree. With a half shudder, he pulled some kind of small scope from his jacket pocket. He pressed his shoulder against the tree and held the scope to his left eye.

When this was over, Ben was going to have to share some of those toys.

Jake turned to his sister.

Rily checked her weapon before meeting Jake's gaze. "I've got your back, Bro."

"I know." An image of Craig wavered in Jake's mind. He shoved the picture away, along with the razor-sharp pangs of remorse that ripped at him with her words. Craig had been reckless. His brother should never have gone in alone. Jake held Rily's gaze. Nodded. "Let's do this."

"I believe there's a house, a rather large house, about two hundred yards in the direction you indicated." Ben pushed himself to his feet then tucked his scope into his jacket pocket. "There's no real clearing around it. At least not from this view. Which could be good for us."

"Especially since she knows we're coming." Rily rubbed the back of her neck with her free hand. "At least Althea does."

"So does Hannah." Ben swung to face Jake, the look in his eyes hooded. "Doesn't she?"

"She should." Jake fixed his gaze forward.

"Will she be able to help? Cause a distraction or something?" Rily closed her eyes for a quick second. "I can't believe I asked that."

Ben's mouth lifted in a half smile, he leaned his back against the pine. "Keep hanging around with us, kid. We'll have you asking all kinds of interesting questions."

She speared him with a dark look.

A sudden hard tug yanked on the thin thread pulled Jake's attention inward to where the thread coiled inside him. Not touching his shirt, he spread his left hand over the center of his chest. His palm hovered over the material before he gave in and rubbed his chest.

"What the hell is that?" Rily stared at his hand.

He glanced down, blinked then took a longer look. Faint shimmering light, like glitter in a room lit only with a small lamp, swirled around his fist. He pulled his hand away from his chest and spread his fingers. The glitter dissipated around his hand, but a small amount continued to eddy at the center of his chest.

"I'd say Hannah definitely knows we're on our way." Ben's eyes narrowed. With his head leaned slightly to one side, he stared at Jake's hand. "And I do believe she'll be able to help."

"But –" Rily glanced at Ben then back at Jake's chest.

"Let's go." Jake rubbed his right thumb over his left palm and ignored the ache in his knees. He moved towards his sister. "You're going to catch flies if you don't close your mouth."

Rily met his gaze then leveled another look at his chest. He kept his own expression blank.

She shrugged. "Let's go get her."

HANNAH LAY MOTIONLESS.

Althea was in the room and hovered somewhere to the right. Close by. Hannah wanted to avoid another of those needle sharp pricks. She wanted to avoid having Althea touch her period.

The woman was crazy. Nutty crazy or foxy crazy, she wasn't sure. Since Althea was obviously the one in charge at this juncture, Hannah had decided to stop fighting.

For right now.

The glitter she saw in her mind, glitter that coated her skin and centered on her palm, still swirled.

Could Althea see it?

How could sparkling dust help? As a defense, what good was it?

She couldn't shield herself from Althea. Not here, not the way she'd done in the void. She'd tried and failed. Even her ability to center on Jake had deserted her.

She was stuck here.

But she had a body. That thought had run around and around in her mind. Althea wanted her to stay in her body. So Hannah wasn't dead. Or if she was, Althea was here in purgatory with her.

If this was purgatory, where was Jake?

He'd managed to touch her in the same way she'd touched him. With his mind. He was coming, here, to find her. Only Althea planned to make sure he actually died this time.

Her heart stuttered in her chest. She couldn't let that happen.

Not to Jake.

"Oh, Hannah." Althea's voice came from the center of the room. "Once we take care of those pesky distractions, we can settle down to some serious work."

A rustling, papers and something else she couldn't pinpoint, sounded closer. Hannah's entire body tensed. In silence she counted to thirty and willed each muscle to ease.

"What have you done to yourself?" Disgust mingled with concern and laced Althea's voice. "Your nose is bleeding."

Hannah flinched inwardly at the sound of a bottle being opened somewhere near her ear. An astringent, antiseptic odor filled her nostrils and her gag reflex closed her throat.

Shock mixed with the stink.

Oh, Lord. She could smell.

The touch gentle, a cold damp cloth wiped several times under her nose, over her mouth.

"There." Althea patted her cheek with the material. "Whatever you're doing, you need to stop. I'd rather not sedate you again. But I will if you force me to."

Chapter Twenty-Two

J AKE KNELT ON THE FOREST FLOOR a few yards from the back of the narrow, two story log house. Ben and Rily came up behind and squatted next to him. The dense, rain soaked overgrowth blocked them from view of anyone in the house.

At least anyone with mundane, physical abilities.

Psychically, he had no clue.

For all he knew, every psychic within fifty miles knew they were here.

He gave Rily and Ben a single nod then glanced upwards. The heavy limbs of the towering pines also blocked any view of the gloomy afternoon sky. Only a low, diffused light penetrated the surrounding trees, keeping everything dim and indistinctive.

Jake focused on the house. Warmed by the passing years, the logs gleamed with a soft richness in the muted forest light. The deep green, metal roof blended with the trees surrounding the structure. If Ben hadn't found the building with his weird little scope, they wouldn't have known the place was here.

The tug on Jake spiraled tight. He rubbed his chest. The shadowy glitter spread out to circle his hand. Rily shot a glance at his chest. With her eyebrows raised she jerked her head at the house. He nodded.

This was the place. Hannah was in there. What else they'd find, he had no idea. But Hannah was there.

Still alive.

"Now what?" Rily touched his elbow.

"We head in." He checked his weapon again.

"How?" She did the same.

"We break in." Ben stared at the house through the thick vegetation. His eyes narrowed. "Stay alert."

"Right." She rolled her eyes. "B and E. Against the law. Remember? Cop here."

"Exigent circumstances." Ben checked his own weapon.

"Right." With the back of her hand, she swiped her hair away from her face. "There better be something exigent in there, guys. Something beyond whatever your questionable mental faculties are grasping at."

Ben cut her a quick, sharp glance. "I'm sure Althea has set booby traps, kids. More than likely the area is laced with them."

"Like the old farm house?" Jake kneaded the back of his neck.

"No. That was an early warning alarm. These will be meant to maim at the very least." Ben held Jake's gaze. "You, they'll be intended to kill."

"Great." Rily pushed herself to a standing position and fisted her free hand on her hip. "Tell me again why we're here."

"Hannah." Jake braced his left hand against the tree-trunk next to him. He managed to stand, more or less, upright.

Rily swung to face Ben. He squinted and stared up at her.

"Look at him." She motioned towards Jake. "He can't even stand without help. What the hell is he doing out here? Why the hell are you?"

"I could ask you the same question, Rily." In one smooth movement, completely belying whatever age he had on him, Ben stood.

Her eyes narrowed and her nostrils flared. "There's no way I'm letting him go alone."

"He's not alone." Ben rechecked his weapon then looked directly at her. "I'm here."

"Yeah." She pushed past them both to press her hand on the trunk of another tree. "That's another reason I'm here. Exigent circumstances my ass."

His stomach tight, Jake met Ben's gaze. His sister was here. For him. As back up. "Let's do this."

Ben nodded. "If Althea actually has any idea what she's doing, the first level of those booby traps will be some kind of ward. Similar to the alarm system, but with more punch." He sent a veiled look at Jake.

"Yeah, I know. Aimed at killing me."

"Exactly. You go in last."

"Last?" Dammit. He clenched his jaw to keep any more words of protest spewing out of his closed throat.

"Otherwise they'll trigger and we'll all be killed." Ben stared at him. Jake refused to look away.

"Makes sense. As much as any of this does." Rily tapped her index finger against Jake's chest. "Last in, Bro."

He pushed her hand away.

Moisture glinted in her eyes. "You'd better make it all the way there and back out again, jerk."

"You, too."

She nodded then turned to Ben. "Let's go."

Single file, with Ben in the lead, they forced their way through the dense overgrowth. Jake ignored the scream of his swollen knees and the way each step ground at his bones. He concentrated on the house.

They moved from under the tree closest to the house. The air around them thickened, pressed tight, and made it hard to draw a deep breath. He rolled his shoulders.

"Is Althea doing this?" In between the two men, Rily turned her head from side to side, constantly scanning the area. "Making the air this heavy?"

"Yes." Ben tossed the word over his shoulder. "It's about to get worse. Stay behind me. Rily keep Jake close."

Vibrations suddenly pulsed around them in waves, knocking Ben back two steps.

"Dammit." Ben straightened. He tucked his gun in the back of his waistband. With his feet braced apart, he lifted his arms out to his side, palms facing forward. "Put your guns away for now. Rily, on the right side of me, please. Jake, behind us."

Jake shared a quick glance with his sister, shrugged. With his lungs burning from the effort to breath, he tucked his borrowed gun away, moved to stand behind Ben. Rily, wheezing a little, stepped to Ben's right side. They both checked the perimeter.

Ben flexed his hands and lowered his head. His breathing deepened.

Jake ran the tips of his fingers over his own chest. The coiled energy sparked glittery dust and coated his hand.

Ben's head snapped up. He darted a fast look behind him. "Jake, whatever you just did disrupted the energy field around the house."

"All I did was rub my chest."

"Maybe it's because you're connected to Hannah." Ben flexed his fingers again. The muscles at the back of his neck stiffened. He squared his shoulders. "Do it again."

Right.

Jake sucked in as much air as his constricted lungs could hold then he drew his fingers in a circle over his chest.

Ben, with his hands spread and his arms rigid, lifted his chin. "Heads up. I think we're about in."

The sudden release of pressure yanked Jake from where he stood. He stumbled backwards. "What the hell?"

"Double that." Rily sucked in lungful's of air. She spun around to nail Jake with a quick look.

"We don't have time, kiddies." Ben jerked his head towards the house. "We need to get inside before she regroups."

They both pulled their guns.

Ben left his in his waistband. "Not sure they'll do any good."

Jake shared a glance with his sister. They both firmed their grips on their weapons and followed Ben across the last few feet of semi-open space then onto the sliver of a back deck. The door leading into the house thrummed with latent power.

Rily threw Jake a spooked glance. Even his sister could sense the contained energy emanating from the heavy wooden door.

Power. Potency.

He ran his tongue over his dry lips. Whatever the hell that vibrating, pent-up energy was called.

"Now what?" His voice low, he braced his aching legs and eyed the closed entryway. "Kick it in?"

"No." Ben's gaze ran along the perimeter of the door. He kept his voice down. "Even if we did, you couldn't be the one to –"

"Yeah, I know." Jake rolled his head from side to side. The tension bunched there refused to budge. "I'm the target and all that crap."

Rily swallowed once then narrowed her eyes. "B and E." Her words barely above a whisper, she tucked her gun in her waistband. She pulled a slim black case from her back pocket then crouched below the door knob.

"What the hell?" Jake squatted next to her and cupped her shoulder. "Where did you get that? How do you know how to use those things?"

Her eyebrows lifted, she aimed a tight smile in his general direction. "There's a lot you don't know about me, Bro."

"Obviously."

Ben covered Jake's hand with his own. "You can't be touching her while she's working. Energy transference –"

"Right." He let go of Rily and shook off Ben's hand before stepping back to quickly scan the area behind them. Not thinking, he covered his chest with his free palm and kneaded the material of his T-shirt.

"Keep that up Jake." Ben jerked his chin towards Jake's chest. "That must be where you're tied to Hannah. Whenever you do that, Althea's energy seems to fumble."

"So I stand here rubbing my chest while you two run in to the rescue?"

"Heart." Rily angled her head and looked up at him. "Your hand is over your heart, Jake."

He glanced down. "True enough." But would it *be* enough? "I don't want –"

"Don't care what you want. Don't want to know. Just keep rubbing." Her mouth lifted in a semblance of a smile. She meet Ben's gaze. He nodded.

Her hands steady, Rily inserted the long, slim pick into the keyhole. Feeling stupid, Jake stood with his fingers over his heart and rubbed his chest.

Ben covered Rily's gloved hand with his. She jerked, glanced at the man.

"Even with Jake and Hannah's help, you could get quite a — Shock. Let's see if we can minimize it."

Rily nodded. She rolled her shoulders and focused back on the lock. With Ben's hand over hers, Jake couldn't see what she did, but in the quietness he heard the slip of the pick. The tightness near the center of his chest contracted inward, the constricting pain quick and sudden.

"It's open." Rily's voice whispered over Jake's suddenly hot skin. "And we're still here."

"The fun is just starting." Ben took a step back while she tucked her tools into her case and the case into her back pocket. "Stay close. And Jake?"

A cold chill ran through him when he met the older man's gaze.

"Whatever you do, keep that connection to Hannah open."

Right.

Like he actually knew what he was doing or how this even worked.

"Guns?" Her weapon already in her hand, Rily eased to a standing position.

"Like I said earlier, not sure they'll do any good, but why not?" Ben pulled his from his waistband. He twisted the door knob then pushed the door open.

Jake brought up the rear. The three of them entered the small mud room. Warm air washed over them along with an underlying aroma of apples and cinnamon.

He shook his head, the picture of Althea baking as foreign as him eating anything she'd created.

Darkened by the lack of light, inside or from the outside, the small room hardly held the three of them. Ben extended his hand, palm down and fingers spread, over the knob of the inner door for a moment before he twisted it open.

They passed through into a long and equally dark hallway. The tug on the thin thread at the center of Jake's chest intensified, the coiled energy sharp and insistent.

"That way." Jake angled his head to the right.

Ben spared a quick glance in that direction. He nodded.

The air thickened again, sudden, and the tug on Jake's chest squeezed tight enough to rob his breath.

He stumbled.

Rily tucked her arm under his and gripped his opposite shoulder. "Jake?"

Shaking his head took focus, but he managed.

Dammit, what was happening?

Vibrations suddenly pounded at him. Sharp and insistent, they warbled around his body. Shocking pinpoints of electricity bit at the skin under his clothes. He stumbled again. Her face tight, Rily wrapped both arms around him, her gun against Jake's side.

Ben lurched backwards. His right shoulder sagged. He planted his feet and had both hands gripped around the handle of his weapon. "Force fields aren't my forte, kids. We're going to have to wing it and dodge this crap as best we can."

"No shit." Jake braced his gloved left palm to the wall for balance. He nodded at Rily. With doubt lining her face, she let go of him. He leaned against the hallway's doorframe.

Hannah?

His fingers wide, he pressed his hand over his heart. The temptation strong to clench the material of his shirt into a fist, he struggled to keep his fingers spread wide. Air thrummed around him and that dark glitter swirled tight over his hand.

Hannah?

JAKE?

A sharpness tugged on Hannah's palm, a twinge stronger than a simple nip of pain. She focused on her hand, on the small swirl of heated vibration centered there.

Not the red-hot, ant bite type of sting, more of a quest to pay attention. Somehow she knew Althea wasn't responsible for this one. She couldn't see her, still couldn't see anything, but she knew the woman hovered to the right. Doing what, she had no idea so she ignored her.

Instead, Hannah concentrated on Jake. Willed herself to join him. Wherever he was.

Jake.

Nothing.

Her breathing ragged, she focused again.

Jake.

"Hannah." Althea's voice, distracted and only a few feet away, chased chills across her skin. "Whatever it is you're trying to do, stop. It isn't going to work any longer."

Dammit it all. Hannah tried to open her mouth, to tell the woman to go to hell, but her lips wouldn't budge. Salty tears stung her eyes. She couldn't even blink the moisture away.

Fine. She pulled her thoughts in tight, struggled to even out her breathing. The bitch wanted her to stop reaching for Jake, she would.

She'd focus on Althea instead.

She grabbed the picture of Althea flitting through her head, sharpened her focus. The energy in her palm pulsed, compressing into a tight swirling circle. In her mind, sparkling dust coated the hand she raised. That dust also coated the thin thread leading outward, away from her. Away from this room.

A part of her wanted to follow that thread, to see if it led to Jake. She prayed there'd be a chance to do that later.

Instead, Hannah pulled her inward gaze back to the image of Althea, of the woman standing across the room with a hateful glee shining in her ice-blue gaze.

"Well." Althea started to move her right foot forward, but then stopped and stood with her hands tucked into the white lab coat she wore. "This is definitely a surprising turn of events."

Hannah blinked, broke eye contact with the woman, allowed her gaze to dart around the room. She now stood several feet away from Althea in some kind of bedroom. A black, ornate wrought iron bed pressed against the far wall.

A body lay on the mattress, covered to its chin by a thin sheet. The only sound in the room was the whisper quiet rhythmic whoosh of monitors attached to the body.

Her body.

With her heart thudding hard in her chest, Hannah pressed her open palm over her mouth and blinked back sudden moisture.

She wasn't dead.

"I don't know how you're doing this, Hannah. But I need you to get back into your body, where you belong." Althea fingered the blue satin ribbon around her neck. She pulled on the cord where it dropped underneath her white blouse. "Now."

Tremors ran over Hannah's skin and down her spine. Her head bowed at the pressure building on top of her skull. She lifted her chin, each increment of motion sending shuddering waves of crushing pressure through all of her muscles. "No."

Still fingering the blue cord around her neck, Althea moved to stand over Hannah's prone body. She ran the tip of her other index finger along the tubing connected to one of the monitors. "Do you really want to fight me?"

"Go to hell."

Althea shrugged. With a quick snap, she jerked the tubing from the body's wrist. "You first, my sweet Hannah."

Bright light pricked at the sides of her vision, but Hannah ignored the dizziness. She ran her fingers through her hair, shook it out around her head. And refused to look away from Althea's gaze.

"This needs to be reconnected, Hannah. Or this time you really will die." Althea held the clear plastic tube in front of her. Clear liquid dripped onto the tiled floor.

"Maybe I will die. But if I do, then your games are over. I don't think you're ready for that. Are you?"

Althea shoved the tube away from her. With her fingers wrapped around the blue satin hanging around her neck, she yanked hard, breaking the cord. Her head low, the cord dangling in her hand, she advanced on Hannah. "I don't have time for this."

Hannah's palm throbbed with energy. She made a fist, swung her arm upward. At the last minute she flung open her fingers. Dark, golden glitter shimmered in the air and seemed to hang between them.

Althea smacked into the sparkling wall. She stumbled backwards, her loafers slipping on the smooth floor. Regaining her balance, she narrowed her ice cold eyes. "That isn't going to stop me."

Hannah sucked in air and tried to ignore the way her heart hammered in her chest and thundered in her ears. She focused on thickening the wall she'd created, on making it denser.

The blue cord still dangling from Althea's fist, she pushed at the shimmering wall. She twisted around then jerked open one of the side cabinets lining the wall next to the wrought iron bed.

Hannah kept her gaze locked on Althea. Looking at her own body laying there would only distract her.

A soft, scrapping noise from somewhere behind her etched itself across Hannah's nerves. Althea hadn't heard, she was too busy rummaging through the cabinet. The woman braced her shoulders then swung around to face the room.

Hannah pushed an extra burst of pulsing electric energy into the barely visible wall between them.

"Okay, bitch." With one hand holding something tight in her fist, Althea held up the cord from around her neck in her other hand. A clear, small glass vial dangled from the blue satin. The vial was two-thirds full of some dark, thick liquid. "Time for you to go back where you belong."

Althea smashed the vial on the floor in front of Hannah's make-shift wall. Fresh, bright red blood, more than what the vial should have held, spread across the tile, crept under the shimmering wall.

Her hand burning, Hannah tightened her fingers into a fist. She took two steps back.

The wall fell in on itself as if it had never existed.

"You're needed for my research. I'm not going to die the way my mother did. The way you would have if I hadn't stepped in." Althea advanced, the soles of her shoes crushing the glass. She held another blood-filled vial held high in her hand. "The way you will if you don't get back into your body and quit giving me so much trouble."

Energy still pulsed in Hannah's palm. The power eddied with heat and pain. She swallowed once then opened her hand. Althea was quicker. She smashed the second vial at Hannah's feet.

The world tipped sideways.

Before Hannah could open her mouth to scream, the door behind her burst open.

JAKE HELD HIS POSITION behind Rily while Ben shouldered his way past the door they'd just busted open and into the softly lit room.

At the center, Althea spun towards them. Dark red splotches were splattered over the white lab coat she wore over her clothes.

Blood?

Hannah's?

Jake shoved forward.

"Don't." Rily blocked him with a shoulder into his side.

Dammit. His stance faltered but he nodded. Rily eased a few inches away.

From a few yards away Althea advanced on them. Fury lined her face. She swung her arm towards Ben and a wave of pure energy knocked him back two steps.

Rily eased into the room low with her gun drawn. Jake followed. His knees threatened to buckle, but until they did, he wasn't staying behind.

"Don't shoot yet." Blood trickled down Ben's chin. "The bullets could ricochet off whatever it is she'd doing."

Althea laughed. With her chin high and her arms spread wide in front of her, she retreated several steps.

Both hands cupped around the Glock's grip, Jake braced his back against the splintered door jam. His lungs ached, each breath more difficult than the last. The coiled thread at the center of his chest suddenly flared, its heat burning from the outside in, straight through to his heart.

Where the hell was Hannah? And whose blood was splattered across the floor? Light glinted off pieces of fragmented glass that lay mixed with the blood.

He gulped air and scanned the room with his borrowed weapon.

Ben and Rily would have to take Althea down. He needed to find Hannah.

Baby? Where are you?

There. Across the room, she lay on a bed with a pristine white sheet covering her body.

No blood. Something inside him loosened a small notch.

He had to get to her. Shoving away from the door, he stumbled when Ben knocked him back against the wall.

"What the hell are you doing?" Jake caught his footing. He ignored the deep shards of pain in both knees. Ignored the fire smoldering in his chest, in his gut. "Hannah —"

"Is over there, too." Rily, still crouched low, gazed at him with wide eyes. She jerked her chin in the other direction.

He twisted to look where she'd indicated and stopped. Hannah stood staring at him. The edges of her body wavered, there but not there. Her dark eyes, full of fear, were too big for her face. Quick, he swung his gaze back to the bed.

She lay there, too. Still and unmoving. He couldn't even tell if *that* Hannah breathed or not. He took a hesitant step away from the support of the wall.

"That's far enough." Althea had taken a position between him and the two Hannahs. With her arms bent in front of her, palms forward, a grim look lined her face. "You've caused enough problems. All three of you."

"We're not the ones holding a woman hostage." Rily settled one knee on the floor. She held her gun lifted and sighted.

"No. You're not. But you're in my way." Althea waved a hand at Rily.

His sister's face tightened. Her jaw worked and her fingers flexed. "Crap."

Her movements abrupt, she set the gun on the floor beside her. Yanking her glove off, she cradled her hand with the other one.

"What happened?" Ben stepped toward her, but stopped when Althea made a small noise in the back of her throat.

"She burned me." Rily held up her hand, the palm already an ugly red.

"Anyone else want to play?" Althea's lips moved into a smile, but her eyes remained a cold, icy pale blue.

Jake glanced once at the bed, then at the apparition of Hannah. He raised his brows then jerked his head towards Althea. *Let's blast the bitch.* Apparition Hannah bit her bottom lip. She nodded.

In his mind he thrummed the fire hot thread curled tight inside his chest. Glittery dust shimmered in the air around him. The tinge of power stretched to the prone Hannah stretched out on the bed.

He glanced at the Hannah standing across from him. The glitter shimmered around her, too. He nodded. There was a sharp tug on his chest then she lifted her hand and flicked her fingers at Althea.

"No." The woman spun in a tight circle. "What are you trying to do?"

Her palm forward, Jake *felt* Hannah shove the pulsing energy outward toward the other woman.

"No." Althea pressed both hands to the base of her neck. Her movements jerky and frantic, she clawed at the collar of her blouse. "Nooo."

Light exploded with sparkling flashes of multi-colored glitter surging through the room. Waves of energy beat an increasing tempo, rising on Althea's sudden shriek.

She crumbled to the tile floor.

Gold and silver glitter dusted the room and shimmered for an extended moment then dissipated as if it had never existed.

Jake took a shuddering breath. His body thrummed with the pulse along the thread that tied his body to Hannah's prone one.

With a grimace, Rily scooped up her gun then rolled to bend over Althea. She pressed the tip of her weapon against Althea's temple. Ben tucked his gun into the back of his waistband. He pulled out a flat, black case.

Jake's swollen knees protested, but he took the few steps to stand over the bed where Hannah's body lay.

My love.

He touched her hair. Tucked a loose strand behind her ear.

She lay so quiet. So still. Her breath so shallow he wasn't sure she really breathed.

He glanced behind him.

Hannah's apparition stood almost as still as her prone body. Her gaze was all that moved and that seemed to envelope him, to sweep over him, to touch the thread still coiled tight in his chest.

"Bitch." Rily's voice broke the spell he swore Hannah was weaving.

Jake glanced at the floor before angling his head towards his sister.

Even with her sore, red palm, Rily had Althea on her stomach with her hands cuffed behind her back. Ben had some kind of red cloth he was sweeping glass fragments into, along with soaking up blood into the cloth.

Ben glanced at him then swung his gaze between the bed and Hannah's apparition. Then he glanced back at Jake. "Rily, why don't we take Miss Sheldon outside so I can call my team? See if there's an easier way into this place. Besides, you need something for your palm."

Rily growled, the sound low in her throat. She sent Jake a dark glance but after a quick look at the two Hannahs, she shrugged and forced Althea to her feet.

Althea didn't resist. If her glazed eyes and slack mouth were any indication, the woman was in shock. Rily and Ben drug her out the door.

"We stopped her." Jake met apparition Hannah's gaze over her prone body. "Together."

The edges of the standing Hannah wavered. She nodded. He rubbed his chest. Energy still pulsed and coiled tight. Hannah spread her hand, palm upwards. Glitter suddenly shimmered in a thin line from her hand to his chest.

"Rily was right." With his gaze locked on her, Jake thrummed a short edge of the thread with his mind.

Hannah's eyes widened. Her lips parted.

He thrummed the edge again.

"How are you doing that?" She leaned forward.

"My heart. Rily said this centers in my heart." He braced his arms on the bed, on either side of the still Hannah's head. Glitter dusted the surface of the sheet, glowing against the whiteness of the cloth. "You hold it in your palm."

Hannah looked down at her hand then held it in front of his chest. "And you hold mine."

He eased himself forward, brushed his fingers over her body's forehead. Warmth spread through his fingers. The body's chest moved, slight, but she still breathed. He angled his head to look at the standing Hannah.

"Now what, Jake?" Her voice thickened. "Do I die? Is it time?"

"No." The word stuck in his throat. He shot a glance at the room's ceiling. "You don't die. You live. With me."

"Jake —"

He fished the ring box from his jean's pocket. "You marry me."

"How?" Desperation lined her voice, filled her dark eyes.

God, this had better work. From under the sheet, he lifted her body's arm then slipped the ring on her finger. "Like this."

He leaned forward, his mouth covering the sleeping Hannah's and he pressed his lips against hers. "I love you, Hannah Dixon."

A harsh gasp of exhaled air swept over him.

His mouth covering hers, his eyes closed, he deepened the kiss. She coughed once then sighed. Her lips softened and moved under his.

God, Hannah. His fingers gripped her shoulders. He pulled away to look at her, at her dark eyes open wide and locked on his. He stole a quick glance upwards. The apparition of Hannah was gone.

He leaned his forehead against hers. "It worked, Baby."

"Yes." Raspy and unused, her voice was the sweetest sound he had ever heard. "I love you, too, Jake Carrigan."

Epilogue

J AKE SAT ON HIS BACK PORCH STEPS with Hannah tucked at his side and his chin resting on her head. The light afternoon breeze toyed with her hair, the strands tickling his cheeks.

Nearly seventy-two hours since they had taken Althea down.

Hannah was still here.

Solid. Real.

She had her left hand on his jean clad thigh, the diamond on her engagement ring glinting in the sun. He rubbed his hand up and down her arm. She sighed and leaned closer.

Sadie chased Nels around the charred shell of the barn. The odor of damp, burnt wood hung strong in the air. The barn didn't matter, though. Hannah, here with him, that's all that was important.

Rily's truck rumbled up the muddy road and pulled to a stop next to his battered Jeep. Ben climbed down from the passenger side. He tucked his hands in his pockets and stood staring at Jake and Hannah.

She stiffened, her tension radiating through Jake. In his mind he sent soothing images along the thread still connecting them. She relaxed against him.

Rounding the hood of her truck, Rily elbowed Ben then strode across the expanse of sparse grass and bounded up the lower porch step. With an arm around them both, she gave a quick hug before hopping back to stand on the ground. Tears glistened in her eyes. She blinked several times.

"Damn it, Bro." Rily wiped at her cheeks.

"Yeah." He squeezed his eyes shut. When he opened them Ben stood next to Rily.

"Mr. Secret Agent Man here must have friends in high places." Rily cut a quick glance at Ben. "Althea's on her way to some super-secret holding tank. They won't tell me where. Half his men went with her, so he gave them his car for the first leg of transport. Portland probably. I got volunteered to chauffeur him to the airport this afternoon."

"Didn't hear you complaining." Ben rocked back on his heels.

"Yeah, well. Now you're at my mercy."

"Heaven help us all." Jake rubbed small circles on Hannah's shoulder. "How's the hand, Sis?"

Rily frowned, her brows low and her green eyes sparking gold. She held up her hand, palm forward. "Fine. Like nothing happened."

The corner of Ben's mouth twitched. Jake looked away to avoid his sister's scowl.

"So what happens to Althea now?" Hannah, her voice soft, leaned closer to him. He slid his hand down her arm and cupped her elbow.

"There are a lot of charges brought against her. The most important thing is making sure she can no longer access your energy. We're taking her someplace where people who know what they're doing will watch her closely." Steel underscored the weariness in Ben's voice. He scrubbed a hand over his face. "She won't be allowed to hurt you again, Hannah."

She nodded then swallowed once. Fine tremors ran over her body, tremors echoed in Jake. He pulled her tight and it was almost as if she sank into him. They both sighed.

Ben covered his mouth with his hand, but it didn't cover his grin. A soft smile touched Rily's lips. There, then gone.

Jake rubbed his cheek over Hannah's hair.

He had her back. That was what mattered.

"I'd like a shot at her. At Althea." Rily pursed her lips.

"No." Ben rubbed the back of his neck.

"Why not?"

"It's better that way."

"For who? Us or her?"

"Everyone."

"What about Dr. Sheldon, her father?" Jake glanced at his sister.

"He's still here." Rily scuffed the toe of her shoe in the grass. "Both he and Althea deny he had any knowledge of her *activities.*"

"You believe him?" Jake glanced between the two.

"No." Ben rolled his head side to side. "We're still going through her notes."

"Detailed notes, if what I saw is any indication." A fierce light flashed in his sister's eyes.

"From a cursory glance through, it appears Dr. Sheldon actually found a marker for the disease —"

"Which is what?" Jake glanced between Ben and Rily. "I've never had a firm handle on what made Hannah sick in the first place."

"Leukemia." Her voice low and weary, Hannah pressed her cheek against his shoulder. Something warm and tender clamped tight at the center of his chest.

They would fight this illness together.

"Yes and no." Ben smiled at her, his eyes warm and the edges crinkled. "PLS. Psychic Leukemia Syndrome."

"I'd been told Hannah had something else, something rare but with leukemia like symptoms. I've never heard of PLS." Rily frowned again.

"Most haven't. It does mimic acute leukemia, hits only psychics and seems to be hereditary." Ben wet his lips. "Somehow, and we're still working on the how, Dr. Sheldon managed to find a marker in your blood. One identical to the one in his daughter's blood profile."

"Althea has PLS?"

"No. But she has the marker and her mother died from it. Althea concocted this plan to use Hannah to find a cure."

"So you're saying the good doctor really wasn't involved?" Rily shook her head. "I don't believe that. Not for a second."

"Since Hannah doesn't remember, we can't bring any charges against him. But we'll be watching."

"My pleasure." A predatory gleam shone in Rily's eyes.

"Don't get in the way." Ben slid a hooded look at Rily. She batted her eyes. His lips twitched again before he turned to Hannah. "The results from the quick physical our doctors gave you came back. Although Althea seemed to be keeping you in some kind of induced coma, you're relatively healthy. Even your muscle tone is half-way decent."

"We found a device that seems to stimulate muscle activity." Rily glanced at Hannah. "Used for coma patients."

"It seemed to work." Ben nodded. "Your blood-work is also back. No sign of the illness. None. Which shouldn't be possible. Whatever Althea did, she may have actually cured you."

Her hand still on Jake's leg, Hannah sucked in a stuttered breath. She sat straighter.

"When you're up to it, we would really like to –"

"Study her? Make a guinea pig out of her?" Derision coated Rily's words.

Ben pulled in a deep breath. "Look. This is a horrible wasting disease. There is no cure."

"Althea must have been terrified of dying the way her mother had." Hannah's eyes misted. Warmth spread outward from where her hand curled on Jake's leg.

"So she tapped into your latent psychic abilities, used your blood to cover her activities, believing that would protect her from the disease." Ben lowered his chin, his gaze intent on Hannah. "Your father died from this. One day I'd like to talk to you about what a good man he was."

"My dad?"

"Yes." Ben sighed. "For him, for you and all the others struck with this disease, we'd like to figure out what Althea did. And how."

"Okay."

"Just like that?" Rily blinked several times. "You're going to let them —"

"Yes." Shaky, Hannah stood, her hand on Jake's shoulder. Energy Jake welcomed pulsed between them. "My mother said...."

"She blamed us, Hannah." Weariness pulled at the lines on Ben's face. "Maybe she was right. He was a strong psychic. The company used as much as he was willing to give. Once the disease struck, it took him fast. I didn't even have time to bring your mother to him."

Jake covered her hand with his.

"My dad." Hannah drew a deep, shuddering breath. "I wasn't psychic. At all. How did I get this disease?"

"We think maybe you were. Are. That Althea had been using your energy, your blood for a long time. And that in itself made you anemic, spurred the manifestation of the disease." Ben shrugged. "Your mother was hell-bent on keeping you away from us. She didn't allow any testing. I kept tabs on you for many years, but it seemed she was accurate in her assessment. So I backed off. Gave her what she wanted."

"You out of their lives." Jake leveled his gaze at Ben.

"Yeah. Now it's looking like everyone was wrong."

"So what do we do first?" Fear and courage warred each with the other in Hannah's eyes. Jake squeezed the hand she still had on his shoulder.

"We test you. Establish what was going on. See where you are now."

"And if I do still have any abilities?"

She did, Jake knew for a fact. So did Ben, if the way the corners of his mouth lifted was any indication. Rily, still frowning, swung her gaze between the three of them.

"Then we'd like to offer you a job." Ben glanced at Jake. "You too. She'll need a handler. I can't think of anyone more qualified."

"Glad you understand that much." Jake kept his gaze direct, no quarter given.

Ben's mouth twitched but then a huge smile spread across his face.

"Wait a minute." Rily planted her feet. With her fists on her hips she glared at them all. "Just like that, you two accept and what? Take off for parts unknown to play Secret Agent Couple?"

"Sounds like a plan to me, Sis."

Tentative at first, Hannah's grin widened. "Especially the couple part."

"Amen." Jake stood, swung Hannah in a circle. Her laughter echoed across the meadow and back. "Amen."

If you enjoyed STOLEN SPIRIT and would like to see more stories in the PSI Sentinel series, please consider leaving a review for this book with your favorite ebook seller.

Every review is appreciated.

To stay up to date with Pamela and to learn more about her upcoming releases, sign up for her newsletter:
http://eepurl.com/bbOUjv

You can also visit her at the following places on the web:

www.PamelaMoran.com
www.facebook.com/pamelamoranauthor
www.goodreads.com/PamelaMoran
www.pinterest.com/pamelamoran/
Twitter: Pam_Moran

Available now:

BLIND SIGHT
(PSI Sentinels, Book Two)

Death plagues Gabe Nicholetti's dreams, but he can't save the people in his visions. The most he can do is bring their killers to justice. But this time, this victim makes it all personal.

Rily Carrigan is a dead woman, or she will be in a matter of days as her past rushes forward to shatter her carefully constructed world. But Rily doesn't believe fate is absolute. How is she going to convince the man who's seen too many die that it's possible to save her life?

Just outside a small, Oregon town, something malevolent lurks, waiting to seize what was once promised then stolen. Together, Gabe and Rily need to find a way to deny fate and keep Rily live.

GAVIN'S WOMAN
(A PSI Sentinel, Darkwater Guardians Novella)

Gavin Dunbar, liaison between the PSI and the government, is a low-level psychic himself. A man of the present who believes the future is too nebulous, too fluid – that it can't be trusted. His reasons are mired deep in a past he has no desire to examine. After all, in his world, having a soul-mate doesn't equate to happily-ever-after.

Tragedy has brought Calea Fontaine to a crossroads and has her reassessing her future without the man she loves. A seer from a long line of seers, Calea knows, firsthand, that while Fate might try to guide a person along a path, Free Will has a way of trumping Destiny.

Or does it?

Along the storm ravaged Oregon coast, a predator stalks Calea with an obsession born of a dark ache, an overwhelming need to control and possess at any cost. The only obstacle standing in his way is Gavin Dunbar's own obsession.

ELSIE'S SECRET
(A PSI Sentinel Novella)

A PSI agent, Sebastian Alexander has secrets that once came between him and the woman he still loves. Finding her prowling around where she doesn't belong turns his simple reconnaissance into a rescue mission threatening to blow everything apart. Is he willing to risk his secrets to save her life?

Elsie Quartermaine has one goal. Save her nephew from a sadistic kidnapper. Sebastian is the one man who can help her. But divulging her secret puts more than her life in jeopardy. Can she trust Sebastian with her nephew's life? Her own? What about her heart?

As dawn creeps over the horizon, can they find enough trust in each other to stay alive?

Coming Early Summer 2015

Darkwater Echoes

PSI Sentinels: Darkwater Guardians, Book One

By Pamela Moran

Footsteps pounded across the deck above. Trent Sawyer, awake at the first thud, rolled from his berth and snatched his gun from under his pillow.

Barefoot and wearing only a black pair of shorts, he moved silently across the dark cabin to the door. He waited several heartbeats before letting the motion of a small wave hitting the side of the sailboat cover the sound of him opening the door a small fraction.

Light from the upper galley spilled through the crack and into his room.

Voices carried down to him, voices that shouldn't have been there – much less arguing over who was going to start the freaking boat's engines.

His boss' boat. Neither of those rough voices belonged to the man.

Trent wasn't letting whoever was up on deck steal _this_ boat. Not on his first night. He hadn't even been on the boat – or in Key Largo – for more than a couple hours.

Not going to happen.

With his gun leading and his body crouched low, Trent slipped into the narrow hallway. He slid one bare foot onto the bottom stair, cringed at the soft groan of weathered wood then shifted his weight to ease his other foot up another step.

On a deep exhale of breath, he lifted his head above the solid railing. Two men, one a blonde giant and the other a squat redhead, both burly and wide through the shoulders, stood across the galley with their backs to him. Their voices lower than earlier, they seemed to be arguing over a sheaf of papers they had spread over the Captain's table.

Now was as good a time as any.

Trent straightened. He aimed his gun at Blondie's head. "What the hell are you doing on my damn boat?"

Both men whipped around, their faces slack with shock.

A small amount of satisfaction welled in Trent's gut.

Mongrels, both of them.

Their eyes brightened and their mouths widened into comical grins. They started forward.

"What the –?" Pain, sharp and sudden, splintered Trent's thoughts.

His world went black.

✧ ✧ ✧

Join Pam's newsletter to stay up to date on PSI Sentinel releases!

http://eepurl.com/bbOUjv

www.ingramcontent.com/pod-product-compliance
Lightning Source LLC
Chambersburg PA
CBHW072116250626

47159CB00007B/2471